# Talio's Codex

# Talio's Codex

J. Alexander Cohen

Space Wizard Science Fantasy
Raleigh, NC
www.spacewizardsciencefantasy.com



Cover art by MoorBooks
Editing by Heather Tracy
Book Layout © 2015 BookDesignTemplates.com

Talio's Codex/J. Alexander Cohen.— 1st ed.
ISBN 978-1-960247-22-3

Author's website: https://www.jalexandercohen.com/

Author's Note

I write a lot of cozy fantasy. *Talio's Codex* is not cozy...I'd call it cozy-adjacent. You might even call it fantasy noir. There isn't much violence, but there is some, and characters go through a lot emotionally.

Content warnings:

- Angst (intense emotional scenes)
- Discrimination (religious, gender, and sexual orientation)
- Dubious consent
- Explicit sex scenes
- Infidelity
- Murder (not onscreen, but there's a trial)
- Cultural/religious conflict
- Social stigma (facial scarring)
- Suicide (mention)
- Substance use (alcohol, alcoholism)
- Violence (two brief attempts on one character's life)

As with all my work, *Talio's Codex* has an unambiguous HEA (Happily Ever After). Getting to that point is a bumpy road for Talio and the other characters. But just as adding a sprinkle of salt makes an orange wedge all the sweeter, I think the ups and downs of the story are worth it.

Thanks for reading.


J. Alexander Cohen

# CONTENTS

# Part One: The Mecomb Murder Case

# Chapter One

Talio Rossa's dowsing rod jerked sideways.

He looked up from the spot where he'd been concentrating. All the other scavengers were bent over their own long, narrow strips of pale blue mineral. None reacted. This was his discovery alone, then. If he could trust the magic in the dowsing rod.

He knew every bit of his rectangular strip of merinite. False merinite, rather. Absolutely worthless, found in abundance, and identical in every way to the priceless specks of true merinite that could still be found here and there. The dowsing rod would only react to true merinite. Talio hadn't seen it twitch this violently in years.

He rubbed his aching lower back and looked past the roped-off sections of false merinite, into the forest beyond. A ragged line of stones inscribed with runes marked the boundary. Talio could just make out the creatures and beasts beyond the translucent barrier. A hovering wyvern. A half-human, half-dragon creature banging its head against the shimmering wall. An immense coiled snake watching him with intent eyes. And beyond them, the Impassable Forest. The bodies of the mages. And if he strained his eyes, Talio could even see the old Royal Palace. The last remnants of the War of the Cities. Live creatures, dead mages and a crumbling palace imprisoned in the Impassable Forest for all time.

Talio bent down again and passed the dowsing rod carefully along the watery-blue merinite. Then the rod touched a woman's beaded dress. He looked up and his former wife, Gawani, stood before him.

Talio froze. He had never expected such a day to come; his body and mind simply refused to react. A small part of him wanted to flee, but where would he go? He had run from her a decade earlier, to the small town of Velos. And now she'd found him, scavenging in the forest like a commoner.

This was not the same Gawani he'd once known. Her face held more lines. Under her beaded bonnet, her hair was darker. The figure she'd once prized was rounder, lusher.

"One moment," Talio said. She did not reply. He glanced around for the two ragged ritual cups that by law accompanied every work site. Someone had taken them. Here they were, alone in the forest with no water for the ritual. But Gawani pulled something out of her purse. It was a small, heavy cube with two runnels and the tiniest dot of pale blue. True merinite. It was a water generator. How she afforded it, he had no idea.

"Source of all things," Gawani recited. "Quencher of fire. Cleanse my soul and purify me." A tiny stream of water sprang from the merinite in the generator and flowed through the source runnel. He took the generator from her while she removed her gloves and washed her hands awkwardly under it, then held it out to him. Talio shook his head. It was common courtesy to offer the waters on arrival, but he did not want to take anything from her, not even symbolically.

"I could not believe you were working as a scavenger until I arrived here in Velos and saw for myself," she said.

Talio handed the generator back to her. Should he hug her? Kiss her? Shake her hand? Instead, he shrugged. "It's all I know how to do at my age."

"You knew how to be a magistrate," she said. "Until you didn't."

Talio nodded. "Just as I knew how to be a husband. Until I didn't."

Her eyes narrowed. He waited for her to lash out at him with her words. But she was still the old Gawani in one way: she retreated from the conflict. She looked at him with a tired glance and said, "I need your help."

Talio gestured to a large flat rock that lay beyond the ring of merinite surrounding the barrier of the Impassable Forest. He and the others took their lunch there, or breaks whenever they wanted. He paid a small amount of silver for the privilege of dowsing for true merinite; it was up to him how much or how little he worked.

Like the dowsing rod, Talio had sensed Gawani was there before he'd seen her. He was as sensitive to her magic as the rod was to merinite. When Talio had started scavenging ten years ago, the rod shook in his hands every day until he'd been able to put Gawani and the past behind him. Even after all this time, she was still like a lodestone drawing him to her.

"Is it your mother?" Gawani Balsamo had lived in the shadow of Lady Dovuta for as long as he'd known her. She'd been adopted by the Balsamo family as a baby and had spent her life seemingly making up for it. Nothing but her mother could have caused his former wife to make the long trip from the Balsamo manse in Nuciferia to the small town of Velos where he now lived.

"No, not this time." Gawani gave him a wry look. "Though of course she is involved with the matter. She is always involved with everything, somehow." Then she grew serious. "There's been a murder."

When Gawani said nothing more, Talio prompted her. "And you are a public defender. Who is the accused?"

"His name is Pazli Mecomb." An unusual name, for a Nuciferian. She gave an airy wave. "It is a simple matter. A local merchant came to visit my mother and ended up dead. Pazli was also present at the manse on other business."

A "simple matter" of a death inside a noblewoman's house. "Did he do it?"

"As a public defender, I should tell you he is innocent until he has gone through the legal system." Gawani gave him a significant look. "But if I were a magistrate, I would find him guilty, based on the circumstances. What's worse, he refuses to defend himself. It's as if he has accepted the verdict already." She sighed. "This time, I am unable to defend him."

Typical Gawani. Playing out the facts like a fisher trawling with bait. "Why is that?"

"He was one of my students," she said. "Some years ago, at the Palace of Justice. It is part of the new conflict-of-interest rules."

She had taught no classes when they had been married a decade earlier. Talio felt a jolting sense of change. "What would you have me do?" he asked. "I do not know this Pazli Mecomb. I cannot provide testimony to his character."

"I want you to defend him."

None of this made any sense. A random man accused of murder. Gawani coming to find him after ten years. Memories flashed through his mind in quick succession. Sitting at the head of a long magistrate's desk. Speaking the words that would forever decide the course of dozens of lives. Until one night...

"You need another public defender, like yourself," Talio said in a gentle voice. "Not a former magistrate." A disgraced one, yet.

Gawani looked up at him, forest sunlight caught in her keen blue eyes. "I need someone who can fight for him." She shook her head. "I can still admit to myself that you are the most intelligent person I know."

"The Crown appoints defenders. I could not defend him, even if I wished to."

"There you are wrong," Gawani said. "The system has changed. For the last few years, anyone with the proper legal education may defend someone charged in a criminal matter."

When he had been a magistrate, only public defenders licensed by the Crown could represent a defendant. He could not remember a change that significant in the years he had sat on the bench.

She smiled with false modesty. "The Queen has asked me to work on other legislative matters." Queen Jaconda. How Gawani—and Dovuta—must have enjoyed that favor.

A shadow fell over them, and he looked up. The skyline hung far above them as it always did, a shimmering stream of rushing blue water stretching across the sky. Along it, the daily skyship ploughed through its waters, sunlight glinting off its copper hull. It was the one Gawani would have taken from Nuciferia, returning along the skyline hanging above the Impassable Forest between the Four Cities.

"I should return to work," he told her. "It has been good to see you."

"Pazli Mecomb is an Incarnite," Gawani said.

It was a day for strange happenings and concepts: the return of his former wife, a murder hearing and now an Incarnite. He had heard of them, as much as anyone in Velos had. "The death cult?"

"Some might have called them that, once." Gawani held up the water generator. "They believe in Sif instead of Felle. If you can imagine." The side of the generator was etched with the image of Felle, the water goddess. Talio could not imagine such a thing. Worshipping a fire god seemed beyond treason, beyond blasphemy. Given the centrality of water to Merin's way of life, it was simply incomprehensible. "Have you not had dealings with Incarnites in Velos?"

"I heard about two who passed through here a couple of years ago. I imagine anyone worshipping Sif would not have been very welcome in Velos." He gestured to his face. "They cover up with a hood for some reason?"

Gawani shook her head. "Their entire body. From top to bottom. Nobody ever sees what an Incarnite looks like, except for their hands." She laughed. "They call themselves embers. After the fire god. The cloak is to protect them when they finally go out into the desert to seek him. All manner of nonsense."

"How do they identify themselves?" Talio jingled the keychain in his pocket. "How does the government identify them? How do you even know which Incarnite you are talking to?"

"Would you stand here discussing the intricacies of identifying Incarnites? Or will you hear my offer?"

He had not found any true merinite in his parcel of land for weeks. The speck in Gawani's generator was the closest Talio had come. "Very well. Let us get away from this forest and the beasts beyond." He turned his back on his marked-off parcel of land. "Come to my rooms with me."

Gawani looked at him in surprise as he directed her away from the long, wide band of merinite where other workers continued to chip away at the pale blue mineral. "Don't you have someone to alert? Somewhere to sign out?"

Talio smiled. A Nuciferian to the end, Gawani's concerns were of schedules and permits. "They charge me a bit of silver to dig in my little portion of merinite. As long as I pay the silver, they care little for when I come or go. I will take a holiday from digging, in your honor."

She handed him the generator once again and prayed, "As I leave, may I always be bathed in your waters. Keep me from the flame of temptation." Gawani washed her hands under the small stream from the return runnel, and he joined her this time.

It took some time to walk back into the town of Velos and what passed for civilization there. They walked along the narrow streets in silence, following the source and return ritual gutters downstream toward the workers' quarters. Every town and city in Merin had the same basic layout: wealthier quarters upstream by the northern exchange, where the source gutters started their flow; and poorer quarters downstream, where the southern exchange station filtered the source water and sent it back upstream as return water. In theory, source and return water had the same level of cleanliness, but the poor were always stuck by the water plants, without exception.

With summer's end, shaded parts of the streets were already cool. The only sound was the burbling of the gutters beside them. Gawani kept the generator in her hands as they walked, and she flicked the lever with the speck of merinite back and forth between its two positions.

After the War of the Cities had ended in the death of the mages and an uneasy truce, soldiers had collected all the remaining true merinite left in the country to power the skylines. Still, there were enough scraps of overlooked mineral among the false merinite that powered the Impassable Forest's barrier that scavengers could make a living...barely. Such remnants were nearly priceless. When Talio was working as a magistrate, he'd stopped at a luxury shop to ask about buying a water generator for Dovuta's birthday. The price the seller had quoted was twice his annual salary. The specks embedded in the false merinite outside the Impassable Forest were smaller than the head of a pin.

Talio watched the lever flick back and forth. "Are you planning on spraying me with water, then?" he asked. "Will you soak me with the source or the return?"

"It's a bad habit," she said. "I'm nervous. I admit that. If I were at the manse, I would..." Her voice trailed off.

Talio looked at her, aghast. "You don't still smoke duhan, do you?"

Gawani shrugged defensively. "It calms me down." Duhan was addictive, he thought. It was bad for her health. They'd argued about her mild habit many times. But fighting Gawani was as foolish as fighting her mother, and just as likely to succeed. After a while, she stopped and stowed the generator in her beaded purse.

Talio marveled at how easily they walked together, how they fell into the comfortable pace they'd once had. He wanted to ask Gawani about her life, about her friends. Did she still have the little cat she'd loved so much? But he had no right to know. The last time she'd seen him, he'd been in the arms of another man. And when he'd looked up at her face in the window, he had seen the death of their marriage in an instant.

"What are you remembering?" Gawani asked.

Talio did not want to lie to her. "That night." He did not need to say which night.

"I was so angry then," Gawani said. *Was.* She had always been an excellent public defender; every word she spoke carried the precision of a knife.

She watched him unlock the door with his meager keychain. "A single lock on your door?" she asked, looking around as if she expected a thief to appear at any moment.

"This is not Nuciferia," Talio said. He slid the warped door open with difficulty and ushered her in.

Unable to afford direct access to the gutters, he kept ritual source and return bowls by the door. Their water was tepid, but Talio was glad that at least he had that to offer. He offered her the bowls first. She said the prayer and dipped her clean fingers into the source bowl. He repeated the words, then scrubbed the soil from his hands in the bowl. He would have to refill it from outside after she left; Talio could not bear asking her to take out the little generator again.

Gawani moved around his rooms. She picked up a prototype circular dowsing rod he'd once thought would be more effective than the usual straight shape. The dowsing master had refused to spare the true merinite to imbue it with magic. Then she examined all the other crafts he'd worked on over the last ten years. She appraised each item with the same frank stare she'd used when they had met long ago. Watching, cataloging, judging.

She flipped through a stack of vellum sheets. "You have children, then? Two?"

Talio shook his head. "Not even one. As far as I know."

Gawani held out the sheets. "Why the birth registration forms?"

"I have been helping some of my fellow workers. The ones at the site. Most of them can't read or write, so when it comes to legal matters..."

She smiled. "You always had a weakness for the less fortunate. Why not become a notary, then? Leave the scavenging to others?"

"That still felt too close to the legal system. Even out here in Velos."

Gawani turned her attention to a small worktable upon which lay a book of vellum. "They never found your codex, did they?" she asked in a quiet voice.

The codex. The most valuable part of any magistrate's life. A list of the laws and sentencing guidelines written by Scodel, author of the Merin legal system. Symbol of the trust the queen and the royal body placed in a lawgiver. Someone had stolen it the same night she had seen him defile their marriage vows.

"I have been trying to reconstruct it from memory," he said in a sad voice. "They will never issue me another one, of course."

She ran her finger down the opening page and read, "'Let the innocent go free. Let the guilty learn the error of their ways.'"

"That is not how Scodel started his laws," she said with a smile, then quoted the man's famous opening words written at the front of every codex, "'It is a grand experiment that I propose...'"

He did not want to hear her read the law, either Scodel's or his own. "No, it is what *I* wrote. I remember how brilliant Scodel's principles were." He shrugged. "Even if his sentencing guidelines were a tangle."

"Will you help Pazli, then? Help him go free, as one of the innocents?" Her eyes turned serious. "The hearing will start in two or three days. By the end of the week, he could be hanged." Scodel's Grand Experiment was noted for its swift justice.

They were too close. There was no room in his tiny quarters for two people to stand, two people with so much space between them. "Gawani, it has been ten years since I was at the Palace of Justice. What will people think?" *And what do you think?*

She looked at him with her direct blue eyes. She had never flinched, not even the first time she'd seen the scar marking his face. "The Palace of Justice has not spent the last decade thinking about your scandal." He wondered how much of the past ten years *she* had spent thinking about it.

"I have appealed to your sense of justice," Gawani added. "Now let me appeal to your self-interest. If you defend the Incarnite successfully, I can have your record expunged. You could return to legal work."

Not as a magistrate. That could never happen. But as an advocate, or in some other capacity? She was playing his feelings like a musical instrument.

"I have two passes for tomorrow's skyship to Nuciferia," she said. "We'll take a carriage to Damiria and leave from there. No more scavenging." Her voice became serious and a bit sad. "You do hate it, don't you?"

"My parents were scavengers," Talio said.

"I object to your answer as non-responsive."

After a moment, he relented. "Yes, I hate the scavenging. But there was nothing else I could work at. I am too old for most manual labor."

Gawani took out her own keychain. She removed a small cylindrical lockbox, the size of her index finger, and gave it to him. At the end of her keychain, next to her identity key, Talio saw something he never thought he would see again. Her marriage key. The one she had used on the day of their wedding, carrying the Balsamo crest. By all rights, she should have thrown it away once their marriage had dissolved.

Their eyes met. "You know," Gawani said, "I did forgive you. Eventually." She crossed to the entrance and dipped her hands in the clean return water, speaking the prayer. "I hope you found a way to forgive yourself." She spoke the last words as if they were part of the ritual. Then she was gone.

The message lockbox she'd given him had the same crest as her marriage key: the clover design of the Balsamo family. Talio opened a wooden box sitting beside his bed. Inside, he found the key with the matching emblem. The same clover crest, but this key was worn and old—the wedding key she'd given him thirteen years ago. He slipped it back onto his keychain. It was a reminder of happier times.

His heart felt lighter. She had forgiven him. His peers had moved on. Talio looked around his quarters. How cramped they were, how lonely. Had he not always believed this day would come? That he would find his terrible decision had not irrevocably ruined his life? There was no taking his sins back, but he could move forward after ten years of penance.

The cavity in the message lockbox was only large enough for the smallest scrap of vellum. Gawani did not want a long explanation or a love poem. He took a bit of vellum from his desk and wrote a single word on it, then rolled it up and slipped it into the cavity, closing the lockbox with a snap.

Once Gawani received it, she could use the matching key to pop it open and read his note. He would have to find a messenger to return the lockbox and its message to her. Her location was no mystery; Velos only had one inn.

Pazli Mecomb. He would devise a scheme to find the man innocent. The Incarnite. Scodel's words would twist like a dowsing rod in the right hands. It was time to repay his debt to Gawani, so he could finally discard her marriage key from his life. Time to rejoin the legal community at last.

# Chapter Two

His beard was the first problem.

Talio had made a deliberate decision not to furnish his rooms with a mirror, or any reflective surfaces at all for that matter. He could feel that his beard had grown bushy and unkempt. He'd avoided the unpleasantness of the barber as long as he could, but it was time. There was no way he could simply shave off the beard; if he did not match the description on his identity key, the guards were within their rights to refuse him passage on the skyline.

The barbershop was a few blocks upstream. After the water ritual, his barber Rani breezed him over into the chair, fussing over him. He pulled a towel around Talio's neck and started combing his hair and beard, humming. "A special occasion?"

"I have a carriage to catch to Damiria. Then a skyship to Nuciferia."

"Nuciferia?" Rani asked, impressed. "What are you doing in the big city?"

"Helping a friend," Talio said.

Rani nodded. "Like you did for me, with the papers?" The man could barely read and write. Talio had helped him fill out the interminable barber licensing forms every year for the last several years and had refused to take payment for it.

A polished reflected metal sheet hung on the wall. Talio kept his eyes trained on the floor, as he always did. Now Rani had the knife and scissors out. He snipped away at Talio's hair. "A great deal of crime in Nuciferia," he said. "Not safe."

Perhaps the barber sensed his discomfort, and soon fell silent. When Rani was done, he held a mirror in front of Talio so he could see his face.

Rani trimmed and shaped his beard well. Over the years, the barber had learned how to comb the hairs so they lay over the deep vertical gash that split Talio's lower and upper lips. If he was careful not to touch it, his beard hid the gash to some extent. Rani could do nothing about the rest of the wide purple scar, which traveled up his face alongside his nose, diagonally across his forehead and disappeared into his receding hairline.

"Very good," Talio said in a curt voice. He turned away from his reflection, and the barber joined him at the front of the cramped little shop.

Talio slipped some extra silver into Rani's hands, and the man was all smiles.

"Watch out for the Incarnites," Rani said in a confidential tone.

"I will do that."

Rani shook his head. "Two came to Velos a few years ago. Fire worshippers. They tried to steal a child. Can you imagine?" Then, leaning even closer, he added, "We chased them out of town."

Talio had not heard this part of the story. "That's good," he said. "That the child was safe."

Rani tut-tutted. "Never mind the child. You take care of yourself in Nuciferia. Incarnites are everywhere there." He dipped his fingers in the source bowl and flicked the droplets over Talio as if in benediction. "And if you see an Incarnite, punch them. Firebugs."

It was a short, jouncing carriage trip from Velos to Damiria with Gawani. Velos had started as a secondary community to Damiria, with cheaper housing for scavengers and the workers who could not afford to live in the large city. As one of the Four Cities, housing in Damiria was expensive—it had a reputation to maintain.

When they arrived in Damiria, the carriage driver stopped at the gate to the city and refused to take them the rest of the way to the skyline station unless they paid additional silver. Gawani cajoled and threatened the driver, wearing him down with endless moral and legal arguments. It was only her ultimate threat to report him to the Damirian carriage licensing authority that convinced the man to drive the extra ten blocks upstream and let them off a short walk from the station. "Is there a Damirian carriage licensing authority?"

Talio asked her as they walked the last block to the skyline station.

She shrugged. "Every business has a licensing authority. Aren't scavengers licensed?"

"If you don't tell the scavenging licensing authority about me, I won't tell the carriage licensing authority what you did today."

Then they turned the corner and Talio saw the skyline station. He felt nausea in the pit of his stomach. He'd forgotten how high the station was above the city.

Talio was almost a standard span high. The skyline station was at least thirty spans above street level. It sat at the top of a tower surrounded by a spiral stairway that went up and up and up. Tilting his head to look at the station made him feel ill, not to mention the sight of three airborne rivers of water splashing out in different directions from the top of the station across the sky.

At the entrance to the tower's base, Gawani gave the passes to a soldier, who then asked for their identity keys. The soldier first compared Talio to the physical description inscribed on his key. The man cross-referenced that key to one of several large volumes of text. Last, the soldier pressed the key into a small square of quick-hardening wax for a permanent recording, before handing it back to him.

As the soldier moved on to confirm Gawani's key, Talio noted the increase in security since the last time he'd ridden a skyship. Other guards stood watch at various points in the base. There had been no accident or incident on a skyline in forty years unless he had missed hearing about one. Was it the Incarnites? He wondered again how anyone could definitively identify an Incarnite. How could anyone identify someone if they did not know what they looked like?

In front of the stairway to the platform above stood a stall with a wizened old man selling souvenirs. Talio knew Gawani was unable to resist such a display. She made a direct line for the stall and examined the wares: Damirian pottery, poorly drawn portraits of a smirking Queen Jaconda with crookedly applied paste jewels for eyes and other trinkets. To his surprise, she picked up a bottle of wine bearing the crest of Damiria and asked the vendor to wrap it for her.

"Are you sure?" he asked, and mimed drinking. "With your mother…"

Gawani shook her head. She lifted the bottle and showed him the bottom: a triangle etched into the glass base. "They call it 'soft wine,'" she said. "Tastes like the real thing. Mother could drink this all day and not even get tipsy." More changes. He'd never heard of such a thing; the workers in Velos drank real wine, not imitations.

Talio had his eyes on the protection amulets from the moment he'd seen the stall. Now he picked one up and judged whether it was worth spending his meager savings. They were superstition, surely, but anything he could do to make a skyline journey safer had to be worth it. He should have bought one in the city proper—the station markup was exorbitant. Gawani nodded. "Take as many as you'd like," she said, drawing out more silver.

The climb up the winding stairs to the platform was the hardest part. Winds buffeted them, and the stairs had only a flimsy railing that did not seem like it would protect anyone from flying out into empty air. At one point, he stopped in fright, holding on to the three protective amulets. He had not had time or the presence of mind to mutter the incantations inscribed on each; they were useless until they were activated.

Talio felt Gawani's hand on his back and remembered the times she'd done so in the past to steady him. "There are other passengers behind us," she whispered. "We can't miss the skyship." He nodded and trudged on.

He felt better once they reached the platform at the top. While the curved stairway had been narrow, the platform was wide and sturdy, even wider than the base of the tower. A post with three arrows pointed the way to the departure gates for the other cities: Nuciferia, Aurania and Rylavia. This close to the skylines, the sound of rushing water drowned out the wind and most noises from the city below.

The skyship was nearly identical to the ships that sailed Nuciferia's harbor, with two critical differences. There were no masts and no sails, since there was no need for them. The rushing waters that made up the skyline would send the skyship swiftly through the air to its destination with no need for wind propulsion. And instead of a typical gray metal hull, the hull of the skyship was a brilliant glinting copper. Talio knew what anyone knew about how the skylines worked. Skyships had to have copper hulls to stay afloat and aloft.

From the departure platform, the shimmering watery curve of the skyline extended out to the horizon, a miraculous river hanging in the sky. When Talio looked back at the tower, he could see where the skyline met the pillar. A round circle of pale blue true merinite was embedded in the tower, the source of the gushing river that formed the path for the skyship. The merinite—and prayer—were the only things keeping the water and skyship in mid-air.

The skyship had ten rows of seats with safety belts for passengers to strap themselves in. Each row had three seats on each side of the aisle, with a section for cargo at the back. A sign at the front of each row read: DANGER! NEVER LEAVE YOUR SEAT ONCE THE SKYSHIP IS IN MOTION. Without asking Gawani, Talio climbed into the far seat by the left side of the skyship, strapped himself in, and gripped the handrail next to it tightly.

In the distance, he could see the treetops of the pine and spruce forest that lay beyond Damiria. The skyline was high enough to pass over the trees; at one point it would bank in a swooping curved rush of water toward Nuciferia. Talio held each amulet in turn, speaking the words that would activate each one. Behind him, he could hear the attendant priests blessing the merinite in the tower and the skyship with their own benedictions.

"There hasn't been a skyline accident in forty years," Gawani said.

"Not since Scodel died in one," he reminded her.

"Do you believe those amulets will protect you if anything happens?"

"Do you believe buying soft wine will prevent your mother from drinking the real thing?"

At that moment, there was a jerk as the skyship pulled away from the station. It bobbed up and down in the suspended water for a moment, then accelerated and launched itself along the river through the sky. He closed his eyes, and gripped the handrail and amulets even tighter. He did not want to see the fog that hid the Impassable Forest below, the monsters and beasts that had been the mages' last, desperate attempt to survive during the war. He did not want to see the remains of the Old Royal Palace. And he especially did not want to see the crushed remains of the skyship Scodel had ridden to his doom. Better to think of his destination.

So many of his memories of Nuciferia were of Gawani. Waking up in the middle of the night to make a late meal with her in the kitchen. Walking home together downstream from the Palace of Justice after the workday was done. Nights spent arguing. Nights spent in bed...

Lying on his back, Gawani's legs around his, as she perched over him with one hand on his chest, the other grasping his crotch. "This," she had said. "This is a noodle."

"I'm sorry," he'd said. "Work is very busy."

She had pushed herself off his chest. "It's not because of work. And you are not tired. Is it me? Is there something wrong with how I look?"

No, she had been as beautiful as the day they had met in the Hall of Reference. It was not her. "If you wanted to," he had said tentatively, "you could..."

"Could what?"

"If you wanted to see someone else..."

She had grabbed him again. "I want you. I want your noodle. And I want it to work."

In the skyship, a gentle spray from the water misted Talio's face and wind blew through his hair and beard. He smiled. "What are you thinking of?" Gawani asked.

"Our times together. The good ones." Good or bad, he'd spent them with her.

"Have you had any good times in Velos?"

He opened his eyes and looked at her. "Sometimes. Velos is a small town. Most of the scavengers are young men and there are few young women for them, so…"

Pain flashed across Gawani's face. The joking, the skylines, the lightness when she talked about the past. All that had been an act. He thought he knew her so well, but it had been ten years. What it must have taken for her to come to Velos, to talk to him after what had happened.

Talio's mind spun back to that night. A handsome stranger had come to his magisterial rooms at the Palace of Justice to ask a legal question. Hints, subtle comments, then outright entreaties. The hand on Talio's leg that he'd allowed to remain there until the man moved it to his groin.

The temptation of the moment, after the dissatisfaction he'd felt for so many years. The affection he'd missed in his marriage. He and Gawani had shared so much, but it hadn't touched the gnawing need he'd felt night after night.

It would have been easier to explain if he had succumbed right there in his chambers. But they had made plans to meet at an inn known to Talio, known to men who preferred the company of other men. He'd had plenty of time to consider the offer and to turn it down.

He'd met the handsome man with olive skin and dark eyes at the inn. He'd never learned his name. Talio had liked how the man looked at him with desire and need, how he'd pushed him backward and pressed his lips to his. Scrambling into a guest room, stripping off each other's clothes and feeling four years of restrictions evaporate, the limitations of his marriage disappear.

Then Gawani's face at the window outside, her shock and understanding. Running home to the Balsamo manse, only to be refused entrance by the servants. Retreating to his office at the Palace of Justice, wondering what to do next. Not being able to find his codex. Thinking he must have misplaced it—he hadn't taken it with him—that it must be on the shelf, in the Hall of Reference, somewhere, anywhere.

Then accepting what he had done, what had been done to him and what he had lost.

"Why did you come to Velos?" he asked her. "Why ask me for help?"

"None of the private advocates would take the hearing. None of them want the stain on their record." Gawani sighed. "The other public defenders will only take up the matter if Pazli pleads guilty. And he will plead guilty unless someone intervenes. There is little time for you to convince him otherwise."

"But you swear he is not guilty?"

"I have an intuition. Only that." She smiled. "You once told me an intuition could be more powerful than any fact, if you can back it up in a hearing."

"I am not a conjurer."

Her tone was painful. "Aren't you, though? Ten years ago, you disappeared without a trace, and now I am asking you to pull flowers from a pretty woman's sleeve." Talio could feel how she was trying to thread a path between what she wished for herself and what she still wished, after all this time, for him.

Gawani reached into her satchel and handed him a set of vellum pages and a stylus. "The summary document for the Mecomb hearing," she said. "The sooner you can become acquainted with the details, the better. Make notes if you'd like."

The facts of the matter were simple on the surface: Selig Ivor, a garment merchant, had paid an unexpected mid-morning visit to the Balsamo manse and had spoken to Dovuta. Gawani was not at home; the servant was out. While Ivor was there, Pazli Mecomb had come by to ask for unwanted household items.

Talio tapped a finger against the vellum. Gawani had said that Mecomb was a former student of hers. Why would an advocate be collecting junk? Was the Incarnite no longer an advocate? He wanted to ask her, but she had closed her eyes and appeared to be dozing. He made a note and read on.

Dovuta had ushered Pazli into the same drawing room where Selig was waiting. While she left to make Selig a cup of tea, she heard the merchant and the Incarnite arguing loudly. She left the tea in the scullery room and rushed back to the drawing room, at which point both men were apologizing, claiming there had been a misunderstanding. Wishing to separate the men, Dovuta took Pazli down to the servant's entrance and promised to fetch the unwanted household items.

Talio imagined how angry Dovuta must have been to have two commoners fighting in the manse. At this point she went back upstairs, leaving Pazli alone in the servant's quarters and Selig alone in the drawing room. The tea was on its own in the scullery for some unspecified period of time.

She gave some junk to Pazli, then remembered the tea and brought it to Selig. He showed her his wares, and she refused to buy any bonnets. Instead, she took pity on him and offered him a sum of money to place as reserve for next season's fashions. Leaving the drawing room yet again to fetch the money, she was in her rooms when she heard Selig cry out in pain. By the time Dovuta returned, the merchant was dead. She called for the peacekeepers. They arrived shortly thereafter and lived up to their reputation for fair treatment by beating and arresting the Incarnite.

Next, he turned to the report of the examination of Ivor's body. It was incomplete and marked *Pending*. Preliminary results based on Dovuta's testimony, and a superficial examination suggested poisoning. Chief Physician Minka Schell had signed the report. Talio smiled. Another name from his past, and a friendly one. They would need the full report to conclude the hearing, unless the magistrate and jury felt that guilt was a foregone conclusion.

Talio considered the summary document once more. As his old professor Clemente Jilani had once said, a hearing contained multiple truths, not one. Which one was correct depended on how you looked at the facts.

He had been denying certain facts for a decade, and now it was time to finally face them. He had kept only one reminder from Velos. Talio put his hand into his trouser pocket and grasped the sole item he'd brought with him as a keepsake. He had not wanted the soldiers or Gawani to see it. It was the dowsing rod he'd used for ten years. Something to remind him he never wanted to scavenge for merinite, ever again. The next few days could reorient his life, if he could get Pazli Mecomb found not guilty.

The people he'd once known and trusted would be waiting for him to make a mistake. The advocates, the magistrates, even the clerks at the Palace of Justice. He did not want to see any of them again, but he would have to show his face if he wanted to regain the legal profession. Perhaps it might not be so bad. He spoke like them; he acted like them. He was an outsider in some ways, but nothing like Mecomb was.

In all his years of scavenging, Talio had never had any trouble with the peacekeepers in Velos. His training in law had served him well, both in speech and bearing. So much easier for a member of a foolish religious cult to run afoul of the law. To be detailed, arrested, beaten, charged with murder.

The people of Velos had seen Talio as a mere day laborer, and his former colleagues had seen him as a fallen man. In the same way, the jury would see the accused as an Incarnite, a masked, hooded junkman of low class and strange religious beliefs. Talio would not let the perceptions of others damn an innocent man. Not himself, and not Pazli Mecomb.

Even if he was a fire-worshipper.

# Chapter Three

Damiria was large compared to Velos, but Nuciferia dwarfed both of them. The familiar streets and canals of Merin's largest city spread out below the waters of the skyline long before they arrived in the city proper; rows of buildings grew ever taller as they approached. The ship glided to a stop at the Nuciferia tower station with a splash of waves coming a moment later. It was now midday.

When Talio unclasped his fingers from the handrail, his hand was cramped and sweaty. If Gawani noticed, she said nothing. The Nuciferia platform was itself larger than the one at Damiria. The four cities—Nuciferia, Damiria, Aurania and Rylavia—were supposed to be equals, but Nuciferia was always grander and larger than the others.

He found himself eager to see the city again. As Talio descended the stairway, the scents wafted up to him. First the canals, the brackish water that flowed sluggishly morning and evening with the tides. Then the chimneys, controlled refuse fires and street vendors. And last, the smell of horses, sheep, animals for sale and the crowds below.

The contrast with Damiria was remarkable. As with the carriage driver that morning, Talio remembered his interactions with the people of Damiria well. They would help only so much and no more. Every single one of them had a limit, beyond which it was clear you were bothering them. They'd looked at him with closed faces, if they had looked at him at all.

The Nuciferians were different. He had forgotten the expression on their faces: fear and mistrust. A Damirian was a closed door; a Nuciferian was a locked door with a hostile guard dog waiting behind it.

It was very subtle, but in the course of his life and legal career, Talio had become accustomed to parsing the expression on another's face. A woman who strayed too close to him suddenly pulled herself back. A man eyed him, then crossed over to the canal side of the street. He was a stranger, dressed in shabby worker's clothes. A threat.

An old woman caught sight of his face, gave him a look of startled astonishment, and bent down to the source gutter to splash herself with water and mutter a prayer to Felle. Talio was also familiar with that reaction. He had prayed to the water goddess himself enough times as a child asking her to take away his scar until he'd become used to it.

"Before anything else," Gawani said, "we must see Pazli. He's at the Palace of Justice."

"Imprisoned, of course," Talio said.

"Of course." She gave him a tired smile. "They wouldn't let an accused Incarnite free without bail, or an overriding policy reason. He might flee." *Into the desert?*

The waterways were busier, too; stationary barges lined up on one side of the canal, some with laundry hanging from their roofs. The other side of the canal was open for moving traffic—boats and barges in traffic to and from the harbor. Talio watched a young girl hop from barge to barge, ducking to avoid the angry hands of the boaters. "Faster to take a boat," Gawani said.

They descended the stairs to the canal and found a captain with a small flat-bottomed boat. "Palace of Justice," Gawani said, handing the woman her satchel. He and Gawani sat at the back of the boat. The captain gave her long paddle a mighty shove against the canal floor, and they were off. With the afternoon sun, lapping sounds of water and the smell of algae, he could almost pretend they were off on an excursion together. Almost.

Then Talio saw the Incarnites.

He could not tell if they were men or women. They were dressed entirely in saffron fabric. Hoods obscured their heads, with a vertical slit in the middle. From the neck down, a long saffron cloak reached to the ground. The sleeves were long enough that only the ends of their hands were visible. How stifling it must be under all that clothing. One out of every twenty people on the crowded street wore an orange-yellow hood and cloak. Against the gray and blue colors of the street, the Incarnites stood out like tongues of flame. Why had he not seen them before? They were everywhere. They had to be baking in the late summer heat.

The boat sailed onward, part of a noisy procession of multicolored boats and barges. The traffic was remarkable for this time of day, but his attention kept returning to the Incarnites above. Children of different ages accompanied some of them. Unlike the adults, the children wore regular shirts, trousers, and dresses, but their clothing was also the orange yellow of faded fire. No beaded fashions for them. They skipped around like ordinary children, laughing and playing, while the cloaked Incarnites fussed and doted on them.

"I did not realize there were so many," he said to Gawani.

"They participate in Nuciferian society. Mostly."

"Tell me about them. All I ever heard in Velos was that they were a death cult."

"That was a long time ago." Gawani shrugged. "Turi Peyor was their leader. An obscure man, but he had a way with words. With persuasion. He was struck with divine inspiration one day and went out into the desert. He was sure he would find a land beyond it."

Talio shook his head. There was nothing beyond the desert, nothing that hundreds of explorers over the centuries had discovered. Merin had the ocean on one side and the desert on the other, with four cities and a few towns sharing its bounty. Nothing more. "He did not find that land, I assume."

She laughed. "No. He nearly died of heatstroke, but he managed to survive. During that time, he claimed he received a divine message from Sif." The fire god. "Sif said that he was the true god, and that Peyor should turn away from Felle. Peyor covered himself from head to toe so that he could survive the desert, and on his return to Merin, he began to gather his followers."

"Who would follow such nonsense?"

Gawani appraised him with her cool, even stare. "To the uneducated, our religion might appear nonsensical. Not everyone follows the Source." She shook her head. "Peyor and his group went out into the desert to await the descent of Sif from the heavens. Most of them died. The rest believed even more strongly."

"Did they not give up at some point?"

She shook her head. "The more devoted you are to an idea, the less likely you will be to give it up, even in the face of incontrovertible proof."

"What happened to this Peyor?"

"He was one of the victims of heatstroke. Or perhaps he had not prayed enough to Sif." She shrugged. "They declared him a martyr, and the Incarnites returned from the desert to the nearest city. Nuciferia."

"And their clothing?"

"They continue to await the word of Sif, the sign for them to return to the desert to find the land of paradise that awaits them. They say they must be ready at a moment's notice." But not the children, clearly.

They came to an intersection now where the harbor was visible in the far distance. The captain used her long paddle to push off against the canal wall and change the boat's direction. "I cannot imagine they get along well with Nuciferians," Talio said. He gave another glance toward the street. "And yet they walk among them."

"Their silver is the same color as everyone else's," Gawani said. "And...accommodations...have been made to enable identification. They remain concealed at all times, even when they are alone with each other." She glanced at him. "It is said that husbands and wives never see each other's faces. It is forbidden for them to marry a non-Incarnite. Or even to fall in love with one."

By all rights, they should have died out long ago. "I never saw one in Velos," he said.

"Not surprising. They are loath to use the skylines unless they absolutely must."

Talio could imagine why. Surrounded by water, held aloft by prayers to Felle...it would be akin to blasphemy. And the ritual gutters? The waters? Surely, they could not—he was unable to contemplate it. "Have you defended many of them?"

"They defend themselves," she said. "Or they accept the guilty verdicts. It matters little."

This far upstream, the barges split off to follow a wider canal to the harbor. The captain guided their boat around one last corner, and the Palace of Justice came into view.

It was a tall, round marble building, with pillars across the front and fountains on each side, with an ornate dock. Gawani paid the captain, and they climbed back up to street level.

*I am home*, Talio thought. *After all these years.*

As per custom, the left fountain was for source water, and the right for return water. He and Gawani waited in line behind a dozen people, each saying, "Source of all things, quencher of fire...," as they performed the entry ritual, then washed their hands and crossed the threshold into the echoing building. Talio knew the way to the detention area. He knew the Palace of Justice, as he knew his own quarters in Velos. He walked as if he were in a daze.

They proceeded down a long airy colonnade, their sabots clicking on the tessellated black-and-white marble floor. *Here, I would have spoken to a clerk about my hearing. And there, I would have quizzed a fellow magistrate on a break. And there, and there...*

The Hall of Detention brought him back to reality. A guard patted Talio down and searched his clothes, then dumped the contents of his satchel onto a table and pawed through it. He gave the dowsing rod a puzzled glance before returning the items to him. Gawani clipped her copper public defender pin to her dress, and the guard let her pass without incident.

The detention master shook her head when Gawani asked after Pazli Mecomb. "They removed the Incarnite from custody a short time ago," she said. "Someone paid his bail."

Gawani shook her head in confusion.

"Was he released?" Talio asked.

The master fixed her gaze on Talio's chest, and he felt naked without a pin identifying him as part of the legal profession—silver, copper or otherwise. "He may still be in administration," the woman said in a grudging voice. "Try the Hall of Registration."

Where the Hall of Detention had been a grim utilitarian structure, the Hall of Registration looked more pleasant, except for the endless lines. When it was finally Talio and Gawani's turn, he was about to ask after Pazli Mecomb when a scuffle started some counters away. An Incarnite was arguing with a clerk and two guards. "Is that him?" he whispered to Gawani.

"How would I know? They all look the same."

One guard grabbed the Incarnite and shoved him against the counter desk. The other guard tried to restrain him while the woman behind the counter looked at them in horror. "Master Mecomb," she said, waving her hands at the Incarnite as if she could make him disappear. "You must remove your hood."

The Incarnite struggled against the guards' hands. "I refuse," he said in a low, deep voice. The hooded and cloaked man was becoming agitated. It would only be another moment before he gave the guards reason to beat him.

Talio grasped Gawani's elbow and pushed his way through the lines of bystanders that separated them. He took a moment to assume his gravest magisterial expression. "Please treat this man with respect," Talio said to the guards. "All accused are entitled to safe conduct and fair treatment." Quoted directly from Scodel's principles.

"We don't need a lecture from a member of the public," the guard holding the Incarnite down said to him. Gawani stepped forward at that point, brandishing her copper pin.

The guards' expressions were deferential at once. "Let him go," she said.

The Incarnite struggled again, and Talio put a hand on his shoulder to calm him. The man stopped and turned to him. All Talio could see were the two halves of the cloth hanging down from his hood. He felt the man's eyes upon him for an instant, somehow. To the woman behind the counter, Talio asked, "Has he not already identified himself to you?"

She shook her head. "He says he is Pazli Mecomb. But I can't read his hand tattoo."

The other guard had Pazli's left hand in his grip. Talio examined it: the tattoo was a circle containing three lines of text, just as his own identity key did. The man's hand was too badly bruised and scratched to make out any information, though. "What happened to your hand?" he asked the Incarnite.

The guard interrupted. "It was already like this when we brought him from the Hall of Detention." No doubt.

"If the peacekeepers charged and apprehended him," Talio said patiently, "then they must already have processed him as Pazli Mecomb. You do not need to identify him again."

The woman wrung her hands. "That is the rule. That is the law. We have to identify anyone discharged on bail before we can release them." Curse the bureaucracy of Nuciferia.

Along with his grave expression, Talio had another magisterial tool: his musing voice. "It could be argued," he said, "that rough treatment of an accused in this manner is a form of tampering with evidence."

The guard holding the Incarnite down blanched and pulled the man to his feet. Scodel's laws were harsh, but nowhere were they harsher than situations where justice appeared unfair. Talio mused further. "Perhaps you could rely on his identity key in this circumstance."

He looked up at the cloaked man, who stood immobile and impassive in front of him. "Do you have such a key, Master Mecomb?" The man nodded. The guard released him, and he produced his keychain from within his robes. The woman behind the counter accepted it and began flipping through her record books. Talio felt the guards relax. For now.

Once the woman processed him, Pazli turned to Talio and Gawani. "Thank you," he said. There was something soothing about his voice—deep and low, confidential, almost inviting. A voice very much at odds with the barrier his robes and hood presented.

"Who paid your bail?" Gawani asked.

"Our sabbath starts this evening. My cousins at the temple took up a collection so that I can spend the next two days in prayer, before the hearing begins. The Palace set the bail at quite a sum." A pause. "No doubt they assumed I would be unable to pay it."

"The hearing is in two days?" Talio asked.

A nod of the hood. "It has been moved up," Pazli said.

"Enjoy your prayer time, firebug," the second guard said with a scoff.

"We were hoping to interview you," Gawani said to Pazli. "For the hearing." She pointed at Talio. "This man was once a magistrate. He will defend you if you'd like."

Pazli gave a shrug. "One advocate is as good as another." Then he gave them a curt nod. "I must get to the temple before first vespers."

He brushed past them, and Talio got a whiff of his scent. It was pleasant, an earthy musk like things grown in the ground. Suddenly, and strangely, he wanted the man. No, that wasn't right. He wanted to know him, find out more about him. The man's diffidence, his foolish costume, only made him more intriguing. What did he look like, under all those robes? Did he laugh, cry as a normal Nuciferian did? Did he love?

Talio and Gawani watched the Incarnite leave the hall. "A strange man," Talio remarked.

Gawani smiled. "I married a strange man. Pazli is something else entirely. Now come with me to the manse."

"I really should find somewhere else to stay."

With only two days until the hearing, Gawani would not hear of it. They ended up walking the short distance downstream to the Balsamo manse. When they were married, Talio had always appreciated how close the Palace was to his home. Now, he wished the walk was longer. He had not seen Lady Dovuta since before the night of the scandal. He and Gawani walked in silence, the sound of water lapping against barges substituting for conversation.

At last, they stood before the door to the manse and Gawani pulled the bell cord. A gong rang in the distance. "Do not worry," she said, putting a hand on his shoulder. "I'll protect you."

A tiny window in the door slid open, and an eye examined them. The window slid shut, and the tumblers of multiple locks slowly clicked. Finally, the door swung open.

Talio had expected a servant, but it was Dovuta, barely more than half his height, much grayer, and fearsome as ever. She took two steps forward and slapped him hard enough that he staggered backward. Losing his balance, Talio sat down hard on a paving stone and rubbed his cheek.

"I have dreamed of doing that for ten years," Dovuta announced.

"It is important to have dreams," Talio said.

Gawani interposed herself between them. "Mother," she said. "He's here to help me."

"He's a monster. A lecher. A cheater. And some other words I will use once I think of them."

A little girl appeared behind her. She was about eight years old, with dark red hair and blue eyes. She ran over and flung herself at Gawani. "Mother!"

The words stabbed at him like a knife. No, she wasn't old enough. And her skin was light like Gawani's, not dark like his.

Gawani's eyes were apologetic. To his unspoken question, she said, "My husband is still at work." Then she added, with less apology in her eyes, "He's not a magistrate. Or a scavenger."

The little girl looked up at Talio with round eyes. "Who is this?" she asked.

"Someone I used to know," Gawani said. "A long time ago."

The girl peered at him. "Why is your face like that?"

"Essa!" Gawani said.

Children had asked this of Talio so many times over the years that he was no longer upset or offended. Instead, he used the response he'd learned was the best reply, "Why is your hair red?" Essa pondered this, then disappeared inside the house.

Dovuta was still seething, fumbling for words. Fortunately, she had a poor vocabulary. Talio gestured in the direction Essa had gone. "I can't stay," he said to Gawani. "I don't belong here." She nodded reluctantly.

"I will return tomorrow or the next day to talk to your mother. I need to consult my client as well." Then he added in a whisper. "Try to keep Dovuta drinking soft wine in the meantime."

"Register yourself as an advocate," Gawani told him. "Charge the fees to my account." She held Dovuta back while he left. Once he passed through the gates of the manse and started down the street, he heard the older woman screaming imprecations at him. She had learned some new ones over the years.

Talio stopped at a street corner. Where was he going? He was tired and there had been too much stimulation today already. With only two days until the hearing, he needed to sleep. He could remember only one lodging house. His feet would take him there if he let them.

He strolled through the streets of Nuciferia in the late afternoon, the cries of the street vendors and the smell of their cooked foods rousing old memories. The Incarnites and the Nuciferians gave each other a wide berth. During the long walk to the place he knew so well, not once did he see an Incarnite talk to a regular Nuciferian.

The quarter had no name; the men who frequented it had never called it anything but "the quarter." It was an open secret for men of a specific type. He had not started out such a man, but had learned about it over the years. Before the night he'd lost his magistrate's codex, he had visited this neighborhood many times.

Talio expected to see men strolling the narrow, cobbled streets, some arm-in-arm. At the very least, he would have expected to see a man or two standing in the shadows, giving passers-by beckoning looks. Even giving him such looks, on occasion. But the shops stood empty. The inn he remembered was still there, a low squat structure with dark panes of wavy glass and a heavy door with three locks and deep scratches in the wood. Two circles hung above the door, and a sign: The Double Moon Inn.

The inn looked as if it had been closed for some time. The panes of glass were dirty and streaked, and one was cracked. Talio walked around to the side to see if the kitchen entrance was open. Someone had drawn a large circle on the wall bisected with two short lines, using heavy black paint. It did not look welcoming.

He sighed. There would be other inns by the carriage station. Not friendly ones, but he needed a place to stay, not company.

Talio was about to leave the quarter when he heard the door to the Double Moon Inn creak open, rusty from disrepair. Then he heard a voice he hadn't heard in forever, a rich tenor voice that sounded hoarser than before, but still full of laughter. "After all this time, you came back," Vinne said behind him in disbelief. "The men are long gone, but let me pour you something and catch you up on everything you've missed."

# Chapter Four

Vinne was the same man that Talio remembered, but there was more of him now: he was rounder, with a larger belly, a bushier graying beard, and less hair on his head. Had he kept the new, longer beard trimmed he might have been a close match for a dissolute Scodel, gone to seed. The architect of Merin's legal system and creator of the skylines would have been horrified at being compared to a man who stayed as far away from the legal system as possible.

Once they'd entered the low-ceilinged main room, Vinne spun each of the three locks on the front door shut with a practiced hand. Then he turned to Talio with a glint in his eye. "Wine?"

Talio looked around in vain for the ritual waters. Finally, he held up his hands to the innkeeper. Vinne rolled his eyes. "Religion," he muttered. "The source of all our problems." He ambled over to a small brown rug and lifted it out of the way, revealing a trapdoor. Grunting with effort, Vinne pulled up the ring of the trapdoor and beckoned Talio over. Two gutters ran below the floor of the inn. The stone of the source gutter was paler and smoother than that of the return gutter, an accommodation for the forgetful and those with poor eyesight. "Do you need bowls, too?"

Talio rinsed his hands in the source gutter and recited the prayer to Felle. "This will do," he said. "It's the substance of the ritual that matters, not its form."

Vinne shook his head. "You must think I'm a heathen."

He shook off the drops of remaining water from his hands and closed the trapdoor. "But an adorable one."

The inn's dim interior had also seen better days. Vinne kept the tankards and silverware clean and shining, but the chairs and tables were now worn, and the rug Talio was now pulling back over the trapdoor was threadbare. The innkeeper busied himself behind the counter, then brought out two glasses, a bottle of wine and a sputtering candle seated in a bowl of water.

They sat down at one of the low tables. Vinne poured himself a full glass of wine and drank it at once. He inclined the bottle in Talio's direction, but Talio shook his head. "Fine," Vinne said, refilling his glass. "Some food, at least." He disappeared into the backroom.

Vinne returned with a loaf of rustic bread and a little bowl of salt. For a large man, he was always moving, always checking on things. He tossed a pinch of salt into the candle flame, which turned blue for a moment. Vinne may have claimed not to be religious, but he was as happy to cast a superstitious curse in Sif's way as anyone else. "They said you were in Velos, scavenging for true merinite," Vinne said. "They" were the informal network of men who lived in the shadows of Nuciferia. Although the innkeeper swore he loved only women, he spent a great deal of time with those who loved men.

Talio nodded. "Ten hard years of dowsing. But where is everyone? The men, I mean."

The gesture Vinne made with his right hand was of a bird flitting away. "Upstream. About ten blocks if you know where to look. The peacekeepers leave them alone these days." He nodded at Talio's surprised expression.

"Aren't the laws still on the books?"

Vinne snorted. "When have you ever known them to take laws *away*?" Talio had been at the Double Moon Inn a couple of times during peacekeeper raids, but Vinne had been able to pay them more silver than their wages from the Palace of Justice. An offer to supply some of the peacekeepers with male companions for the evening also worked, more often than one might suspect.

"They don't enforce them anymore," Vinne said. "Unless they find two men in an alleyway." Talio smiled. The alley behind the Double Moon Inn was well known for anonymous encounters. He had had his fair share of experiences there with other men—one or more at a time—before he'd gathered up the courage to enter the inn itself.

Vinne shrugged his rounded shoulders. "As for me, I own the inn, and I didn't want to move. So, I decided to stay." He smiled. "The occasional fellow comes by to rent a room for the night. Or a shorter period, like you used to."

Talio saw again the pain in Gawani's face as they'd sat in the skyship. "It was wrong." He broke off one end of the bread to occupy his hands. "I was married, and it was wrong."

Vinne nodded. "They say the heart wants what it wants."

"Other parts of the body want what they want as well." The innkeeper tipped his now-empty glass toward him in agreement. Again, Vinne poured himself wine from the bottle.

It took Talio some time to explain why he was back. Vinne nodded and made noncommittal noises at intervals while he drank two more glasses of wine. He laughed when Talio raised the matter of Incarnites. "They are a wonderful people."

"Are they?"

"Honest to a fault," Vinne said. "At least where silver is concerned. And some of their men have been known to stray to our side of Nuciferia, if you know what I mean." Talio could not picture it.

When Talio recounted Gawani's visit to him in Velos, Vinne burst out, "She misses you!"

"She has moved on with her life." Talio did not mention Essa or Gawani's husband.

The bottle was finished, and so was Vinne. "Well," he rumbled. "If you want to stay here while you're defending that Incarnite, I'd be happy to take you in."

It was late. Talio was exhausted and did not want to double back upstream to the carriage station. Stumbling with every step, the innkeeper showed him to a small, clean room. All the rooms in the inn were alike: narrow, with a tiny bed and washbasin. They had been built with a single purpose, and it was not lodging.

His room had only two types of vigil candles, eight-hour ones or twelve-hour ones. Talio wanted to be at the Palace of Justice as early as possible, so he lit two of the eight-hour ones and placed them in a bowl of water on the table by his bed. He made sure that they were far from the window or any other draft.

Even though the quarter was mostly deserted, the night was loud compared to the quiet of Velos. The clattering of horses and carriages, men and women carousing and a faint scream in the distance at one point all kept Talio awake.

In the middle of the night, the door to his room opened. He heard heavy, uneven footsteps and smelled wine. Then Vinne drew back the sheets and climbed in unsteadily beside him. A moment later, he wrapped his arms around Talio and pressed his belly to Talio's back. He was naked.

Vinne had done this a few times before, on the rare occasions when Talio spent an entire night at the inn. He only did it when he was very drunk, and he had never made any further advances than holding him from behind, his soft beard rasping against the back of Talio's neck. Talio suspected Vinne might not have refused something more, but nothing had ever happened between them.

Having someone in bed with him comforted Talio. He had spent ten years alone in a small bed in Velos starved for companionship, hungry for the touch of another man on his skin. He felt cradled by Vinne's hairy arms and fell asleep easily.

The next morning, he awoke to the sound of one of the vigil candles sputtering and hissing its alarm after having burned for exactly eight hours. The second candle had gone out during the night; Vinne did not buy high-quality supplies.

Vinne had somehow spread out his naked bulk to occupy the entire bed, and Talio awoke compressed into a corner. He dressed and let the innkeeper sleep. When he returned, Vinne would have retreated to his quarters. They would never speak of anything that had passed between them the previous night. Much as Vinne kept the secrets of the men who came to the Double Moon Inn, his mind kept secrets from himself.

The next morning, the Palace was much busier. Talio had to wait in line to use the ritual waters, then again to be searched by guards. In the Hall of Registration, his heart sank as he recognized the man behind the counter this time. Ten years had not improved the appearance or expression of Delmar, who always looked as if he'd smelled something bad. His greatest joy was refusing the requests of others.

"May I assist you?" Delmar asked.

"I am here to register as an advocate."

"And you are?"

*No other man in the Palace of Justice has this scar on my face.* "Talio Rossa."

Delmar bit his lip and looked skyward. "Rossa...Rossa. Why does that name sound familiar?" He snapped his fingers. "You were a magistrate here, right? Twenty years ago?"

"Ten years," Talio said, gritting his teeth.

"What was it?" Delmar's voice was quiet, innocent. "Something happened. Some kind of scandal." Then he raised his voice until the entire hall could hear. "You lost your codex!"

Talio hung his head. He had a sudden wish to be an Incarnite, an ember of anger and shame hidden under a saffron cloak and hood. "I'd like to apply for a private advocate's license."

"Is there anything in your previous record that would prevent you from acting as an advocate?" Delmar's tone was silky. "Aside from losing the codex, of course." He glanced at the woman staffing the counter next to him. "He lost his codex. Can you imagine? Quite remarkable."

Talio recited Scodel's Advocacy Pledge, which every officer of the court knew by heart. "I have not been convicted of any crime or immorality. Nor have I committed any violent acts against any representatives of the government or the royal body." *Yet.*

Over the years since his injury, Talio had learned to smile in public, to hold his head in a certain way and to appear pleasant, or at least non-threatening. This often forestalled comments about his scar. It was a simple matter to do exactly the opposite now, and lean his forehead toward Delmar, glaring at him and angling his face to show his long scar to full effect.

Delmar blinked and drew back. "Yes," he stammered. "That is good to hear." In an instant, Talio recomposed his face and resumed his pleasant smile.

The license fee was enough to make him gasp, and that was only for the expected length of the Incarnite's hearing—a week at the most. Talio couldn't imagine how advocates could survive unless they were independently wealthy. Delmar credited the fee against the Balsamo account.

"Sign here," Delmar said at last. He presented a copy of the form to Talio along with the silver private advocate's pin. "And now you are Advocate Rossa." He rolled his eyes. "Don't lose the pin."

Talio fastened the pin to his jacket with some pride and turned to leave the Hall of Registration. Then he saw the one person he thought he'd never see again. All sounds stopped. All motion ceased. He was alone in a crowd of people.

Leaving the Hall of Registration was the handsome man who had stolen his codex and destroyed his life.

Talio wanted to run after him, pound him with his fists, and demand to know why he had done it. Long ago he'd accepted he was as much to blame for the events of that night, but he still could not forgive the man for instigating the seduction.

Instead, Talio watched him retreat down the colonnade. He was wearing prosecutorial robes. Talio was grateful that the man was not a magistrate; he was not sure he would have been able to restrain himself if the man had not only ruined his career but had usurped his avocation.

He was as Talio remembered him. They'd only been together less than an evening, but his image was burned into his mind: tall, slim, black-haired, with dark eyes. Handsome and assured. Ten years ago, he'd had long black locs tied back behind his head. Now those locs were short and dyed blond. They hung free, swaying slightly as he walked.

Talio considered hiding behind a pillar and watching the man, but once he turned down the hall, Talio realized he had nothing to conceal. He had just as much right to be in the Palace. Talio caught up to him, walking directly behind the man. Part of him hoped he would turn around.

The prosecutor came up to a young blonde woman in casual clothes and handed her the vellum he was carrying. Her face was all hard angles, broken up by vivid inquisitive hazel eyes. "Emara," he said.

She nodded at him. "Cale." Her gaze moved to Talio, though he was some distance away. She examined his face but did not react to his scar in shock, revulsion, or anything but a cool interest.

Cale turned to follow her gaze. Recognition, surprise and embarrassment all played quickly across his face. "Prosecutor," Talio said in a quiet voice.

The handsome man stood silent, which Talio imagined was rare for him. Emara looked at each of them, then shrugged. "You two have something to discuss. Let me know about the paperwork, Prosecutor Faro." With that she took her leave and Talio approached the man.

It was an effort for him to stay calm. "You owe me an explanation," he said in a low voice. "That is the least of what you owe me."

"I do." Cale's voice was soft. "But not here." He glanced around the hallway. "Can we meet later? After the workday?"

The man was so handsome, Talio thought, and hated himself for thinking it. Ten years had not dulled his looks. The new fine lines on his face only enhanced his large, dark eyes, and his lips were still as red and full as ever. "I am staying at the Double Moon Inn," he added. He did not have to tell Cale Faro where it was. Their assignation had been there ten years ago, the night his life had forever changed.

Cale nodded. "I will come to see you. I promise."

He would not show. It would not serve him to stir up the past. Talio balled his fists at his side, watching Cale walk away down the hallway.

The past. The Palace of Justice was filled with echoes from his past. Gawani and Cale were part of his past. He could not reach back through time, make different decisions. He had to stay focused on the present: Pazli Mecomb's murder hearing. And keep one eye on the future. Clearing Mecomb's name was the first step in regaining his permanent license. Cale Faro was an unwelcome distraction.

Putting the prosecutor out of his mind, Talio made a mental list of tasks. He needed to compare the summary document with any peacekeeper reports and evidentiary submissions. He also needed to interview those present at the Balsamo manse at the time of the murder: Mecomb and Dovuta.

How would he even find Pazli? If he went to the Incarnite temple, would he have to yell out the man's name? The Incarnites' anonymity was maddening and foolish at the same time. Did the Incarnites even use message lockboxes? Did they refuse to identify themselves beyond their tattoos and identity keys?

First, though, the Hall of Documents. As the advocate of record, he requested a copy of the full documentary set for the Mecomb hearing and received a thick packet of vellum pages.

It was as he remembered, the same convoluted story of people dashing back and forth, an abandoned teacup and the death of Selig Ivor. The victim had been a garment merchant. Talio knew nothing about the Nuciferian garment industry, but he knew someone who might.

The newest wing of the administration building was the Hall of Commerce. When Talio left Nuciferia, there had only been two booths in the wing, but now there were several private vendors and service providers. He stopped at one that provided general message services. The generic lockboxes they offered were of cheap wood and only came in one unadorned size, but he could not afford to be fussy.

The form of a lockbox did not matter, except for those concerned about image and the judgment of polite society. Vinne would not care if the lockbox was made from the cheapest of woods. Humble or ornate, all lockboxes shared the same properties. A small chunk of false merinite lay inside the keyhole, preventing anyone but the intended recipient from picking the lock. It was all false merinite was good for. And in this case, it didn't even matter.

When Talio had lived in Nuciferia, he'd given colleagues, friends and acquaintances keys corresponding to his personal lockboxes. He could pop a confidential message into a lockbox meant for Gawani, and only the key he'd given her for that lockbox would open it. He'd been away so long he had yet to equip himself at a lockmaster. The wooden lockbox he'd bought would open to anyone, but custom and courtesy meant he should not simply send a plain vellum message without one. As Gawani had once told him, "It just isn't done."

On a strip on vellum, Talio wrote out a request to Vinne: *Can you ask around? See if any of your friends know about the garment merchant who was killed? His full name was Selig Ivor.*

When Talio had last lived in Nuciferia, the men who preferred men had a circle of contacts that spread into every sector of society. If anyone in that network could find out about Selig Ivor—the truth, not a description in a legal document—it would be Vinne. It did not matter whether Selig preferred men, women, both or neither.

Talio rolled up the message and poked it into the hole at the end of the cylindrical lockbox, then snapped it shut. It had a keyhole, but it was only ornamental. He gave it to a gawky girl with the instructions to take it to the Double Moon Inn.

She wrinkled up her nose at him in disgust. "Then you're one of those men?" She gestured to his face. "Even with that?"

He nodded. "Even with that." She shrugged and headed off on her task.

While he was at the booth, Talio also sent out a generic message lockbox to the Incarnite temple to ask Pazli Mecomb to make himself available that afternoon. It was less a request than a demand; there was no time to waste, and the hearing's expedited nature was a bad sign. He bought a few extra spare generic lockboxes, promising himself he would go to a proper lockmaster once he'd won the Mecomb hearing.

Dovuta would be at the manse. She did not like to leave it, as she claimed going out into Nuciferia made her angry, which was bad for everyone involved.

He needed a pad to take notes. There was no booth selling supplies, but he found one of interest: an enterprising woman renting out scribes by the hour for note taking and other writing tasks. A group of scribes sat idly against the wall, bored. He was not expecting to see a familiar face, but one of them was Emara, the blonde woman Cale spoke to that morning. She gave him a nod. "Emara Ravil. Do you need a scribe?"

"How much to take some notes for me?"

Emara named a steep price. "Are you flexible on that?" Talio asked.

She pointed to a sleepy, gap-toothed scribe. "Ask him. He doesn't use punctuation, though." She puffed out her chest. "I can read and write Ancient Merin."

"That will be useful when my ex-mother-in-law starts speaking in tongues. Follow me."

Dovuta was at the manse that morning, and Essa joined them in the drawing room, playing with a toy skyline station and mouthing mildly blasphemous incantations. Gawani was at the Palace of Justice. He hoped that the presence of Essa and Emara would prevent any outbursts from Dovuta.

Talio was almost disappointed by the lack of drama. He asked Dovuta to recite the events of the morning Selig Ivor died. Her recollections matched the summary document. Next to him, Emara took notes. Only once did Dovuta falter. "Did you know Ivor previously?" Talio asked when she described looking over the wares he'd brought for sale.

Her gaze flicked down to Essa for a moment, then back to him. "I buy many clothes. Of course I receive visits from traveling merchants."

He tried again. "But had you met him before?"

Dovuta looked at him with guileless eyes. "Not before that day."

After the interview, Talio and Emara walked downstream through the midday crowds toward the Incarnite temple. "What did you think?" he asked her.

She gave a brusque shrug. "I'm not paid to think."

He faced her. "For the silver I'm paying you, you can afford to think a little."

"Fine. There is something strange about her testimony. Not sure what it is."

The Incarnite temple was in one of the older quarters of the city, far downstream. From the design of the building, they had purchased a normal shrine and repainted it. The outside was a bright saffron, like their cloaks and hoods, but with uneven vertical brushstrokes reminiscent of leaping flames. They had also painted over any windows that had once existed. The other buildings on the narrow street were the usual older gray and blue Nuciferian limestone; the warm orange-yellow color gave the temple a set-apart look.

Inside, Talio looked around for fountains, gutters or even ritual cups in vain before remembering the Incarnite devotion to Sif. Instead, there were small votives everywhere, flickering spots of yellow-orange light. He rubbed his hands together and murmured, "Source of all things, quencher of fire..." in an abbreviated prayer. Without the ritual waters, he felt unclean.

They approached the front desk inside the temple, and Talio explained his purpose. The cloaked man nodded and asked them to wait while they summoned Pazli from his cloister. Incarnites walked past them, but Talio's eyes were on Emara; there was something about her neutral, curious gaze which took in all sights with the same regard that fascinated him.

One Incarnite finally approached them. Talio saw the scratches on the figure's left hand. "Hello," Talio said. "Is there somewhere we can speak?"

Pazli stood motionless under his saffron cloak. Hidden, and yet present. Seen, and yet unseen. A light, but not for anyone's eyes. "There are tables within the temple," he said. "One of my cousins will make room."

Incarnites filled the inner part of the temple. Talio heard bits of conversation as they walked past and wondered if any of it was about him. He wished again that he could wear the Incarnite cloak and hood, that he could walk through the temple—or Nuciferia for that matter—without drawing attention to his face. This was an isolating costume. There might be a religious overlay to it, but the purpose of their cloak and robes was to separate themselves from the rest of Nuciferia.

Pazli sat down at an empty table, and they joined him. "Where do you work?" Talio asked.

"I told the peacekeeper this. I am a junkman. I do not 'work' anywhere specific. I go through Nuciferia, collecting goods. Then I salvage what I can and sell what will sell."

Again, his voice was warm and soothing, but he was like a Damirian: straight to the point and no more. Had he grown up in Damiria? Or was this his attempt at hostility or indifference? Talio changed the subject. "You were a student of Gawani Balsamo. Did you complete your education?"

"I have trained as an advocate." Pazli spoke with a hint of irritation among his mahogany tones. He sounded as if he were reading from an old scroll. There was suppressed anger there, though, and bitterness.

"Then why do you work as a junkman?"

A sigh. "Are you familiar with the costs of licensing?"

Talio recalled his shock at the fee to become a private advocate. "Then you know how the system works," he said, stumbling over his words. "I mean, how the hearing will proceed."

Pazli inclined his hood. "I know very well how it works. They will find me guilty."

Again, the resistance. His law school professors had impressed upon Talio the need to make a connection with a client, to draw upon any shared experience. How had this man managed to finish law school with this attitude? When he was so...alone? Talio rubbed the part of the scar on his forehead, then shook his head. "Before we go into strategy, let us review your testimony."

Again, he went through the summary document and listened to Pazli tell his story in a voice better suited to a fairy tale. When Dovuta brought Pazli into the drawing room with Ivor and left them, the man paused. "Did you and the deceased exchange words?" Talio said.

"We screamed at each other."

"Why is that?"

Another pause. "He is—he was a thief."

It took all of Talio's control not to bang his head against the table. "So you knew Ivor before that day?"

Pazli folded his arms. "There are many traveling merchants in the city. If someone buys from the first one who visits, they are unlikely to buy from the second." He shook his head. "Ivor watched me. He learned my route. Memorized it. And then, that day, he made sure he went to all the houses, all the canal boats and barges ahead of me. By the time I showed up, nobody would give me anything. I finally caught up to him at the Balsamo manse."

The prosecution would see an obvious motive. "But you weren't selling anything. You were collecting junk."

"You do not understand the rich. To them, giving away junk is like giving away money. They regret having to part with anything."

Here was motive and opportunity. Pazli had plenty of time to poison the tea in the scullery room and return to the servant's quarters before Dovuta took the tea to Ivor. Talio asked a question he'd been told never to ask as an advocate, "Did you kill Selig Ivor?"

Pazli said nothing. He was a statue with folded arms. Talio glanced at Emara, who shook her head in puzzlement. He tried again. "Did you murder the deceased? Did you poison him?"

Still no response. This was not panic or anxiety. The man simply would not answer.

"I am trying to help you. I cannot be your advocate if you will not be honest with me. Tell me you are innocent, and I will believe you." *Or tell me you are guilty.*

Silence.

He had no more patience with the man. "They'll take off your hood, you know," Talio said in an offhand voice.

At this, Pazli tilted his head toward him. "They will not."

"Oh yes, they will. When it comes time to hang you, they will take off your hood, and your cloak, and whatever else they choose. You will be on display for all to see."

Pazli started to speak, but Talio waved him off with a hand. "I was a magistrate many years ago. In my training we learned about a young woman who wanted to wear her lover's bracelet to her hanging." He shook his head. "They wouldn't allow it. Once they have found you guilty, you are the property of the royal body. They can do anything they want to you." For once he was glad Pazli had a legal education. Talio did not want to explain the confusing concept of the "royal body" that lay behind the Merin legal system. The royal body symbolically represented all of Merin, with Queen Jaconda as the head, the nobles as the arms and heart, and the commoners as the legs.

"Then you must defend me," Pazli said at last.

"Then you must help me do so." Progress. Extracted at the point of a knife.

After a pause, Pazli asked, "What happened to your face?" The directness of it shocked Talio; usually only children were so bold or tactless. He put a hand to his split lips for a moment.

"I was a child living in Aurania." Talio spoke in a quiet even tone. He wished he could speak of it in the storytelling voice that Pazli always used, to distance himself from the memory of it. It had been twenty years after the last battle of the mages. The Smiling Queen-in-exile had launched her last desperate attack against the old Royal Palace in the royal forest. The other mages had followed, and all of them were slaughtered. She had just enough loyalty among the remaining soldiers to command them to build the barrier of runes and merinite and create the Impassable Forest.

Ancient history. Twenty-some years ago and as close to him as yesterday. "There were still Damirian soldiers alongside the Forest between Damiria and Aurania. Even all those years after the War of the Cities. Leftovers. Convinced that some of the mages had survived, that they hadn't all gone into the royal forest. Waiting to launch a counterattack on the Smiling Queen. They said Scodel was a fraud. Any attempt to tell them the truth was dismissed as enemy propaganda."

No response from Pazli, except the slightest incline of his hood. "Three soldiers came into Aurania looking for trouble. They killed seven people before they came across me. My parents begged them to spare me, but they wanted me to remember who won the war." He touched his lips. "I never forgot."

"I am sorry." Pazli's voice held a tinge of regret, or of sadness.

"That is something that happened a long time ago. We have more pressing matters. Let us discuss how you will answer the prosecutor's questions—and mine. No more silences."

Afterward, on the street, Emara asked him, "Was that true? About the bracelet?"

"Yes, I remember it very well." Talio did not add that the Incarnite cloak and hood, as religious symbols, would be legally protected. But what was more important, convincing an accused to fight for his own rights, or the truth?

He was standing in the middle of the street, hesitating, and finally Emara told him she had to return to work. "I'll be at the Palace of Justice," she said. "If you need me." Then she marched off upstream and left Talio in front of the temple.

He also had business at the Palace of Justice, business that he did not particularly want to attend to. But that was not the reason he stood there. Talio gazed up at the Incarnite temple, a solitary saffron flame in a gray-blue sea. He waited another moment, then walked back in through its doors.

Talio was embarrassed to go back up to the desk and ask for Pazli again. Instead, he stood amid the swirling crowd of Incarnites, hands in his pockets. Then he smelled something, an earthy smell. From behind him, or perhaps all around him. "Pazli," Talio murmured.

The man came up from behind him, and Talio saw the scars on his left hand. "You recognized me, then," Pazli said.

"In a manner of speaking."

The man folded his arms. "Were there other questions you had for me?"

"Not exactly." Talio did not quite know why he was there himself. "Can we sit down somewhere?"

Pazli led him to a table similar to the one they'd sat at earlier. "Sometimes Nuciferians come to our temple," the man said without preamble. "Young ones, mostly. Men and women who want to see how the mysterious Incarnites worship. To see if Sif will come down and praise us, or Felle will come down and smite us." He shook his head. "It amuses them."

"That's not why I'm here," Talio said.

"You are curious. About me, about the Incarnites. Me and my cousins are so far outside of your point of reference that you cannot imagine being one of us." His voice was lulling Talio, smooth and rich, despite the words.

Talio changed the subject. "Why did you not become a public defender? I understand the fees for private advocacy, but Crown work does not require a paid license."

Another hint of bitterness, now. "Gawani Balsamo put my name forward. They did not want an Incarnite. There was no reason to try further."

Talio leaned forward. "But there is a reason to defend yourself in this hearing. You know that Scodel's legal system is meant to protect everyone. Incarnite or Nuciferian."

"The water rituals are described in Scodel's laws. The prayers to open each hearing refer to source waters and return waters. Scodel speaks endlessly of rivers, oceans, seas." Pazli clasped his hands. "Will I see justice under those laws?"

Talio said nothing. "Why are you trying to help me?" Pazli asked. "An Incarnite?"

"Maybe because I see something familiar in your eyes."

"You cannot see my face."

*No,* Talio thought. *But I know what loneliness sounds like. How it feels to live in a world, apart from that world.* "Let me help you."

Pazli sighed. "I do not believe the Merin legal system will give me a fair hearing."

"Then let me believe for you."

# Chapter Five

Walking back upstream, Talio wished he'd asked Emara to wait while he'd talked to Pazli. When he'd first arrived in Nuciferia, the city had seemed like home. But after his second conversation with the accused man, he felt somehow alone.

Perhaps it was the sense of loneliness that radiated from him. Loneliness, and the barrier Pazli put up. The entire Incarnite religion seemed designed to keep outsiders away. Though on reflection, Talio realized that could not be entirely possible. They had started from a small group, and many of them must have perished in the desert waiting for Sif. Somehow the ranks of the Incarnites had grown rapidly over the last several years. Not through proselytization, neither Pazli nor any of the other Incarnites at the temple had attempted to preach to him. But certainly, the religion itself was not attractive enough to draw converts. It was an odd puzzle.

Back at the Palace of Justice, Talio waited for access to the ritual waters and the inevitable search, then walked to the administrative wing. It was in the old part of the Palace; he could feel a change in the air as he crossed over from the marble floor to the older granite.

Fifty years ago, the Nuciferian Palace of Justice was confined to this space and the rooms off of it. After the War of the Cities, when the Royal Palace relocated to Nuciferia and the city took on more prominence, the government started the physical expansion under the orders of the Sleepy Queen. It was now a sprawling complex of interconnected halls and rooms.

Behind the fountain at the back of the rotunda stood an immense statue of Ennio Scodel. It seemed to be hidden behind the fountain. There was no way to stand before the statue and examine it directly. He had to view it from an angle and strain to make out any details.

Scodel stood with hammer and chisel, facing an obelisk—the Obelisk of Justice—about a span high. He had already inscribed several lines onto the obelisk and was poised to chisel the next letter. Scodel's most famous quotation was engraved upon the wall behind the statue of the man, followed by the names of the four cities and their mottos:

*Let four streams flow and may four cities bloom.*
NUCIFERIA: City of Strength
AURANIA: City of Compassion
DAMIRIA: City of Honor
RYLAVIA: City of Equality

Scodel's brow was furrowed in noble concentration. His half-ripped suit revealed a magnificently muscled body. Talio doubted that anyone who spent a lifetime studying the law would be that muscular. His chin sported the equally magnificent long, bushy beard he was known for. Most male law students tried to grow a beard in imitation; Talio still had his after all this time.

Gawani walked up beside him. "Standing in Scodel's shadow. As always. Have you ever seen the original obelisk?"

"When we were studying to be advocates. It's in the Hall of Antiquities, isn't it?"

She nodded. "They've kept the Hall locked up for years now. Some Incarnite woman broke in and tried to smash the sentencing section of the obelisk with a hammer." Every magistrate's codex was a direct copy of the text from the obelisk. Since the magistrates used the codices and not the obelisk itself, this would not have affected the law in the slightest.

She hung her shoulders and looked at him with weary eyes. "I am rather tired, and the day has been a long one. Meetings, always meetings. May we sit?"

Talio had been on his way to the law school, and he wanted to delay that visit as long as possible. They found an empty bench in the colonnade. "Your meeting was with the Judicial Review Committee?" he asked.

She nodded. "I will give you an example of what we are facing. Today we were discussing public indecency."

Talio smiled. "How did that come up?"

"Peacekeepers caught one of Queen Jaconda's maids wearing nothing but her undergarments in the public fountain outside the palace one evening. No soft wine for her." She looked at him. "You've heard the saying, 'It is the noisy stream that attracts the swimmers'? Since the matter involves the royal houses, they tasked us with reviewing the law about indecency. Each of the committee members had their own views." She twirled her index finger. "And so we went around in circles."

"They couldn't touch the sentencing, of course."

She shook her head. "That is the strict purview of the magistrates." Gawani caught his eye. "But enough shop talk. Do you need anything?"

Pazli Mecomb. He needed a way to get him to care, to fight. Or an ironclad alibi, a trick, anything. "Clothes," Talio said. "I can't defend him wearing this." He pointed to his scavenger's outfit.

"I'll have something sent over. Where are you staying?"

He looked down. "The Double Moon."

Gawani's voice was quiet. "Very well."

A bell sounded. "The roster," she said. "They've updated it." A young page was slotting new vellum sheets into position on wall brackets. They listed upcoming hearings, dispositions, sentences.

They went over to the nearest posted roster and Gawani ran her finger down the list. "There. You're a provisional advocate now."

Talio followed her finger and read the line for the Mecomb hearing. He was indeed listed in the Advocate column, but that was not what surprised him. In the Prosecutor column was the name Cale Faro. As little as he wanted to see the man again, he relished the idea of facing him in the arena of a legal hearing. In the Magistrate column was the name of someone he planned to visit that very afternoon: his old law professor, Clemente Jilani.

After how things ended ten years ago, Talio knew he had to see Jilani, talk to him. It was even more critical now that the elderly man would be adjudicating the Mecomb hearing.

He could put it off no longer. He had one day until the hearing started and barring any surprising findings from the chief physician's examination of the body, Pazli Mecomb would be found guilty.

Motive: previous acrimony with the deceased. Cale would be busy digging up witnesses who could testify to previous altercations. There might even be evidence of Pazli declaring his hatred of Ivor, or Ivor declaring his hatred of Incarnites.

Opportunity: Pazli, Ivor and Dovuta had each been alone, without witnesses, at the critical point before the deceased had consumed the tea.

Means? Easy to imagine that a junkman could have access to poisons. And yet, something nagged at Talio. Something was wrong. It all seemed too neat. Or was that the superstitious fear of an advocate with no trick to play in this particular hearing?

He approached the law school wing. Students filed into gray-walled rooms as the afternoon chime sounded.

Clemente Jilani always had the lecture room near the second noticeboard. Talio performed the water ritual, said the prayer and took a seat in the back row. Jilani looked exactly the same. At his advanced age, ten years meant little. He kept his arms behind his back, leaning slightly forward, bobbing his head up and down. The students in Talio's year had called him The Pigeon, until he'd found out.

Legal History was a required course for first-year students. Talio would only need to hear the first few sentences of Clemente's lecture, and he would know where they were in the fifty-year history of modern Merin law.

Clemente rapped on the podium for attention. "We resume our exploration of legal history after Scodel's death, forty years ago. As Scodel began to craft his brilliant legal system, he worked with an intermediary named Amina to communicate with the Sleepy Queen, still in exile. Amina was an ambassador, but after the War the last thing Merin needed was an ambassador. We know little of her. So little, in fact that we do not even know her last name..."

Talio did not need to hear any more. The War of the Cities had ended fifty years ago with the death of the rogue mages. After the mages in the Royal Palace had commandeered the grounds and surrounding forest, the Sleepy Queen had used her power in exile to send mages from the Four Cities to the Royal Palace under the pretext of brokering a surrender. Instead, her soldiers and the few mages still loyal to her had trapped the rogue mages and their monstrous creations in the forest using the runes and merinite, turning the Royal Forest into the Impassable Forest for all time.

Following this strategic victory, the Sleepy Queen had called upon Scodel to craft a unified legal system. He had also been responsible for designing the skylines. Being powered by merinite, they were an excellent excuse to gather up all the remaining true merinite, putting it out of the reach for all time of any mages that might have yet escaped her clutches.

The irony of Scodel's creation did not escape Talio. Ten years later, he had died in a tragic accident when the skyship he was riding slipped off the skyline waters and fell out of the sky into the Impassable Forest. They had never been able to recover his body; only the copper hull of the skyship remained visible to skyline passengers overhead.

Talio shuddered. Skyships had taken tens of thousands of trips before and since without incident. They were supposed to be completely safe. Not for Scodel. No matter how many prayers the attendant priests spoke.

How would it be to die out of reach of civilization? For your body never to sail down a canal toward the harbor of heaven? There were rumors he'd simply disappeared. There were rumors the skyship had been sabotaged, that Scodel had never been aboard, that a surviving mage had predicted the disaster, that the Sleepy Queen had orchestrated it all. Clemente Jilani did not give marks for rumors.

Talio let the rest of the lecture wash over him. He already knew the rest of the story: justice prevailed, as it always had.

Praise Scodel. It was only when Clemente concluded the class that he realized his old professor was waiting for him by the podium. Talio came down the shallow steps, letting the other students flow past him toward the ritual waters. "Master Jilani."

"Gawani Balsamo has brought you back to defend the Incarnite." Clemente looked down his nose at him and shook his weak chin. Talio felt like a student all over again.

"Is that a problem?"

Clemente folded up the vellum sheets he had not referred to a single time during his lecture. "There is no rule that a disgraced magistrate is barred from being an advocate." His voice was thoughtful. "That does not excuse what happened ten years ago."

"Master, I have been paying for that mistake ever since."

"No, you have not." The professor gave him the full force of his withering stare. "You did not stay to explain. You did not take part in the disciplinary hearing. You did not even come to me for help." He shook his head. "No, you fled. As you always do."

Talio flushed and said nothing. Clemente went on. "When you broke your stylus during the first-year examination, you ran out of the room in a panic. When you asked that foolish question during your mock hearing, you stood in silence and let the other student come to your rescue. And when you lost your codex, you ran all the way to Velos."

"There was nothing I could do here."

Clemente shook his bird-like head. "When Pazli Mecomb is found guilty, you will run again."

"He is innocent."

"Is that so? Or will you pull another trick from your satchel? A surprise witness? Some documents out of nowhere? A novel legal interpretation?"

Anger rose in Clemente's face. "The Merin legal system is not a game. The law is not a puzzle. Scodel gave his sacred life so that the citizens of the Four Cities could live in peace." He scowled at Talio. "Whether or not you save the Incarnite from the noose, you will not find a place here among your peers."

Clemente walked past him and ascended the steps to the exit. As he washed his hands in the return bowl, he made one last remark. "I do not like you at all, Advocate Rossa."

Talio sank into a seat. His old professor's anger had had ten years to grow and fester. Now he would have to convince Magistrate Jilani that Pazli was innocent. He could appeal the choice of magistrate for the hearing to the review committee, but Clemente Jilani was the longest-serving and highest-regarded legal mind in the Palace of Justice—if not in all of Merin. It was what he had been afraid of all along. The judgment of others. The anger of others. Gawani had forgiven him, but of course she had once loved him.

When Talio returned to the inn in the early evening, Vinne presented him with a package of three suits she sent along. They buoyed his spirits. The suits were much finer than he was used to, high-quality material tailored to his frame. There was no mirror in the inn, but Talio tried on each outfit for Vinne, who gave his tipsy approval.

Talio was debating how to spend his last evening before the hearing when there was a knock at the door. It was the last person he wanted to see.

He and Cale Faro sat in silence across from each other, the past hanging between them. Finally, Talio spoke because somebody had to. "When did you become a prosecutor?" he asked. "When I was a magistrate, I knew every Crown prosecutor in the Palace. You were not among them."

"I wanted to be a defender. To work at the Palace of Justice." Cale's voice was quiet. "My family could not afford law school. So I worked at the Palace as a cleaner."

Talio nodded. His parents had been poor scavengers; he had his own story about his legal education, but he'd never trusted anyone enough to tell the truth.

Cale went on. "Someone started leaving notes in my locker. Every now and then."

"Who?"

"I never found out. The first notes were innocent enough. Telling me to leave a door open or erase a slate. And once I did so, they left silver in my locker the next night." Cale shook his handsome head. "I think the initial ones were a test. To see whether I'd do what I was asked."

His dark eyes contained a plea—for sympathy, for understanding? "Then the instructions became more detailed. More serious. Things that were on the edge of legality. Then a bit over the edge. Like following a path into the darkness." Now Cale could not meet his gaze. "I had already gone this far, and the notes indicated they would pay for my legal education if I followed them. If I complied. So, I kept doing what they told me to do."

Cale took a long time before continuing, looking down at the candle standing in a bowl of source water that lay on the small table between them. "I received a note asking to distract you that night. I did not know why. Until the next day when I heard that your codex had been stolen from your chambers." He put a hand on Talio's wrist. "But I didn't take it."

Talio withdrew his hand. He could not bear the man's touch. He did not want Cale to ever touch him again; he made that mistake long before. "Whoever set up the theft of my codex also told my wife to come here so she could see us together. She already had her suspicions by then. It must have been easy for them to convince her."

Their eyes met. Talio hated him in that moment, hated those easy good looks that the prosecutor could apply to whatever problem faced him. He hated him all the more because he could not simply blame Cale for all of his problems. Cale had provided an opportunity and a temptation. But Talio was the one who had taken him up on it. He had already started down the stream leading away from the ethical path, well before that. His marriage to Gawani would not have lasted much longer, and his magisterial career would likely have ended either way. If only he were blameless and Cale were completely responsible, but life was never that easy.

Cale looked down once more. "As my reward, I received a legal education and was selected for the prosecutorial track. They left me a few more notes after that, but I tore them up without reading them. The price had become too high."

Talio felt a reluctant, sneaking sense of sympathy. "I have done a few things that have fallen on the edge of the law myself," he said grudgingly. That was all he would allow him.

The other man leaned over and took his hand again. "Might I stay the night? Continue what we started all those years ago?"

He was remarkably handsome. But wasn't that what Cale was relying upon? That night ten years earlier, all he'd had to do was look at Talio to start the dance of seduction. Now Talio felt nothing but wariness. "I regret I have a hearing to prepare for," he said stiffly, forcing himself to pull away and get to his feet. "We will see each other tomorrow morning."

Cale looked disappointed, but he stood as well. "The Incarnite hearing. You have your hands full of fire with that one."

Talio could only repeat what he had said to his old professor. "He is innocent."

"None of them are innocent," Cale said. "They're Incarnites."

Talio turned away before Cale could say anything further, or before he himself could change his mind. He had to focus on the hearing, his chance for redemption. Like Cale, he would do anything he needed to right his career. Anything to win Pazli's freedom and get his license back.

In his room, Talio sat down hard on the unyielding bed. He picked up the dowsing rod from Velos and turned it over and over in his hands. His body wished that Cale had stayed. He was angry with himself for wanting the man physically. The prosecutor had easily been the most attractive man he had ever slept with. Now he knew why Cale had seduced him ten years ago. Not because of attraction, but as part of a Siffian bargain.

Talio put down the dowsing rod, stretched out on the lumpy bed and pressed his face into the pillow. He might not have the good looks Cale had. But those looks had no doubt given the prosecutor an easy life and a fool's overconfidence. He would convince Jilani of Pazli Mecomb's innocence. He would remove that sly smile from Cale Faro's face. And most of all, he would show him what an advocate whose soul had been shaped by the raging currents of adversity and scandal could do.

# Chapter Six

The next morning, Talio put on the most formal of his three new suits and pinned the silver advocate's pin to his chest. Vinne was up early enough to give him an unsteady hug and mumble in his ear, "Kill them all." Killing them all would be an easier task than the one he was facing. Save an innocent Incarnite from the gallows and get his license back. Simple.

The hearing room was nearly full. Pazli—he assumed it was Pazli—had already seated himself at the defendant's desk in the first row. Talio washed his hands in the ritual basins and spoke the prayers, adding a silent one for his law license and the somber Incarnite in front of him. "Are you ready?"

Pazli's voice was low and nervous, though still smooth and clear. "Yes." He sat still and quiet, but when Talio looked more closely, he could see the man's hands gripping each other, his thighs stiff and straight under the cloak.

Cale took his seat next to Talio's at the Crown's desk. It was as if the previous night never happened. They nodded to each other while the audience seats filled up. Talio glanced behind him and saw Gawani, who gave him an encouraging smile and waved a gloved hand in his direction. In another row, Emara sat watching. She gave him a curt nod.

In the far corner of the audience, a man and a woman were whispering back and forth. The man pointed to Talio, and the woman nodded and laughed. It was always the same; his face spoke for him even when he did not want it to.

The scribe rose before them and recited from a scroll. "In the hearing of the Royal Body versus Master Pazli Mecomb, the Incarnite, enter Magistrate Jilani." Talio got to his feet and heard the scraping of chairs as the rest of the gallery stood. Clemente entered the courtroom and washed his hands at the source basin, mouthing the prayers ostentatiously. Then he sat behind the magistrate's desk and rapped his fingers twice on its surface to open the hearing.

The scribe continued. "Prosecutor Faro and Advocate Rossa." Talio and Cale inclined their heads toward Clemente. The magistrate reached into his robes and placed his codex upon the bench. He rested his hand on the red book. Talio knew how the cover felt, the leather that became softer over the years. He had a pang for his own lost codex then, wherever it had ended up.

"We pray for guidance," Clemente intoned. "And wisdom. May your knowledge flow through us and grant us the ability to make the correct decision in this legal matter." He was addressing Felle, even if he did not say her name. Talio thought suddenly of Pazli's comment about the Merin legal system. From the ritual waters to the opening prayers, it was canted against the Incarnites, or anyone who was not a follower of the Source. But he had to put that out of his mind.

"Welcome in the jury," Clemente continued. Five jurors—three men and two women—filed in and sat at the jury desk. Jury selection was by lottery to ensure a range of ages and backgrounds. Talio knew of advocates who would try to read jurors' faces, telling fortunes in tea leaves. Would they be kind or merciless? There was no point. He had learned long ago a kindly old lady was as likely to harbor bloodlust as a thuggish sailor was to spare an accused.

The next step was the reading of the summary document. Talio followed along with his copy. When the scribe reached the part about Ivor's wares, he presented the bonnets and admitted them into evidence. Talio looked at the samples and frowned. They were gaudy and bright, very much the sort of thing he knew Dovuta disliked. Strange. He made a note on his pad as a reminder.

"Chief Physician Schell sends her apologies," the scribe read. "The results of the examination of Ivor's body are still pending, but she expects them within a day." Minka would not even hint at the possibility of poison until she was absolutely certain it was the cause of death. A consummate professional—and a stubborn one.

This was not unusual. The Chief Physician's office was overburdened and chronically under-funded. Clemente nodded. "Very well." He pointed to Cale. "Begin the preliminary questioning of the defendant."

Cale walked to the defendant's desk. "Are you ready to swear your testamentary oath on the ritual waters?"

"I am not," Pazli said. A stir among the crowd. Talio wanted to slap his forehead. After their discussion on religion and the law, he'd spent a fair bit of time coaching Pazli on the answers to questions he knew would arise. Swearing an oath was one of the first and most fundamental. Talio nudged Pazli under the desk.

Pazli cleared his throat. "I apologize. I am not a believer in the Source. I cannot take the oath on the ritual waters."

Cale looked from Clemente to Talio in surprise. "Then on what basis are we accepting the accused's testimony?"

Talio had prepared for this. "The Incarnites take a somewhat different oath, but with the same result." He drew out a small bowl of ashes soaked in alcohol and a flint, then lit the ashes and passed the flaming bowl to Pazli amidst the murmurs of the crowd. He nodded to the man.

Pazli made an exaggerated show of placing his hands over the flame. "I am like Sif, I am like fire," he said quietly as the murmurs fell to silence. "I am a flame that cannot be quenched. Let my speech burn true."

Clemente did not look pleased. "Felle will be watching. I do not know whether Sif is in attendance, but let your words be stated plainly and honestly."

"You are the Incarnite, Pazli Mecomb?" Cale asked.

"I am." Pazli raised his battered hand. Cale peered at it closely, but finally shook his head. He called the scribe up to read the tattoo, confirming Pazli's name, date of birth, Damiria as his birth city, and his height.

From his years of experience, Talio could sense the feelings of the audience. Pazli was a spectacle, an outsider. Worse, he was someone not to be trusted. These were feelings he had to overcome in the jury's minds...and in Clemente's.

Cale went through the expected questions: who Pazli was, what he did for a living, where he had grown up, the nature of his religious beliefs. "The gods of fire and water made a pact long ago," Pazli said. "They would keep the two elements in balance."

Talio had heard the origin of Sif and Felle every year at the water station shrine growing up; he'd insisted Pazli speak of it first, grounding the audience before he began to speak of his beliefs. The Incarnite blasphemy would be bad enough.

"There were those who worshipped Felle as the more powerful god," Pazli went on. "Since she was able to extinguish fire. Then there came a group that sought to worship the vestal flame of Sif." He pointed to the dish of ashes that was still blazing in front of him. "Not evil, not wicked. The necessary counterpart to Felle. No matter what some may say." Talio hadn't asked him to say that last part.

"Is Sif equally as powerful as Felle?" Cale asked.

"My beliefs are my own," Pazli replied carefully. "I wear this cloak and hood so that one day I may join my brothers and sisters in the desert to receive Sif's blessing. As you receive Felle's today."

Cale raised his eyebrows and shrugged, while Talio gave a silent sigh of relief at having passed this preliminary point without an outcry. "Master Mecomb, we turn now to the events of the day of the death of Selig Ivor."

Pazli had been taking his usual route that month. The Balsamo property was the next manse on the route. He had brought his pushcart that morning and knocked at the servant's door. Dovuta had let him in, and when he explained what he wanted, she promised to look for anything the household no longer needed. "She was distracted," Pazli said.

"Please confine yourself to direct observations."

"Lady Dovuta *seemed* distracted."

At that point, she'd taken him from the servant's quarters to the drawing room. "Was there anyone else in the drawing room at that time?" Cale asked.

"Ivor. The deceased."

Talio gave a silent groan. He'd told Pazli not to use the words "death," "dead" or "deceased"—anything that might link him to the murder in the jury's mind. The Incarnite might well have replied, "The man I poisoned at the Balsamo manse."

"What happened next?"

"Dovuta—Lady Dovuta introduced us. Then she went to make Selig a cup of tea." Now the Incarnite admitted he knew about the tea. Soon he would ask to make Cale's closing argument for him.

"And then?" The information was in the summary document, but it was far more damning for the accused to say it.

"We had words," Pazli said.

"What words were those?" Cale's voice was light. "Pleasant words?"

Talio raised his hand. "Objection. The information is in the summary document. The accused has already pled acceptance of the preliminary facts of the hearing."

"Withdrawn," Cale said. "You had an altercation with Ivor. What did you fight about?"

"He was poaching on my territory. He had been doing so for some time."

"Then you knew each other before this day?" Talio could see the trap closing.

"Yes," Pazli said.

"What was your opinion of Selig Ivor?"

Again, Talio raised his hand. "Objection. Irrelevant."

"Magistrate, this goes to motive. I am not looking for an objective assessment of Ivor."

Clemente nodded. "Overruled. Proceed, prosecutor."

Talio cringed. *Don't say it. Please don't say it.* "I hated him," Pazli said. And with that, the hearing might as well be over, with his license floating away on the canal waters.

"Did you want him dead?" Cale asked.

Talio leapt to his feet. "Objection!" This time, Clemente agreed with him. But the damage had already been done.

The rest of Pazli's testimony was uneventful. Dovuta had taken him back to the servant's quarters. He had waited, explaining, "It would be inappropriate to wander through a noblewoman's manse unescorted." Dovuta had brought him some pots and broken dishware, then excused herself to bring Selig his tea. Pazli heard a scream, but did not know if it was Dovuta, Selig or someone else. He ran back to the drawing room and found Dovuta and the garment merchant, who was dead.

On cross-examination, Talio paced a triangular path between the magistrate's desk, jury desk and defendant's desk as he spoke. "You said you would not leave the servant's quarters in a noblewoman's manse," he said. "Why did you leave them when you heard the scream?" He knew the answer very well, but wanted it spelled out for the jury.

"Lady Dovuta could have been in danger." *Good.*

"This 'poaching' you mentioned. Was it the first time Selig had done so?"

Pazli shook his head. "It is common among junkmen and other wandering sellers to fight about things. Ivor was known to fight with many others." He turned his hood in Cale's direction. "To *have words* with them." Excellent. Again, forestalling a potential line of inquiry.

"One more question," Talio said. "At any point that day, did you pass through the scullery room?" He knew the answer to this question, having lived in the Balsamo manse for years. Dovuta would not have taken anyone, let alone an itinerant merchant, through the scullery room. Nor would it have been necessary.

Pazli nodded. "Yes. Not when Dovuta brought me to the drawing room, or back to the servant's quarters. But when I heard the scream, I took the shortest path."

*And how did you know the shortest path lay through the scullery room?* Then it struck him. Pazli called her "Dovuta." Talio had asked him during their meeting if he'd been to the Balsamo manse, and he'd said yes. But calling a noblewoman by her first name? He likely knew her quite well. Well enough to know the layout of the manse. With so little time to prepare for the hearing, Talio had missed this vital point.

He needed time to think. "No further questions at this time." He sat down.

Cale was on his feet at once. "I wish to redirect. Now."

The prosecutor smelled blood, and Talio knew exactly where it was coming from. "How did you know the path through the scullery room would be faster?" Cale asked.

"Objection," Talio said. "Irrelevant."

"Overruled," Clemente said. "But please go somewhere with this, prosecutor."

Talio saw the exact path Cale's mind had taken, and he was powerless to stop it. He had been out of the game too long. He was not as fast as he should be, as prepared as he should be. He could not let Cale outsmart him.

"I had been to the Balsamo manse before."

Voices rose in the courtroom. "Order!" Clemente barked. "There will be silence."

Talio could predict the next questions before the prosecutor asked them. Had Pazli been to the scullery room before? Yes. Did he know where they kept the teacups? He supposed so. Did he know how to get from the servant's quarters to the scullery room without being seen?

"Objection," Talio said.

But before Cale or Clemente could say anything, Pazli answered the last damning question in a quiet voice, "Yes."

"No more questions at this time."

Talio got to his feet once more. "I wish to redirect at this time as well."

"Really, advocate?" Clemente asked. "Would you care to dig a deeper hole?" When Talio did not reply, he nodded. "Be quick. Midday break is approaching."

Talio asked for the redirect on impulse. He did not want Pazli's admission about being able to sneak from the servant's quarters to the scullery room to be the last thing the jury heard before the break. He had one question he could ask to surprise the jury and Clemente. After Pazli's odd silence, he'd coached him on how to answer the easiest of inquiries: had he killed Selig Ivor? "No" was such a simple response.

"You are aware of why we are here today?" Talio asked Pazli. Cale threw up his hands, and Talio added, "Question withdrawn."

"If you had pled guilty, we would not be in a jury hearing." Before Cale could object to this, Talio went on hurriedly. "To confirm: You did not kill Selig Ivor, correct?"

Silence in the hearing room. Was the jury leaning forward? Was the audience craning their necks? Talio only had eyes for the hooded and cloaked man before him.

Pazli folded his arms and said nothing. *No.* Talio gritted his teeth. *You can't. Not now. We agreed you would plead innocent. Don't ruin my second career, firebug.*

"Please answer the question." No response.

Clemente spoke in a thundering tone. "The Incarnite will answer the question, or I will find him in contempt of this hearing. Failure to answer will result in summary judgment."

Talio leaned down and spoke under his breath. "Say you didn't do it."

Pazli's words were lifeless and grating. "I did not poison Selig Ivor."

Talio felt the assembled audience and jury release their breath. "No further questions at this time." He sat down shakily.

The scribe rose to his feet. "Following midday break, we will call the following Crown witnesses: The arresting peacekeepers. The detaining guards. The identifying official at the Hall of Documents..." Talio ignored the words. He had a fool for a client, and a suicidal one at that. *So you say you did not poison Selig Ivor, did you?*

Pazli wrote something on a scrap of vellum and slid it over to Talio.

It read: *But I know who killed him.*

# Chapter Seven

"Then what happened?" Vinne asked.

Talio rested his head against the top of the inn's bar. "Then I realized I had a client who was withholding material evidence. Then I told nobody he was withholding material evidence. Then I realized I was in contravention of the advocacy ethical guidelines."

The innkeeper topped off his wineglass. "You have ethical guidelines?"

Talio grabbed the glass and took a swig. "In theory." He sighed. "Scodel was quite clear that failure to report a known criminal was itself grounds for disbarment. I could claim that since I remain unsure Pazli is telling the truth, I am not contravening any ethical rules *yet*." Two days on the job and he was already sliding over the ethical line.

"Did you ask him who killed Ivor?"

"I tried. No answer, of course. I used to think foolish clients spoke too much, until I met Master Mecomb." Talio continued with the recitation of the day's events. "I managed to convince him to give me a list of the customers on his route. Then I told him to stay in his cloister tonight."

"And his note? Tell me you burned the note."

"As soon as I found the nearest lit taper."

Cale had spent the rest of the day examining the first of the crown witnesses. Talio had tried to raise the issue of Pazli's beating both during the testimony of the peacekeepers and that of the guards, but Scodel had magnanimously allowed for "discretionary use of force" in his laws pertaining to arrest and transfer of "problematic" accused. From the expressions of the jury during Talio's objections, any Incarnite resisting the law had it coming to them. The hearing was proceeding swiftly and inexorably. Talio was almost out of time. "What's next?" Vinne asked.

Talio shrugged. "I could call character witnesses. The cleric at the Incarnite temple, for one." He sighed. "But I saw the faces of the jury when Mecomb was testifying. One

Incarnite in the hearing is bad enough. And Pazli does not seem to have any non-Incarnite friends." He had less than a day to come up with something. Anything. If only he were the conjurer Gawani believed him to be.

Vinne picked up the remains of their light fish supper and bellied his way into the back room. "What's he like as a person? Any redeeming qualities?"

A person? Talio had thought of Pazli as an accused, a client, a menace. Anything but a person. "He smells nice. His voice is...soothing."

He heard the sounds of Vinne washing up. "You really struggle when it comes to someone you can't look at, don't you? It's always about the looks."

"I'm not about to be attracted to a man I'll never see."

"Are looks the only thing that matters?"

"He pouts like a child." Talio ticked off points on his fingers. "He is standoffish. He treats me like I'm trying to get him to believe in Felle. He puts up barriers between us." He chuckled. "Of course, we could lie in bed discussing Scodel's judicial principles. I imagine he wears the cloak and hood there, too."

"There's something to be said for someone who smells nice and has a soothing voice. Maybe you could do it without candles."

Talio sat with this thought until someone knocked at the door of the inn. It was a message boy. "For Vinne Canto." The youth's voice cracked. He had no lockbox in his hand.

"I'm Canto."

The boy shook his head. "He's fat. No scar."

Talio passed him a silver. "Are you sure?"

The boy pushed a sealed note into Talio's hands and disappeared.

Vinne smiled when he read the note. "One of my friends has information for us about Selig Ivor."

Given the urgency, the man agreed to meet them that evening in the garment district. As they walked across the city, they passed a saffron group of Incarnites. "Does it matter what Pazli looks like under his robes?" Vinne asked.

Talio did not answer. Of course he was attracted to handsome men; such was the way of the world. Appearance was the bait and personality the hook. He admitted it was hypocritical. Even with the scar, he had found lovers and had married Gawani. He had never worried about his own looks. Others had looked startled, or made remarks, or asked questions. Like Pazli, he'd put up barriers in his mind against being hurt by such things long ago.

What *did* Pazli look like under all those layers of saffron cloth? Did he have a beard? Was he hairy? Without his distinctive deep, soothing voice, he looked and sounded like every other male Incarnite.

The garment district was part of another old quarter of Nuciferia, with narrow streets similar to those surrounding the Incarnite temple. Despite being a commercial district, the neighborhood was subdued and quiet at this hour. "Are we going to visit the man's garment shop?" Talio asked.

The innkeeper shook his head. "Hope you like the smell of duhan."

Talio groaned. Perhaps he would be stabbed next if he were lucky. Vinne surprised him by guiding him to one of the barges. They hopped carefully onto the top of the swaying boat, then took a rickety flight of stairs down to an unmarked door. "Give me two silvers," Vinne whispered. Talio sighed and handed over the coins.

Vinne rapped twice on the door, and it opened a crack, the aromatic and faintly nauseating scent of duhan wafting out on the breeze. "Two," he said, proffering the coins. The door swung open, and they crossed the threshold into the darkness of the interior.

The air was heavy with duhan smoke. A man and a woman danced a sinuous Rylavian dance as another man thumped a large drum to the slow rhythm. Vinne looked around and went to the table of a man with a long face and nose. He had ears that stuck straight out from each side of his head. The man looked like a mouse—a giant mouse smoking duhan from a water pipe. The mouse extended a hand to Talio, removing his mouth from the mouthpiece for an instant. "Oran Keel." Curls of gray smoke coiled out of his nose.

Talio looked around, but saw no water bowls, basins or gutters. He paused, hand half-raised to meet Oran's. Vinne laughed. "My friend here isn't used to anywhere he can't dip his fingers in water." He put a hand on Talio's back. "This isn't the time for bathing."

Talio gave in and shook Oran's hand. "You the type to get in some trouble like the rest of us?" Oran asked, gesturing to his face. The scar. As with most comments about his appearance, he ignored it. He did not have time to do otherwise.

"Oran here knew Ivor." Vinne did not elaborate if they'd been friends, lovers, or something else.

"Tell me about him," Talio said.

Oran withdrew his lips from the mouthpiece once more. "He was a fine man, Selig was." Duhan had stained his teeth, and the tips of his fingers were deep green—fabric or dyes, Talio guessed. "He had a source for Auranian bonnets. I had a source for Rylavian sabots. Our lines matched well enough, so why not sell them together?"

Talio remembered the bonnets admitted into evidence in the hearing room: gaudy colors, cheap manufacture, shoddy beadwork. Dovuta wore elegant clothing. Gawani favored subdued outfits. Selig would not have been able to sell such a bonnet to either of them. "How was his business going?"

"Not so well," Oran admitted. "We've all had some setbacks lately. Fickle customers, cost hikes, those dyes. That's the nature of the garment trade. Often, I pay my bills late." He took a puff on the pipe and Talio wondered how long he could go without it. "But Selig had troubles."

"Money troubles?"

"You could say that."

"Did he owe money?" Talio asked. "Loans?"

Oran shook his head and blew a quick burst of duhan smoke from his mouth. "Selig knew better. You don't borrow silver from anyone around here. He didn't have enough money to buy new stock. I pay my bills late, but he couldn't even manage that." Again, he glanced at Vinne. "Cash flow problems. If you can't follow the fashions..."

"Was he upset about his situation?"

"More than upset. He said he wanted to end it. I don't know if he meant his business or his life." Oran pursed his lips. "I tried to talk to him a few times. He said he had one chance left."

"Go on."

The man was clearly dragging his story out as long as possible, savoring the moment before he revealed his best bit of information. "He said he had the chance to make a lot of money. Something he didn't want to do. He said it wasn't much of a chance, but he had to try."

Talio leaned forward. "Did he say what it was?"

Oran shook his head and went back to the duhan pipe without answering. He had given what information he knew. But Talio had more questions to ask. "Did Selig know Lady Dovuta Balsamo. Before that day, I mean?"

"It's possible. The Ivor family used to be rich. Lost it all in some scheme a few years ago. Banking? Investments? I don't remember. He never mentioned her."

Extortion? If Selig had known Dovuta long ago. If he had incriminating evidence he could threaten to release. If he'd visited the manse to extort her. It was a tantalizing line of inquiry, and a potential alternative explanation for Ivor's death, but for it, it was simply too far a leap across the river of logic.

"Do you know an Incarnite named Pazli Mecomb?" Talio asked.

"Nope." Oran shrugged. "Lots of Incarnites around here. They stick to their own. Make their own garments if you get my drift."

Talio was nearly done. "Did you speak to the prosecutor's team?"

Oran shook his head. "They asked around if people knew Selig. Everyone said no. We don't like outsiders."

"Did you tell them Selig was despondent? That he had money problems and wanted to make a big score?"

Oran was losing interest now. "As I said, we don't like outsiders."

Back outside on solid ground, Talio pawed at his suit, which now stunk of duhan. "Did that help?" Vinne asked.

Talio shrugged and started making quick, concise notes on a scrap of vellum he'd brought with him before he forgot any salient points. Did it help? Three people had been in the manse that day: Dovuta, Selig and Pazli. Possible motives: Dovuta reacting to a farfetched extortion attempt. Selig committing a farfetched suicide. And Pazli eliminating a hated rival—unfortunately not farfetched enough.

They started toward the inn in the darkness. Talio had no proof of any extortion, and unless he could draw a connection between Selig and Dovuta, it would remain an outlandish theory. He could not afford to suggest a noblewoman had committed murder with no evidence—not to mention Gawani's likely response. And why would Selig go to a customer's manse to commit suicide?

It was Pazli's silence that Talio could not explain or understand. Or the note he'd written. The man was dangerous. All Pazli had to do was admit to an official that he told Talio he knew who'd committed the murder. Failure by Talio to produce material evidence with a reasonable probability of truth would be fatal to his second career in law. If only Pazli had admitted to committing the murder; in such a case, Scodel permitted the accused's advocate to hold their tongue in order to ensure a fair hearing.

"Reasonable probability of truth." Was that how the advocacy ethical guidelines stated the matter? He needed to review them. And he wanted to go to the Palace, where he could think and plan.

"The Palace of Justice?" Vinne said. "I'm too sober for that nonsense."

After they parted ways, Talio made his way upstream through the empty nighttime streets. Even the canals were empty of traffic except for the occasional pleasure boat festooned with garlands. Once inside the Palace, he was glad most people had already gone home. The guard on duty wrinkled his nose at the scent of duhan on his clothes. "Narcotics hearing," Talio said vaguely and walked hurriedly past.

The Hall of Reference was in the old administration building and stayed open late at night to accommodate law students and their last-minute cramming. A clerk pressed an imprint of Talio's identity key into wax.

Candles and lamps seated in bowls of water lit the gloom of the hall at intervals. After performing the water ritual, Talio found an empty reference desk. A chain held the codex to the wooden table to prevent theft. He hefted the book of scalloped vellum pages and ran his fingers across the watermark on the first page.

The one he was holding was an abridged version. It contained Scodel's principles and laws at the front and the addendums at the back. Between them was a single red page with the words SENTENCING GUIDELINES OMITTED. Only the magistrates' codices contained the sentencing guidelines and the impenetrable concordance that linked the laws to their respective sentences. He'd tried many times to understand Scodel's reasoning behind organizing the codex. The laws were straightforward, but the sentencing was opaque.

Talio drummed his fingers. Why *were* the sentencing guidelines missing? Sentencing was the strict purview of magistrates, but removing the pages themselves smacked of censorship, or excessive control.

Talio flipped to the addendum section and began reviewing the advocacy ethical guidelines, most of which could be simplified to "Do not do anything wrong or foolish, or take any action that would cast the Palace of Justice or the royal body in a negative light."

He remembered only two phrases from his ethics in practice course. The first was "conduct unbecoming." It was a catch-all: the charge for censuring an advocate where the Ethics Review Committee could not point to a specific principle they had contravened. His record likely contained the words "conduct unbecoming" on every page.

It took him some time to confirm the second phrase. The guidelines required an advocate to disclose that a client was withholding material evidence if they had "reasonable belief" in that regard. Did he reasonably believe Pazli knew who killed Selig Ivor? Why had the man refused to say he was innocent?

Talio tapped his stylus against the desk. Perhaps Pazli was protecting someone. *But I know who killed him.* A strictly moral man might find himself trapped between not wanting to lie and implicate himself, or tell the truth and implicate another...

He heard soft footsteps. A young messenger boy was walking through the dark hall carrying a slate with the word ROSSA written on it in chalk.

He waved the boy over. The messenger gave him a universal lockbox and shuffled away. The message was written in handwriting he had not seen in a decade:

*Pazli Mecomb murder hearing. Selig Ivor, preliminary cause of death identified. Contact Chief Physician Schell.*

# Chapter Eight

The Chief Physician's rooms were in the same wing of the Palace as the Hall of Reference. Talio signed out, walked across the rotunda and opened the door to Minka Schell's outer rooms.

They were empty, but he heard sounds from the workroom beyond. Without thinking, Talio opened the inner door. The first thing that struck him was how much Minka had aged in ten years. The second was the smell of death coming from the bench in front of her.

Minka was gaunt, with a long red robe and matching bonnet. As he approached, she looked up at him and gave him a smile. "Would you like to hear about it, or see it for yourself?" Talio glanced down at the remains without thinking, and his body swayed.

Minka was by his side in an instant, guiding him back into the other room and onto a bench. "My apologies. The assistant is out. Normally, you could not simply wander into the workroom."

His mind still held the vivid image of sliced organs. "I am not good with violence."

"Neither was Selig Ivor." She smiled. "But there is no violence here, old friend. Any violence occurs before the bodies reach us. Our cuts are very deliberate and precise." She caught herself. "I am sorry. I will stop with the talk of cutting and violence."

"You are working late."

"People have the impolite habit of dying at all hours. The work is overwhelming." She bowed her head. "I apologize for how long this examination is taking." Then another smile. "I should have waited until I had the full report, and then sent it on to Clemente Jilani. But you were always my favorite magistrate. A kindred spirit. Consider the message advance notice."

"Thank you." But Talio saw something he could not understand. "Brown. Why was Ivor brown on the inside?"

The Chief Physician pursed her lips. "Not all of him. The inside of his mouth, his throat, his stomach. And the tips of his fingers. Some kind of coloring. Poison, without a doubt. The cause of death."

Talio remembered Oran Keel's green-stained fingers gripping the duhan pipe. Minka went on, "My educated guess is bonnet dye. But we will know eventually."

"Bonnet dye. Is there such a thing?"

She nodded. "One moment." Minka went to a shelf on the other side of the room and pulled out a thick, worn registry. "This is a list of the common poisons we encounter." She flipped through the pages. "Most dyes are poisonous, if ingested. Bonnet dye is remarkably flavorless, I've been told. And brown dye would be the perfect color to slip into a visiting garment merchant's tea." She looked up at him. "Women who cannot afford a new bonnet every season find it cheaper to purchase dye and paint their bonnet a new color."

She had not been eating. The Minka he remembered from ten years ago had been a plump woman. Her skin was now pulled taut across her cheekbones. "Do you use bonnet dye?"

Minka barked a short laugh. "I could buy ten bonnets every season if I wanted. Fashion is for the simple-minded." He had missed her.

The bonnet dye was not something a noblewoman like Dovuta would need. "Where do they sell this dye?"

"Everywhere." Minka closed the registry with a thump. "You could never track down the purchaser or point of sale. I keep a vial in the workroom as a sample."

"When will you be able to confirm the exact nature of the poison?"

"Another day or so. But Magistrate Jilani is becoming impatient. I will submit a preliminary report stating the cause of death was poison." A grin, now. "And you will hold your tongue until then."

The peacekeepers reported no vial of bonnet dye or any other container on Selig's body. He imagined Selig begging Dovuta for financial help. Dovuta refusing, turning away, promising to bring him a cup of tea to soothe his feelings. Then Selig, alone—despondent, his last chance gone. Drinking the brown liquid in the vial. Screaming, falling to the floor in agony. The vial rolling away under a piece of furniture.

Then he imagined Selig threatening Dovuta with extortion. Something about their past together? Dovuta laughing at him, saying it would be the word of a noblewoman against that of a poor garment merchant. Going into her servant's quarters, taking the vial of bonnet dye she had purchased before their meeting, pouring it into the tea and serving it to Selig. Going to look for junk for Pazli and waiting for the sound of screams.

*But I know who killed him.* "May I see the bonnet dye?" he asked.

She brought him a small bottle cut into a rough jeweled shape. Talio twisted off the top. The base of the stopper ended in a purple brush.

Talio bent closer to smell the fluid and accidentally touched the brush with his fingers. Minka barked out another laugh. When he refastened the lid, his fingers were purple.

"You will have the dye on you for two weeks at least unless I fetch you some solvent." She looked down at her own hands. "Even I have a few spots from handling it."

The solvent was clear and oily and smelled of spirits. Minka rubbed his fingertips with a soaked cloth, then her own. She put the bottle and cloth aside and looked at him with affection. "It will take some effort not to call you magistrate." She leaned against her desk. "Advocate Rossa."

"It is strange for me to hear it too."

Minka considered her next words. "There were those who did not appreciate your unconventional approach to the law." She clasped her hands. "Or your disbarment. You are not the only one keeping secrets about your personal life."

Talio leaned forward. "What do you mean?"

"There are women in the Palace of Justice who have a vested interest in such things. I was not always as you see me before you. Once, I—"

The outer door opened, and a young man entered in red robes. The Chief Physician looked at Talio and put a finger to her lips. Talio raised his eyebrows, and she shook her head no.

Cale had told him someone asked him to distract Talio that night. But who had directed Cale? Had this been a part of a plot to remove him as a magistrate? And how was a group of women involved?

Talio stared at the faint purple splotches remaining on his fingertips. If anyone in power had wanted him out as magistrate, there were many options: review and censure were but two. Even "conduct unbecoming." Why frame him? His unconventional approach to the law? He had interpreted Scodel's principles fairly. There had been the usual complaints to the Ethics Review Committee. Perhaps more than the average magistrate. Perhaps many more. But any magistrate's decisions made them a target for complaints.

And women? Every magistrate was a man, and most of the administration as well. Despite the overwhelmingly male nature of the Palace of Justice, Talio had tried to take a balanced approach, treating male and female petitioners and accused the same. He had met Minka during a contentious marital abuse case, where the defendant's advocate had claimed that "altercations" between husband and wife could not be considered anything but a private matter. Minka's detailed report on the wife's injuries had been critical to the conviction.

At the moment, it mattered little. He was out of time and out of options. Clemente had told him he would permit no tricks. But what did he have aside from tricks? The shakiest of defenses, and an accused who would neither save himself nor identify the actual killer. It was clear to Talio that Pazli was innocent, but without proof, he needed a spectacle.

He wanted to follow up with Minka about the mysterious cabal of women, but the following day was the last day of the hearing. The morning heat was stifling. Talio arrived early at the Palace, having asked Gawani to meet him for morning meal. She was wearing yet another stylish dress with a matching pink beaded bonnet and gloves. They sat across from each other and drank tepid water with lemon; it was too hot a day for tea. "Are you ready to conclude your argument?" Gawani asked.

"I am worried Magistrate Jilani has reached a foregone conclusion."

"It is your task to convince the jury—not Clemente. What is it about him that bothers you so?"

*The fact that he could bring a complaint to the Ethics Review Committee on various charges?* "I feel he is passing judgment on me."

She gave him a wry smile. "He *is* passing judgment, but he is not your father."

"No, but he has always felt like one. A most disapproving one, at that."

Gawani finished her water and put down the glass. "Your own father approved of you enough to send you to law school, even though he was a scavenger. Wasn't that enough?"

His own father had not approved, and he had not paid for his law school either. Talio shook his head. "I will tell you that story someday. And you can tell me the story of the orphanage."

Gawani looked away. She would claim to be Dovuta's daughter until the end of time, but Talio knew the truth: she had been a foundling. It might explain her singular devotion to her mother—she had rescued baby Gawani from poverty, after all.

He looked down at his fingers, which still bore the faintest of spots from the bonnet dye. Dye. Selig and Dovuta and Pazli. Then he had an idea, an idea Clemente would despise. An idea the jurors might listen to. One that might save Pazli, and his license.

Talio excused himself. He had a favor to ask the Chief Physician before the hearing. Her assistant was present, but he managed to get his point across in vague enough terms that Minka understood what was required. Any stories of conspiratorial groups of women would have to wait.

The morning was blisteringly hot, and the hearing room was windowless. The water in the source basin was warm. Most of the audience was sweating. Dovuta sat in the second row, fanning herself with a sheet of vellum.

The scribe cleared his throat and addressed the room. "Chief Physician Schell has submitted her preliminary report on the death of Selig Ivor. She cannot be here in person this morning because of the backlog."

Talio permitted himself a small smile. Not even Clemente Jilani could compel Minka to appear. The evidentiary rules allowed for testimony and evidence to be submitted on its own, or in the absence of the person testifying.

Clemente grumbled and ordered the scribe to read the report.

"The cause of death for Selig Ivor is confirmed on preliminary internal examination to be poisoning. The type of poison used has yet to be identified. Positive identification is expected within two days, depending on its characteristics. Signed, the Chief Physician."

Talio was relieved she had followed his request that morning and had given no specific details. Without Minka to berate, Clemente turned on Cale, "Why is it taking so long?"

Prosecutor Faro held up his hands in supplication, "From what I understand, many poisons have similar symptoms and mechanisms of action. It can take some time—"

"Enough." The magistrate glared in Pazli's direction. "We know that *someone* poisoned Ivor."

Cale asked for Dovuta's testimony to be read into evidence. Although she was in the audience, nobody expected a noblewoman to sully herself with such matters as verbal testimony. Talio had already had the chance to review her testimony and submit questions for cross-examination. He was on the edge of his seat; not because of Dovuta's testimony, but because of the trick he'd planned once Cale finished questioning the witnesses.

The scribe read the document aloud: Cale's questions and Dovuta's terse answers. Did Dovuta have items to give to the Incarnite? Yes. Had she been expecting Selig at the manse? No. Here Talio confirmed the line in the summary document: "An unexpected mid-morning visit to the Balsamo manse."

He glanced at Dovuta. One would have expected her to be watching the scribe, or the prosecutor, or even the jury. But she was staring in his direction. Not at him. At Pazli.

Talio could read a witness's face at twenty paces. She had lied in her testimony. She'd been expecting Ivor that morning. That "unexpected mid-morning visit" had been prearranged.

# Chapter Nine

Talio's stomach sank. He waved his hand at Magistrate Jilani. "It is quite hot in here. Could I have some water?"

Clemente shook his head wearily. "Let us take a quick break before the remainder of Lady Dovuta's gracious testimony, so that our thirsty advocate may refresh himself."

Talio got to his feet, walked to the back of the room, and poured himself a glass from the pitcher of water that stood in every hearing room. Unlike many flustered advocates, he'd never made the mistake of scooping up water from the ritual basins. He muttered a silent prayer to Felle. Then he added a prayer to Sif—who no doubt watched over the Ethics Review Committee—for what he was about to do next. On the way back to his desk, he stopped beside Dovuta and pretended to sip the water. "When did you meet Ivor before?" he asked from behind the glass.

Her eyes were full of fear. "That was the first time I met him." She fanned herself at an increasing pace.

"Dovuta."

She held the paper up in front of her mouth. "I am a noblewoman, Advocate Rossa. They will not find a noblewoman guilty. Even if you speak out of turn."

Such was the majesty of Scodel's justice. "What really happened that morning?"

"I did not kill him. Do not pursue this, or you will not find work again, even as a scavenger."

He could not stand there all day. Talio walked back to the defendant's desk. She and Selig had known each other, and she did not want that fact disclosed. Extortion? Possibly. A clandestine relationship? Perhaps long ago, but not now. He could not dwell on it. It was time for him to put his trick into action.

The scribe completed the recitation of Dovuta's testimony, which was unremarkable. Magistrate Jilani eyed him. "Advocate Rossa, do you have any additional witnesses you'd like to question?"

"I would like to question Pazli Mecomb once more."

Cale rolled his eyes. "Magistrate, Advocate Rossa has examined the accused. He has re-examined the accused on redirect. And now he wishes to repeat the re-examination. This seems excessive."

He was getting under the prosecutor's skin. Good. "There is no testamentary rule against multiple redirects," Talio said.

"I will allow a brief redirect," Clemente said. "With the understanding that we will hear something determinative." His narrowed eyes held another message: No tricks.

Talio turned to face Pazli, who had been silent so far. The man was rigid and unbending, a fire behind his hood and cloak. One last chance to save him, before that fire burned away his new law license. There was nothing to be done but to seize the moment.

He took the vial of purple bonnet dye he'd borrowed from Chief Physician Schell that morning out of his pocket. "Master Mecomb, have you ever seen anything like this vial?"

"Is it ink?" Pazli shook his head. "I am not familiar with it."

Talio pushed the vial at him. "Would you take a closer look, please?"

Cale got to his feet, exasperated. "Is this necessary? This is not admitted evidence, and the accused has stated he is unfamiliar with it."

"I beg your indulgence, magistrate," Talio said. "No doubt the Crown would want justice to be served here." He gave the sweetest smile to Cale. Clemente waved his hand in irritation.

Talio showed Pazli the vial once more. The accused shook his head. "As I said earlier, I have not seen anything like this before."

"Thank you." Talio turned back to the jury. "It is very warm in the hearing room today."

"Magistrate," Cale said, fuming.

Talio wiped his forehead. The audience and jury erupted in laughter, as he'd expected. Cale was looking at him wide-eyed. He knew what they were all seeing: a smear of purple dye across his forehead.

Talio walked over to the scribe. "I wish to enter this vial as secondary evidence. Reference material in advance of the Chief Physician's final report." He placed the vial down on the scribe's stack of vellum. When he picked it back up, the top sheet came with it, stuck to the bottom of the vial.

More laughter. "My apologies," Talio said and peeled the bottle from the sheet. "Here you are."

Instead of releasing the vial, Talio managed to run it along the edge of the man's wrist. "What is this?" the scribe asked in alarm, rubbing at the stain. This only transferred the purple dye onto the fingers of the man's other hand.

The laughter was turning to conversation and buzzing confusion. "My patience has come to an end," Clemente said. "Your redirect is finished."

Talio put the vial back in his pocket. "That was a vial of bonnet dye. Tomorrow, the Chief Physician will testify that Selig Ivor's body contained a large quantity of brown bonnet dye. Swallowed. The cause of death."

Cale shouted this time. "Magistrate, it is not the advocate's place to admit expert testimony!" *And it was not your place to seduce me, ten years ago. But here we are.*

Talio raised his purple-stained hands. "One more question and I will be finished. One more." Jilani's eyes held daggers. "Lady Dovuta. Master Mecomb. Would you hold up your hands, please?"

Slowly Dovuta removed her gloves, then raised her hands. Pazli raised his in front of him. They were both clear of dye.

"This proves nothing!" Cale burst out. "That was several days ago. And surely there is some way of removing this dye. This is nonsense." Talio was quite enjoying the prosecutor's reaction. Revenge a decade later was still as sweet. Cale had proven far more emotional than he'd hoped, as opposed to the morose Incarnite who sat by his side, silent.

"If we asked the peacekeepers who detained Pazli Mecomb, would they remember any brown dye on his hands? Or on Lady Dovuta's?" Talio asked. "Wouldn't they have noticed a noblewoman with stained hands? As for the Incarnite, they had to inspect his hand closely on two occasions that day to identify him. Isn't it odd that nobody reported his hands were stained brown?"

Cale was livid. "Gloves. He could have worn gloves. This is a specious argument."

Talio walked back to the defendant's desk. "I did think of that." He took a pair of gloves he'd borrowed from Minka that morning out of his satchel. "These are the heaviest industrial gloves available for sale in Nuciferia. Would you care to try them on?"

Cale hesitated. Talio could read his thoughts; if he refused, it would be an instant admission of defeat. Finally, the man slipped the gloves on and faced him. Talio handed him the purple vial and he took it with reluctance.

Talio waited a moment, then took the vial back. His own fingers were now completely purple. "Please remove the gloves."

Cale peeled them off without saying a word. His fingertips were stained purple.

Talio turned to Clemente. "Magistrate Jilani, I submit that whoever poisoned Selig Ivor would have had dyed hands. Neither Lady Dovuta nor Pazli Mecomb would have had the time to completely clean off the dye before the peacekeepers arrived."

The murmuring of the jurors rose to a din, and Clemente rapped his fingers on the desk. Talio did not like what he saw in the magistrate's eyes. "Pending the expert testimony of Chief Physician Schell," Clemente said stiffly, "I direct the jury to return a preliminary verdict of acquittal for the Incarnite, Pazli Mecomb."

A verdict of acquittal was not the same as one of not guilty. Acquittal simply meant the evidence was insufficient for a conviction. The verdict would follow Pazli and prevent him from acting as an advocate. It was not Talio's place to challenge a magistrate's direction to the jury, but what was one more ethical violation?

"Magistrate," Talio said. "I have heard rumors that Selig Ivor was having money problems." He ignored Cale's incredulous look. "Since he was the only person in the Balsamo manse with stained fingers, I suggest a theory. When Lady Dovuta refused to purchase his inferior bonnets, he could take no more and committed suicide then and there. Would that not be a more sensible finding?"

Clemente was not having it. "Rumors. Unless we hold a side hearing to investigate."

He would have to go even further, then. "This hearing has been a blot on the fine reputation of Lady Dovuta and the Balsamo name. I suggest we no longer try her patience." Talio pretended an idea had suddenly come to him. "One might check the Hall of Registration and review the renewal payments made by Selig Ivor for his business license. Any irregularities or delays would be suggestive of financial troubles."

He watched the magistrate weigh the options. The garment business was risky. What were the odds a vendor of shoddy goods such as Selig Ivor had made every license payment on time? Talio was now out of tricks, but there was no way for Clemente to know that.

"Very well." Clemente's tone was deadly. "I accept your reasoning. Pending the testimony of the Chief Physician and a final report, I direct the jury to return a preliminary verdict of not guilty. I issue a second preliminary verdict that the death of Selig Ivor was a suicide. I also note that Lady Dovuta is blameless." He rapped his fingers twice on his desk. Without a further word, he rose and strode from the hearing room. Talio knew from experience that Clemente had a set of ritual basins in his private rooms.

Cale gave Talio a rueful, wondering shake of his head and went to talk to the scribe. Talio returned to the defendant's desk, and Pazli whispered in his ear. "What if they review Ivor's records at the Hall of Registration?" Of course. Now that the hearing had concluded, his client suddenly was interested in the details.

He whispered back. "I suspect there will be some payment issues. Someone told me recently the garment industry is not a stable one."

Pazli's shoulders slumped. Talio sensed a tremendous tension leave the man. "Thank you," he whispered. "I did not think it was possible, that I would escape the gallows."

Talio patted him on the shoulder, felt the muscle under his hand and the cloak. "You should trust in Scodel's legal system. Or, at the very least, in your advocate." In the end, Selig Ivor committing suicide at the Balsamo manse was a nonsensical finding. But he did not believe Dovuta could have done it, and Pazli certainly was innocent. He felt like every law student making a convoluted argument in a mock hearing, sailing away further and further from the island of rationality into a sea of doubt.

"This is not a legal system for Incarnites. Perhaps my advocate is unable to see that from his position." Then it was as if Pazli remembered himself. "But I am still grateful."

Looking around the hearing room, Talio did not see smiles, congratulations or approval on the faces of the audience. As Clemente had said: *Whether or not you save the Incarnite from the noose, you will not find a place here among your peers.* He offered to buy Pazli a midday meal, and the man surprised him by accepting. They walked out of the hearing room, and Talio tried to ignore the words he heard in passing. *Improper. Incarnites. Firebug.*

The canteen was nearly full, but Talio spotted a free table and walked toward it. An attendant approached him and Pazli. "That table is reserved."

"Is it?" Talio asked. "I do not see a placard."

He looked around and saw another free table. The attendant followed his gaze. "That one is reserved as well."

Pazli put a hand on Talio's shoulder. "Let us go."

"Do you know who I am?" he asked the attendant. He had always hated it when Dovuta would say this, but he had no other weapon to deploy.

"It would be hard not to recognize you," the attendant said with a pointed look at his scar. "Even after ten years." Talio looked around and saw the closed faces of the patrons.

He and Pazli walked to the front hall of the Palace, where he examined the updated roster. Under the Mecomb hearing, he read "Preliminary disposition: not guilty" and felt satisfaction.

"You are free to return to the Temple now," Talio said. "For vespers, if you like."

A smile in Pazli's voice. "Vespers are in the evening. But I will be busy the next while earning the silver I need to pay for this legal adventure."

Talio was confused. "The bond for the bail payment will be discharged. Your cleric will get the money back."

"I meant your fees."

Talio shook his head. "I took on this work to regain my law license. Do not trouble yourself with thoughts of payment."

Pazli's voice was suddenly cold. "I see. Not because you thought me innocent. Not because you wanted to help someone who could not afford your fees. Congratulations on your law license." He turned and walked toward the exits without a word.

Talio stood shaking his head. How could anyone deal with a man who heard every word as a weapon?

# Chapter Ten

Celebrations of Pazli's acquittal were few. Talio was not surprised, and yet a part of him had hoped someone might send a congratulatory message lockbox that evening, or even come by the Double Moon Inn. He slept poorly that night. A simple trick and some quick thinking were all that saved Pazli Mecomb from the gallows. Had Jilani found him guilty, sentencing would have been merciless. Scodel's sentencing guidelines might remain hidden from view, but every citizen knew that murder was a hanging offense.

He slept late and awoke to find three messengers bearing generic lockboxes waiting in front of the inn. The first was from Gawani. She wanted to see him at the Palace of Justice. Congratulations—finally—were in order.

The second lockbox was made of the flimsiest wood he had ever seen. Pazli invited him for dinner in two days, after the weekly Incarnite prayer period. Would Talio meet him at the temple? He wrote the word "yes" and sent the lockbox back with the messenger.

The final lockbox bore the symbol of the Palace of Justice. Talio opened it with dread.

The title read "Conduct Unbecoming" in red. They had charged him with ethical violations based on his antics in the Mecomb hearing. The note did not mention his license, but it was ominous and reeked of Clemente Jilani's involvement. Talio very much did not want to go to the Palace, but they were holding his license over his head.

The Conduct Unbecoming charge occupied his thoughts on the walk upstream. It would mean the end of his second legal career before it even started. Nobody could come back from both a disgrace as a magistrate and a finding of ethical malpractice as an advocate.

In the Hall of Documents, he reviewed and signed the acknowledgment of ethical malpractice, which was as vague as the lockbox message had been. Then he found Gawani's rooms at the end of the administrative wing. He heard the scratching of her stylus within and opened the door without knocking. Her rooms mirrored her personality—cozy and tidy, with soft rugs and old lamps. She looked up from her worktable and motioned him to sit down.

"Today is a happy day." Gawani stood and brought him a wrapped package—small, heavy and angular. "Go ahead, open it."

It was her merinite water generator; it even bore the Balsamo clover insignia, along with the image of Felle and the required incantation inscribed along the side. "I can't," Talio protested. "This is far too much."

"You defended Pazli Mecomb in an impossible hearing. This is the least I could do."

"What would your mother say if she knew?"

Gawani waved her hand. "Mother, mother, mother." She shrugged. "Being raised by a noblewoman can be a double-edged sword."

Gawani the foundling. "Where were you actually born?" She had always been so reluctant to discuss it, but a good advocate knew to keep asking.

After all these years, she finally relented. "Rylavia. She travelled there on a charity mission before her wedding to Father. Said she fell in love with me at the orphanage and couldn't let me go."

"You are indeed very lovable."

Gawani smiled, then showed him a sheet of vellum from her worktable. Even at a distance, he could see the red letters: *Conduct Unbecoming.* "The Ethics Review Committee, however, has somewhat less love for you."

He shook his head. "Is there any hope?"

"I told you successfully defending Pazli would get your license back. This makes it impossible." She drummed her gloved fingers on the sheet. "But there is another option."

"Jump into the source fountain in front of the Palace and make a public prayer to Felle?"

Gawani laughed. "Nothing so dramatic." She handed him a pamphlet with the title: *Program for Wayward Advocates.*

Talio shook his head. "Wayward. You are joking, certainly."

She did not reply directly. "Two years ago, there were some irregularities with the law school's graduating class. Instead of disbarring every student, they needed an alternative. Clemente put together this framework."

Jilani. Talio did not have to flip through the pages of the green-bound text to know it would be cruel and punitive. He did not feel like playing Gawani's usual game of pulling each word from her, so he kept silent until she spoke.

"You have until the end of the judicial season to earn one hundred points and regain your license," she said. "Each hearing you successfully argue counts for a certain number of points. The more serious the case, or the more public the matter, the more points you can get."

His anger was fading. Here she was, still trying to help him after all this time. "The judicial season ends in six months. Less than that. How much was the Mecomb hearing worth?" Talio asked. "In points." The question was sickening in its implication.

Gawani would not meet his eyes. "Thirty. You are well on your way."

He got to his feet, water generator in one hand and the hateful pamphlet in the other. "Nobody will hire me," he said. "Except perhaps the Incarnites. Do day-to-day Incarnite matters earn points in Jilani's system?"

"In some cases. Again, it is matters brought before a magistrate that you should focus on." She did look at him, then. "Clemente was very civic minded with this project. You can also earn points if you advance the state of the law. Even more if you perform a service in the name of the queen."

He wanted to laugh. "Appoint me to the Judicial Review Committee or get me an audience with Queen Jaconda, then. Unless you have some other ideas."

"There's a noticeboard in the Hall of Commerce. Put up a sign asking for clients. Ask around."

Talio crossed to the door. "You won Pazli's freedom," Gawani said. "Nobody thought it was possible, except me. You can do this."

"And if I were to leave it to the next judicial season?"

She shook her head. "By registering as an advocate for the Mecomb hearing, you've set the river flowing. Either you succeed this season, or—" Back to scavenging.

He hesitated, debating whether to say one last thing or go. He saw the question in her blue eyes. "I never told you, ten years ago," he said at last. "You caught me, and then I fled. I ran from you, from the Palace, from everyone." He closed his eyes. "I am sorry for what I did to you."

Gawani sighed. "I know you are, Talio." He nodded and left her rooms.

He spent the next two days reacquainting himself with details of the legal system. Scodel's laws were the same, of course, but he had forgotten a great deal of peripheral matters. There were also changes to procedure, such as the new private advocates. Talio re-accustomed himself to the rhythms of the library in the Hall of Reference and pored over the forms in the Hall of Registration.

All the while, he tried to find clients.

The noticeboard in the Hall of Commerce was crowded, but Talio found a spot to post his notice. He agonized over the wording. Could he say "reasonable pricing" if he had to adhere to the advocacy fee schedule? What about "fast service"?

It ended up mattering not a bit. A day after he posted the notice, he came back from the Hall of Reference to find it torn down. Talio rechecked the posting rules, but he hadn't done anything wrong.

He put up another notice. Again it was torn down, faster this time. Talio experimented: a notice for a lost dog stayed up; once he added "Contact the Double Moon Inn," down it came.

He could not guard the noticeboard at all hours; he had to sleep. It occurred to him to hire Emara to watch it for him, but even if she could be there day and night, Talio could not afford what she would undoubtedly charge.

His next idea came from seeing a jar of quick-sealing wax for sale in one of the Hall of Commerce booths. Talio spread the wax over the back of his notice sheet, then stuck it to the board. There was no way anyone could tear it down now.

He came back later that day to find two words scrawled upon it: FIREBUG DEFENDER. He would have to find another way.

Vinne's network of men was no help, either. They stayed far away from the law if they could help it, and those unlucky enough to be ensnared by the legal system either pled guilty or had contacts that could help them outside of the courts. Talio was out of ideas.

* * *

The next evening, he walked downstream to the Incarnite quarter. Incarnites were milling about outside the temple in the early dusk light. One Incarnite was standing at the exterior of the temple entrance. There was something in the way the figure stood, the way they moved.

Talio came up to him. "Hello, Pazli."

"How did you know it was me?" came the deep muffled voice, speaking in the distinctive way Talio had come to know.

"I recognized your handsome face."

Silence. "Ah, I see. A joke."

"It was supposed to be, yes."

Pazli folded his arms. "We have ways of telling each other apart. Your kind usually think we all look the same."

This was not going to be a pleasant evening. Talio cleared his throat. "Where shall we have dinner?"

Pazli pointed toward the temple. "Join us. We are about to serve the evening meal."

A dinner with Clemente Jilani sounded preferable, but Talio followed Pazli into the dining hall. Two dozen rows of long, dark orange benches and trestle tables covered with candles filled the hall. Hundreds of Incarnites filed in, taking their seats in an orderly fashion. Pazli gestured to Talio to follow him, and they sat down at one end of the room. He was the only one not wearing a cloak or hood.

Talio braced himself for prayer and songs, but there were none. After a moment, doors set into the far wall opened and more Incarnites came out bearing trays of food. Each Incarnite at a table passed the trays down along to the far ends until everyone was served. There was a quiet, meditative quality to their rhythmic motions.

Talio hesitated with his spoon above the food. "Do you need salt?" Pazli asked.

Talio shook his head. "No, it's not that." He hesitated. "When do you pray?"

"We prayed when we came into the hall. We prayed when we passed the trays down the line. And I prayed just a moment ago. Would you like to sing aloud?"

"No, no," Talio said, horrified. He settled into his meal. Based on Pazli's dour personality and the ascetic decoration of the temple, he'd expected dinner would be institutional. But the food was good. There was a bit of meat, vegetables, a hunk of dark bread and even some fruit. The Incarnites ate in silence, with occasional hushed murmurs.

After the meal, Pazli took Talio for a walk around the building. "You were expecting something different at supper?"

Talio flushed. "Singing. Prayer. Exhortations."

"Is that what you do when you pray?"

"I go twice a year." Talio did not know why he felt so defensive. "The water purification ritual at the end of fall and the winter thaw ceremony in spring. There's a bit of singing. Some prayer. No exhortations."

Pazli guided him up the stairs to the third-floor cloister. "I am sorry for you," he said to Talio. "To have so little prayer in your life. But do not think we are a cult."

Talio wondered if he had somehow set the man off again. "My father once said the difference between a cult and a religion is about half a century."

They stopped in front of a door with Pazli's name stamped onto a nameplate. "Scodel created Merin's legal system fifty years ago," Pazli said. "Would you call it a cult?" *Praise Scodel.*

When Talio did not reply, he added, "Would you like to see my room?"

"If you'd like." He could not imagine why Pazli was doing this. Talio might feel some curiosity, intrigue, perhaps even attraction toward the other man, but Pazli had shown nothing but indifference.

The room was saffron, with furniture in shades of orange and yellow. He would have thought that an all-saffron room would be oppressive, but every piece of furniture had its own shade, slightly different from the walls and floor. It had a soothing harmony. There were two cups of water on the side table. Pazli watched as he performed the usual water ritual, and Talio realized the man placed them there for his benefit. It felt odd to speak prayers to Felle in the middle of an Incarnite stronghold.

They faced each other in the small room. "I wanted to apologize," Pazli said with some difficulty, folding his arms yet again. "If I have seemed distant. Or hostile."

Pazli's posture and voice seemed distant and hostile at that very moment. "You don't have to apologize," Talio said.

"I believe I do." Pazli sat down on the bed. "Whenever I speak with a Nuciferian, there is always...something within them. Derision. Pity. Hatred, even."

"I don't hate you," Talio said gently, standing before him.

"Simply because we are on opposite sides of a religious divide," Pazli said as if he had not heard him. Then, as if catching himself, he added, "The cleric says I have the habit of putting up a wall between me and other people."

Talio sat down next to him. "Does the wall help?"

Pazli shrugged. "Sometimes. Does your wall help you?"

Talio rubbed his hand across the scar on his forehead without thinking. He had no answer to that. Instead, he glanced around the small room. He was surprised to recognize a wooden box on the shelves. He hadn't seen the game since he was a child in Aurania. "Do you play, then?" he said, pointing to it.

"Four Cities?" Pazli asked. "When I was younger. Not so much, now."

After what had happened to his face, Talio's parents had forbidden him from playing a game based on the war, but they had not been able to stop him from sneaking out at night to play the copy a neighboring girl owned.

He wanted to leave, to go back to the Double Moon. To figure out how to get clients, before he lost his last chance at staying in Nuciferia for good. Four Cities was a game of building walls, but perhaps this was a night for tearing them down. "Would you care for a game?" Talio asked.

"If you'd like." Pazli took down the box and emptied its contents onto the bed. They sat on either side, Talio stacking the worn and battered playing pieces and cards while the other man assembled the board.

"I'll play Aurania," Talio said. "If you don't mind. I grew up there." Aurania also had the advantage of an extra agricultural unit per turn, but this he did not mention.

"I choose Damiria, then." Pazli dealt the cards, and they took their starting positions on the board.

Pazli played a typical Damirian approach to the game—acquisition and conquest, risking his position and leaving himself open to flank attacks. Though Talio was in the Auranian role, he employed a variety of strategies to keep the other man off balance, from the retrench-and-build tactic of Nuciferia to the citizen-pleasing infrastructure/agriculture combination beloved by Auranian players.

All the while, he kept his eye on one of the pieces in the tower stack. He'd noticed the cannon piece at once; it was unusually worn compared to the other tower pieces. Pazli had knocked the tower stack over just before they began to play, and when he'd put the cannon piece back in the stack, he'd turned the cannon away from Talio. An old trick to get him to pay less attention to the piece. Another round and the piece would be available.

Talio found himself invested in the game. He had always been competitive, always focused on winning. During the hearing, he'd enjoyed sparring with Cale and ultimately beating him. But here in the cloister with Pazli, he found the other man a challenge. His strategy was excellent, his mid-game formidable. For an Incarnite.

Time for a distraction. "I know why you sent me that note," Talio said. "During the hearing." He'd had a few days to contemplate this and deduced a logical explanation.

Pazli laid down a spy card and picked up two knowledge cards in return. "Is that so?"

"You said you knew who killed Selig Ivor. I assume you thought it was Dovuta."

He sensed a sudden tension in the other man. Pazli nodded. "You were sure Dovuta had done it," Talio said. "Why not tell me?"

Pazli folded the knowledge cards into his deck and shifted position on the bed. "The first time I came to the Balsamo manse, she had broken some crockery. She yelled at me. The next time, she apologized, and I showed her how to piece it back together. Then there was a second conversation the next time I visited, and one after that." He looked up at Talio. "I had been Gawani's student, but I became Dovuta's friend. Do you understand?"

"Didn't Dovuta care what people thought?" Pazli's hand tightened around his cards, and Talio regretted saying it.

"When we were alone, she was a different woman than she is in public. A much kinder one. Just as Gawani can be less kind in certain situations."

Pazli had wanted to shield Lady Balsamo, protect her. But he would not implicate himself. And so, his response: frozen silence. He and Dovuta had wanted to protect each other when the true culprit was neither of them. The whole business of Selig Ivor's death still bothered Talio. He'd convinced the legal system that it had been suicide, but he had yet to convince himself.

The cannon piece was now in play. Pazli had played his spy card instead of holding it for this moment. "Do you have any new hearings coming up?" he asked. "I imagine it is busy at the Palace."

Talio looked up from the board. "I admit to having some trouble finding new clients." He smiled. "As a newcomer to Nuciferia."

Pazli picked up a grain card, but his hand stopped in mid-air. "And as someone who defended an Incarnite."

Talio ignored this, and casually dropped two stone cards into the discard pile. He moved the cannon piece from the stack onto the top of his Auranian tower. The game was all but over.

"Would you like to place a wager?" Pazli asked.

He was one turn away from firing on Pazli's undefended tower, and the man wanted to make a bet! "What do you offer?" Talio said in a neutral tone.

"I may have some clients who could make use of your services." Incarnites. Worth few points, in Clemente's view. But he needed the silver.

"And if you were to win?"

"Then I have a favor to ask you."

Talio suddenly felt warm. "That could mean anything." Had Pazli invited him to his room as a sexual overture? But this was madness. He was clearly misinterpreting the signals from the other man. Why was he playing at this pretense?

"It is a legal matter. Quite simple, I promise you."

Talio nodded, relieved but somehow disappointed. "Then I accept your wager." He wanted to shake Pazli's hand as confirmation, but the man was holding his cards before him. Cale was as intelligent as this man, and he'd been able to easily resist the prosecutor's charms. It was that wall that he'd spoken of; he wanted to break past his defenses, see the fire that lay behind it.

He swiveled the cannon piece atop his tower until it was facing Pazli's. "I strike, using five stone." Talio laid down the stone cards between them. "Defend yourself."

Pazli said nothing.

He would not permit this nonsense again. If the Incarnite was going to be silent in anger, he would get up and walk out. "Your response?" Talio said.

"I have won."

He laughed and pointed to Pazli's tower and cards. "You do not have enough defensive resources. You have lost, quite plainly."

Pazli's voice was mild. "As you know, any cannon attacks from other players on Damiria are automatically repelled by virtue of its military might."

There was no such rule. The man was trying to make a fool of him. He would show him who the fool was. Talio grabbed the box and started reading the instructions.

After a while, he slowly put it down. "Were you not familiar with the rule?" Pazli asked. "As Scodel would say, ignorance of the law is no excuse."

It was a little-known, niggling, foolish rule, but it was a rule, nonetheless. Nobody ever had reason to use the rule, because those playing Damiria always took the cannon piece. The piece that Pazli had carefully positioned to make Talio think he wanted it for himself. The piece Pazli maneuvered him into taking. He had planned it all, from the moment they'd sat down at the board. Or even earlier, perhaps—had Pazli placed the game on the shelf to catch his attention? Was the favor he sought that important?

Talio crossed his legs. He had been outmaneuvered. By an Incarnite. A junkman. By someone who could grasp the advantage as well as he could and turn it to their benefit. Here was an intellectual equal, someone who was not afraid to challenge him, wall or no wall. He was aroused. Pazli's deep voice, his physical presence, his scent that faintly hung in the room about them. He had conquered Talio...in the game, at least.

They faced each other on the bed in silence, the game board between them. He sensed the other man getting up his courage to say something. It was odd. Heavy cloth obscured all but the most obvious of Pazli's movements. The slightest motion of his head, the way the cloak moved about his shoulders, the position of his body—these cues spoke to Pazli's thoughts and feelings as if he sat before Talio, unburdened of his disguise.

Pazli placed his hand on Talio's. "As I said, I need something from you."

He felt a jolt as their hands touched. It was the one part of Pazli that was open to him, unencumbered by cloth. Long, tapered fingers laying atop his. Their sturdiness excited him. How strange, to respond to someone hidden from him, except for the electric touch between them. He longed to lean over, to touch—but what would he touch? He could not remove Pazli's hood or his cloak. This had to remain a one-sided attraction.

After a long moment, Pazli withdrew his hand. "I require your help as an advocate."

"The system has exonerated you."

Pazli shook his head. "Not me. My younger cousin. His name is Amaury."

"What has he done?"

Pazli's voice was unhappy. "Nothing. They are investigating him. He is involved with a bad business, but he is innocent. I know it."

"What have they accused him of, then?"

The single word Pazli spoke was devastating, "Clipping."

Talio did not know how to reply. The queen considered defacement of currency of Merin the most serious crime next to murder and rape. It was more serious than assault. Anyone who snipped off the edges of coins hoping to make more coins was a fool. Or desperate and poor. He spoke as gently as he could. "Pazli, every accused ever charged with clipping has been hanged. There have been no acquittals."

The man's voice shook. "I know, but he is not guilty. He has made the wrong friends. The peacekeepers are investigating them, and they will follow the trail to Amaury."

What could he do? He had an ethics review committee investigating him, and Clemente Jilani watching him. This was no game. "You could defend him yourself. I could borrow some money for your advocate's license."

"You have been a magistrate and an advocate. I need your help."

"I'm not sure I will even stay in Nuciferia." The eyes of his contemporaries in the canteen still haunted him.

Pazli set his shoulders. "Very well. You will not defend an Incarnite."

Talio would not let him escape that easily. He took Pazli's bruised, tattooed hand in both of his. "Once they arrest him, they will make an example of him. Whether or not he is an Incarnite."

Pazli withdrew his arm, but brought it up to Talio's face instead, stroking the back of his hand along Talio's beard. The contact was intimate, shocking. He shivered at the touch.

"I have wanted to touch you," Pazli whispered. "Ever since you intervened on my behalf with the guards."

Then he drew back, and the moment passed. It had been too much. Too close, too intense. For a moment, Talio had broken through the impenetrable wall surrounding the man, and Pazli would not allow it.

"You should go." Pazli's voice was distant. "It is late." He folded his arms. Talio did not wait. The wall would not come down again.

On the street, Talio ignored the Incarnites and walked along the edge of the canal, kicking pebbles into the water below. *You should go.* Yes, he should. What was keeping him here? A ruined career? A man who was fighting his own desires?

He would follow Pazli's direction. He would go all the way back to Velos.

# Chapter Eleven

Talio asked Vinne to intercept any message lockboxes that came for him unless they were from the government or the Palace. He did not want to hear from anyone, and he did not want to be summoned anywhere unless forced to go. Talio did not expect the Ethics Review Committee or Jilani would make a move right away.

At the conclusion of Pazli's hearing, Gawani deposited some money into his account. It was enough to pay his expenses long enough to decide whether to stay or return to Velos. If he sold the water generator, he'd have enough money to stay for a few years, but Talio did not want to give it up. The little device represented something few would acknowledge: his success in Pazli's murder hearing. Tricks aside, he'd saved an innocent man from the gallows.

Talio made a mental list of the reasons he wanted to leave Nuciferia: his inability to get his law license back immediately, the reaction of the other advocates, his failure to get any new clients and the sheer cost of a legal license. The contradictory reactions of a certain Incarnite did not figure into his calculations in the slightest.

The next morning, silence and boredom got the better of him. Talio walked upstream to the Palace of Justice in his shabby suit from Velos. It was early enough that advocates and others were streaming through the halls, on their way to hearings or other meetings. He stood in the warm rotunda and closed his eyes, listening to the echoing footsteps. There were also several arguments for staying in Nuciferia: Had he not defended Pazli successfully? Was he not a stellar advocate? Did Pazli's nephew not need him?

But the one argument that swayed Talio more than the others came from Clemente Jilani. *You fled, as you always do*, he'd said. He was right. The moment he could be anything less than brilliant, anything less than what others expected—that was when Talio gave up.

He stood in front of the fountain and took what might be his last look at the statue of Scodel. What would it be like to be remembered for such a legal mind? Scodel had benefited by being immortalized in marble. He would look forever ennobled. Talio was only human.

"Advocate Rossa," Cale said from behind him.

"Prosecutor Faro."

"You were quite clever the other day." Cale wore a surprisingly friendly smile. "Have you been assigned to a new hearing yet?"

Talio shook his head. "I will likely go back to Velos. Within a few days."

"Oh?" Disappointment showed in the prosecutor's face. "Then I would ask your advice on a legal matter before you leave."

His knowledge of hearings was ten years out of date, but Talio was loath to leave the Palace. He nodded and followed Cale to the prosecutorial wing, where the man unlocked the two locks to his rooms and held the door open for him to enter.

"What was it you wanted to ask me?" Talio said, folding his arms defensively. Then he thought of Pazli and dropped them to his sides.

"I was hoping you might stay in Nuciferia. Perhaps I might convince you."

Sif damn him. Trying to play on his feelings, on his attraction. Talio walked forward until he was a breath away from Cale. He meant to push him away in anger, but instead he pulled the prosecutor to him. His lips sought Cale's and his tongue hungrily explored his mouth.

*It has been too long*, Talio thought. *Here I am kissing the first handsome man I see.*

After a long moment, Cale drew back and looked at him with naked attraction. "I have missed you. I still think of that night ten years ago."

The man had a roguish charm, but Talio was not about to forgive him that easily. "I am very fond of you," Cale murmured. He tilted Talio's head back with his hand and kissed him again, then pulled him into a tight, hard hug and nuzzled his ear with his beard. "You handsome, handsome man. When will you know if you are staying?"

This was another factor to consider. Cale would pursue him if he let him. He had no interest in letting the prosecutor into his heart, but every man had needs.

Talio disengaged himself. "I will let you know if I stay." He did not want to risk remaining in Cale's rooms and losing himself to the prosecutor's physical charms once again. Sexual congress on the grounds of the Palace of Justice was beyond a doubt Conduct Unbecoming.

He wanted to seek Gawani's advice on leaving, but she was not in yet. Talio walked to her rooms and stood before the locked door. He waited there a long time, no longer sure of his decision. It would be so much simpler to return to Velos. The idea of turning his back on all this galled him. He belonged here.

A sheet of vellum was protruding from under the door. Talio kneeled and retrieved it. It was a copy of the latest roster that hung at the entrance to the Palace, carrying tomorrow's date. He skimmed the page, looking to see if Cale was listed as prosecutor in any hearings.

Talio recognized one name on the sheet: Amaury Mecomb. The hearing category was "Clipping—Capital Offense." The sentence was "Guilty—Hanging." The disposition read "Complete."

Talio sagged against the wall. It wasn't his fault. The man had received a fair hearing. He had to have been guilty. Scodel's justice was fair and swift. Wasn't it?

Here he was dallying with Cale, playing games with Pazli, when a man's life had hung in the balance. Why would the public defenders have cared about an Incarnite?

*Flee,* he thought. *Run away. Go back to Velos, where you belong. Forget Amaury Mecomb and forget Pazli.*

He hadn't thought it would be this fast, but Queen Jaconda hated any interference with the coin of the realm. He should have helped, should have put himself forward when Pazli had asked. It was so easy to push aside the concerns of a group of people he did not know, especially when they looked and acted so differently. So easy to simply turn away.

Talio had arrived at a fork in a river, with neither stream offering a clear advantage. If he stayed, how could he face Pazli again? But if he left, how could he face himself?

He replaced the sheet under Gawani's door. He did not need to talk to her. He did not need to consider the matter any further. It had been one thing to be a magistrate, all those years ago. Impartial, unemotional—or at least projecting that image. Advocates were supposed to get deeply involved in their hearings and with their clients. In one of his famous addendums, Scodel had referred to the legal system as an "arena" and advocates as "warriors" on behalf of the public.

Walking back into the rotunda, Talio thought of Pazli, of Amaury, of all of the other people who needed a voice in the Palace of Justice. He could be that voice for them.

He laughed, drawing the attention of a few people nearby. This was conceit. Any public or private defender could have defended Pazli or Amaury. But he had something they never would have.

He was Advocate Talio Rossa, after all.

# Part Two: The Incarnite Cases

# Chapter Twelve

*Three days later.*

Talio awoke to Vinne shaking him. He sat up in bed, groggy, and rubbed his head; it was morning.

"You've got company." Vinne pointed a thumb toward the front door. "Outside. You won't believe it."

Talio stumbled over to the ritual basins and splashed water on his face, making a mistake he hadn't made since he was a child: using the return bowl instead of the source bowl. "Felle, forgive my transgression," he mumbled, stumbling over the words of the apology prayer. Talio wiped away the return water and did his best to flatten down his hair and beard before he did the correct ritual with the source water. *Cleanse my soul and purify me.* More and more, this seemed like a tall order.

Then he dressed in his casual clothes and went out to look. Vinne hung behind him, holding the big stick he kept by the door and grumbling about intruders.

A line of Incarnites stretched from the door of the Double Moon Inn around the corner to the alleyway. Most were adults in hoods and cloaks, but there were some children, standing impatiently in their simpler street clothes. He saw with incredulity that one adult was leading a horse.

Talio peered around the corner of the inn to see how long the line was. Two Incarnites stood in front of the mysterious, black-painted circle he had noticed his first night back in Nuciferia. They were gesturing to it and whispering while a cat watched them.

Another Incarnite was standing next to the line about halfway down, with an air of authority and folded arms. Talio sighed and approached him.

"Good morning, Pazli."

Pazli inclined his head. "I see you have recognized my face once more."

"Your folded arms are most distinctive." Talio gestured at the crowd. "What is going on here?"

Pazli took out a stack of vellum from the folds of his cloak and handed it to him. "These are your new clients. I told you I could help."

"You won the game of Four Cities fairly."

"And you saved me from the gallows. Or did you think I had forgotten?"

Talio wanted to ask about Amaury—apologize—but he could not bring himself to do it yet. "Come with me." They entered the inn, and he explained the situation to Vinne.

"The Double Moon Inn is not a law office," Vinne said.

"Do you have any other paying clients besides me?" Talio asked. When the man did not reply, he rubbed his eyes. "I will make it worth your while. Silver is silver. But we need somewhere to receive them."

Pazli began giving orders, "Start moving the chairs and tables out of the way. We will need a row of chairs along that wall. Push three tables together to make a worktable. Put it at the other end so we have some privacy."

Vinne gave a questioning look to Talio, who nodded back. Pazli was the expert on Incarnites. The three of them set to organizing the furniture. Vinne grunted and sweated, and Talio's scavenging and digging muscles had already weakened. But Pazli pushed the tables into place without complaint. He had a pleasant, earthy scent to him when he exerted himself, like a field after a fresh rain. Talio wanted to follow along behind him, to catch a whiff of that unusual scent, but he had to move furniture instead.

Talio had thought Pazli thin, but under the cloak and hood, he must have a strong, wiry body. Hopefully covered with hair. There was something appealing about his efficient strength. Far more interesting to have to picture his body than to actually be able to see it. His imagination gave rise to all sorts of unclothed images. The things he could picture doing with the man...

Vinne poked him in the shoulder. "Are you helping or supervising?"

When they were done, Talio was alert enough to give the innkeeper his own set of instructions: how to let in each client, how to use the row of chairs as a waiting area, and so on. "There's a horse that needs tying up. And whatever you do, don't go offering any ritual waters to the Incarnites. Some candles would be better."

He took a moment to collect himself, then he remembered Amaury Mecomb. Once Vinne went outside to deal with the horse, Talio spoke quietly. "I am sorry about your cousin."

Pazli nodded. "They acted faster than I thought. As you said, coin clipping always leads to a conviction." He paused. "Amaury needed help long before then. It was my fault as much as yours."

"I don't want that to happen again," Talio said. "Not your cousin, I mean. I can acknowledge the deficiencies in Scodel's legal system and try to remedy them."

"Will you defend every Incarnite, then?" Pazli's deep voice sounded somewhere between sarcasm and belief.

"Every person who needs help. Incarnites and regular Nuciferians."

Pazli folded his arms. "Of course. Regular Nuciferians."

He'd slipped up again. It was like trying to handle a spiky fish without gloves. "Let's help these people," Talio said. "As best we can."

The first client was a woman in a worn cloak and hood with a squalling baby who refused to settle down, even when Pazli dandled him on his knee. Her landlord raised her rent without notice, and when she'd complained, he'd posted a notice to rent her room—No Incarnites Allowed. "This is a common occurrence," Pazli said. "A means of getting rid of us indirectly."

"He said I'd burn the rooms down," she said in a sad voice. "Even when I promised to put the candles in bowls of water. At first, he'd taken my silver just fine, but some of the other roomers had complained. That I was a follower of Sif and all that." *Firebugs.*

Since she could neither read nor write, Talio helped her to draft a letter to the Hall of Equity, which oversaw contractual disputes and lesser civil matters. Pazli explained to her how she could file the complaint. "They may not accept your identity key at first, even with your tattoo."

The woman was grateful, until Talio mentioned the fee, quoting the lower end of the standard advocacy rate schedule. "I do not have enough silver with me today," she said, handing him slightly more than half of what he'd asked for.

Pazli withdrew his own purse and added the rest to the pile. "Go deliver the letter." He gave the baby back to her.

Talio shook his head after she left. "You cannot make up every shortfall. Are you going to ask the cleric to take up a collection again?"

They took a break between clients so that Talio could take notes. "Is housing a typical problem with Incarnites?" he asked.

"What do you think?" Pazli's voice was even.

"They could stay at the Incarnite temple."

Pazli shook his head. "There is no room for every Incarnite there. And would you have us all confined to the Incarnite district? We have as much right to live in Nuciferia as 'regular Nuciferians.'"

Talio did not want to fight. "The legal system cannot force people to accept Incarnites."

"The first step to acceptance is living side-by-side. And the Palace of Justice can certainly force that," Pazli said.

The next client was a man who sounded very young. "I went into a wine shop, and they said I'd already been there earlier, causing problems. I hadn't been there in a week. They got me confused with another Incarnite. Does that sound fair to you? I think they owe me an apology."

Talio wondered what really happened, given the man's belligerent attitude. "There is no provision in the law for apologies that I am aware of."

Pazli broke in. "What happened next?"

The man shrugged. "The shopkeeper called the peacekeepers. They insisted on taking an impression of my identity key and barred me from the shop. Fools."

This they could work with. Compelling someone to make a key impression under threat of arrest was an infraction of the peacekeeper's code. Pazli suggested that the young man file a complaint in the Hall of Equity and explained how to phrase the wording to ask that the shopkeeper readmit him in the future.

"Aren't you going to write me a letter?" the man asked Talio. "You did it for that woman."

"Can you read and write?"

"Well, yes, but—"

"Then I suggest you apply stylus to vellum."

He quoted a bit less than the standard rate, but the young man claimed to have even less silver than the woman. After he left, Pazli reached for his purse again, and Talio waved him off. "Don't bother."

"The majority of Incarnites have little money. Most of the time, manual labor is the only type of work we can get," Pazli said. "'Regular' Nuciferians do not want us working in their shops and offices."

Talio sighed. "You may continue to use that word as a weapon, but I would prefer a more direct attack. Would you accept an apology from me?"

There was a pause. "There are some words we hear very often. They mean nothing to you, and everything to us." A smile came into Pazli's voice. "Though I admit you are certainly no 'regular' Nuciferian."

There were eleven clients in all that day; Pazli had counted twelve, so perhaps one had grown tired of waiting and had left at some point. Or, Talio thought with some amusement, Pazli had counted the horse.

They were all minor disputes. Minor under the law, not to the Incarnites. These were the frustrations of everyday life: rent, education, money matters. And always the issue of identification.

As the day wore on, Talio started charging less and less silver. By the afternoon, he was asking the last clients, "How much can you afford? Can you pay some more next time you get money?"

The paperwork was exhausting. Pazli took over note taking at one point, but it was impossible to both give advice and document client concerns at the same time. Talio wondered if Emara might help, and how much she might charge for the privilege.

It was sundown by the time the last Incarnite client had left. "There is something I have noticed our clients have in common," Talio said to Pazli as they were pushing the furniture back into place. Vinne was in the back room preparing supper. "They are all so downtrodden."

"And do you go to a physician when you are feeling well?"

Talio considered the remark. The hearings where he had been an advocate or magistrate had all involved rare life events: murder, high-value crime, fraud and so on. The petty matters the Incarnites presented were not within his usual scope of practice. To them, they were far from petty.

He sat down in one of the chairs. "In a way, this seems somewhat hopeless. We can nibble away at the edges of the problem, fix the day-to-day matters. But it is like patching holes in a ship's hull when the bottom is missing."

"Thank you," Pazli said.

"For what?"

He put a firm hand on Talio's shoulder. "For nibbling around the edges. You are far more likeable when no tricks are involved."

"Would you stay for supper?" Talio asked. He had not broached the subject with Vinne, but the innkeeper would complain no matter what happened—then get roaring drunk.

Pazli shook his head. "Vespers." Talio watched him go. An entire religion, seemingly designed to keep its people isolated and separate from society. From "regular Nuciferians." He vowed never to use that phrase again.

That evening, Talio reflected on the problems the Incarnite clients brought forward that day. With a bit of shame, Talio realized he would not have encountered such "petty matters" years ago as an advocate because the Nuciferian legal system was too expensive for the Incarnites to get any help. They would have had to use public defenders like Gawani, who were overwhelmed with hearings and more likely to pressure them to settle or drop their concerns.

Grimly, he totaled up the silver he'd earned and multiplied it by the number of workdays in a month. Even if he worked every single day, he would not be able to afford to pay for his advocate's license. Today's earnings gave him barely enough silver to buy a coded set of keys and lockboxes at a lockmaster—critical for participating in Nuciferian society and commerce. Not to mention paying Vinne room and board.

Even more grimly, he went through the *Wayward Advocates* pamphlet and determined how many points the previous day's work had earned. Not one. He was unsurprised; the point system was geared toward hearings— the higher profile, the better. A hearing involving a matter over a thousand silver would get him twenty points, on top of the thirty he'd earned for Pazli's acquittal. None of the clients today had concerns involving anywhere near that amount. Even if they had, Talio was not about to push any of his Incarnite clients to file for expensive hearings they could not afford when their concerns could be handled more affordably through other methods. Regardless, he had to find another way to earn his law license back.

The next morning, a messenger girl from the Palace of Justice brought him an official lockbox. Talio opened it with dread, but the contents were a pleasant surprise. Gawani wrote that the Judicial Review Committee had named him as a member. He would represent the views of the legal profession, receiving a small stipend for his work, and five points each month toward his license. Only Gawani could have managed such a deal. The note listed the other committee members: Gawani, a queen's representative named Darra Quiere, and a magistrate named Verrane that sounded vaguely familiar.

The committee was to meet that afternoon. He asked Pazli to continue seeing clients in his absence. Then Talio dressed in his second-best suit and took a leisurely stroll upstream to the Palace of Justice. In his enthusiasm he was early. Talio went to the Hall of Registration and waited in line until he came face to face with the functionary he knew so well.

"Delmar, I am interested in finding out the fees for operating a law office." Gawani had paid his licensing fees under the advocate sole proprietorship provision, but it had occurred to him that partnering with another advocate could halve his expenses.

Delmar flipped through vellum forms. "Moving up in the world, are we? Here is the form for simple partnership." He pushed one sheet at him. "And the one for limited-liability partnership." Another sheet. "Try not to lose them. At least you still have the pin."

Talio reviewed the forms in growing frustration. On a per-advocate basis, the simple partnership fees were higher than those for a single advocate. The limited-liability partnership fees were worse. All partners would also have to be licensed separately, on top of aggregate costs. Only independently wealthy advocates would be able to launch partnership firms. Queen Jaconda insisted on getting her share, even to the detriment of the legal system.

Vinne might let him use all the space in the Double Moon Inn if he shared some profits. Judging from the Incarnite clients so far, Vinne was going to have to be generous for the first while.

There was still time before the committee meeting. Talio used the restroom by the rotunda. While he was washing his hands, Emara joined him in the small chamber. "The canteen is selling flatbreads," she said to him. "Two for one." She was wearing her scribe's cap, but loose strands of blonde hair had escaped it.

"I'd rather not eat at the canteen. For now."

Her hazel eyes bore into him. "The best approach to conflict is often the direct one." Just as he'd said to Pazli.

"Let me be direct with you on another matter," Talio said. He explained what he wanted her for: she would be part scribe, part assistant, part errand-woman.

"I'd rather join you as an advocate. I'm looking to specialize in medical hearings."

He shook his head. "Not yet. I cannot pay you." Then Talio asked, "How much to work for me?"

Emara named a price that was high, but not eye-watering. Talio put out his hand flat at eye level, then dropped it to knee level. She took his hand and raised it back up to the level of his chest.

He dropped his hand to his waist, and again, Emara took hold of it. Now Talio resisted, and they started pulling his hand up and down in a representation of her relative salary. Her strength was remarkable.

Finally, he'd had enough. "Half now. We will revisit the matter in a month. If you're any good, I'll raise it to three-quarters."

Emara let go of his hand. "I'll need to leave early one day a week. And you'll include lunch every day." It was settled, then.

He needed the name of a lockmaster, and Emara was happy to give him her considered advice. After he left her, there was still time before the committee meeting for one last errand. He asked the quavering old man behind the administration service desk to locate Minka Schell for him.

The man shook his head. "She is on leave."

"Since when?"

The man tapped his fingers on the desk. "Off the active register since last week."

Talio turned this information over in his mind as he walked to the committee room. He thought of her gauntness; it worried him now. The door to the committee room was open, and voices came from beyond it. Since he was not late, they must have started early.

As committee organizer, Gawani sat at the head of the heavy wooden table in a severe gray dress and peaked bonnet. A scribe sat behind her against the wall, stylus poised over a vellum pad.

To Gawani's left was a fashionable young woman with the red pin of the Royal Palace: the queen's representative. She was leaning back with one hand on the arm of her chair, watching him.

To Gawani's right was a short, round man in a magistrate's robe. Seeing him, Talio finally remembered him from his own time as a law student and magistrate: Verrane. He delivered solid, by-the-book verdicts, notably in the medical field.

But the face that gave him a jolt belonged to the man sitting at the other end of the table from Gawani. A name that had conveniently been omitted from her note.

At the foot of the table, wearing the green pin of the law school, was his old professor, Clemente Jilani.

# Chapter Thirteen

The ritual basins gave Talio an excuse to gather his thoughts. "Cleanse my soul and purify me." *And may Sif strike down Clemente Jilani with a swift blow.* Then he sat down while Gawani made introductions.

"This is Queen Jaconda's representative, Darra Quiere." Darra gave a languorous nod in his direction. "And you may know Magistrate Verrane." The round man smiled and waved. Talio remembered the little blue pamphlet, *Verrane on Medical Hearings,* and how the magistrate forced every law student who took the elective on medical negligence to buy that year's edition—regardless of the hundreds of used copies available for sale.

Gawani went on. "Professor Jilani is also joining us for the first time as of today. We are privileged to have his guidance for the remainder of the judicial season." Talio felt Clemente's unblinking eyes on him. He must have maneuvered his way onto the committee once he'd found out Talio was joining.

Gawani gave another smile. "Advocate Talio Rossa is well known for his work on the recent Mecomb hearing. We have not had an advocate on our committee for some time. It was agreed that having a voice from outside the government and the administration would be beneficial."

*It was agreed. By someone.*

Darra and Verrane murmured words of welcome. Clemente remained silent.

"Our purpose here is to streamline the legal system as best we can," Gawani said. "Forms, processes, administration. Anything which falls outside of Scodel's laws. The Palace is overburdened with hearings and its budget continues to be cut." She smiled at Talio. "Do keep that guiding principle in mind." Now she was all business, as he'd expected.

She rapped her fingers twice on the table. "I call this meeting to order."

She started by listing the attendees and their titles. The scribe started writing, and Talio noticed a vigil candle next to her. From the height of the candle and the red alarm line, it was a one-hour candle. What could they hope to accomplish in a single hour?

"Let us return to the work of the last meeting." Gawani straightened the stack of vellum before her. Darra, Verrane, and Clemente all had similar stacks of paper. Talio raised his eyebrows at Gawani.

"Make a note," she said to the scribe. "Advocate Rossa will require copies of all documents for future sessions."

Darra slid closer to Talio and placed her stack of vellum between them. "Thank you," he whispered. The top page of the stack had the heading "Licensing Term Assessments—Summary Findings."

Gawani continued. "The discussion from the last session centered on renewals for barbers, stylists, and other personal grooming service providers. Please turn to page three."

Talio's excitement at having joined the committee slowly evaporated as the candle burned down to the halfway mark. Everyone in the room had an opinion on whether or not they should extend the licensing renewal periods for these service providers from one to two years. It went on and on. The only thing this committee seemed to be good for was earning him five points every month for the rest of the judicial season.

Finally, they ground to a halt. "Do we vote now?" Talio asked her.

She looked over at him in surprise. "No, now we review the submissions from the other cities. Nuciferia cannot make law for all of Merin." Gawani pulled yet another vellum sheet out of her stack. "We will start with Aurania. The representative magistrate there has petitioned for relief for personal service providers..."

It was endless. Aurania, Damiria, and Rylavia had all provided submissions on extending the renewal period. There was no consensus; Talio could not determine how they would make any final decisions.

Once they reviewed the last of the submissions, Gawani closed the topic. "Next week, we will consider the potential timeframe to implement the license renewal change and review the administrative changes required by the Hall of Documents." She sounded as tired as Talio felt. "Are there any more items before we leave the matter?"

Talio raised a hand. "Will there be any discussion of licensing fees?"

"Do you have a concern for the fees of barbers?" He thought he heard Clemente snicker.

"I meant fees in general. Licensing fees for advocates are quite high, for example."

Darra leaned forward, clearly bored. "The government has set licensing fees to be equitable and affordable. They have not risen in the past two years."

"Have we received any complaints on advocacy licensing fees?" Gawani asked the scribe, who shook her head.

Of course not. What advocate would complain about fees to the officials in charge of their license? Would a complaint ever make it as far as this committee?

The vigil candle hissed and spat. The scribe wet her fingers and pinched out the flame. Gawani rapped her fingers on the table. "Thank you all for your work today. We will meet again next week."

Talio sat back as Gawani, Verrane and Clemente filed out. Darra straightened up her vellum but made no move to leave. Finally, she spoke to him. "What did you think?"

He wondered how much he could trust her. "Applying a bureaucratic process to reducing bureaucracy is quite an interesting approach."

The young woman laughed and readjusted her bonnet. "Yes, that is an excellent answer." She rolled up her vellum and put a band around it, then hesitated. "Someone has a message for you."

She was fiddling with the red pin on her dress. Queen Jaconda. "What is this message?"

"She is watching you." There was no malice in her voice, but no warmth, either. "The Incarnites are a question that must be resolved."

"A question?"

"They are citizens who have separated themselves from the royal body." Darra shook her head. "They live among us, and yet they are not part of us. We cannot live as two separate peoples in one country. The Queen would have them integrate with us. This will require accommodations on their part."

*But not on ours*, he thought.

"I have a proposal," Talio said. She nodded.

"Put an Incarnite on this committee."

Darra put the roll of vellum under her arm and headed to the exit. "Good day, Advocate Rossa."

"You want them to integrate with the rest of Merin." He joined her at the door. "Show them they are a part of the royal body. Invite them to be a part of the committee, symbolically at least." Talio gave her a sly smile. "And what would it matter if an Incarnite had an opinion on licensing intervals?"

Darra did not return the smile. "Professor Jilani told me you would be cunning."

Talio opened the door for her. "He also ruled in my favor in the Mecomb hearing, did he not?"

She stepped out in front of him and walked away. The committee was slow, hidebound. The rest of them might want to delay reform. The sooner it came, the better. And if Talio could somehow force faster changes in the law, there was the tantalizing possibility of more points toward his law license. "Advancing the state of the law" was worth an incredible forty points in Clemente's pitiful program. No doubt he expected nobody to ever achieve it.

Talio walked downstream through the city in the early afternoon during the lull after midday, watching a group of men and women struggle to right a listing barge blocking a canal from traffic. He had been thinking of Pazli. Why could the man not serve on the committee? He would bring the viewpoint of an Incarnite. Aside from a tendency to be somber or silent, his advocacy skills were solid.

Talio imagined Pazli and Clemente facing each other with folded arms in sullen silence. The idea made him laugh. In good spirits, he took a side street to his final destination of the day before the Double Moon Inn.

At his request, Emara had given him the name and address of a moderately priced lockmaster that met the needs he'd voiced, "Reasonable. Not cheap, not bad."

Emara had written the information on a scrap of vellum. "Here's one I trust. If she tries to overcharge you, tell her Emara Ravil sent you."

The keys and lockboxes were expensive, but when he mentioned Emara's name, the lockmaster raised her eyebrows and gave him a hefty discount. Talio ordered a starter set of ten lockboxes and five keys. He could only think of a few people who would need his keys right away: Pazli, Emara, Gawani, and Vinne. Once he had sent ten messages, he could order replacement lockboxes. If he truly did not have the silver to buy more of them, he could be graceless and ask for the lockboxes back. He splurged and chose larger lockboxes, cylindrical ones about the size of his hand. They would be large enough for a letter or even a few sheets of vellum rolled up tightly. Enough for the types of matters the Incarnite clients were bringing him.

"Would you like an insignia?" the woman asked as she prepared the order.

"Yes. Do you have some vellum and a stylus?" He sketched out what he had in mind. The lockmaster nodded and transferred the image onto a stencil.

He decided to ask Pazli to dinner at the Double Moon. He wanted to send Pazli a message with his new set, but Pazli could not open a lockbox without the corresponding key. Instead, Talio sent a messenger boy with a generic lockbox and vellum message to the Incarnite temple.

By the time he returned to the inn, Pazli had sent his response: *yes*. The man arrived after Incarnite vespers. The sun was low in the sky, and Vinne had lit two tapers at a table in the corner. First came turtle soup, then sweetbreads. Despite grumbling over having to provide dinner for two, Vinne kept the wine topped up, but otherwise remained behind the bar.

"We have a problem," Talio said to Pazli once they started on the main course.

"Do we?" Pazli had a delicate way of spearing the sweetbreads with his fork and navigating them between the curtains of the hood into his mouth.

Talio put down his cutlery. "The Incarnites cannot pay enough for me to start a law office. Not even enough for my sole proprietor license."

"Is payment all that matters?"

He thought of the lockmaster, the rent, and all of the other expenses. "It is not everything, but it matters if I can't afford to do the work."

Pazli said nothing. "There's another problem," Talio said. "I am still trying to regain my law license after my spectacle in your murder hearing. I need to have higher-profile cases in order to do so."

"The other day may have left you with a mistaken impression of the Incarnites." Pazli took a generous sip of wine. "Not all of us are poor."

Talio matched his sip. "Oh?"

"I know some Incarnites—not many—who are quite wealthy. I would be happy to refer them to your law office. On two conditions."

The flickering candlelight and drink was making Talio warm around the ears. This was not soft wine. "You have my undivided attention."

"First, you will accept some clients who can pay little, or not at all. The wealthier clients will make up the discrepancy."

He would still earn points regardless of the silver paid. "That seems fair," Talio said. "If the amounts balance out. And the other condition?"

"I will join your law office."

At that moment, Vinne came out to refill their wine glasses. Talio and Pazli did not speak until the innkeeper returned to the backroom. "Why?" Talio asked.

"We are facing an unfair legal system." Pazli gave a shrug. "The Incarnites need advocates they can trust. Advocates who know how they think, what matters to them. I will fight for them on my own terms."

Talio nodded. "Scodel always said the law was meant to be blind."

"That can be a good or a bad thing." Pazli shook his head, as if to banish the thought. "Are you in agreement then?"

"I am sure we can come to an arrangement." Talio raised his wine glass.

Pazli clinked his own glass against Talio's. "When it comes to the Incarnites, we have complementary skills. I think we'd make excellent partners." Once again Talio felt the undercurrent of the man's words. Was there a double meaning, or was he only wishing it was so? Cale would no doubt make a direct overture, but somehow that was not as exciting as imagining what Pazli might be thinking behind his cloak and hood. Even if an Incarnite could not have a relationship with a non-Incarnite. Or did that extend to intimate relations?

They drank, and Talio contemplated the offer. Wealthy clients would solve his financial issues. Pazli's presence would be invaluable, given the cultural issues he faced with the Incarnites. He also could not deny that he would appreciate the company; law could be a lonely business. And Pazli had shown himself to have a keen grasp of everyday legal issues already. With enough wealthy clients they could easily afford the man's law license.

When the meal was over, they moved to a pair of low chairs that faced each other with no table between them. Distant tapers cast warm yellow reflections onto their glasses.

"I will let you know my decision tomorrow," Talio said. He reached into the pocket of his jacket and drew out one of his new message keys. "Take this."

Pazli turned it over in his hands. "The insignia—what is it? A slingshot?"

"A dowsing rod."

"Is it a metaphor? Are you searching for something?"

Talio smiled at him. "Maybe I am. For ten years I used to scavenge merinite." He expected Pazli to ask why. But Pazli was a junkman and advocate—why not a scavenger and advocate?

"Did you like scavenging?" Somehow, they had gotten closer to each other. Talio had leaned in, or Pazli had; he was not sure which.

"No." He took another sip of wine. "No, I did not."

They sat in silence, and Talio felt the man's gaze upon him, a quiet contemplation. "What are you looking at?" he asked in a soft voice.

"My future partner. Perhaps." Pazli's voice was soft as well. He was leaning toward him, closer than a fellow advocate should. Talio wondered what it might be like if he leaned closer still.

He gazed back at him. He had to switch the subject. The wine was going to his head. "You may have heard that I am on the Judicial Review Committee," he said in a rush of words. "Would you like to be with me? On the committee?" That had come out all wrong.

"It might give them a certain legitimacy." Pazli's voice made it sound as if this would not be a good thing. "Although I could see the benefit of being with you...on the committee."

"It would be good for both of us to stay close together." Talio was trying to keep his tongue straight. "I would like to take advantage of your experience." Now his words were getting all mixed up. "But you would not be a passive participant. I would want you to get deeply involved." He coughed. "In the matters of the committee."

A longer silence. "If someone makes me an offer, I will consider it," Pazli said. So many meanings in those words. Talio imagined a pendulum in the man's mind, swinging slowly back and forth between approach and retreat.

He was so close to him. All Pazli had to do was reach out, touch his lips, his cheek. Talio leaned even closer. "I would be happy to entertain a counteroffer."

He felt Pazli's knee brush against his own. It stayed there, pressing against him. *Do something*, Talio urged him silently. He sensed Pazli's hesitation and felt his own. He let the fingers of his left hand rest lightly atop Pazli's knee—an invitation. No man would let another man touch him in such a manner unless he were interested in more than friendship. Talio could do no more without a clear sign from the other man, but he felt himself responding regardless. The flush rising in him was not from the wine. Could Pazli not see the message in his eyes?

The other man put down his wineglass on the arm of his chair instead. "I should not drink too much," Pazli said. "There could be consequences."

Consequences. If only. Talio sat back, pulling away from Pazli's knee. He set his own glass aside. "I have drunk more since I came to Nuciferia than in my ten years in Velos."

Pazli sat back as well, straightening up. "Ah, Velos. Two of our congregants passed through it some years ago. The townspeople attacked them. One was never heard from again." His voice was horrible in its calmness. "The other escaped."

"I don't believe that," Talio said with a thick tongue. Not the town where he'd lived for a decade. He knew of the Incarnites who were rumored to have visited Velos, but...

Pazli rummaged through the folds of his cloak and withdrew a book. A large codex, in the saffron color of the Incarnites.

"This is the Yellow Codex," Pazli said. "We keep a list of towns and villages that are friendly to us. And those who are not as friendly."

"I thought that Incarnites refused to take the skylines."

Pazli shook his head. "That was true, once. After our leader Turi Peyor died, we lost many followers. His acolyte Zielle sent out missionaries to the other cities. And towns like Velos."

"On foot?" Talio was aghast. "How long did it take?"

"Months between cities. Sometimes longer." Pazli sighed. "There were even some magical beasts left from the war that had not been restrained inside the Impassable Forest. Eventually the clerics relented and allowed parishioners to use the skylines, if they sought a dispensation. There are dispensations for everything. Staying out past vespers, using the skylines..."

*Loving a non-Incarnite?*

Pazli held the Yellow Codex so that Talio could see the interior. As Pazli flipped through the pages, for one tantalizing moment Talio saw a circle with two horizontal lines: the same mark on the side of the Double Moon Inn. But before he could ask about it, Pazli had moved on.

He stopped at a page with an entry for Velos. Two emphatic strokes crossed out the town's name. The rest of the page was blank.

Talio could think of nothing to say. He recalled his barber, Rani, telling him about the wicked Incarnites. A bit of light fun about these strange people. "They said an Incarnite stole a child in Velos," he murmured, then wished he had not said it.

"Did they." Pazli's words were not a question, but a condemnation. Talio had expected him to be angry, but the man only sounded weary and resigned. He closed the codex and put it away. "Do we strike you as child snatchers, then?"

Talio recalled the happy Incarnite children he'd seen and shook his head. It had been easy to believe anything about the Incarnites before he'd met any of them. Easier to imagine they were kidnappers or criminals. People who deserved whatever happened to them. *And if you see one, punch them. Firebugs.*

The other man got to his feet. "I must return to the temple. Second vespers." Had he driven away Pazli yet again? Talking to him felt like riding a skyship; he could only stay on the narrow path of swiftly rushing water. One step to the left or the right and he would plummet out of the sky, like Scodel.

They stood at the open door to the inn, Talio not wanting him to go. From the way Pazli hesitated, he did not want to leave either. For all the times Vinne had yelled at him not to let cold air in, the innkeeper was silent. "Thank you for inviting me to supper." Pazli lifted up his hand as if unsure what to do with it.

When he did no more, Talio dared to reach out himself, then traced the circle of the tattoo on the back of the man's hand. "I...I am glad your hand is healing."

"Yes. Fortunately, the scars will not be permanent." Pazli bowed his head. "I am sorry. I did not mean to—"

His face. He meant Talio's face. Of course. "It is all right. My scar does not hurt." After a moment, he added, "You may touch it if you like."

Pazli raised his hand to him and gently placed the tips of his fingers on the part of Talio's scar between his nose and his mouth. They stood in silence for a long moment. He wished he could see the expression in Pazli's eyes, but the meaning of that touch was very clear. At last, the man pulled away from him. "Thank you," Pazli said. "For trusting me."

"And perhaps someday I might touch your face," Talio said, his heart leaping with the daring words.

"Perhaps on a night when I have had more to drink." He disappeared into the street.

Talio closed the door to the inn and tried to shake the haze of wine from his head. Vinne had also been drinking; he staggered out from behind the bar. "He was trying to seduce you."

Talio blushed. "You could not even see his face."

"I saw how close he sat to you. The way he turned toward you. He leaned forward when you talked. He touched your cheek. And did I mention he was rubbing himself under the table while you were eating?"

Talio raised his eyebrows at Vinne's last sentence, then he laughed. "You have quite the imagination."

"Get him drunk, like he wants you to." The man clapped a powerful hand on Talio's shoulder. "Get him drunk and see what happens next time."

He stumbled backward toward the kitchen, leaving Talio to put away the wine glasses and extinguish the tapers. He was about to set the locks on the front door when he changed his mind and went outside.

The night was brisk and held the promise of fall. His footsteps a bit uncertain from the wine, Talio walked around to the side of the inn and gazed at the painted symbol he'd seen reproduced in the Yellow Codex. It was a message to fellow Incarnites. Was it a warning, or a welcome?

Pazli had crossed the inn's threshold for dinner, but the touch of his hand was as far as he would go, for now. There were signs of that wall within him cracking, opening a bit to let the light inside shine out. Talio suspected that there was more than religion keeping him closed like a book. Just as he was able to wriggle around Scodel's laws, Pazli might be able to maneuver around the Incarnite tenets. There was more to life than words, after all.

He would accept Pazli's offer of a legal partnership and see where the river took them. As to a more personal partnership, Vinne was right. Talio would have to make the next move.

# Chapter Fourteen

Talio needed to talk to Vinne, and it could no longer wait. They spent much of that night discussing the inn and sharing profits, as best they could in the innkeeper's inebriated state. Vinne agreed to leave the furniture in the front room organized as worktables with chairs, but he drew the line at removing the beds and converting the rooms to private working spaces.

"When was the last time you had anyone stay at the inn?" Talio shook his head. "Aside from me?"

By that point in his alcohol consumption, Vinne could only manage a garbled set of syllables from which Talio picked out the words "property values."

When Talio awoke the following morning, eight adult Incarnites were waiting for him outside the Double Moon Inn, as well as several children and Pazli. There was no horse.

"I have a client who may be more profitable," Pazli said to him. "Once we see everyone waiting in line." It was not the thought of a rich client that made Talio's heart soar, but the possibility of earning twenty points in one go.

Fortunately, Emara arrived at that moment. Talio could not have been happier to see her. She showed no concern that the Double Moon Inn was a house of ill repute, or that her work involved Incarnites. Her concerns were practical: she had one schedule written on vellum for Talio and another for Pazli. They would each see a maximum of five clients per day, no more. Clients could wait outside, or inside if they promised to be quiet.

Once he and Pazli explained to her they needed the afternoon off, Emara revised their schedules and announced to the Incarnites which ones could see the advocates that afternoon and who would have to return the following day. Her voice and attitude brooked no disagreement; Talio wanted to hug her but did not dare.

"We will be back before supper," he called over his shoulder as he and Pazli headed out of the quarter and upstream. The last Talio saw of Emara, she was surrounded by a throng of Incarnite children and looked bemused.

"How much are you paying her?" Pazli asked once they escaped.

"Not enough. She wants to work for us as a medical advocate someday."

They crossed over a footbridge and waited for two carriages to bounce by. "There is something about Emara I dislike," Pazli said in a musing tone. "A fundamental toughness to her. The Incarnites need some measure of compassion."

"I suspect that her compassion is not far from the surface."

They walked on. Pazli withdrew a paper from his cloak. "The cleric lent me some funds from the Temple savings."

The gilt edge of a licensing form was all he needed to see. Talio smiled at him. "Congratulations, Advocate Mecomb. Shall we go visit our first wealthy client, then?"

The shadows of the buildings felt markedly colder and damper than they had only a week ago and wind rippled the canal waters; fall was in the air. "Her name is Lady Zielle," Pazli said. "She was once Peyor's disciple. Her manse may surprise you."

"Disciple?" Talio had heard so little about the Incarnite religion, but it surprised him that one of their religious figures might be so ostentatiously wealthy.

Pazli assumed the voice of a parent telling a bedtime story. "About twenty-five years ago, Peyor received a vision telling him that Sif would descend from the sky in the desert surrounding Merin. He took his hundred disciples out into the sands to await the god."

And most of them died, but Talio did not say this. "After the tragedy," Pazli continued, "the small remaining group returned to civilization. The nearest city was Nuciferia. Zielle had been one of Peyor's favorites, and she inherited the church's wealth. Naturally, she used the money to found the

Temple and the Incarnite district. Peyor had also left instructions on developing the further tenets of the Incarnite religion."

Pazli pointed to the large roof of the manse they were approaching across the canal. "She is old, but no fool." No fool to keep a good portion of Peyor's inheritance for her own.

A servant led them through the front gate into a sumptuously appointed gathering room lined by ceremonial torches and candles. The manse was immense, twice the size of the Balsamo estate. Talio had thought his mother-in-law had been wealthy, but he had not been prepared for the scale of Zielle's residence. There were no ritual gutters or bowls, of course. Expecting this, Talio had scrubbed his hands at the inn in advance.

A stooped Incarnite in a cloak and hood of fine fabric walked through a door toward them, supported by a cane. "Thank you for coming." She extended a gnarled hand. "I am Zielle."

He bowed. "Lady Zielle."

She turned and hobbled back the way she came, beckoning them to follow with the cane. Two Incarnites were waiting for them in a study. Back when Talio had been courting Gawani, a comedic duo had been popular in the theaters. Even with their cloaks and hoods, these two men reminded him of that pair. Joban was tall, nervous, and affable, while Birk was shorter and the quieter of the two.

"These two men are the minds behind the Skyways Construction Company," Zielle said. Birk was the principal of the firm, and Joban its natural scientist. Zielle had invested a substantial sum of Incarnite funds in the company, and they were there to show Talio and Pazli why.

Joban had with him a scale model of a skyline and skyship. It reminded Talio of the toy that Essa had been playing with, only far more detailed.

Joban pointed to the model. "Surely you are familiar with the mechanism underlying the skylines and skyships?" Talio shook his head. Merinite and prayer was all he knew of it.

The scientist cleared his throat. "Merinite provides the propulsive force. Two disks of merinite, one on each tower, cause the waters of the skyline to form between them."

Talio coughed. "I don't mean to interrupt..."

"What is it?" Pazli's tone was unusually sharp.

"The skylines are not a natural science phenomenon," Talio said. "Merinite is only the spiritual tool the magic flows through. The incantations, the prayers to Felle—however you care to characterize it. This is not science."

He sensed rather than saw four pairs of Incarnite eyes exchanging looks. There was a long moment of silence. "Then let us assume that the merinite is a channel for the incantations to the goddess Felle," Joban said, as if to a child. "Putting aside metaphysical concerns, may I proceed?"

They were treating the magical skylines as if they were nothing more than a horse and carriage. But this was a potential client, which meant silver and points. Talio nodded for Joban to continue.

The natural scientist turned one of the two towers in the model to face the other and a tiny spray of water sprang out between them. "Once the skyship starts on its trip, surely it cannot stop."

Talio peered at the model more closely. Each tiny tower had a speck of blue at its top. "This is a working model with actual merinite, then?" He could not believe it. The cost of these grains of true merinite alone would be remarkable.

"Yes, yes!" Joban nodded, placing a tiny skyship model complete with copper hull on the river emanating from the tower at one end and giving it a push. The skyship splashed along the skyline and stopped at the other tower. "Now, surely you have noticed the drawback inherent in the skyline system?"

Talio wished he would stop using the word "surely," but that would *surely* never happen. Some of his law professors had fallen prey to their own favorite words that they would repeat without realizing; it was nervousness, or insanity. He hazarded a guess. "The cost?"

Joban shook his head. "No, not at all." He sent the skyship sailing back to the other tower. "There is surely a limit to the amount of people and cargo that can travel the skylines. Only one skyship can move along a given skyline for each trip. Travelers from Nuciferia cannot travel to Rylavia until the skyship returns from its first trip."

Birk took over at this point. "We believe we have solved the problem." There was pride in his voice. Joban removed the skyship and replaced the existing two towers with two new ones. It was hard for Talio to tell given the scale, but the merinite speck looked slightly different. "We have reconfigured the merinite from a disk to a star pattern."

Joban sent the skyship along its path and it cut through the watery stream between the towers much faster this time. "We estimate we can surely double—at least—the speed of each trip. Twice the passengers every day, up to sixty. Twice the cargo. That is the mission of the Skyways Construction Company."

Talio imagined riding in a skyship at double the speed, which did his stomach no favors. "It seems quite dangerous. Even testing it would be risky."

Joban waved his hand in the negative. "Not at all. We have constructed a track outside of Nuciferia where we will run full tests later this week. Assuming the tests are positive— and surely they will be—the city officials have agreed to let us run an actual test on the Nuciferia-Aurania skyline next spring, when the service shuts down for maintenance."

"It is an audacious plan." Pazli sounded impressed. "But why do you need an advocate?"

"The government has stolen our idea," Birk said in a sober tone. "The Department of Distance Travel, specifically."

Talio looked at him in confusion. "You do realize there is no cause of action here."

"We have already filed a request for a hearing. Our first advocate refused to continue and removed herself from the action."

Talio could not understand. "What did she write on the form for the cause of action?"

Birk hesitated. "She left that part blank. The Palace of Justice processed the form regardless." Only a fool like Delmar would have accepted it.

Talio faced Joban, Birk, and Zielle. "Nothing has been 'stolen,'" he said, spreading his hands for emphasis. "There has been no 'theft.'" First, he offended their understanding of science, and now he was going to offend their understanding of law.

He'd heard these arguments from fellow students in school, and even once as a magistrate from a desperate complainant who had been sure the type of knot she'd used in her sabots was unique. This situation was far more awkward, where he was merely an advocate and stepping very delicately around what he supposed were Incarnite beliefs.

Joban and Birk looked at each other once more. He would have to explain in simple terms. "Theft is the taking of property with the intent to deprive the rightful owner." Talio felt ridiculous repeating words from his very first lesson on criminal law. "An idea is not property. If the government had taken this skyline model from you instead, we might have a cause of action."

Birk shook his head. "But they say they had the idea independent of us. And we know that is not so."

"Did they deprive you of the use of your idea?" Talio continued. "If I take your model, I have deprived you of it. If I copy your idea, you still have it. No theft has occurred."

"But we had planned to sell our idea to the government. And now we cannot."

"Ideas are like fish," Pazli said. "You may throw a hook into the water and catch what is there for anyone to take." Talio felt relief that Pazli was backing him up. If his fellow advocate had also persisted in this foolish belief, it would have been one against four.

Zielle spoke for the first time since the meeting started. "Without a sale to the government, my investment will have been for nothing. The Skyways Construction Company will have no reason to exist." She stepped forward. "At least review our documents."

Talio walked away from Zielle's manse with a stack of vellum and mounting irritation. "Are all Incarnites fools?" he asked Pazli as they walked upstream toward the Palace of Justice.

Pazli's tone also held irritation. "Surely only those who retain you as their advocate."

"Do not start with the 'surelys.' There is no cause of action for Skyways' claim. How did their claim even get this far? It is madness."

"Do you refuse to take Zielle as a client, then?" Pazli asked.

"Scodel was always very clear that hypotheticals and imaginary ideas had no place in his system of law. A woman who receives a marriage proposal that is then withdrawn cannot launch a cause of action against the man and force him to wed her."

Pazli folded his arms. "And if a claimant in a negligence hearing has been injured, they may very well receive damages based on projected losses to income. Or is that insufficiently hypothetical for you?"

Now Talio was getting angry. Not because Pazli was right, of course, but because he could not immediately marshal his arguments against him. "Property has a physical form. Scodel's laws on land are quite clear. I will not argue this with you further."

"Then you will not take Zielle's case?"

"I will," Talio said. He did not mention the points. "Out of deference to the lady's position within the Incarnite church."

"I see," Pazli said, in an unconvincing voice that suggested he did not see at all.

Talio instructed Pazli to research Palace of Justice records for any mention of Skyways or the Department of Distance Travel. Then he hefted the stack of vellum, which contained designs for the test skyline track and the research documents that Joban provided. "I shall try to make sense of this, and I will see you at the Double Moon later."

He spent an hour in the Hall of Reference reviewing the Skyways papers in annoyance and frustration. The designs and plans seemed plausible, but any changes to Scodel's brilliant original design troubled him. Perhaps he was being dogmatic. He had been so quick to quote Scodel to Pazli about property; wasn't religion nothing but beliefs without proof?

At one point, Talio spotted an error in the elevated illustration of the test location and made a note. Each skyline tower held three merinite disks, or stars in this design: one for each destination city. But one of the test towers had a sketch of a fourth star pattern with a dotted line going off the edge of the sheet. He frowned. If the Skyways Construction Company could make such a fundamental error, he worried about the accuracy of their merinite redesign.

Talio pushed the vellum away from him and rubbed his forehead. He could not let Lady Zielle and her ridiculous cause of action affect him. The professor of his advocate-client relations course had often pointed out that the higher the billings for a hearing, the higher the level of aggravation. He would assist Zielle as much as he could, and he would bill her handsomely for the privilege. Perhaps there was some way to twist this into a real cause of action that could result in a hearing.

Back in the administration rotunda, Talio stopped before the statue of Scodel. What would he have made of the Incarnites? Would he have rewritten his laws to accommodate them? And what of their secular view of the skylines, Scodel's second-greatest creation?

A cheerful voice spoke behind him. "Advocate Rossa." Cale was confident and well-dressed in his prosecutorial robes. "Are you at a hearing today?"

He shook his head and lifted the roll of vellum. "Research. Well-paid, infuriating research. Then back to my workrooms."

"Might I invite you to lunch?" The man's brown eyes sparkled. Did Cale wake up every morning looking so beautiful?

Talio shook his head. "I have work to do back at the Double Moon." The man's smile only made him more wary. He did not want to spend any more time with him than necessary. Then his stomach growled.

"Your words say one thing, and your body another," Cale said with a grin. He took him by the elbow and started ushering him through the administration building toward the Hall of Education. "Indulge me. Please."

A door beyond the last classroom led outside to an area that had not existed when Talio attended law school. Stone-paved paths and benches crisscrossed a manicured lawn where students chatted, flirted, or sunned themselves. Cale called it "the square." The trees along the edge of the square were on the verge of bursting into fall color. Some students dared to smoke, and the scent of duhan wafted through the air.

"He reminds me of you, you know," Cale said as they sat on a bench and ate lunches they'd bought from a pushcart vendor. Talio did his best to distance himself from the prosecutor—mentally and physically—but it was a pleasant afternoon, and the man had a sweet charm to him.

"Who is that?"

"Scodel. I've seen you looking at the statue. He would have found in you a kindred spirit."

Talio laughed. "Quite the opposite, I'm sure."

"Why do you say that?"

If Cale wanted to be serious, he would be serious. "Scodel set out the laws of Merin, and I spend my time finding ways around them. My task is tearing down what he spent years building up."

Cale shook his head. "No, there you are wrong. Scodel's laws were never meant to be the definitive answer to our justice system. They were only the starting point. There is a reason he called it his 'Grand Experiment.' 'Let four streams flow and may four cities bloom,'" he quoted. "Bloom, not wither and die. The laws were supposed to evolve and change along with us." He smiled at Talio. "That's why you are on the Judicial Review Committee, is it not?"

"True. We are discovering legal situations that Scodel could never have imagined." The Incarnites. Skyways.

Cale finished his flatbread and slid down onto the grass, leaning against the bench. "I would like to serve on that committee. I'm an excellent prosecutor." He stated his competence without arrogance. "Why did they never seek my assistance? You could put my name forward."

Talio's voice was low. "My former wife is the head of the committee."

"Ah." Cale's face fell. It did not take much to connect Gawani with the night she'd seen them in bed at the Double Moon Inn ten years ago. "That is an egg I cannot un-crack."

Talio said nothing. Gawani had not recognized Cale during the hearings so far, but if he introduced them, she might remember. And he had no desire to help this man.

"And you?" Cale said, looking up at him. "Do you hate me?"

"I hate what you did," Talio said with difficulty. The man had done what he had to do in order to go to law school. His own path to the law had had its own ethical hurdles. Neither of them was blameless.

Cale gave a sad smile. "That would seem to be the narrowest of differences."

"Victory or defeat in a hearing often rests on such differences," Talio said.

"This is not a hearing. I am not a prosecutor here, and you are not an advocate. Although you and I shall be seeing a lot of each other in the future, along with Magistrate Jilani."

"Why is that?"

Cale put his hands behind his head. "The Palace likes to pair up the same advocate, prosecutor and magistrate as often as possible, if the scheduling permits it. The last advocate I faced regularly retired this year. You'll be in front of Jilani from now on...or Magistrate Verrane, if you're familiar with him."

"The pamphlets."

Cale grasped his hand. "I'm glad we will be in each other's orbits from now on. Your actions in the Mecomb hearing impressed me. A worthy opponent." Talio looked at him in surprise. "Will you let me try to win your heart?"

The man was painfully handsome. Telling him he was flattered would be an insult. "Could I stop you if I tried?"

Cale grinned and held his hand closer to him. "I can win you over. I know I can." He squinted at him. "Or is that the problem? Would you prefer someone more distant? Someone who plays games with love?" Someone more distant. There was only one man who fulfilled that requirement, and Talio found him more challenging than romantic. Pazli did not play games with love; he pushed any opportunities away from him with vigor. But Cale? So tempting, to let this striking man sweep him away. A man who had deceived him ten years earlier. What was this feeling inside of him, all of a sudden?

"Let the record show that the witness declined to give a response at this time."

Cale gave him a regretful look. "Perhaps Scodel would not have approved of you after all."

* * *

Back at the Double Moon, Pazli reported that neither the roster nor the register held any mention of previous meetings or hearings for the Skyways Construction Company. The roster was posted, however, listing a new "pending" hearing, with Verrane as magistrate, Talio and Pazli as advocates of record for Skyways, and Cale Faro as advocate for the government. "I am surprised a hearing was scheduled at all," Pazli admitted.

"There is something unusual here," Talio said. "And I would never turn down the opportunity for a hearing." Or for twenty potential points.

They received a gilded lockbox with an invitation to the test skyship demonstration that weekend.

Talio and Pazli took a carriage an hour out of the city. As they sat on either side of the swaying carriage, Talio broached the subject that had been on his mind. "Do you not find it surprising that the government agreed to contract with Skyways in the first place? An Incarnite company, I mean."

Pazli sat up straighter, and his voice held pride. "Incarnites are known for their ingenuity and enterprise."

Many things had changed in ten years. "Are they?"

"Most of the booths in the Hall of Commerce are owned by Incarnites. The idea of renting a scribe came from an Incarnite. Quick-sealing wax was created by one of my cousins."

"Quick-sealing wax was invented thirty years ago."

He could hear the scoff. "Yes, and the woman who invented it became an Incarnite some years back. It happens more often than you may think."

Talio sat back. He still could not understand the timeline of the Incarnites. He'd come to Nuciferia twenty years ago as a young man. Pazli had said a small group of Incarnites had arrived in Nuciferia five years before that, but he hadn't heard of them until this year. "Does your religion proselytize?" he asked Pazli. "Deliberately seek out new converts?"

"Not at first," Pazli admitted. "We let the word of Sif find new congregants. In recent years, however, Zielle discovered a trove of Peyor's writings, once thought to be lost. They directed us to go forth and speak the word of Sif to those who would be receptive."

A trove of writings discovered later. A wealthy acolyte of Turi Peyor. Talio couldn't help but think that Lady Zielle had invented many of the trappings of the Incarnite religion for herself and had done well financially in the process. "You have never tried to preach to me."

"I might argue you are already in the throes of another religion," Pazli said. "Praise Scodel." Talio did not reply.

Birk and Lady Zielle met them at the entrance to a set of white bluffs overlooking a disused quarry. A matronly woman named Wynn wearing a reinforced cap gave a brief introduction; she was there from the Department of Distance Travel as an observer. "Our department maintains the skyline station and skyships," Wynn said. She had a professional, friendly expression.

It was a bright, windy day. The company had erected a span-high skyline tower atop two bluffs on opposite sides of the quarry. Talio could make out the small blue merinite stars on each tower. The narrow gushing waters of a diminutive skyline hurtled through the sky between them. A copper-hulled skyship sat in place at the farther tower.

Private peacekeepers surrounded the towers, and he asked Birk about them. "Security," the man said. "The amount of merinite we are using is priceless in value. Why do you think we needed Lady Zielle's investment?"

Talio looked around for Joban. When he did not see him, he asked Lady Zielle. "He is up there." She pointed to the furthest skyline tower.

"He's going to ride the skyship?" The towers were only five or six spans up, but still...

Lady Zielle's voice was admiring. "He believes in our cause. We have used five times as much merinite as necessary to ensure complete safety."

The little group stood at the area marked off for observation. Birk cleared his throat. "This is the first test of the Skyways Construction Company merinite redesign. Natural scientist Joban will pilot the craft." Lady Zielle waved a signal flag. Talio saw Joban face the merinite and mouth the appropriate incantations. No doubt he had received a dispensation for the blasphemy of praying to Felle. Fortunately, it did not matter whether he truly believed or not, as long as he spoke the words. Then Joban climbed into the skyship. Nothing happened for a long moment.

The skyship slid away from the skyline tower through the waters hanging in the sky toward them. Lady Zielle cheered, and Birk waved. For Talio, it was as if he were sitting next to Joban, feeling the ground drop away from him. He could not breathe. *It is all right*, he thought. *Surely Joban is safe.*

Talio watched the skyship gain speed. What would this speed increase mean for Merin? More trade, more visitors, more merchants. More hearings, no doubt. More Incarnites.

The skyship skimmed to a stop, hanging motionless in the sky, surrounded by water. Something was wrong. Talio looked at Birk, who was waving his arms toward the skyship in alarm. Lady Zielle had a hand to her chest. Pazli stood silent as always.

A moment later, the skyship tumbled through the waters of the skyline and plummeted toward the ground. Lady Zielle screamed. Talio tried to look away, tried not to see what would happen when Joban's body struck the surface of the quarry.

He did not see the impact. But he heard it.

# Chapter Fifteen

Talio lifted the wineglass to his lips with a trembling hand. He sat across from Pazli in the front room of the Double Moon Inn, eating what was becoming a regular dinner together.

Pazli broke the silence. "Clearly, the project was not yet ready for testing."

Was that a joke? No, Pazli was simply drawing a conclusion in his usual understated manner. "They attempted to deviate from Scodel's original design," Talio said in a shaky voice. "This test was doomed to failure. Joban arranged his own death." There was something fundamentally unsafe about skyships, even with Scodel's brilliance. The few times he'd ridden in one, he'd felt it tip from side to side as it rode the airborne river. This incident did not help. Talio grasped the edge of the table to try to stop his hand from quivering.

Pazli put his own hand over Talio's for a moment, and his tremors stilled in an instant. "Are you all right?" In moments like these, he could believe the barrier around the man was coming down, brick by brick. Cale had no barrier around him; why did he still mistrust him?

He closed his eyes for a moment. "I...I do not like high places. It is difficult for me to ride the skylines. Seeing what happened today did not help." Talio shrugged. "Or the way the peacekeepers interrogated me afterward."

"I imagine they were more respectful to you than the rest of us. The one who spoke to Birk, Lady Zielle and me could not understand how Incarnites had come into possession of so much merinite."

"I would have thought they would treat Lady Zielle with appropriate deference."

"The lady is still an Incarnite." Pazli's voice held a trace of the bitterness he knew so well. "But I do not believe the crash was caused by a design flaw."

"Are you suggesting another cause for the fatality?"

"There is something odd here," Pazli went on. "The test should have been a mere formality. Now the Skyways Construction Company is ruined. Lady Zielle will never see a return on her investment." Then he changed his tone. "I suppose this means that our work for the company is at an end, is it not?"

Having finished their meal, they moved to the worktable Talio reserved for himself. "Not quite yet." He pointed to the stack of vellum related to the hearing. "I would like to review the government's documents for the project they were working on before Skyways contacted them. The Hall of Documents should have them on file." He frowned. "It does not matter that there is no cause of action here. Why would Skyways claim the government copied them? Only one of them can be telling the truth."

"Perhaps the dates on the documents will show who was the first to develop the merinite redesign proposal." The Hall of Reference was already closed, but they decided to check the documents there the following day.

At Pazli's suggestion, he and Talio saw clients separately the next morning. They found they could see twice as many clients if they worked on their own. When they had questions for each other, it was a simple matter to step into a disused storage room Vinne had converted into a small gathering space and confer on matters of law or Incarnite customs.

He had to send Pazli to the Palace of Justice that morning to look up a point of law in the Hall of Reference. Then that afternoon, Talio needed to send Emara to confirm the text of an addendum, but it was the one day of the week she left early. All this travel back and forth to the Palace frustrated him. It would not do. They needed to buy a set of reference texts.

Talio was keeping track of the issues the Incarnites brought to him on a strip of vellum. Housing and employment were the primary subjects—anywhere discrimination was likely. A full set of reference texts for those two areas alone would cost more than their law office could bill in two months, even assuming each Incarnite client paid the full amount listed on the fee schedules. The Skyways crash had not only been a disaster for the construction company, but the Double Moon as well.

Then they received an official message lockbox from the Palace late that afternoon. Only Talio's identity key would open it. Here was another problem: he would have to purchase corporate identity keys and lockboxes for the law office so that Pazli and Emara could send and receive messages in his absence. Another expense.

He handed the message to Pazli. "Magistrate Verrane has summoned us for a meeting tomorrow morning. The pending hearing has been cancelled."

Pazli examined the vellum. "Why do you suppose he is continuing this pretense?"

"Skyways' cause of action is built on sand," Talio said, shaking his head. "I wonder if there is some overriding policy reason we are not seeing."

It was a bright and balmy day in Nuciferia, a surprise final reappearance by summer ahead of the fall. Magistrate Verrane received Talio, Pazli, and Cale in his chambers. Talio and Cale busied themselves with the ritual water basins and prayers, then joined Pazli sitting across from Verrane at his massive oak worktable.

"Faro here has moved to dismiss the hearing," Verrane said without preamble, lacing his fingers over his belly. "Scodel couldn't be clearer: an idea is not property. In addition, the government already studied a similar proposal and concluded that it is unfeasible. The Skyways test was unsuccessful, to say the least. Is there a reason I should not formally dismiss this matter right now?"

Talio leaned forward. "Magistrate, I would like to call a witness."

"This is not a hearing. We cannot take testimony under oath."

"Consider this additional information to inform your decision. It should not take long."

Cale looked at him with narrowed eyes. Outside the workrooms, he was happy to pursue and take the lead. But under the eyes of the law, it was Talio who would show him who was in charge. "Who?" Cale asked.

"The government worker who was at the test site the other day. She is called Wynn, but I do not know her last name. She is with the Department of Distance Travel."

Cale left to find Wynn. "How are you finding the Judicial Review Committee?" Verrane asked Talio during the ensuing silence.

"Very interesting. It is a pleasure working with such an experienced group of legal minds."

Verrane puffed his chest out. "Well, well." He smiled. "My pamphlet on medical hearings is modest, but the students seem to like it." *Except for the expense of having to buy the latest edition every year*, Talio thought. That they did not particularly care for.

Cale returned with the matronly planner, an irritated look on her face. "I told Master Faro I am quite busy. What do you need to know?" Quite a change in attitude from the other day.

Verrane's voice was brisk. "Advocate Rossa has some questions for you, Planner." Wynn's face was polite at once. The advocates made room for her at the worktable.

*Don't interrogate her*, Talio told himself. *She is not under oath.* "Can you tell us how Skyways Construction Company approached your department?"

She pursed her lips. "Well. It was all very odd. We had put out a bid for tenders for station maintenance, and the first one we received was from Skyways. They said they could double our travel speed. We weren't even looking for skyship upgrades."

"Then why did you accept their bid?"

Wynn became even more irritated. "We didn't. I had already worked on the same idea as Skyways—the merinite redesign, some months earlier. A promising idea, but modifying the existing towers without testing seemed quite dangerous." She shook her head. "As Skyways demonstrated."

"In any event," she continued, "the department head felt we should give them a chance. Maybe they knew something we didn't. Even if they were Incarnites." Pazli did not react.

"When did the government work on its version of the merinite redesign?" Talio asked.

"A year ago, I believe. Eleven months."

"And when did Skyways approach you?"

She thought about it. "Six months ago."

There was something he was missing. "How did your department handle Skyways' cause of action?"

Wynn fidgeted in her chair. "We had already worked on this concept. Suddenly, Skyways said we were copying them. Our legal department advised us that an idea is not property. In any event, we did not copy them. This was a frivolous hearing."

"I would like to review the Skyways design with you." He lifted his roll of vellum onto the worktable.

Wynn turned to Verrane. "Magistrate, I am quite busy. There is always work to do." Then to Talio, she added, "Why not ask the head of Skyways to go over the drawings? Birk?"

He wondered why she seemed so eager to depart. "Birk has been very busy with business matters since the tragedy," Talio said. This was an invention on his part, but a plausible enough excuse for the magistrate to keep Wynn present.

Verrane lifted a hand in Wynn's direction. "Another few minutes, please."

Talio spread the Skyways document over the worktable. He pointed to the dotted line he'd noticed the other day. "This is a schematic of the test tower, but Joban drew in the additional skylines that would exist on the actual tower." He looked at her. "There should be three skylines departing from Nuciferia—one for Aurania, one for Damiria, and one for Rylavia. Where is this fourth merinite star and unlabeled line supposed to lead to?"

Wynn laughed, an unexpected sound in the small chambers. "The Fifth City."

"I'm sorry," Talio said in sheer surprise. "What?"

She waved a hand in dismissal. "The mythical Fifth City. A departmental joke. Every junior planner makes the same mistake. They think: four cities, four skylines, four disks. I have made the mistake myself. It is so common, we barely notice when it happens. But of course, each skyline station only has three disks—or stars, in this case. Joban was a natural scientist, not a planner." Was that a frown on her face? Some dawning realization?

She got to her feet. "Now I must go. As I said, there is much work to be done. I must close the files on the Skyways matter."

Talio had nothing more than a suspicion, and Wynn's odd behavior. "Thank you, Planner Wynn. You are free to return to your work."

"Then we are done here," Verrane said once Wynn left. "No cause of action and no working merinite redesign." He drummed his fingers on the worktable. "I am considering issuing a magisterial note to the effect that no cause of action may be brought against the government in such a matter."

There it was. The overriding policy reason that Talio had suspected. Causes of action against the government were extremely rare, but this felt like someone attempting to forestall any future claims. Perhaps someone from the Royal Palace.

Scodel's system did not recognize the concept of precedent, but it was still an ominous sign. Talio did not like the idea of such a frivolous case being used to deprive citizens of any of their legal rights.

"I would request that you hold off on that note for the time being," Talio said. "More testimony may be about to come to light."

"The only testimony we have yet to hear from is from someone at the bottom of a quarry," Verrane said gravely. "Unless you wish to depose someone from the Fifth City."

Talio and Pazli conferred in the administration rotunda. "What did you hope to achieve?" Pazli asked.

"I'm not sure. I was thinking of Master Verrane's pamphlet."

"The one on medical hearings? What does that have to do with Skyways?"

"Did you ever take his course?" Pazli shook his head.

"In my second year at law school, I took the elective. He was teaching in Aurania that year, but the substitute still made us all buy copies of his little blue pamphlet. New copies, naturally. And then, two weeks into the course, we had to return them."

"Why?" Pazli asked.

"An error on one page." The memory of that day was still vivid. "Instead of the words 'not liable,' whoever had copied that edition's text had written 'liable.' They sent word to Verrane in Aurania. It was only one mistake, but given the potential for future liability, he paid to have new pamphlets copied. He ordered every single existing one destroyed."

"I still do not see your point."

"This is an issue of copying. Skyways claims the government copied them. The government made no counterclaim, but Wynn was clearly implying they had the idea first. Skyways must have copied them in return. I suspect this extraneous detail—the fourth star and the dotted line—will show who copied who." Talio put the roll of vellum under his arm. "We need to go to the Hall of Documents. And we need to go there at once."

At the Hall of Documents, Talio explained what he wanted: any prototype design documents from the Department of Distance Travel from eleven months ago. He showed his silver advocate pin and explained that they were the advocates of record for a related hearing.

Normally government documents were restricted, but their association with the hearing convinced the clerk, who showed them several sheets of designs from that period. Only one had a skyline tower with the familiar merinite star design. Talio gave an imprint of his identity key to borrow the copy for an hour, and he and Pazli sat down in the library to examine it.

The design for the revised merinite shape was identical. "Here is the fourth star." Pazli pointed to the vellum. "And the dotted line. Exactly as they were on the document Skyways prepared. Something is very wrong."

Talio could not make sense of it. "Now *I* am confused. If Skyways copied the design from the Department of Distance Travel, they could have copied this fourth star and line. This does not prove culpability. It only proves that some form of copying has occurred. We are naturally assuming Skyways is guilty because the Department's design predates theirs."

"I am starting to see," Pazli said. "How did Skyways get the department's design in order to copy it? We were only able to request a copy because we are listed as advocates on this hearing." He pointed at the drawing again. "And the Department of Distance Travel created this design six months before Skyways approached them. Why did they draw a design that contained the same error?"

"This is an impossible situation."

Pazli shook his head. "I have been thinking like an Incarnite. I jumped to the conclusion that the government was wrong and the Incarnites were right. The truth is more complicated."

He rolled up the vellum. "I am concerned we may already be too late. Where would someone go if they wished to make sure no Nuciferian peacekeepers would follow them?"

The entrance to the skyline station was busy with the morning's passengers waiting to be checked and processed. Pazli pushed his way through with Talio by his side, brandishing his advocate's pin. Surprisingly, the peacekeepers let him pass without comment.

Wynn was in line at one of the inspection stations. She gave a start when she saw them, but there was nowhere for her to go. Pazli stood before her. "Please open your satchel."

She clutched it closer, but he would not move. "I can wait until the peacekeeper opens it, if you'd like."

Wynn sighed and spread the contents of her satchel out on a counter. It held a dress, underclothes, toiletries and four white dinner plates with Nuciferian designs.

Pazli picked up one of the plates. Wynn looked at him in protest. "Those are a gift for my sister. In Aurania."

He used his fingernail to scratch at the surface of the plate. Nothing. Pazli held up his other hand to forestall the planner's protests and picked up the next plate. Again, he scratched the surface. This time the white peeled away to reveal the watery pale blue of merinite beneath.

"It's false merinite," Wynn said defensively.

"I will let the authorities make that determination," Pazli said. When Talio fetched a peacekeeper, Wynn did not resist.

That afternoon, Talio and Pazli were back in Magistrate Verrane's rooms with Cale, Birk and Lady Zielle. "Explain all this, please," the magistrate said.

"I will try," Pazli said, "although some of this is mere supposition. Wynn may choose to be more forthcoming in exchange for a finding of reasonable doubt in her hearing for Joban's murder."

Pazli stood before them. "About one year ago, Joban and Wynn had an idea. He may have approached her; I do not know. But together they decided to defraud one of our most respected congregants, Lady Zielle."

He spread out a large sheet of vellum on the worktable: the design from the government. "First, Joban gave Wynn the redesigned pattern for the merinite. She presented it as her own work to the Department of Distance Travel. It was, as she said, unfeasible."

Then Pazli spread out the second sheet of vellum: the Skyways design. "Next, Joban produced the same design in his own hand. This explains how the error of the fourth star and the dotted line showed up on both plans."

"He used the second plan to convince Birk to join up with him and launch the Skyways Construction Company," Talio said.

Birk nodded. "He was most persuasive. But I am not a natural scientist. I trusted his expertise."

"Joban knew the government would never run a test on the live skyline system," Pazli said. "His plan hinged on the test site. The small amount of merinite required for the two tower stars would be remarkably expensive." He turned to Zielle. "And that is where you became involved, my lady."

"Joban claimed to be such a devout Incarnite," Lady Zielle said. "I allowed the fires of my heart to override my mind." *And you allowed yourself to be dazzled by the silver that would be involved had Skyways become a major supplier to the government*, Talio thought.

"We were all fooled," Pazli said. "After Lady Zielle invested, Joban used the funds to purchase the merinite required for the demonstration. He promised they would sell it back afterward, but he had no plans to return it. Ever."

"Joban submitted his design to the government and claimed the government stole it. Then Wynn claimed Skyways had stolen the government's design."

"But why?" Verrane asked. "He could simply steal the merinite on the day of the test."

Birk shook his head. "This, I can answer. The government would have rejected us outright if we had approached them with an untested idea. Since Wynn said she had done most of the work on it, they were curious to see if we had a solution for the remaining issues."

Verrane threw up his hands. "Then why did Joban die if he was part of this scheme?"

Cale broke in at this point. "I have a theory. Wynn must have wanted everything for herself. All she had to do was to sabotage the demonstration. But I still don't understand how she got the merinite when it was under such tight guard. And how did she kill Joban?"

"I am hypothesizing here," Pazli said. "Lady Zielle said they had used five times as much merinite as necessary. Joban and Wynn had to steal the merinite before the day of the test, when it would be under guard. Before they mounted the star, they had removed much of the merinite for themselves—leaving just enough of a margin to keep the skyship aloft. Joban thought he would be safe, until Wynn removed quite a bit more on her own. Enough to cause the skyship to fail and remove her partner from the scheme. But we will have to wait until the peacekeepers conduct a full investigation."

Verrane harrumphed and pushed up his glasses. "All of this is theory and supposition. We know Joban died. Wynn was caught with her hands in the stream, as you might say. We have a murder case now, not any sort of 'stolen' ideas."

Cale stood at once and smiled. "Regardless, what we learned today proves there can be no Skyways claim, whether an idea is property or not. Thank you for an enlightening lecture, Advocate Mecomb, but you have proven our argument. Since Wynn was acting in collaboration with Joban, there was no 'copying' by the government."

"Wasn't there, Advocate Faro?" Talio asked in mock surprise. "Didn't Wynn present Joban's original plans as her own? She was acting as an agent of the Department of Distance Travel. I would argue in this case, this was effectively the government copying his designs. And we've clearly established the detriment to the company here."

Magistrate Verrane rapped his fingers on the worktable, as if they were in a hearing. "You still have no cause of action, advocate. And with no cause of action, you cannot have a claim for damages. Your deductions have been quite clever, but the matter ends there, I'm afraid."

"If you will forgive me, magistrate. I believe you are incorrect. And if you will adjourn this gathering until tomorrow morning, I would be happy to prove my argument definitively."

Verrane looked skeptical. "The peacekeepers will return the stolen merinite. Lady Zielle will recoup her original investment. I will continue to say that ideas are not property until Scodel himself breaks free from the Impassable Forest to tell us otherwise. What more can be done?"

"Will twelve more hours make such a difference in the administration of this matter?" Talio gave the magistrate an innocent look. Cale gazed skyward in frustration, but the prosecutor was repressing a faint smile.

The magistrate pursed his lips. "Very well. I will see everyone tomorrow morning in a proper hearing room. Don't disappoint me, please."

Pazli caught up with Talio in the hallway. "You do not have any ideas at all, do you?"

Talio gave him a serious look. "I do have one, but time is very short. I will need your help—and the help of the Incarnites. We are a hair's breadth away from dismissal." And losing the twenty points involved.

"They can pray for intercession, if you wish."

Talio shook his head. "I need something else from them. Magistrate Verrane's little blue pamphlet on medical hearings has given me an idea."

# Chapter Sixteen

Talio and Pazli sat on a bench in the colonnade while Talio explained his plan. Pazli stayed silent with his arms folded. There was a certain tension in the way that he held them that delivered a clear message: disapproval. "We have very little time," Talio said. "I would rather hear your disdain in verbal form, to expedite matters."

Pazli nodded. "Very well. I do not wish to participate in another of your tricks. The one at my murder hearing was quite enough."

Talio stared at him. "It saved you from the gallows! Or would you have preferred I had said nothing and let the jury convict you?"

"I believe the professor who taught my logic course might have something to say about presenting only two choices when others are available."

They waited until a group of law students—laughing and joking—passed. "Your logic merely opens the door to any type of deception, if the desired result is virtuous enough," Pazli said.

"I will not have you judging me like Clemente Jilani." Now it was Talio's turn to fold his arms, this time in anger. "Have you never found a way around the words of your catechism?"

"Never."

Talio spoke more softly this time. "And if you were to meet a situation that fell outside of its principles?"

"There is nothing outside of being an Incarnite." Now Talio had his answer to a question that had been hanging over him since that drunken night at the Double Moon. He put the thought out of his head.

"This is an object lesson. A way to convince someone that will not harm anyone," he said. "I promise. It will also help Lady Zielle."

A long pause. "I will help you," Pazli said at last. "And I will seek a dispensation from the cleric. You may expect a lockbox with my invoice shortly."

There was no time to argue about silver and invoices. "We will need a large amount of vellum," he told Pazli.

"I assume each sheet needs to be the size of a pamphlet." Pazli said. Talio nodded.

That was harder than it seemed. They stopped at a stationer's Talio had passed several times on his walks to the Palace of Justice. The middle-aged woman behind the counter couldn't help him. She had small strips in stock, the type that Talio used to take notes. She had larger vellum, such as the one used for the Skyways Construction Company designs. But there was nothing the size of a pamphlet or a codex. Talio could have bought larger sheets and cut them, but the pages he needed had a particular scalloped edge and watermark that he could not hope to reproduce.

"Is there another store I might try?" Talio asked, panicked. "Anywhere?"

She shook her head. "We are not permitted to sell vellum cut to that size." But they did have stiff red leather covers that could be cut to size; Talio bought twenty of them.

Back out on the street, Talio shook his head. "I feel as if I've gone mad." When Pazli did not reply, he looked at the Incarnite. "You are of course free to disagree with my assessment."

"It is indeed odd. I have never noticed this restriction on vellum before."

They continued downstream toward the Double Moon. True, the registers, the rosters, the pamphlets, and the codices were all the same size. Allowing anyone to procure vellum of that size could result in all kinds of mischief.

Vinne was of no help, either. "They're regulated by the printing and copying guild. Something to do with preventing fraud."

Talio gave his head a glum shake. "It is a conspiracy of codices. I thought Nuciferian bureaucracy was bad, but I had no idea."

"I don't know anyone in the guild." The innkeeper grumbled. "They're pretty law-abiding, if you know what I mean."

Talio followed Vinne into the kitchen, where Pazli could not hear them. "What about someone like Oran Keel?"

Vinne started chopping vegetables, his sharp knife a blur of motion. "Why would he have anything to do with vellum?"

Talio sidled closer. "Doesn't he have interests in other businesses?"

The knife stopped mid-slice. "Don't ask Keel."

"Fine. Then I should see Pazli back to the temple."

"Don't talk to Keel. I'm telling you as a friend and your landlord. Don't ask him or anyone else down there."

Once they were outside the district, Talio gave Pazli instructions for the Incarnites, and they parted ways. He was a grown man, and he did not have to listen to Vinne. He had dealt with enough criminals in his time.

Halfway to the garment district, Talio found his way blocked by two wagons whose owners were in a heated dispute about right of way. He sighed, put his hands on the stone railing and watched the candlelit barges silhouetted against the canal as a flock of birds angled across the sky. Despite the urgency of his errand, he couldn't get certain thoughts out of his head.

A conspiracy of codices. He'd said the line in jest, but something was indeed wrong. Talio had spent his career looking for the single fact that did not add up, the one witness whose testimony did not match the others. He could not understand the pattern he was seeing.

Why were codex-sized vellum pages restricted? Why were unabridged codices impossible to see unless one was a magistrate? And for that matter, why was there such an air of secrecy around the codices at all?

In the law school magisterial track, the professors treated the codices as holy relics. Losing one's codex was almost a capital crime. Look at how he had been shamed, shunned ten years ago. *Praise Scodel,* law students would say as a joke. To Talio, it was no longer amusing at all.

The laws of Merin were meant to be straightforward and accessible; Scodel's principles described them as such.

Talio—and any advocate, prosecutor or even member of the public—could review them in the Hall of Reference.

Except the sentencing guidelines. And the civil equivalent, the guidelines for damages. Nobody could see them except magistrates. Why? It had never occurred to him to consider this when he'd been a magistrate; Talio had gloried being in on the secret, having access to something that few people had. To be on the outside raised all sorts of questions.

Talio watched a couple in an illuminated pleasure boat drift by, hand-in-hand, with eyes only for each other. He smiled for a moment but returned to his previous thoughts with a frown.

In Scodel's legal system, sentencing was uniform across Merin. Rape, for example, was a capital crime. The sentencing guidelines gave a magistrate no leeway; hanging was mandatory. Lesser crimes offered a range of sentences at the magistrate's discretion. Talio had always tried to impose the lightest sentence available. He was particularly creative and could often twist the facts of a case to have it reclassified to a crime with even lighter penalties.

Why hide the sentencing guidelines from public view? Why obscure them with the tables and concordances? Why were they so poorly organized, when the rest of Scodel's laws were a model of organization?

Talio continued on his way. He had run away to Velos partly because Gawani caught him in bed with Cale, yes. But the main reason had been because he had lost his codex. They are only *books*, he thought. And now he wanted to know why the legal system was treating them like they were gifts from Felle. Take Vinne's comment about the printing and copying guild. Nuciferia reproduced the codices for all of the Four Cities, but even as a magistrate, Talio had never been granted access to these facilities. Why?

The garment district looked seedier at night; hanging laundry flapped in the breeze, and the few people that were about did not look friendly. The barge with the duhan lounge was not where it had been; he had to search a few streets to find it. Presumably they moved it frequently to avoid detection. Talio slipped the man behind the door two silver and went in.

It was a gamble that Oran Keel would be here, but it was fair odds. The man could not go a minute without sucking on a water pipe. Where else would he be, on some other barge?

Keel was sitting at the far corner of the stage, alone. Nobody was dancing or playing music this evening, and the lounge was somber. "May I join you?" Talio asked him through the haze. The mousy man did not reply.

"I need your help." Still nothing. "I need some vellum. A few hundred sheets. Tonight." Talio angled his thumbs and fingers together to make a small, rectangular shape. "That size. Scalloped edges. In an hour or so."

Keel put down the stem of the water pipe and blew smoke in his face. He was cold tonight, cold and still. "So, you *are* on our side of the law."

Talio shook his head. "No, but I need your help this evening."

Keel leaned forward. "What happened to your face? Who did it?" This was not the quiet question that Pazli had asked him. He said it with a fascination and an insolence that chilled Talio.

Talio had no desire to share the truth with this man, but if it would get him the vellum, he would say something. "There was a mudslide. When I was a child. My parents pushed me under a cart to save me. They died. The cart collapsed and..." He drew a line with his finger down his scar. His parents had indeed died in a mudslide. He had not been present, but every advocate knew that a lie mixed with the truth was more believable. "Can you help me with the vellum, then?"

"What makes you think I have a source?"

Talio fought the urge to cough from the thick duhan haze. "Do you?"

Keel named a price that made him flinch, nearly half the advance Lady Zielle paid them. "Can you get it to me in an hour?" Talio asked.

The garment merchant stretched out a hand in the gloom. "Payment first."

"I don't have the silver on me."

Keel looked at him, calculating. Then he gestured at Talio's chest. "Give me the pin." Talio looked down. He'd forgotten to remove his advocate's pin after leaving the Palace of Justice. Hopefully nobody else had seen it or understood its significance.

Talio hesitated, then removed it and handed it over. "I had better get this back."

"When I get my money."

He thought again of the conspiracy of codices. Maybe this was what he wanted to ask for all along, and the vellum plan had merely been an excuse? It was dangerous, but he had to try.

"There's something else you could get me," Talio said.

"Is there." As before, Keel lost interest in the conversation.

Talio dropped his voice to a whisper. "A magistrate's codex." For a while, the only sounds were the lapping of the water against the sides of the barge.

"You can't pay what it would cost you," Keel whispered back at last. "And I wouldn't take your money for it, anyway. You don't cross the magistrates. At least, not the important ones." He refused to elaborate further.

The man gave him instructions for the vellum: he was to wait in a nearby street and the "materials" would arrive shortly. When Talio arrived in the street, it was dark and deserted; there were no lamps or tapers in any windows.

Little more than an hour later, someone with a high collar obscuring their face rolled a cart up to Talio. "Get going," the person said. He could not be sure if it was a man or a woman.

"Can I take the cart?" The person slapped him on the back of his head and disappeared into the night. As he headed toward the Incarnite temple, Talio felt ridiculous rolling a cart around half of Nuciferia, but it was better than carrying the vellum by hand.

In a few minutes, he and Pazli were in the temple's dining hall, watching twenty Incarnites writing on twenty sheets of vellum. As each one finished a page, they placed it in a pile and picked up another blank sheet from a second pile. A second group was hand-lettering the red leather covers. "How did you convince them to help?" Talio asked.

"Lady Zielle is considered near holy. More than that, it is the principle of the matter."

"How do you mean?"

The man gave his characteristic shrug. "An injury to one Incarnite is an injury to all."

When Talio returned to the Double Moon, the sun was rising over the rooftops. Vinne was asleep; Talio was glad that he would not have to endure a lecture from the man. He had only enough time to change into a formal suit and meet Pazli at the Palace of Justice. He pretended he'd forgotten his advocate's pin and borrowed a temporary one from the service desk. It would be a few days before he would have the money to reimburse Keel. He was fortunate that advocates and others often requested spare pins; their clasps were sadly known for falling off or jamming at inopportune moments.

In the hearing room, Magistrate Verrane sat behind his desk, Cale at his, with Lady Zielle and Birk in the first row of the audience seating. Pazli gave Talio a brief nod and excused himself.

The magistrate rapped his fingers on the desk. "I adjourned our meeting yesterday afternoon so that Advocate Rossa could prepare his argument. Now I am ready to hear it."

Talio strolled up to the magistrate's desk. "I have reviewed every one of Scodel's laws. I believe that one from the medical field might be applicable here."

He pulled a red pamphlet from his pocket and read aloud, "In cases of medical negligence, it must first be determined whether the injured had any pre-existing conditions that might mitigate damages. Further to this principle—"

The magistrate was leaning over, looking at him, looking at the pamphlet in his hand. "Where did you get this?" he roared. "Give me that!"

Talio handed the red pamphlet to Verrane, who flipped through it in agitation. "This is not my pamphlet. The words are the same. But it has a red cover—and no mention of me. The printing is different."

"I am selling them," Talio said. "Would you like to purchase a copy?"

The door to the outside opened, and Pazli wheeled in a cart of red pamphlets. It had taken the Incarnites hours to copy each page of Verrane's original blue pamphlet. At first, they could make only one copy of the original. Then they used the originals as the basis for further copies before hastily binding them with the red leather covers. There were only twenty pamphlets on the cart, but Talio could not guarantee which one Verrane might pull from the pile. They all had to be perfect. He could have produced a single copy, but a pile of them would deliver his message far more effectively.

The magistrate stood up from his desk and rushed over to the cart. He pawed through the pamphlets, grabbed one, and started reading. "You cannot do this."

Talio shrugged. "Why not, magistrate? Which law would you say I am contravening?"

Verrane sputtered. "It's against all the laws of morality!"

"I do not believe you can recoup damages for an offense to morality," Talio said gravely. "At least not without a proper cause of action."

The magistrate was beyond speech. He looked at Talio and seethed, red-faced, gripping the pages of the pamphlet.

"Would it damage your reputation if someone started selling these copies?" Talio asked. "Even without your name on the cover, they might confuse them with the ones that you have published. And if they contained an error—the words 'not liable' instead of 'liable'..."

Wary, Verrane nodded. "Yes, yes of course."

"Then perhaps that principle might apply in the Skyways matter." Talio addressed the rest of the room. "A loss of investment of this magnitude would cause damage to Lady Zielle's reputation. We can call witnesses to that effect."

"Objection," Cale said.

Verrane looked up from the pamphlet. "What is it, Faro?"

Cale got to his feet. "Damages to reputation must be based on proof of financial loss. Advocate Rossa may be able to call witnesses to the effect that Lady Zielle had a loss of reputation emotionally, or that she suffered embarrassment. But can he prove she suffered a specific monetary loss?"

Talio's mind was whirling. Yes, damages to reputation had to be quantified. And yes, Lady Zielle had recouped her investment. The recovered merinite would be returned to her once the peacekeepers had held it long enough to teach her a lesson as an Incarnite. He could not even show she had been a fool; this had been a conspiracy between a third party and a government employee. There was no way she could have known.

For once, he did not know what to say. He had bet his entire strategy on the pamphlets. He had claimed that he'd read every one of Scodel's laws. That might have been a better use of his time.

"In a battle between Advocate Rossa's pamphlets and Advocate Faro's legal interpretation," Magistrate Verrane said drily, "I prefer the latter. I would normally conclude the hearing now, but there is no cause of action here, and therefore, no hearing ever took place." He rapped his fingers on the desk with finality.

Verrane pointed to Talio. "Advocate Rossa. It occurs to me that the matter of copying of documents—and the ownership thereof—is something I should refer to the Judicial Review Committee. You have identified a gap in the legislation as it stands." He pursed his lips. "It is inevitable that in such a young legal system, new situations will arise that even the great Scodel never considered. Such as new religions." He nodded in Pazli's direction.

"And dispose of those pamphlets, would you?" Verrane added in a colder voice. "The Hall of Documents will burn them for you. Unless you'd care to fill us in on the specific process you went through to create these spurious documents...and all of the citizens involved." Talio shook his head no, vigorously.

Verrane went on. "The issue of mediation and government causes of action will be paused for the time being."

"I'm sorry," Cale whispered to him as he passed him on the way to the exit. Remarkably, he seemed sincere.

"I prefer strong opponents," Talio whispered back, which earned him a smile from the prosecutor.

Talio wanted to get home as soon as possible. Skyways had held such promise: twenty points toward his law license, and the prestige that a case dealing with the skylines would bring. Cale had dealt him as fatal a blow as the one he'd dealt the prosecutor in Pazli's murder hearing.

Zielle put a comforting hand on Talio's back as they left the hearing room. "You did what you could. Birk and I have other plans for Skyways now."

"What are those?"

"We are going to blaze a trail from Nuciferia to Aurania," Birk said. "Through the Impassable Forest."

It was unthinkable. They would be eaten by monsters or repelled by the magical barriers. But as Pazli said, the Incarnites were ingenious. "Perhaps you'll find the Fifth City," Talio said, and Birk laughed.

He and Pazli returned to the Double Moon Inn, where Vinne had decorated the inside with festive streamers and flowers. "Oh," the innkeeper said when he saw their faces. "Well, we can celebrate the fact that they haven't thrown you in prison. Yet."

Emara joined them for drinks, but the mood was somber. Pazli sat with folded arms, and she watched him with keen interest. At one point, Emara folded her arms and sat like Pazli. Talio wanted to laugh; with the same height, the same build, and the same body position, it was as if he was facing two Pazlis. He could not imagine double the sarcasm—or double the silence.

At Emara's request, Talio explained Skyways and how their trick failed. She shook her head. "You mustn't subvert the words of Scodel."

Ah, a strict constructionist—to her, one should only apply the laws as Scodel had written them, with no deviations. Emara's black-and-white thinking did not surprise him. "He never contemplated the theft of an idea."

Was that anger in her eyes? "Then we should clearly leave it alone. Praise Scodel." He did not press the matter further, and they returned to their drinking. Scodel had never had to worry about earning points, either. Her dogmatic nature worried Talio a bit; if he took her on as a partner in the Double Moon, how would she manage when faced with the inevitable compromises arguing the law entailed? Or was Pazli right, after all? Was he simply using Scodel's laws as a framework to bend and shape to his needs?

Talio waited until later, when Vinne collapsed, and he'd put a pillow under his head and a blanket over him. Then he snuck out and returned to the garment district.

This late at night, the district was even eerier. A mangy cat carried an enormous rat in its mouth down the street. The duhan barge had not moved, but the man behind the door now demanded four silver.

Keel peered at him through the duhan haze. "What is so important about a magistrate's codex?"

"Secrets always intrigue me." That was not the real reason. A codex had ended his legal career. Upon rational reflection, there was no reason for it to have done so. Something very important was being hidden from view, and he wanted to know what, and why.

"I can offer you more money," Talio said.

Keel shook his mousy head. "Can't get you a codex. But I spoke to my source. We can get some ruined pages." At Talio's questioning face, he explained. "Whenever a copier makes a mistake, they discard the page. They're supposed to burn the discards. They don't always get rid of them."

"I'll take the ruined pages. But they must come from the sentencing guidelines section." Keel's source should know what that meant. He handed over the money for the previous night's printing he'd withdrawn from the bank earlier that day.

Keel gave him back the advocate's pin and named a price for the ruined pages that would hurt the Double Moon. It would not be for long, if Emara was able to bring on contingency clients. "Is it really worth all that money to you?"

Everything in the Merin legal system seemed to obfuscate how those laws were to be interpreted. He nodded. "Yes, I think it is."

It would take Keel some time to get the pages, he explained; Talio should not expect them right away. He wasn't sure if Keel would ever provide them, but at least he had taken the one action he could that was not under the eyes of the Palace of Justice.

His sleep was sound, but when Talio awoke, he found the point of a spike protruding from the door of his room. He swung the door open and stared. Someone had nailed a dead rat to his door. Blood dripped down the door and congealed at the base. A note read: NO MORE TRICKS.

Talio wrapped his arms around him to stop himself from shaking. He did not want to wake Vinne; gathering his sheets around his shoulders, he went through the rest of the inn and checked all the windows. They were intact. The kitchen door remained rusted shut. And all three tumblers on the front door remained locked. None had been tampered with.

# Chapter Seventeen

He hadn't wanted to tell Vinne about the rat, but he would not have been able to explain the hole in the door to his room otherwise. Vinne hung an ugly painting of three big-eyed fish over the hole; it reminded him of the rat every time he came home from the Palace.

Ever since that night, Vinne hovered around Talio. The innkeeper insisted on accompanying him on errands whenever he was sober. Talio appreciated the company but was not worried. He'd walked through the garment district at night without being accosted. Nuciferia was a frightened city, but a safe one.

"Do you know someone who might hate you enough to do this?" Vinne asked.

"Many people." He had Pazli and Vinne on his side. The Judicial Review Committee tolerated him, although Magistrate Verrane now treated him with frosty indifference. Talio hadn't thought far enough ahead. He'd figured Verrane would see the brilliance of his arguments, would simply grant him the Skyways judgment and the points involved. But perhaps, he admitted, there was a part of him that wanted to needle the magistrate and his infernal pamphlets. Had it really been worth it?

Talio was still unsure about Emara. She came to the Double Moon and did her work with briskness and a stern efficiency. Her attendance was stellar, although he missed her the one day a week she left early. But was she on his side? She had stayed on, despite them not being able to hire her as an advocate. She had her degree, though. She could have paid for a license. The answer became clear a few days later.

One afternoon she stood by his desk with folded arms, looking very much like Pazli. They were of similar height and build, except for the cloak. With Pazli, folded arms signaled trouble, but with Emara, Talio could never tell. Finally, she passed him a scrap of vellum with an address. "Please come to dinner tomorrow night," she announced. "At my parents' rooms."

Talio nodded, not sure what was more surprising, the formal, stiffly voiced invitation or her use of the word "please." When she'd gone, Vinne came out from behind the bar and asked him, "Do you think she needs an alibi?"

*Alibi* was the term used by men who preferred men for a particular arrangement. Once such a man reached a certain age without marrying, people started asking questions. Procuring a pleasant woman willing to accompany the man on social errands was often enough to quell any suspicions. The woman could be paid to become a regular companion, or in some cases even a wife. Talio had never heard of a woman seeking a man for a similar arrangement, but he supposed it was possible. "I'm not sure," he said. Emara was still quite young to be expected to marry.

The address was downstream from the Double Moon, halfway to the Incarnite temple. He walked down there the following evening, dreading the dinner. Talio had already gone through the possibilities of her parents' origin based on Emara's own personality and the stereotypes every Merin citizen knew. Nuciferians were passive, docile and easily frightened. Auranians like himself were kind-hearted but sometimes too kind. Rylavians...well, Rylavians kept to themselves, and they were odd. Like Pazli, Emara's parents had to be Damirian; both her own militant personality and the concern over an alibi pointed to it. That meant endless questioning, heavy foods, and uncomfortable furniture.

But their rooms were cozy and bright, with worn edges and abstract artwork everywhere. To Talio's surprise, they were not Damirian at all, but dreamy, impractical people— Rylavians. They both gave his scar several surreptitious looks over the course of the evening but said nothing. After spending time with them, he could not understand how they had produced someone like Emara.

Her mother was an inventor. She showed him the device she was working on, a series of staggered bowls through which dripped water. "Once it's perfected," she said with enthusiasm, "you'll always know what time it is." She had sent letters to several nobles outlining her ideas; Talio didn't have the heart to tell her that given the findings about ideas in the Skyways hearing, she had given away her idea for free.

Emara's father was a painter. After a pleasant dinner of root vegetables and savory pastries, he gave Talio a tour of their rooms, including his studio. The artwork was bold and dramatic; it was out of step with the style of the times, but her father was sure he could make a large sale to the Royal Palace, if only he could get the chance. Emara's parents were dreamers; perhaps she had taken it upon herself to confront reality, as she saw it.

While Emara helped her mother clear off the table, her father showed Talio her old room. "It's just as she left it." Unlike the rest of the house, her room was orderly. Only a stray paper poking out of a sheaf of vellum betrayed any disorganization.

Emara's mother called for the father, and Talio stood alone in the impersonal room for a moment. There were only superficial clues to her personality here. He looked again at the paper, a legal certificate of some kind. He touched his fingers to it but hesitated. Why did he always feel the need to explore any potential mystery?

"Go ahead," Emara said from behind him. Permission granted, Talio drew out the sheet. It was her legal license, dated two years earlier. There was a green border he was unfamiliar with, and a watermark that read: *Provisional License.*

She took it from his hands and gave it the same clinical gaze she gave everything. "There were some problems at the law school. Two years ago."

Gawani had mentioned some scandal. "You were caught?"

Emara shook her head. "I was one of the 'innocent' ones." She gave a smile that was half-grimace. "Professor Jilani's exams had been getting harder. Harder and harder, all semester. Half of us would have failed or dropped out. Several students decided to cheat. They were the ones who got caught."

She closed the door to her room. "The rest of us decided we wouldn't let them get expelled. So, we all said we'd cheated too."

Talio could only imagine the pandemonium. An entire graduating class, disqualified. Who would Queen Jaconda have addressed at the ceremony? A solitary Clemente Jilani?

Her voice was brittle. "They created a program. Something for 'wayward advocates.' You can imagine how well that went over." She shoved the license back into place on the shelf. "Jilani designed that system well. It looks like you can get your license, but it's almost impossible. We all found out eventually."

"I'm familiar with it." A thought occurred to him. "I could help you with the points. Or lend you the money for your license if you'd like."

She shrugged. "Whatever you can do to help."

"We'll set aside a bit of time every day from now on and see what we can do." At that point her mother came in to offer them tea and cakes.

At the end of the evening, Emara gave Talio a hard peck on the cheek as he was leaving. Walking home, he was still unsure what that night meant. Was he an alibi for her parents, or had this been her way of opening up to him a bit, taking a brick out of her own wall?

Talio wanted to believe it was an overture of friendship. He liked Emara for her simplicity and straightforwardness. She was hot or cold, black or white, good or bad. He wanted to remain on her good side.

The following afternoon at the Double Moon, once Pazli left for the day, Talio asked Emara how many points she'd managed to amass under the *Program for Wayward Advocates*. "Seventy so far," she said glumly.

"Seventy!" Talio could not believe it. "Perhaps there are some pages missing from my pamphlet."

She flipped through it and shook her head. "Mine's different. Ours was for students. This one looks like it's for experienced advocates. And I've been working on my points for two years."

The student program was quite different. There was no time limit. It also tried to encourage new advocates by awarding points for small administrative tasks. The downside of that approach was that those tasks could only be rewarded once. Emara was now in the same situation as Talio; she needed hearings to get past the one-hundred-point threshold.

"You can assist me and Pazli with hearings from now on," Talio said. "That should help. And keep trying to get some work for those medical hearings you mentioned."

She nodded. "I am trying. They are dying to become my clients." Emara flashed him a tight grin. For the first time since they'd met, she'd made a joke.

One morning a few days later, a boy came up to him at the Double Moon, tugging on his cloak and urging him some distance away. The youth was dirty, with sharp eyes.

They stood outside the kitchen door. "Keel wants you," the boy said. "He has them."

Talio's heart skipped a beat. When he gave the messenger some silver, the boy looked up at him with a frown.

"Your face looks weird," he blurted out, and disappeared around the corner. Talio sighed and rubbed his eyes; at least he hadn't told him not to pull any more tricks.

That evening, he begged off dinner, claiming his stomach was upset. Vinne left a tray outside his door. Talio waited until he was sure the innkeeper was asleep, then made his way downstream to the garment district in the chilly, purple night. The man at the barge charged him six silver this time.

Keel's eyes were bloodshot and wary. He pushed a packet of vellum toward him. "Don't come back," he said, and turned away, his protruding ears wreathed in a halo of smoke. Talio walked back to the Double Moon with quickening steps. When he'd returned to his room, he propped the chair up against the door and examined the package.

He wasn't sure what to expect. Talio's memories of the sentencing guidelines from his codex from ten years earlier had dimmed. He remembered the instructions at the start of the section, the tables and concordances, and the pages of sentences that followed.

Talio spread the pages from the package on his bedsheet. At a glance, none of the fifteen pages comprised instructions, the tables or concordances. The absence of the introductory sections disappointed him, but he would have to make do.

After reviewing the pages in more detail, he separated them into two piles: criminal hearings and civil ones. The civil section was, by necessity, much smaller than the rest of the guidelines. The section name was a misnomer; there was no sentencing in civil hearings. The section described the remedies available to a magistrate: damages, specific performance, and other types of non-monetary compensation.

He could link none of the sentences back to the criminal charges or civil causes of action; he would need the tables and concordances to make those connections.

The partial text of each page ended with a word or phrase struck through with a line. Talio assumed these were the errors that resulted in the pages being discarded. That suggested that the preceding text was an accurate copy of the original.

What surprised him was the harshness of the sentences. He remembered certain sentences from his days as magistrate: Serious acts of violence always merited the penalty of hanging. And regardless of Talio's feelings on the subject, Queen Jaconda was firm that coin clipping, counterfeiting, and other major currency offenses were all capital crimes.

But the pages in the criminal pile were far out of proportion to the range of sentences he'd expected. Whipping. Flogging. Beheading, of all things! The prison sentences ranged from five years to an incredible twenty-five years. He had never sentenced anyone to more than six years, and that was only because the guidelines offered him no lenience.

Without knowing which causes of action linked to which civil damages, he could not determine their severity.

Damages would be based on actual monetary loss, as Cale mentioned, or non-monetary losses such as emotional harm or inability to work due to injury.

Talio put the pages down and drummed his fingers. These were not as he remembered them. He could not have forgotten so much in ten years. Of course, he had never sat down and read the hundred pages of sentences; nobody read all the sentences from start to finish. As every magistrate did, he'd relied on the tables and concordances to guide him to the range of sentences he needed. But his codex had never guided him to such severe sentences, ever.

He needed a second opinion. He could not talk to Pazli about this. The man took his ethics too seriously; he would not even consider the implications of what Talio had potentially found. He could hear Pazli already, talking about the immorality of how he'd obtained these pages. No, he would leave the man to his catechism.

The next morning, Talio received a lockbox from Cale. The prosecutor had handed him a personal key before the Skyways hearing, but Talio hadn't thought he would ever need to use it. *We need to meet*, it read. *I'd like to clear the air. This evening.* It gave the address of a downstream dormitory. Very well.

The dormitory building and furnishings were threadbare. Talio could not imagine why a successful prosecutor was living in such a noisy, ramshackle building. He was no elitist, but Cale could certainly afford better.

The clerk told him Cale was out and returned to her needlepoint, observing him with careful eyes. Talio waited in the lobby, watching people come and go, until Cale appeared at the door in a dark cloak that set off his brown eyes and made him look even more handsome.

"I am glad to see you," the man said with a smile. "Let's go up to my room." Talio had to sign in, and he could tell that by the shake of the clerk's head that she did not approve of Cale having company.

The prosecutor's single room was tiny but well-furnished. Cale's eyes were far away. "I am sorry I was so late," he said. "I was at the hospital visiting my father."

"Is he all right?"

"I pay for nurses to care for him. He forgets, then he remembers, and then he forgets again." Cale shrugged. "But he never forgets to remind me what a failure I've been all my life."

His tone was light, but anger barely hid behind it. "Then why visit him?" Hospital attendants were expensive; now he understood why Cale lived in such shabby accommodations.

"When I was a child, my father did everything but keep me locked in a room, for years and years. He was my whole world once my mother passed away. And now I get to see him locked in his own little room. Unaware. Unable to leave. Seeing the pain in his eyes gives me some small, sick pleasure."

Talio could not think of a reply. "At least you go to see him," he said at last.

"At least your parents loved you enough to send you to law school," the prosecutor said.

Talio shook his head. "They did not want me to go to law school. Even if they had supported my wishes, they would not have been able to afford it. But I was able to get my license, somehow."

Cale sighed. "I have heard from the river of gossip that flows through the Palace that you are trying to get your license back once again." Talio nodded. "Something about points," Cale went on. "I am sorry for beating you in the Skyways matter."

"You have nothing to apologize for," Talio said. "I expect you to do your job. Just as you should expect me to trounce you at our next hearing."

Cale gave a sad smile. "Perhaps I still feel guilty about what happened all those years ago. It's not easy thinking that I ruined a man's life, once."

Talio thought of Gawani, how she'd managed to forgive him, even after all that time. He put a hand on the man's shoulder. "I bear some responsibility for it, too."

Cale looked at him with troubled eyes. "There is something I must tell you," he said. "I have been trying to think of a way to do so ever since you came back."

"What could be so terrible that you could not say it?" Talio asked. "I know you were instructed to seduce me that night, all those years ago. There could be nothing worse."

Cale looked as if he might cry. Talio waited while the handsome man mustered up the courage to speak. Finally, he spoke four quiet words, "I stole your codex."

There it was. Talio should have known he'd lied about it earlier. Of course he'd taken it; what other purpose had their night together all those years ago served? But he did not feel angry, or resentful, or even sad. There was a more important question now. "Do you still have it?"

Cale laughed in disbelief. "That is your first response? Do I still have it?" He shook his head. "No. They told me to go directly from the Double Moon back to the Palace, then leave it in a special spot." Then it had been a deliberate effort to end his career, not just his marriage.

"You have confided in me," Talio said. "And now I will confide in you." He had brought the ruined pages with him, unsure whether he should mention them. But he needed Cale's help. He could not do this alone. He explained to the prosecutor what the pages were but omitted any mention of how he had obtained them. Talio did not need to ask Cale for secrecy.

Cale flipped through the pages and listened to Talio's commentary about the sentences. He motioned Talio off the bed and moved the bedding to reveal a hole in the bedframe. "I also have something to show you."

Inside the hole was another codex. Talio knew it was not his, that it was only a book, but it still felt intoxicating in his hands. He remembered how the leather of his own codex had softened and cracked over the years. "Where did you get it?"

he whispered, running his fingers down the scalloped edges of the vellum.

"I go for long walks in the Palace at night," Cale said. "When I can't sleep. I became familiar with the guards' patrol schedule. One night I was in the Hall of Documents, and I found it partly wedged behind a service desk."

"Who could have lost it?"

"There were some sudden retirements during that time. One of those might not have been voluntary." Or another magistrate had been seduced and their codex stolen.

They spread the pages Keel gave him over the bed and compared their contents with the pages in the codex. With the help of the instructions, tables, and concordances in Cale's codex, Talio could finally trace the sentences back to the appropriate criminal charges and civil actions.

"They don't match," Cale said at last.

"It can't be an earlier edition."

Cale shook his head. "No. You know sentencing is inviolable. Scodel set it down fifty years ago and it has never changed. Nuciferia prepares the codices for all four cities. This codex has a copy date from one year ago. Your ruined pages are from codices that are currently in production." He stared at Talio, his voice low. "What have you found?"

"Maybe there were other errors on those ruined pages. Besides the struck-out text."

"No. Look here." Cale pointed to the top page in the stack. "Under *arson of government buildings*, the ruined page mandates a sentence of whipping, but in my codex, it states three years' imprisonment. That is not a mistake a copier would make. They might have written the wrong number of years. But whipping instead of imprisonment? Never."

Talio put the pages back in the packet and looked at Cale, helpless. "What do we do now?"

"Nothing. You keep your pages and I'll keep my codex. Hide them as best you can. And tell nobody." Cale's face was grave. "But we will find out, somehow."

After the revelations of the evening, they had little else to talk about. "Thank you for bringing this to me," Cale said as they stood at the door to his room. "What led you to trust me?"

"I wasn't sure," Talio admitted. "Not until you told me about stealing my codex." He smiled. "Somehow you seem to be telling me the truth these days." He looked into Cale's brown eyes. His expression was open and direct. If this man felt something, he would express it. On impulse, he leaned forward and kissed Cale on his soft, full lips.

The man smiled. "Why did you do that?"

"Because you did not do it first."

Cale's arms enfolded him, and their lips met again. Talio let himself relax in the man's embrace.

Cale drew back and shook his head. "If I'm caught kissing a strange man here, I'll be in trouble."

"I'm not a strange man, merely an advocate."

Cale laughed. "That is subject to debate. You know, there may come a time when I won't let you go."

Talio disengaged from the other man's arms. "Good night," he said, and turned away. He took the flights of stairs with a giddy step, but the taste on his lips was bittersweet. Cale's revelation that he had stolen Talio's codex did not upset him as it once might have. The events of ten years ago had set many changes in motion, but in retrospect they had been for the better. Without them, Talio would still have been married to Gawani. She would likely never have chosen him to serve on the committee. He would have dismissed the Incarnites as a mere nuisance. And he might not have met Pazli or become close to Cale and Emara.

He and Cale were on opposing sides of the law, but in many ways, he felt closer to him than he did Pazli. Cale would let him in emotionally all the way, if he wanted. Pazli was determined to put as many barriers between them as possible: religion, morality, ethics.

Talio smiled. One could never accuse Cale of overly rigid adherence to morality or ethics. He supposed he should be angry with him, blame him for stealing ten years of his life. Hadn't Cale simply taken advantages of the opportunities he'd been given, much as Talio had made the decision to explore darker, more hidden parts of his life? They were more kindred spirits than he and Pazli were, in that regard. Dealing with Pazli felt like being summoned before the Ethics Review Committee.

Talio was indeed fond of Cale, but was he fond enough? Like so many, they were both broken people. As he stepped out into the frigid street, he wondered: Were they broken in the same way? Could they somehow fit together as one whole?

# Chapter Eighteen

Toward the end of fall, Pazli joined the Judicial Review Committee.

He had not told Talio of any offer; the first Talio knew was when he came in for their weekly meeting and saw Pazli sitting next to Magistrate Verrane. Talio still had to tread with care when dealing with him—a valid disagreement would lead as easily to stubborn silence as to reasoned discussion.

"Good morning," Gawani addressed the group once Talio completed the water ritual and seated himself next to Darra, the queen's representative. "We are privileged to have another member of the Double Moon Law Office on our committee, Pazli Mecomb."

Darra cleared her throat. "Certain parties made it clear that involving the Incarnites at a higher level of advocacy might improve their participation in the Nuciferian legal system." A delicate way of phrasing it.

Gawani nodded. "Advocate Mecomb, would you like to say a few words?"

"Thank you," Pazli said. They all waited in silence for several moments. He said nothing further. Verrane and the others started fidgeting, and Talio realized with uncomfortable amusement that those were the extent of Pazli's few words. The man did not seem to care. He sat still and silent, not looking around, facing forward. As if he were sitting alone in an empty room.

Gawani raised her eyebrows. "Very well. Welcome, advocate." She rapped her fingers twice on the worktable. "I now call this meeting to order."

As promised, Magistrate Verrane referred the legal issues raised by the Skyways hearing to the committee. Through Darra, Queen Jaconda provided her assent for the committee to study the matter and provide a set of recommendations.

For this topic, Talio got to witness the process from the beginning, and all the obstacles it brought. The first week, Clemente played professor, and gave them a long lecture on what he called "intangibles" in the law. The second week, Clemente took on the role of magistrate and spoke at length about why new legislation covering "theft" of designs or documents would tamp down expression and what he called the "wellspring of creativity." The third week, Magistrate Verrane spoke as the author of the renowned pamphlet *Verrane on Medical Hearings*; he dedicated most of his time to how he had written it and the marvels it contained. The fourth week, Darra read prepared remarks the Royal Palace provided for her. They had to do with the royal warrants Queen Jaconda issued to companies that produced products on behalf of the Crown. The law, the remarks said, should protect these products, above all, from copying, fraud, or other infringement.

Despite the bureaucratic foolishness, Talio was eager for the opportunity. He'd rechecked the *Program for Wayward Advocates* pamphlet on this very subject. Advancing the state of the law counted for forty points, depending on the scope of the work. If he could get the committee to move forward—and show that he was driving force behind it—he could ask Gawani to petition the Ethics Review Committee to grant him those vital points. He was still only sitting at forty-five points, but any little bit helped.

A week later, it was Talio's turn. "You have asked me to speak from the advocate's perspective," he began. "Since a large part of the advocate's work takes place in the Hall of Reference, I have spent the last weeks researching the matter."

He looked around the table with a prickle of fear. Did they see this as a trick? Had he strayed too far from his ambit? But Clemente's face was neutral.

Talio went on. "I should point out the Palace does not compile official statistics on hearing outcomes. I did this work by hand, requesting each set of hearing documents from the Hall of Documents."

"Yes, yes," Clemente said. "We looked at the issue of statistics years ago. The Magistrate's Committee felt that it would prejudice a magistrate to know how others had ruled on similar issues." He shook his head. "And we would not want advocates basing their arguments on how often a magistrate ruled one way or another, of course."

Talio gritted his teeth. Another way the legal system obscured the details of sentencing. No reports, no statistics. This project provided a convenient disguise for his work on the codex, however. For each set of transcripts he sought from the Hall of Documents related to intangibles, Talio also requested a single transcript for a hearing related to the sentencing guidelines from the ruined codex pages. He was compiling his own set of sentencing statistics.

"I identified the causes of action that would likely have involved intangibles." Talio spread the pages across the worktable. "Theft, fraud, damages to reputation and the like. Then I looked at transcripts of dismissed hearings." Many of these hearings involved Incarnites, their business ideas and inventions. Most magistrates had found against them, of course.

"Why not all hearings?" Darra asked.

"A successful cause of action would suggest the matter was grounded in physical property. As with the Skyways hearing, a magistrate would properly dismiss anything related to 'intangibles,' since they fall outside current law."

Talio was afraid he'd gone too far by mentioning Skyways, but Verrane was nodding; he enjoyed the confirmation he'd properly dismissed the hearing.

"I disagree with your methodology," Pazli said.

"What would you suggest?" Talio asked. It surprised him that Pazli should speak so soon, and against him.

"There may be hearings where the magistrate incorrectly accepted the argument around intangibles and found for the plaintiff. Not everyone is as wise as Magistrate Verrane."

Verrane beamed. Talio was about to object that reviewing all the hearing transcripts in those categories would involve far more work, but then he realized Pazli had done him an inadvertent favor. More work meant more statistics related to the sentencing guidelines. "Yes, of course. You are quite right."

The meeting concluded with the decision that Talio's research was a fruitful direction. He would continue with his work while each member drafted a conceptual underpinning for legislation related to "intangibles," which they would present at the following session.

"There is one more item," Darra said before they adjourned. "We are not the only ones working on judicial review in Merin."

She explained that Kallis, a magistrate in Aurania, petitioned Queen Jaconda with an idea for shunting causes of action against the government into a separate mediation process. Although most hearings used to be completed within two days, the number of hearings was increasing as more private advocates joined the system. The queen was interested in anything that could ease the backlog. Talio thought back to Verrane's attempt at shutting down Skyways' cause of action but said nothing.

"Ask Magistrate Kallis to join us at our next session," Gawani said. "We have a travel fund."

Darra shook her head. "He refuses to use the skylines. Thinks they're dangerous." She and Verrane shared a hearty laugh, but to Talio, this Kallis sounded like an intelligent fellow.

After the session adjourned, he pulled Pazli aside into the restroom off the rotunda. "I would appreciate it if you would support me at these meetings. Clemente and Verrane are already against me."

"Will you provide me with a written transcript of what you would like me to say at the next session?" Pazli asked. Talio sighed. A prickly discussion with a fiery porcupine. This was why he did not wish to confide in the man about the codices; he could not imagine Pazli's reaction.

He wondered how he could explain that he wanted Pazli's broad support, and not the slavish devotion that Verrane showed to Clemente. But the other man spoke before Talio could continue. "I have found more wealthy clients."

"Excellent news." With the silver Talio appropriated to pay Keel, the Double Moon had nearly exhausted the fees from the Skyways hearing. The Incarnites that passed through its doors only contributed enough to cover basic expenses. And there was his ever-present worry about points and the approaching end of the judicial season. "Tell me everything."

"Not just yet," Pazli said. "Have patience. Take the day tomorrow and come with me, out of the city to meet them." He added, "I do not want you to prejudge the matter."

For a wealthy client and potential points, he was not about to press the matter. "Very well."

The next morning was cold and sunny. They met at the carriage terminal at the south end of the city. It was much larger and more elaborate than the ones Talio had seen in Damiria and Velos. Nuciferia did everything on a grander scale.

Incarnites crowded the terminal, forming orderly lines and waiting to board carriages that could carry up to twenty people at a time. Pazli came up to Talio and handed him a carriage ticket. "We are going to the fair."

"The fair?" Judging by the attendance at the terminal, it was for Incarnites only.

"It is our harvest festival. And you are welcome to join."

Talio and Pazli sat wedged in with Incarnite adults and children. The adults were quiet, but the children raced about the carriage, chattering and laughing. One little girl peered between a gap in the seats and waved at Talio; he smiled and waved back.

None of the children paid any attention to his face. There were no looks of alarm or questions. What did they imagine their parents or other Incarnites looked like under the hoods and cloaks? Did facial appearance not matter to them? Talio could not imagine how it would feel, to know that they were only years away from losing their own faces, their own individuality.

The carriage jounced out of the city and along a rural lane. At first, Talio felt self-conscious being the only uncovered adult in the group. But there was a festive atmosphere in the air, and when a woman handed around a sausage wrapped in wax paper and a knife, he accepted it when it passed his way and cut a hunk off to eat.

"A festival seems at odds with the Incarnite religion somehow," he whispered to Pazli at one point.

"As I mentioned, when Lady Zielle assumed prominence within the church, she discovered a cache of documents Peyor had left behind. Along with instructions on integrating the Incarnites with the rest of Merin, he wanted us to flourish culturally as well." Yes, the documents Zielle had so conveniently discovered once Turi Peyor was out of the way.

"Did they also instruct the Incarnites to become wise in the ways of business and invention?"

"Peyor used to say that necessity was the driving fire of invention. When you cannot succeed in everyday commerce, does it not make sense to strike out on your own, with your own ideas and plans?"

The carriage wound through farmland for an hour. At last, they arrived in a large open field dotted with tents, Incarnites milling about. "Where are our clients?" Talio asked after they disembarked.

Pazli shook his head. "They cannot see us until midday." To Talio's unspoken question, he added, "They are the owners of this fair."

"At least give me some information before we meet them," Talio said.

Pazli nodded. "They have a child, age eleven—the youth recently assumed the cloak and hood. The child is neither male nor female."

Talio stared at him. "I don't understand. Is this a medical issue?"

Again, Pazli shook his head. "The child does not wish to be called a boy or a girl. And now the government has filed a request for a hearing."

Talio could well imagine. A fundamental part of any identity key was identifying the holder as male or female. Not doing so was equivalent to a refusal to identify, one of the most serious non-capital crimes. "But the child was either born male or female. There are records."

"The child wishes to be known as neither. And refuses to show their identity key as a result. They want a new key."

Talio shook his head. This was madness. "You cannot be serious." The only alternative was…

"They want a key that has neither male nor female inscribed on it."

"No, no, no, no!" Talio threw up his hands. "The government will not change an entire organizational system to benefit one person. One person!"

"There are others." Pazli considered him before going on. "I tell you this in confidence, but many Incarnites believe themselves to be neither male nor female. Have you not wondered why we use the term 'cousin'? It is precisely for that reason."

This could not be part of their religious catechism, or they would all feel this way. But why? Perhaps there was something about concealing oneself that made one feel less attached to being a man or a woman? "Then why do they not all come forward?"

Pazli shrugged. "How successful would they have been? And how would the people of Nuciferia treat the Incarnites if they knew?"

In such an unthinkable matter, he had to appeal to Pazli's reason. "When I was in law school, I spent a summer seconded to the documentation branch of the government." Talio remembered the hot dusty summer spent among boxes and boxes of vellum. "The entire population of Nuciferia is categorized by male and female. Thousands—tens of thousands of records." He put out a hand to Pazli. "Every form has a checkbox for male and one for female. They would all need to be discarded and recopied. All the keys recalled and exchanged. Not to mention the effects on medical legislation: pregnancies, birth leave, adoption, abortion! It is impossible." Easier to abandon the skylines and skyships.

Pazli was impassive. "We will talk to the parents. You will see the child. And then we will discuss what is possible." He refused to speak further about it.

The carriages would not leave the fair to return to Nuciferia until late that afternoon. Talio was trapped. No wonder Pazli had been unwilling to discuss the matter ahead of time.

At midday they were ushered into a finely furnished tent. The parents were Jani and Ulric Tamm. He could not see their expressions, but they had the same air Talio's mother and father had when he'd told them he wanted to go to law school: loving, concerned, reluctant. It would have been easier if they disapproved. Easier to explain why their request was impossible.

Honell Tamm was the child. Having spent days with the Incarnites at the Double Moon, Talio felt he could distinguish man from woman. Honell gave no signs of being either. When they spoke, Talio heard the voice of a boy, then a girl, then a boy again.

Jani explained the situation. As soon as they assumed the cloak and hood, Honell had felt different. They did not want to take part in traditional boys' activities—fishing, fighting, and similar hobbies. Nor did they want to join the girls in sewing or knitting. They felt set apart, different from the others. At one point, they had refused to show their identity key. And now the government had filed suit.

"What are you hoping for?" Talio asked, helpless. "What would you like me to do?"

Ulric leaned forward. "We know the government won't change anything. Not for one person. But we want them to listen. To hear us. And to hear Honell."

Honell sat in silence and listened while their parents spoke. "What about you?" Talio asked them. "Are you willing to be questioned in a hearing? I do not know if they will even allow you to testify if you refuse to identify yourself properly."

Honell nodded. "I will speak. I will tell my story. Will you convince them?"

Talio sighed and shook his head. "I do not think so." But he considered the Judicial Review Committee. As with the concept of intangibles, a magistrate might refer the matter to the committee if he raised enough of a fuss at the hearing. If there were enough others like Honell, and if he could convince the committee. If, if, if. "We can try."

"You know I cannot refuse a sad story," Talio told Pazli after they left the family's tent. "Incarnite or otherwise." His frustration had faded, replaced with the powerlessness he often felt when faced with the way Incarnites were treated in Scodel's legal system.

"It is a fine quality to have," Pazli said. "Perhaps you shall become a folk hero someday."

Talio laughed. "I would rather not." He remembered Cale comparing him to Scodel. "I dislike the expectations that history places upon heroes. Maybe Scodel should have given the Obelisk of Justice a rest once in a while and gone to a fair."

He couldn't help but think of his law license. The hearing would earn him points, of course. He hated the points by now, hated how they figured into his every consideration. Jilani had managed to turn Talio's love of the law into a game of scavenging for points. But that was not why he would fight Honell's battle.

They came upon a booth where one could toss a ball at dozens of bottles to win prizes. Talio had little ability with games of chance, but the prizes attracted his attention. One was an enormous stuffed wyvern half a span high he found adorable. The woman behind the booth noticed his interest and tossed a ball behind her without looking, knocking over a bottle. "Easy, easy," she said. "Three balls for a silver. Try your luck, cousin?"

"Let me," Pazli told him. "Which prize would you like?"

"I was only looking," Talio said in protest.

He felt the other man scrutinizing him. "It is the large wyvern, isn't it?" Could Pazli tell that much from a single glance? "If you'd like it, you need only ask."

Talio shifted his feet. "I would hardly reject the wyvern if someone were to give it to me."

The man stood at the booth counter and assumed a formal throwing pose. Then he threw the balls, one after the other. Three bottles fell over in quick succession.

The woman's face was sour. "Good throwing, cousin." She all but shoved the wyvern at Talio.

"That was incredible," Talio said as they walked away. Because the wyvern was so large, he had to hold it straight out in front of him. "Are you an athlete?"

"My parents worked at a fair. There are always some loose bottles for the attendant to knock over. The audience needs to see it is possible. The positions never change."

They walked on. "What was it like growing up in a fair?"

"You may think it was all pennants and dancers," Pazli said. "My parents wanted more for me. I sat for hours studying and reading old, discarded pamphlets. They did not like me playing with the other children or engaging in any frivolity." Talio imagined a young Pazli surrounded by pamphlets, chastised or punished if he dared move, show emotion, do anything but study. A well-read, solemn, silent boy with folded arms.

He was struggling with the giant wyvern, and after a while, they had to stop. Pazli found a discarded rope from a tent and tied the wyvern to Talio's back. "You look like a porter on an expedition. I can see you as a hunter of monsters, traveling the impassable forests between the Four Cities." A bit of light shone through the chinks of Pazli's wall on this unusual day.

A man accosted Talio in front of another booth. "Guess your age? One silver. If I'm off by more than five years, you win a prize."

Talio gambled that his scar and prematurely receding hairline might give him an advantage. He passed over the silver and waited while the man walked around him. "Thirty-seven," he said at last.

"Close enough," Talio said. "How did you know?"

"The way you stand. Your voice. The rest is irrelevant." In an insinuating tone, he added, "Now what about your 'friend'?"

Pazli paid and went next. Talio palmed two silver and put his hand out behind him, slipping the money to the man so Pazli could not see.

Another examination. "Twenty-five."

Pazli shook his head and produced his identity key. "Not even close."

The man had a small selection of prizes, but nothing like the giant wyvern. Pazli selected a small bird and carried it with him like a trophy. "How much did you give him to miss?" he asked Talio once they were some distance away.

"Two silver."

"Good. Any more, and you would have insulted him."

"How can he succeed at this?" Talio shook his head. "With everyone hooded and cloaked?"

Pazli tossed the bird into the air and caught it as it fell. "Masks do not matter. You recognize me, do you not?"

*Sometimes,* Talio thought. *But not always.*

They reached the edge of the fairground. "Everything is so inexpensive," he commented. "The Tamms can't make much money from this fair."

"Your attention to the finances of the Incarnites is commendable. Most of them have little money, and so the prices have to be low."

There was a large, flat rock and Talio sat down atop it, putting the wyvern to one side. "Why not work to change the circumstances of the Incarnites, then? Instead of making allowances for their poverty?"

Pazli sat down next to him. "You say this as someone who finds every trick and loophole in the law, yet you continue to support Scodel's Grand Experiment."

"I *am* trying to change things. Look at the Judicial Review Committee."

"We have seen how swiftly they work." Pazli was silent for a while. "You said you would defend Honell at the hearing. Do you believe in the youth's cause?"

Now it was Talio's turn to pause. "I accept it. But I do not believe in it."

"What is the difference?"

"The magistrate in this hearing must believe in order to find on their behalf. Acceptance is not enough." Talio looked over at him. "We will do what we can for Honell. I will not pray to Sif or plan a pilgrimage into the desert, but I will still help the Incarnites."

"Is there anything that you do believe in, then?" Pazli asked in an idle voice. Talio refused to answer a question based on such foolish premises.

The carriages returned to Nuciferia in the early evening. The night was humid, and the air was thick; tendrils of fog hung in the air.

Talio agreed to meet Pazli at the Hall of Documents the following morning and set off on his own upstream toward the Double Moon, holding the giant wyvern. The Nuciferians had a dislike of fog, so the streets were deserted.

He glanced down at the stuffed animal and frowned. This hadn't strictly been a client meeting. The walks, the chatting, the festival games. His day together with Pazli had more of the air of a romantic engagement, given the man's roundabout way of expressing his feelings. Or had Pazli meant it to be romantic at all? Was Pazli simply drawn to him without realizing it?

Two uniformed boatmen stood in animated discussion on a footbridge in Talio's path. One of them was waving a long oar as he spoke.

"Excuse me," Talio said. "May I pass?"

Their gaze turned to him, and they started walking toward him, oars raised in their hands, in silence. This was no random encounter, he thought with a sudden prickle of fear. They were waiting for him.

Talio backed away, the wyvern in his hands. He looked around: there was the canal and its lineup of barges and boats; and there was the street, but he doubted he could outrun the burly boatmen.

His first year in Nuciferia, he and friends had made a game of jumping from one barge to the next. Now this game might save his life. Making a split-second decision, Talio hopped onto the first barge, which dipped slightly under his weight. He ran forward and hopped onto the next one. Footsteps sounded behind him.

He knew he should drop the wyvern. But as he leaped from one barge to the next, Talio gripped it tighter. It was the only physical thing Pazli had ever given him. The only aspect of him he could touch, hold with his hands. Even as he raced forward, Talio drew comfort from that moment of connection.

The next barge was angled partway around the curving canal, but when he got to the other end of its roof, there was only dark water ahead. The barge was too far from the street for him to jump back.

Then they were upon him. The boatman without the oar grabbed Talio, pulled him forward, and with a quick push shoved him and the wyvern over the edge of the canal.

It was a long fall to the water.

# Chapter Nineteen

The water closed over Talio's head. He paddled against the water, trying to surface. It was no use. His heavy cloak was filling with water. He could not open it; his fingers scrabbled at the slick buttons. The side of the barge slammed into his head. He was dizzy, stunned.

He surfaced once and gasped for air. Then a sharp pressure on his head. The oar. They were pushing it down on his head.

He held his breath. Tried to remember how to stay afloat. It was pointless. They would stand above him. If he surfaced, they would push him back down, or hit him with the oar.

Talio felt the air tearing at his lungs. He pressed his lips together. Bubbles flew upward around him. He pumped his arms in a fury. And then—

And then the oar was gone. He surfaced and drew in great gasps of air, spitting up water. Talio splashed about, waiting for the next blow, wondering how they would finish him. The oar lowered toward his head again.

This time he heard Pazli's voice, "Grab hold."

The oar was slick with water and algae, but Talio's cloak was leather and clung to the oar as he wrapped himself around it. With agonizing slowness, he rose out of the water, pushing against the side of the barge with his feet as leverage. When at last he was on the street by the canal, he collapsed to the paving stones, shaking and gasping and vomiting up water.

When Talio had the energy to look up, Pazli was holding the oar like a weapon and scanning the streets. "Where did you come from?" Talio said in a feeble croak.

"I came back this way to talk to you. To apologize for forcing the Honell matter upon you without asking you first."

"Apology accepted." Talio's shoulders heaved. "And the boatmen?"

"They fled." Pazli put down the oar and extended his hand to him. "Can you walk?"

The chill had seeped into Talio's flesh. He tried to rise, but his legs folded underneath him. He looked up at Pazli, helpless, and shook his head no.

The man bent down and lifted him up easily, arms under Talio's back and knees. *So strong*, he thought. Shivering, he lay his head against Pazli's chest, taking ragged breaths as the man carried him back to the Double Moon.

As soon as Vinne saw Talio, he pulled him from Pazli's arms and stripped off his cloak and soaked garments. Next came warm blankets and hot tea. Talio grimaced at the first sip. Vinne had added rare, fermented spirits to the mug. They were far stronger than wine.

"He fell into the canal," Pazli explained, cloak dripping with water. It did not sound convincing to Talio, and he knew it would not sound rational to Vinne. No six-year-old would ever wander close enough to the edge of a street to fall into a canal.

"Right." Vinne retreated behind the bar and kept watch on Talio, wiping the same wine glass over and over.

The blankets and tea helped warm Talio, but he continued to shake as he gripped the sides of the mug and looked up at Pazli through the steam. "If you hadn't been there..."

The Incarnite nodded. "Yes. I am sorry that we lost the giant wyvern, however." He withdrew the small bird he'd "won" at the fair from his cloak and placed it on the table. "Take this instead."

Talio put down the mug and held the bird tight to his chest. "Will you stay? For a while?"

Pazli leaned forward and touched Talio's cheek. He stopped trembling at once. How he'd missed that simple touch. With Cale, he could see the man's emotions play across his face, how he stood, even the position of his arms. With only Pazli's fingers visible, being touched by them took on so much more significance.

The other man shook his head. "I am late for second vespers. The cleric will no doubt forgive me for missing first vespers to save a friend's life, but his forgiveness extends only so far. Dispensations for breaches of conduct are few and far between. And costly. I seem to need more than my fair share of them when I am with you."

After Pazli left, Talio sat staring into the flickering fire, holding the tiny bird. *A friend's life*, he thought. A friend. Pazli was more than that to him now. The man who saved his life. The man who worked with him every day. The man he had come to rely upon. The man whose touch could calm him in an instant. Cale had never seen him vulnerable like this, having just escaped death. While Pazli put up a wall between him and Talio, it was Talio who did the same when confronted with the prosecutor.

Pazli was more than a friend now, but so was Cale. Pazli and Cale, fire and water. One excited, burned, challenged Talio. The other one soothed and salved and nourished him instead.

Vinne circled around him, checking the blankets and refilling his mug. At last, he pulled Talio to his feet and put him to bed surrounded by a mountain of pillows.

Talio waited until he was sure that Vinne had gone back to his rooms, then pushed back the sheets and sat on the edge of his bed in the dark. He used a flint to light a vigil candle in a bowl of water and watched its orange flame dance across the shadows of the room.

If Pazli had not followed him...Talio paced the small room. He kept the dowsing rod from Velos on the far table; he placed the bird next to it. Now he picked up the dowsing rod, holding it like a talisman as it tugged gently toward the true merinite in the water generator.

Who hired the boatmen? Clemente Jilani? He could not imagine the birdlike professor hiring assassins, even clumsy ones such as these. It was easy to conjure Clemente as a monster haunting little children in their dreams. Would the magistrate really try to resolve a problem through murder?

This was no random attack; it was a specific reaction to something Talio had done. He reviewed the events of the last few weeks. The dead rat and the NO MORE TRICKS sign: those could have been the result of the Skyways hearing. The duplicate pamphlets were a noteworthy trick, and the rat came shortly thereafter. What might have triggered the boatmen's attack?

Oran Keel. Despite his appearance and trade, he was a gossip. He might easily have told someone, or one of his associates had. Or someone could have followed Talio during his visits to the garment district. Vinne had been right to warn him away from Keel; he'd been a fool. He had no business dealing with criminals.

That suggested a link to the codices, and whatever secret lay behind them. This all started with Talio's suspicions and requesting the ruined pages from Keel. He'd been foolish enough to wear his advocate's pin on one visit, which would have made him easy to track down. Even his requests for odd hearing transcripts from the Hall of Documents could be raising suspicions.

Another thought struck him. The scandal ten years earlier. Minka's elliptical comment. Cale's seduction and the theft of his codex had also been a reaction to something Talio had done. Some might not have appreciated his freewheeling approach to justice. The current situation had the same flavor; it suggested the same people were involved in the long-ago theft, the dead rat, and the murder attempt.

Nothing dangerous happened that day, or the next. Talio returned to the Palace and continued with his research. He saw Cale, and ran across Gawani in the rotunda restroom, and met with Pazli at the Double Moon. The normalcy was frightening. *Someone tried to kill me*, he thought. *There is nothing I can do to stop them from trying again.*

Vinne spent more time with him, and Pazli was reluctant to leave at the end of a long day. Even Cale found excuses to visit him at the Hall of Documents. "You look somewhat vulnerable," he explained. Talio welcomed the company; he dreaded being alone. He did not confide in the prosecutor this time. It was not that he did not trust him. Rather, Talio did not want anyone to know who did not have to. It was bad enough for Vinne and Pazli to watch over him.

A week later, he and Pazli stood at the door to the Double Moon after a long day. Talio marveled he could already see his breath in clouds of vapor. An unexpected face appeared in front of them: Darra Quiere, in casual clothes. "This is your law office," she said, taking in the dilapidated exterior and heavy locks on the door.

"For now."

They sat down at one of the makeshift worktables. "The Queen has authorized a committee trip to Aurania," Darra said. "To meet Magistrate Kallis."

Talio tried to remember. "Mediation? For causes of action against the government?"

Darra nodded. "You, me and the Incarnite." She inclined her head in apology. "Advocate Mecomb." Pazli made no reply. "Advocate Balsamo is busy with a hearing, and Magistrates Clemente and Verrane are proctoring examinations."

"I will ask the cleric for another dispensation to use the skylines," Pazli said. "It has been a while since I've requested one. He must think something is wrong."

Talio did not want to leave the safety of the Double Moon. That night, though, he reasoned it would be safer in Aurania; assassins were not likely to book passage on a skyship.

The skyline station was as intimidating as it had been on the trip from Damiria to Nuciferia. Talio told himself he could not show weakness in front of Darra or Pazli. He managed the long climb to the platform by keeping his eyes on the comforting bulk of Pazli's cloak as the man walked in front of him. He could smell his earthy scent, even through the breezes at the upper levels. His cloak brushed the top of the stairs, never quite revealing whatever Pazli wore underneath: pants, slacks or leggings. Talio had to hand it to Peyor or whoever had designed the Incarnite robes. They remained impenetrable visually.

There were no other passengers. Talio marveled at the expense of reserving an entire skyship that sat thirty, just for the three of them. Then again, to Queen Jaconda, what did silver matter?

The wind was higher on the platform, and the priest attendants had to hold on to their headgear. Talio took a seat by the railing. Darra raised her eyebrows and looked at his hand gripping the handrail but said nothing, sitting down two seats over from him. Pazli took a seat on the other side of the aisle. Talio closed his eyes as the attendants spoke the launch prayers to Felle. At last, the skyship glided away from the station, splashing through the airborne waters of the skyline.

Darra had brought along vellum pages in her satchel, and he peeped at her now and then, bent over the pages and making notes. At one point, she caught him looking. "Royal business."

"That is good," Talio said, and felt foolish.

"Queen Jaconda is observing you."

He did not know how to respond to this either. "That is also good," Talio said. Now the queen's representative must think him stupid as well.

Darra smiled. "She wants to ensure that you can carry out your work unobstructed." She returned to her pages, and Talio closed his eyes, the wind whipping through his hair and beard.

He must have slept, because the next time he opened his eyes, they were arriving at the Aurania station platform with another sudden jerk and splash of water. *I made it*, Talio thought. Unlike Scodel. Unlike Joban.

Talio had grown up in Aurania, but he hadn't been there since his parents moved away to pursue better scavenging opportunities when he was eleven. Not much had changed; banners with Auranian sayings hung in the streets, covering the damage to the quaint buildings that had never been completely repaired after the War of the Cities. Much like Talio, Auranians had a complicated relationship with the war: they appreciated it had concluded without total devastation but abhorred the violence it took to subdue the rogue mages.

The three of them were staying at a small inn with the usual colorful Auranian folk art on the walls. He had some time before dinner with Kallis. Talio excused himself and took a quick stroll through the nearby streets until he found a wine shop. He went back and forth in his mind about the plan he'd devised since he'd learned about this upcoming trip with Pazli. Finally, he purchased a bottle of wine and returned to his room, placing it on the table in a prominent position.

That evening, they met the magistrate at a small, cozy tavern. Kallis was a tall, gangly man with an unfashionable frizz of white hair. The smell of duhan hung about him. He had one pair of spectacles in his magistrate's robe pocket, and another perched atop his head. In the pantomime plays, there was often a figure much like Kallis: absent-minded, bumbling but pleasant.

"To business," the magistrate said once they ordered. "Let us talk mediation."

"Before we begin," Talio said, "I would ask, with respect, whether we need a separate mediation system for causes of action against the government at all. Scodel was against a two-tiered system of justice." He tried to frame his objections gently. "And there are barely any hearings against the government as it is. Doesn't this seem like a waste of resources?"

"Excellent," Kallis said, clapping him on the back. "Excellent points. But you are wrong." He chewed the hunk of bread in his hand with great relish.

The other three looked at each other. "Do you have a response to Advocate Rossa's objections?" Darra asked.

Kallis blinked and looked up. "Well yes, of course." He waved the bread at Talio. "My plan would require a separate group of arbiters to administer the mediations. Not our dear magistrates. Possibly promoting some of the existing private advocates to these positions, so they could become experts on the issues at hand."

Their bowls of stew arrived. Now Kallis could wave at them with his spoon instead. "Scodel may have wanted advocates to be generalists, but he created his legal system when the courts were still tiny in size. We are at a very different place today."

"Do you imagine the mediation would still follow the underlying principles Scodel set down?" Pazli asked. "Or would there be a need for a separate framework?" And the conversation continued.

After the meal, Kallis took them on a tour of the utilitarian Auranian Department of Justice building which stood in sharp contrast to the grandeur of the Nuciferian one. They ended up in the magistrate's rooms. Except for notes scrawled all over the walls, it was a study in stark austerity; it reminded Talio of Pazli's cloister.

Darra and Kallis started an animated discussion about how the Judicial Review Committee might be able to construct a framework for the mediation he was proposing. Pazli flipped through pamphlets on the magistrate's shelves.

Then Talio saw the codex.

The top of it was peeking out from under Kallis's robes. When they entered his rooms, the magistrate took them off and draped them over the back of his chair.

All he needed was a distraction. Something to get them away from the codex, just long enough. Then he shook his head. He could start a fire or spill a ritual source basin, but those were the antics of pantomime plays. "Magistrate," he said once Kallis and Darra paused for breath. "Might I see your codex?"

The man looked at him, surprised. "Surely you have referred to codices in Nuciferia. Mine is the same." If only.

Kallis's rooms were full of notes. There were notes on the walls and all over his pamphlets. It made sense that he would write within his codex. "I am always interested in the notes that magistrates leave in their codex."

Kallis looked doubtful. "I'm not supposed to show it to anyone."

Talio had heard the same argument directly from Clemente in his magisterial track courses, over and over again. Scodel's received wisdom on sentencing was sacrosanct. It was not for ordinary citizens to see how the fish was sliced. He'd heard it so many times he'd believed it himself. Until now.

To Darra, the magistrate asked, half-joking, "Can I trust the young man?"

Darra shrugged. "The queen has trusted him enough to appoint him to our committee. Make of that what you will."

"Very well, very well," Kallis said, handing him the codex with reluctance. "Be careful."

The Auranian codex was full of inscriptions and other marginalia but otherwise looked identical to the Nuciferian ones, down to the scalloped pages and watermarks. Talio waited until Kallis and Darra resumed talking, then flipped to the back matter.

He wished he had the ruined pages with him, but he could not have taken the chance of having the skyship guards search him. Talio started reading with mounting frustration. What could he even remember of the sentencing guidelines he and Cale had examined?

Arson. Cale had mentioned arson. *Under arson of government buildings, the ruined page mandates a sentence of whipping, but in my codex, it states three years' imprisonment.* Talio flipped through the sentencing guidelines section faster and faster, looking for any mention of arson. Had Scodel never thought of using alphabetical order?

He found the section at last. For first offenses, the sentence was probation. For second offenses, community work in service of the royal body. And for third offenses, six months in prison. Once again, completely different. Far gentler punishment, in this case. But why?

He could not spend any more time examining the codex without arousing suspicion. He returned the codex to Kallis as the evening drew to a close.

Darra suggested that she and Kallis should discuss his ideas further. Darra did not seem the type to work after hours, based on how she fled committee meetings the moment the vigil candle started hissing. Talio suspected she might want to smoke some duhan with the man. Parting ways with them, he and Pazli walked back to the inn.

"Come sit with me a while," Talio suggested when they reached their rooms. "I bought some wine."

There were no wine glasses in their rooms, but the inn had provided each room with tumblers. He uncorked the bottle and poured generous portions.

"What did you want with Kallis's codex?" Pazli asked.

"If I tell you, will you keep it a secret?"

Pazli sipped at the wine. "Is it trouble?" Talio did not answer. "Then I had best not know. A Nuciferian's trouble is an Incarnite's disaster."

"As you wish." Talio poured another drink.

They continued to go through the bottle of wine. He found himself fascinated by Pazli's hands. They were strong, but not thick or square. The nails were neat but not trimmed. The scratches on his tattoo had healed long ago. If he did not know Pazli, he would not be able to tell from his hands if he were a man or a woman, though Pazli's deep voice made it immediately obvious.

"What are you looking at?" Pazli asked, putting down his empty tumbler. Talio reached over and refilled it.

"Your hands. I have a question about them."

"You have already seen my tattoo."

Talio shook his head. "Why do the Incarnites expose their hands?" He struggled to express his idea. "Should you not wear gloves or something, if you are shielding yourself from the desert sun?"

Another sip from Pazli. His responses were coming slower. "When Sif revealed his wisdom to our founder, Peyor covered himself completely. Including his hands."

Pazli leaned over and breathed fumes of wine in Talio's direction. "And do you know what the peacekeepers did to him?" He shook his head. "They beat him, of course. For refusing to identify. The peacekeeper's code can be shortened to three words: 'Beat the Incarnite.'"

"Then you *are* willing to make compromises for your religion."

Now Pazli refilled Talio's glass. "There was no compromise. Peyor chose to continue living, to practice his religion and tell others of the Incarnite beliefs, and he chose wisely."

Talio shook his head. "What is it now?" Pazli said with some irritation.

"I still do not understand how your religion managed to grow so quickly." Talio asked. "What would make anyone want to become an Incarnite?" He blushed. "I am sorry to be so blunt."

Pazli gave a great heaving sigh, his shoulders set. "It is not my task to convert others to the Incarnite faith. We have evangelists who go forth at certain prescribed times of the year." He leaned closer and spoke more quietly in the same rolling, deep voice. "But let me tell you. It is not a matter of speaking of Sif, or of the desert, or of Peyor or fire or any of the trappings of the Incarnite faith. Do you know what they say to prospective converts?"

Talio shook his head. Pazli continued in a tone that resembled a recitation. "Have you never wanted to be unseen? To walk through the streets of your town and be unremarked? To speak your mind and be unheard?" He reached out and unsteadily touched the cleft of Talio's lower lip.

"Never," Talio lied.

"Then you will never be an Incarnite," Pazli said, withdrawing his hand.

"Do you never see each other without your cloaks and hoods?" Talio asked. Pazli gave a slow shake of his head. "Not even when you are intimate?"

"Not even then. We only do so in absolute darkness. Or there are other methods. An Incarnite must always be prepared."

The wine was almost gone. Talio dared one more question. "And have you ever been intimate with a man?"

"An Incarnite may only lie with another Incarnite," Pazli recited. "But that is not what you are asking, is it?" His voice took on a sudden sharp tone. "What have you done to me?"

Talio did not reply. "Is this what you have wanted all along?" the man asked, struggling to his feet. "Did you plan to get me drunk?"

He stood in front of Talio and gave him a sharp jab in the chest with his index finger. "Get up."

Talio stood uncertainly before him. The man's earthy musk was stronger now. "Remove your clothes," Pazli said in a harsh tone.

Talio flushed. His cheeks burned with shame and desire. Pazli folded his arms and stood there. "Remove your clothes or I will leave."

Talio's throat was dry, and he had trouble swallowing. He slid off his jacket. Then he unbuttoned each button of his shirt, letting it fall away from his body. He stepped out of his trousers and undergarments and stood before the other man, naked, hands covering his groin. He was hard to the point of pain.

Talio felt but could not see Pazli's gaze sweep over his body. Then the Incarnite withdrew something from his cloak. It was a long strap of heavy black fabric, the length and shape of a wide belt. Did he mean to restrain him?

Talio held his wrists together in front of him, but Pazli shook his head. "Turn around." His voice was guttural now, thick with lust. Talio turned away from him to face the wall, lifting his hands behind his back.

To his surprise, the other man reached around and wound the strap over his eyes instead, tying it behind his head. Pazli's voice was a whisper in his ear. "Do not take this off. Not ever. Do you understand?" Talio nodded. He could no longer see a thing—all was blackness.

He heard the sound of cloth behind him; Pazli was removing his cloak and hood. With a hard shove, the man pushed Talio down on the bed, onto his belly. His hands worked at Talio's rump, moving his legs apart. "Spread them." Pazli's words were a command, not a request.

"In the satchel," Talio mumbled through the sheets. "Some grease." He'd brought it to pleasure himself. Or had he hoped this would happen all along? He was so hard that rubbing along the sheets was painful.

Pazli was gone for a moment. Then he returned and spread Talio's legs wide. Talio felt the slick grease as the other man prodded and pushed at his rump, sliding slick fingers inside him. Pazli had a rough efficiency to his work; the jabs of his fingers deep inside him gave Talio sharp waves of pleasure.

He felt Pazli's other hand pushing his head sideways against the sheets, pinning him in place. The man grunted in anger and lowered himself onto him. Then in one swift stroke, Pazli penetrated him and Talio cried out. It was pain and pleasure mixed. Pazli did not stop. He slid in and out, faster and faster, hand pushing the side of Talio's head down into the bed as he rode him in a fury. Pazli was not angry with him. He was angry with himself. There was a battle within his mind between curiosity and shame, and this was the stage for that battle. Pazli's earlier coldness had not been indifference, but inward-directed rage.

The long, slow strokes were bringing Talio closer to the brink. How he had longed to submit to this man. Unable to see, the darkness heightened all of his other senses. He felt the sheets scrape against his hardness, Pazli's sweat drip onto his back, the pressure of the man's hand on his cheek, the harsh smell of his body and always, his grunting, animal noises.

A few more thrusts and Pazli slammed into him, then shuddered and gripped his shoulders. As he pulled out, it was as if he were taking Talio's guts with him. Pazli shoved him aside, then collapsed onto the bed. A few moments later, the man was asleep.

Now was his chance. He could remove the strap and see what Pazli looked like. Talio started to remove the binding from around his eyes. Then he stopped. No, he had made him a promise. As much as he wanted to know, he would not betray Pazli in that way.

Instead, he lay next to him, exploring Pazli's body with his fingers: his furry chest, so lean that there were horizontal ropes of muscle across it; his stomach with a bellybutton that protruded outward instead of inward; his hard, hairy thighs; the firmness of his rump. Talio wanted to remember how it felt to touch the man, in case he never got another chance.

When he awoke the next morning, the strap was no longer around his head and Pazli was gone. The door between their rooms was closed but unlocked. Pazli was standing in his room wearing his cloak and hood as if nothing happened.

"I was very drunk last night," he said. "I remember nothing."

Talio expected this. "Is that so?" Walking back to his room, he picked up the empty bottle and took it back to Pazli. He lifted it up so that the other man could see the triangle insignia on the bottom: soft wine.

Pazli took the bottle from him. Would the Incarnite strike him? Dash the bottle against the wall? "You do nothing but play tricks," Pazli said in a low, tense voice. "In the hearing room, at the Double Moon, in the bedroom. You are dishonest with everyone."

"Last night I was trying to get to the truth."

Pazli set the bottle down. "Here is my truth, then: I wished to be drunk last night. I wished it, so that I could be with you." Talio could hear the torment in his voice. "There is another truth. What I did was wrong." With that, he left the room.

During the skyship journey back to Nuciferia, Pazli sat with folded arms in utter silence. Talio did not try to speak to him. Darra glanced between both of them, a silent question in her eyes, but Talio shook his head and concentrated on gripping the handrail.

A sense of unease was settling over him. He'd indulged his curiosity with Pazli, just like he'd indulged his curiosity with Cale all those years ago. It had not hurt Cale; the only one he'd hurt was Gawani, who was never supposed to find out. This time, he'd pushed Pazli too far, and discovered just where the line between attraction and religion lay.

Talio did not want to think of it. Instead, he considered another, vitally important matter: Kallis's codex was different from Cale's, and from the pages Keel provided. Why? And for what reason?

# Chapter Twenty

When Talio entered the front room of the Double Moon the next morning, Pazli was not there. Emara handed him a lockbox containing the message: *Doing research at Hall of Documents on Honell hearing.* Pazli had stamped his identity key instead of signing the note.

"He came right up to the inn with me," Emara said. "And then he gave me the lock and walked away." She examined Talio's face. "Is everything all right?"

"Nothing is ever all right with that man," Talio said. "When he does not get his way, he turns into a child." But that was unfair. He forced Pazli to confront something he would rather not. He had taken away his choice.

There was no legal term for what he had done. It was seduction by way of a lie. At first, Talio wished desperately that he had not followed through with his plan. But then he had to admit he had wanted it, badly. And he'd enjoyed it. The morning after Pazli had taken him, he discovered he'd spent himself on the sheets while the man was pounding into him, without even touching himself. Talio had been so focused on the man that he hadn't even felt his own climax. How could something feel so wrong and so pleasurable at the same time?

What could Talio say to him? That he was sorry Pazli had done something he'd truly wanted? Just as there was no law to break, there were no words to express his apology. Nothing but a feeling of having done wrong, and not knowing how to correct it.

He put the matter out of his mind for now. "With our favorite Incarnite absent," Talio told Emara, "you and I have work to do."

Since their dinner together at Emara's parents' house, Talio had gradually been drawing her into the work of the practice: filling out forms, client meetings for notary work, and accompanying him and Pazli to the occasional hearing.

Now that Pazli had started to give him and the Double Moon a wide berth, he would have to rely on her more and more.

This morning, they were seeing a new Incarnite client named Vedan. "He was referred to us by Lady Zielle," Talio told Emara. "Be especially polite."

"I'm always polite," she said.

Vedan was part of Zielle's retinue, and she'd tasked him with traveling to Rylavia to scout potential locations for a satellite temple. Upon arriving at the skyline station, Vedan had been detained for an unusually long time by the station guards, and missed his skyship, forfeiting the ticket price.

"Did you do anything wrong?" Emara demanded of Vedan. Talio gave her a look with raised eyebrows and a discreet hand gesture to tone it down.

The tall Incarnite folded his arms, and Talio sighed. Another student of the Pazli Mecomb School of Behavior. "They said something about my robes. That I didn't look like a typical Incarnite. Imagine." Talio examined the man's cloak and hood. They were of a finer fabric than the usual Incarnite garb, like Zielle's had been.

"They do look different," Emara said. Then, glancing at Talio, she added hurriedly. "What about your hand tattoo?"

Vedan held up his hand. "They claimed it could be forged with ink. Imagine." He shook his head. "Only someone at the Palace would have the skill to do that."

"Where did you get your clothing?" Emara asked. "Is there a shop? We could ask if they'd had dealings with peacekeepers before." Talio saw where her mind was going, even if she wasn't explaining herself well. Government officials were expected to know how the Incarnites dressed, but if Zielle's retinue wore a special fabric or design, liability could turn on whether they were expected to be aware of this as well.

Vedan explained that each Incarnite's clothes were made individually for them and blessed by the clerics on behalf of Sif. "I remember something from law school," Emara said thoughtfully. "Peacekeepers are supposed to be trained in dealing with foreign cultures." Talio cringed. "We will investigate this and advise you on a potential hearing."

After Vedan left, he sat Emara back down. "A bit more gentleness. Please."

She looked at him, uncomprehending. "I am following what I was taught in law school."

"Think of the client first. Scodel's laws come afterward."

"Don't forget the points." If Vedan had a cause of action, that would be another ten points for her, and five points for Talio for assisting her.

With the work Talio gave her, Emara was forceful, dogmatic and often successful. But her heart clearly lay elsewhere. She was still convinced that her legal career lay with medical hearings.

Talio had taken Verrane's course on medical practice because he heard the magistrate's substitute was an easy grader. He'd regretted it because of the cost of Verrane's infernal pamphlet, and what he'd discovered later. There were almost no medical hearings, and the few that took place were monopolized by the same few advocates. Medicine was generally a simple matter: the healer performed a visual diagnosis, prescribed herbs or minerals, and the patient either lived or died. Advanced illnesses like cancer were even simpler: the patient died.

Emara kept going on about one particular client. "Lady Safana," she explained one afternoon, "I finally have a meeting with her at the Palace." She looked around the Double Moon's dim interior. "She'd rather not come here."

Talio wasn't surprised. "Would you like me to come along?"

"If you'd like."

She explained the case to him on the walk upstream to the Palace. "She broke her right arm, and a healer named Malmo set it. Now she's in constant pain and can't use her hand for anything."

They found a curious situation when they arrived at the entrance to the meeting rooms that could be rented in the

Hall of Commerce. Lady Safana sat, cradling her arm, with three women arguing around her.

"Leeches," Emara muttered. She shooed the other women away and whisked Lady Safana into a meeting room. "They're all advocates looking for medical clients," Emara whispered to him. "I got there first."

"They're all women," Talio said. Very unusual. Gawani was one of the rare women advocates he knew of.

"With your sharp eyes, you could be a medical advocate yourself," Emara replied drily. Then she composed herself. "Lady Safana, thank you for meeting with us."

Talio sat back and let Emara run the meeting. Why were there so many women advocates in the medical field? Minka was Chief Physician; had her unusual presence as a woman in the higher ranks of the Palace drawn others to the specialty? Or was there something else going on? He sensed an undercurrent he was not privy to. A trick, perhaps.

That night, Talio contemplated the matter of tricks. There was always a trick he could pull, or that was how it had seemed until recently. Pazli and the soft wine. Skyways. When he had been a magistrate, he enjoyed finding legitimate ways around Scodel's laws. More tricks.

Tricks like the bonnet dye or the duplicated pamphlets put him at the center of things, noticed by others in the way he wanted to be seen. *Look what I have done. Look who I am. I am more than the face you see in the street.* Other tricks were outright deceptions: overcoming Pazli's defenses to take him to bed.

He did not want to use tricks anymore. Not with Pazli, and certainly not in the upcoming hearing. Honell was seeking dignity and justice. It was easy to pull a trick when you cared more for your reputation than the person whose life would be forever affected by the hearing. Victory had been more important to him than Pazli's acquittal. Victory and the accursed points had both been at the front of his mind during the Skyways hearing.

If Scodel's laws spoke to a fundamental truth, he would find that truth. For Honell's sake. For the sake of all

Incarnites who felt the same way. And for the sake of justice. Tricks—misdirection—had their place, but he would no longer use them in place of legal arguments. Or in place of telling Pazli his feelings, if he could ever bring himself to do so.

The Palace posted the roster for the Honell hearing. Cale would be Crown prosecutor, and Clemente the magistrate. Talio, Pazli and Cale. It seemed that they were doomed to reenact this triangle over and over again, at least within the hearing rooms. Talio was fortunate that so far, the three of them had yet to meet together in private. That was not a comparison he wanted to make. Was it not enough that the two men intrigued him in different ways, much as their styles of practicing the law did? Cale had a loose, organic approach with a singular goal always in mind. Pazli was intense and focused, and channeled his emotions into precise speech and actions. It was a luxury, Talio knew, to have the attention of two intelligent men. One of them extraordinarily handsome, and the other...the other he found his mind straying to during random moments when the hearing preparations became too intense.

What surprised him about the roster posting was the hearing date. The government put it off for three months. Hearings were normally within a few days of the filing of the cause of action. Was the government afraid of the hearing? Did they want so much time to prepare?

Talio's cloak was no longer enough to ward off the cold. He bought a vest to wear under his suit jacket and a pair of boots to replace his sabots once the snow started falling. At the Palace, women wore shawls over their dresses and groups huddled around the braziers in the ventilated public spaces. Pazli had switched from a light cloak and hood to heavier material. At Emara's request, Pazli investigated the Incarnites' garment fabrication process. It was still unclear whether the special fabric used in Zielle and Vedan's robes counted as official religious decoration, or simply ornamentation.

People spoke with longing for the end of the judicial season. Talio viewed it with dread. It might be his last ever practicing law, given his struggle with the points. He was at sixty-five points and Emara at eighty-five. She would easily reach one hundred given the lighter requirements for recent law graduates, but Talio was no longer confident of his ability to get there before the end of the season.

He was writing numbers down on a scrap of vellum late one afternoon with the *Program for Wayward Advocates* pamphlet by his side—going over the points situation again and again—when Emara dismissed the last Incarnite client and locked the door to the Double Moon. "Does writing down the points help you worry less?" she asked. Talio thought she was being sarcastic, but her expression was genuine.

He sighed and pushed the vellum away from him. "I continue to hope I've made an error in addition. Only Clemente Jilani could have come up with this system. How was he when you were in law school?"

"Fine, at the start. As I said, his exams started getting harder and harder." Emara frowned. "I don't think he hated us. He thought every year's students were worse and worse. Further away from the legal principles, that sort of thing. 'Insufficient deference to Scodel' and all that."

At that point the door to the Double Moon opened, admitting a gust of chill wind and an Incarnite with frost at the bottom of his cloak.

The frost was not only on the outside. "What is that?" Pazli said, gesturing to the *Wayward Advocates* pamphlet. Talio had not wanted to discuss it with him at any point, but Emara clearly felt no compunction.

"Getting our law licenses back," she explained. "Points for each hearing, basically."

"Points," Pazli said in a flat voice. "Earning points by helping the Incarnites."

Talio sighed. "Once again you are twisting the interpretation of things."

Emara slammed her hands down on the worktable, and both he and Pazli flinched. "Enough!" she said. "If this is some kind of lover's quarrel, I suggest you two kiss so that we can get on with the business of bringing in silver."

Pazli straightened his robes. "And points. Let us not forget the points."

He stalked off toward his own worktable, and Emara glared at him and Talio in turn.

Talio shrugged and muttered very quietly, "He started it."

# Chapter Twenty-One

Nuciferia marked the end of fall with the water purification ceremony. Talio did not have to worry about encountering Pazli there, as the Incarnites did not attend any religious events but their own. There were parties all around the city, but as a member of the Palace of Justice, Talio could celebrate it at the northern exchange.

The exchange was at the most upstream tip of the city, a reservoir with high walls and the thundering sound of waters collecting from various pipes and gutters. Here, all the return water collected, to be filtered and returned downstream as source water.

Cale asked Talio to accompany him, and he stuck close to him, hand on Talio's elbow. If anyone thought it odd, nobody said a word. They waited in line to dip their arms into the newly filtered water and receive the blessings of Felle from the deacon. Talio saw Gawani, her husband, and Essa further back in line, talking and laughing. Elsewhere, magistrates discussed recent hearings, and traded jokes with advocates.

Then he thought of the Incarnite temple, its flickering flames, the quiet solemnity, even while eating. It did not make the Incarnites better than Nuciferians who believed in the Source and Felle. It did, however, set them further apart. Just as the points were now another matter of contention between him and Pazli.

Talio had been relying on the five points a month he was receiving for his work with the Judicial Review Committee, but he received an unpleasant surprise at the final meeting before the year-end break.

"We're asking you and Pazli to both recuse yourselves from the committee," Gawani told them in private after the meeting concluded. "For the time being."

What had they done now? "It's the Honell hearing," she explained. "Queen Jaconda has asked us to put together a position paper on the matter. Your presence would be an obvious conflict of interest." He saw the points flying away in his mind, but what could he do?

They broke down the work for the Honell hearing into two parts: Talio would research the legal implications and Pazli the social issues. Then something happened that changed the importance of the hearing altogether: a month later, the committee's position paper leaked.

Someone on or near to the committee reproduced the paper's conclusions and sent copies to a selection of nobles and business leaders. The paper focused on the expense of changing the administrative systems, balanced against the "unnatural" request of one claimant. The language was that of an internal government document: blunt and dispassionate. The public might expect the government to be bureaucratic and monolithic, but to see a bloodless argument marshaled against a child was something else entirely. Talio heard rumblings at the Palace, and imagined the ones at higher levels were deafening.

Nobody admitted to the leak, but from Talio's experience with the Skyways matter, producing that number of copies would require a substantial amount of silver. Or a large number of people working together with a common goal.

Magistrate Clemente stopped him outside a hearing room a few days later. "Did you leak the position paper?"

"No, Master Jilani," Talio said with all sincerity.

"Are you very sure?" His eyes were those of a hawk—pale, sharp, and frightening.

"If I were to pull such a trick, I would like nothing more than to take public credit for it."

Clemente seemed satisfied. "Every copy of the original paper had a unique identification code. We will find out who distributed it."

The committee never released a statement about who leaked the document. The next time Talio was in Pazli's presence without the other man walking away, he whispered to him, "Are you aware there were identifying codes on that paper?"

"I am no fool," was all that Pazli said in reply. Talio agreed; no fool would have thought to get the Incarnites at the temple to copy the paper's contents, as they had for Verrane's pamphlet. He doubted any amount of public opinion would sway Clemente, but he was pleased Pazli had learned from his example.

Through Emara, Pazli provided Talio with copies of his research, but the scholarly works eluded Talio's understanding. A man was a man, and a woman was a woman. He read of intersex individuals, and the special certificates the government issued for those rare situations. Honell was not claiming to be intersex, merely that they did not feel they should have to make a choice between "male" and "female." The vagaries of sex and gender were beyond Talio's understanding. He needed to speak to a medical expert. One he could trust.

The frail old man at the administration service counter agreed to forward a generic message lockbox to Minka Schell if Talio donated to the administration upkeep fund. *The old man upkeep fund,* Talio thought, but he paid.

A few days later, he received an invitation to tea with the chief physician.

Minka lived in a cluster of rooms in the mid-priced west end of Nuciferia. The two of them sat across from each other by the crackling fire. She had been busy, she said. Working on a treatise about the decomposition of bodies. She did not speak of any illness, and Talio did not want to pry. "You look well," Minka said with a smile.

"The law agrees with me," Talio said. He would not lie and tell her she looked well. "Your rooms are beautiful."

She nodded. "All the money I would have spent on bonnets goes to my furnishings."

A pretty, plump woman with smiling eyes brought them a tray with mugs of tea. "Thank you, Neri," Minka said. Neri leaned down and kissed her on the lips. When they were alone again, Minka raised her eyebrows at Talio.

"You have good taste in women," he said after a moment.

"As you once did," Minka said, then they both burst out laughing. It was good to hear her laugh.

She grew serious. "But you are here to discuss the Honell hearing," Minka said.

He nodded. The details were common knowledge among the citizens; the odd facts of the matter had sparked the public interest during a dull winter. "I cannot make sense of it," he admitted. He could not yet *believe* it, as he had told Pazli.

"Do you believe there can be something other than male or female?" she asked.

Talio shook his head. "I've seen the research. Babies born with two sets of genitals. Intersex individuals. The government has an identity key notation for that situation. That is not the case here. Honell was born with either a penis or a vagina. It is on his—her—their identity key."

"Honell believes they are neither male nor female," Minka said, leaning forward. "That deep inside, they are something else." Believe. Again, with that word.

"I may believe that I am a sabot, but that does not make me one."

He expected one of her abrupt laughs, but Minka shook her head. "Do you honestly believe that? Deep in your heart?"

"And if a madwoman were to honestly believe she was Queen Jaconda? Should the queen abdicate her throne?"

Minka got to her feet and placed her mug on a table. "You have the advocate's habit of following a thought downstream to its conclusion without considering logical paths." She tapped her fingers together. "Have you ever felt placed into a situation where you did not belong? Where society labeled you as something, but you knew you were something else?"

Talio remembered his discreet visits to the Double Moon Inn during his marriage. Avoiding the judgment of Gawani, of the Palace. As long as he did not admit to his desires out loud, people would turn a blind eye. "A long time ago."

"Then you might use that memory," Minka said, pulling her shawl around her too-thin form. "As a source of some fresh stream of thought."

Something else had been on Talio's mind since his meeting with Emara and Lady Safana. "Are you familiar with the advocates that argue medical hearings?" he asked, changing the subject.

"Of course," Minka replied. "That is one area I tend to be called as a witness, more than any other legal field. Why do you ask?"

"Are they mostly women?"

"All of them," Minka said. "Without exception."

He sat there wondering how to phrase his next question, but she saved him the trouble. "There is nothing specifically feminine about medical hearings," she said with a sharp laugh. "Being an advocate is not easy for women, and medical hearings are a generally unprofitable sideline. It stands to reason that it would attract a group of women who stick together."

"Stick together?"

She paused. "Most women at the Palace help each other. Information, gossip, favors. Going around the official channels. Like digging a tributary to bypass a blocked canal." Talio thought of Vinne's network of men and nodded.

Before he left, Talio asked her, "How did you come to your beliefs about those like Honell? Was it some pamphlet or report? Something I could read?"

The former chief physician considered him. "When I was a child, I knew I was female. No matter how much my parents dressed me in boys' clothes. I knew otherwise. I waited and waited until I could be the person I wished to be." She smiled. "And now I am."

"Thank you, Minka." He could think of nothing else to say.

"We live in a city of secrets," she said with a shrug. "I feel no shame, and I imagine you do not, either. But the systems of Nuciferia were designed for *them*, not us."

A thought occurred to Talio. "How did you have your identity key changed?"

"The women, again. They are surprisingly powerful. We do not control the pressure of the water, but we can influence the direction it flows." She shook her head. "Regardless, this is not a question of keys. You don't need to change the words on Honell's key," she said. "You need to change the law."

On the walk back to the Double Moon, Talio saw Minka Schell's face in his mind. In a way, her revelation changed nothing about what he knew of her; in a way, it changed everything. So many of us with secrets, he thought. Secrets kept for reasons of self-preservation, in a society that refused to believe, or even accept. She trusted him with a truth about herself, and now he would take that truth forward with him, as part of who she was.

It was easy to see Minka as a woman; he had only ever known her as such. Talio could see Honell as something other than man or woman if he thought hard about it. It was such a small sacrifice on his part and meant so much to them. But the sacrifice from all of Nuciferia, all of Merin, would be enormous, especially if so many Incarnites felt the same way as Honell. Pazli had always scoffed at Talio's focus on money and the cost of things, but was that not what this hearing turned upon—the cost of retooling the identity key system? Or were there those who would simply refuse to believe regardless?

Later that evening, Talio sat on the stoop of the inn. The night was frosty, and he had his cloak pulled tight around him. Gray clouds skittered across the dark purple sky.

He heard the door to the inn open, and Vinne sat down beside him in the dusk. "It's freezing out here," the large man said, putting a burly arm around Talio's shoulders.

"I could use some companionship," Talio admitted.

"What do you call this?"

Talio smiled and leaned his head against the man's broad shoulder. "Male companionship."

"Last time I checked down there, I was male."

"Sex," Talio said.

"Can't help you there," Vinne said. "But it's not sex you need."

"What do I need, then?"

Vinne gave his shoulders a squeeze. "You're the romantic type. Always knew it. You'd only bring one guy at a time back to your room at the inn. If you wanted more than one, it was into the alley with all five of you."

Talio laughed. "I will be sure to remember that definition of 'romantic.'"

They sat in comfortable silence. "How about the prosecutor?" Vinne asked. "The handsome one?"

"He has a fine mind. Ambitious. But sometimes, I feel he is too beautiful."

Vinne nodded. "The prettier they are, the easier they break. You sure forgave him fast, though."

Talio shrugged. "He did what he had to in order to get into law school. I made a similar bargain, once." He knew the other man would not pry any further. Favors done in exchange for money were no secret to either of them.

Vinne shifted his bulk a bit. "What about Pazli, then? Anything there?"

"Next, you'll be asking about Master Jilani." Talio relented. "By all rights I should have no interest in Pazli whatsoever."

"He's a bit of a mystery, all right."

"One I may never unravel. An Incarnite may not love a non-Incarnite. He has reminded me of their rule."

"Maybe he's reminding himself. I've seen how he is with you." Vinne smiled. "I know you'll bring the right one back to your room eventually. Leave the alleyway for the cats."

They sat quietly a while longer. Then Talio remembered something he'd been meaning to ask the innkeeper. "Where did the symbol on the wall come from?" he asked. "Did the Incarnites paint it?"

"I did. A while back, when men of our—your kind stopped coming to the Double Moon." Vinne shook his head. "One of the hooded fellows I know thought I might get some Incarnite clients if I drew it. They have their share of curious men, too. It's a code they use. Little did I know you'd be the one with all the customers."

"What does it mean?" Talio asked, exhaling a cloud of mist that hung between them and the stars.

"Everyone is welcome," Vinne recited. "You're safe here. We don't judge." He grinned. "And be sure to try the stew."

The next day, Talio sent a message lockbox to Pazli: *We need to talk this evening.* He had originally written that he wanted to talk to him, but that was incorrect; Talio needed to hear from him as much as he needed to say what was on his mind.

When he showed up, they sat down at Talio's worktable. Pazli picked up the little stuffed bird from the fair Talio kept there, examined it, then replaced it without comment.

"I would say that I am sorry," Talio began, "but I know it is far from enough."

"That is true. It is very difficult for me to be around you now." Pazli fell silent.

"I wanted you," Talio said, pushing through the discomfort. He had to say the words, give form to the thoughts in his mind. "I wanted you on my skin, in my arms. And I thought you felt the same way. That you only needed a gentle push, and that I could provide it."

"I wanted you as well. But I was not ready." Pazli's voice was low. "I am still not ready. I may never be. And you know what our catechism says about being with non-Incarnites."

"I know. I will wait. And if—" He could not bring himself to say the rest. If Pazli's religion came first, then he would never speak of it again. But he would go on waiting.

He changed the subject. "I need your help to win the Honell hearing. We need each other's help. Not to mention the other Incarnite hearings before the end of the judicial season. Please."

"I will make more of an effort to work with you," the Incarnite said in a grudging voice. "If you promise you will not serve me any more wine. Soft or otherwise."

Talio nodded.

He should have been relieved at that point. But he was not telling the truth. He still wanted Pazli, but now that they had been together physically, he wanted him in a different way.

And unless Talio's sense of human nature was inaccurate, Pazli saw him as more than a business partner, though his desires were all tangled up with the Incarnite teachings. Their feelings would have to remain unsaid for now.

It was time to take another step. If he could trust anyone, he could trust Pazli. Talio took a deep breath. "There is something else I need to tell you." This was the moment of no return. "It's about the magistrate's codices."

# Chapter Twenty-Two

Talio took Pazli to see Cale the next night. The prosecutor's dormitory had a disused recreation room on the first floor. They sat down at one of the dusty game tables, surrounded by old athletic equipment.

He and Cale took one side of the table, and Pazli the other, by silent agreement. The man's arms were folded, as if he had already decided he would sit in opposition to them. Talio wanted to sigh. Even at this point, at this critical juncture, Pazli was still throwing up barriers, denying him the emotional access that Cale would freely offer. Was this the first time the three of them had sat together outside of the Palace? Pazli continued to glance back and forth between the two of them, and Talio could not shake the feeling he was drawing a conclusion about their relationship, whatever it might be.

Cale brought his codex, and Talio the ruined pages. It did not take long for them to explain the source of each document, the discrepancies Talio found, and the mystifying circumstances that protected the codices from being examined.

Pazli flipped through the pages, then the codex. "It is obvious," he announced at last. "Each city has their own version of the codex."

"That is quite the deduction," Cale said. "Why not conclude that every codex is different?"

Pazli shook his head. "It is a matter of administration. How many codices are there in Merin? Hundreds? Imagine the work required to create different versions for each magistrate, and then to track these versions from production to distribution."

Cale looked doubtful. "The position paper that leaked had identification codes," Pazli said. "To track hundreds of codices, there would need to be some way of telling them apart without going through the sentencing guidelines line by line." He tapped the codex's cover. "I see nothing of that nature here."

It made sense. Cale's Nuciferian codex differed from Kallis's Auranian one. The ruined pages could have come from a Damirian or Rylavian codex. Nuciferia produced codices for all cities centrally.

"But why?" Cale asked. "And who is behind it all?"

Again, Pazli shook his head. "No, the question is not *why* or *who*. It is *what*."

"Explain," the prosecutor said.

"There is only one Obelisk of Justice. What is written on that obelisk? And which set of codices matches it?" Pazli sat back while they considered this.

The man's deductions and logic were remarkable. Talio had been so used to taking charge at the Double Moon, to calling on him only for information about Incarnites, that he had treated him as little more than an assistant. In contrast, he'd paid more attention to Emara's advice. It was easier to listen to her because she pressed her opinions on him. Or, Talio realized with embarrassment, because he'd thought himself superior to Pazli.

"You believe that three of the four cities are dispensing faulty justice?" Cale was incredulous. "And have been doing so for years?"

"No," Talio said. "The *laws* must be the same. They are taught everywhere; most of us have memorized at least some of them. It always comes back to the sentencing guidelines." He thought of the tables and concordances. "Someone organized the codices to hide the differences in sentencing. Perhaps Scodel himself."

They could not determine why anyone would do such a thing, or to what end. If a group wanted more lenient or harsher sentencing, why not change the codices in all four cities?

After much fruitless discussion, Cale put a stop to it. "We agree then that we need to inspect the Obelisk of Justice. Determine which city has the correct codices."

"And alert the authorities," Talio said. "But there is no way to see the obelisk." He recalled his conversation with Gawani in front of the Statue of Scodel. "The original is in the Hall of Antiquities. Ever since an Incarnite attacked it, they've kept it locked away."

"That attack was a lie," Pazli said with bitterness. "The cleric asked the entire congregation, and nobody came forward."

Talio would not comment on the efficacy of that method of investigation, but locking the obelisk away was yet another way that the sentencing guidelines remained hidden. Just as the Palace's decision not to collect statistics on the disposition of hearings prevented anyone from comparing sentencing outcomes in each city.

"I told you I take regular walks around the Palace late at night," Cale said to Talio. "When I am working late, I can get to the door of the Hall of Antiquities without any of the guards noticing. I know their schedule."

"Then we go tonight," Pazli said.

Cale shook his head. "The door to the hall is quadruple-locked. Given the importance of the obelisk and the codices, the keys to that door must be highly guarded."

He promised to find more information about the keys. They had little else to discuss besides theories and suppositions. At this point, they needed hard evidence.

Pazli stood abruptly. "You will excuse me. Vespers." He gave them one final glance. "I will leave the two of you together."

Talio shook his head after Pazli left. "Should I ask?" Cale said.

"Please don't."

"Allow me some leeway," the prosecutor said with a frown. "Are you involved with him?"

Talio laughed. "As partners in law, certainly."

"And partners in love?"

He stared at Cale. "I wouldn't put it that way."

Cale shook his head. "You cannot dangle both of us at the end of a string. I would like you to choose. Either me or Pazli."

"There is no choosing Pazli." Talio wanted this to be over. He did not want to be free of either man, but he admitted it was unfair to both of them.

"If that is true, then you should be able to give your heart to me right now." Cale smiled with the bright expression of a student achieving a high grade in his ethics in practice course. When Talio said nothing, that smile vanished. "I see. Then let us discuss something a bit less fraught."

Talio breathed a sigh of relief, then took the seat across from him so they could look at each other more easily. "I am struggling with the Honell hearing," Cale admitted.

"That is good to hear."

"You would think so. But I am grappling with a dilemma. A moral one, or an ethical one." Talio raised his eyebrows.

"If this were a murder hearing," Cale went on, "then I could paint the accused as someone wicked. A monster. We never speak directly to the character of an accused, but we imply. Insinuate."

Talio knew the procedure well. "And for Honell?" he asked.

"She is a child," Cale said. "Perhaps no longer in the eye of Scodel's laws, but in my mind, she is. I have met her." He shook his head. "*Them. They*. The words are so difficult."

"Everything about this hearing is difficult." Talio considered the various approaches. "If I were you, I would focus on the facts of the hearing. As admitted, and as you see them."

"That is all I can do," Cale said. "There is no legal interpretation to argue. The law on refusal to identify is clear and final. The alternative is to accept the parents' argument that we must change every Nuciferian law that exists, all the ones in Merin." An exaggeration, no doubt.

"Or is that one of your tricks?" Cale continued, musing. "I have become so familiar with them over the months."

Talio shook his head. "I am behaving myself. This is not a hearing of tricks. But I do intend to beat you soundly."

"We shall see," Cale said with a roguish grin. He was wearing a red snood that held his locs, his soft brown eyes as intelligent as ever. *How would it feel to be so handsome?* Talio wondered. No doubt the man's looks had unlocked many doors. Just as Pazli's had closed so many.

What would it be like to wake up to Cale every morning, to caress his olive skin whenever he wished? The legal conversations would be scintillating. And they would have few silences in their lives. Unlike the ones he experienced so often with Pazli.

The government claimed one delay, then another. By the time the Honell hearing started, there were only two months before the end of the judicial season. At seventy-five points, Talio's chances of regaining his law license were looking slimmer and slimmer.

The audience area in the hearing room was full. A line of people waiting to get in stretched down the hallway before the guard closed the door. The government miscalculated; the delays had only aroused more curiosity from the public.

Honell sat nervously next to him, their parents in the first row of audience seating. Talio smiled and patted their arm. There was not much more he could do. Pazli sat at the far end of the desk.

Cale's opening statement began with a discussion of legal principles. Merin society was based on the principle of identification. Any large, modern society must have a means of identifying its citizens—for matters of administration, authentication and prevention of crime.

Honell had refused to identify. This was a simple violation of the law. They were guilty of contravening the statute in question and must identify themselves or suffer the consequences. "I should add," Cale said in conclusion, "that Honell is in possession of an identity key. The Nuciferian government knows if they are a boy or a girl. That is not the issue. What we discuss here today is compliance with the law. A law required for Merin society to function."

Poor Cale. He took the logical path Talio had known he would. And now, this early, he had already lost the hearing.

"Your statement?" Clemente asked Talio and Pazli. By agreement, Talio had asked Pazli to hold back. Only one person could make this argument effectively.

Talio rose. "At this time, I reserve my right to make an opening statement." This was unusual, but not odd enough to be a "trick" to Clemente. Talio had heard hearings as magistrate where advocates reserved their opening statements. The typical reason was so they could expound at length at the point in testimony where it would be most advantageous.

Clemente narrowed his eyes. "As you wish." He turned back to Cale. "Proceed with the witnesses."

The first witness was a section chief at the government's document division. Cale spent much of the morning asking her about procedures and protocols, focusing always on how the division categorized records separately for male and female citizens.

"And what would you say the cost of unifying this system would be? To enable someone such as Honell"—Cale pointed to the youth sitting next to Talio—"to avoid stating whether they were male or female? In round figures, please."

This was the other part of Cale's error. Unless he simply wished to point to the statute and call Honell guilty, there were only two ways to argue the hearing: analysis or policy. Cale could make no impact by analyzing the refusal-to-identify statute; Talio would be the first to admit it was valid on its face. So, he turned to policy.

The implications were obvious. The cost to Nuciferia and Merin to make these changes was enormous. The change was impractical. It would take years. There was no way that an entire society could accommodate one individual.

Talio declined to cross-examine the section chief.

Cale continued that afternoon with a second witness from the government's Department of Security to testify about the costs of modifying the identity key system.

Talio rose once Cale finished questioning. "I will use my reserved statement at this time," he said. "If I may."

Clemente nodded. "Very well. Proceed."

During the Skyways hearing, Talio had claimed he'd read every single one of Scodel's laws. This time, he had actually done so. Partly for the Honell hearing and partly because he would need that knowledge when they examined the sentencing guidelines on the obelisk. What had been of particular interest was the beginning of the codex.

Law students hated the opening section: flowery sentences by Scodel about justice, the inherent rights of citizens and his Grand Experiment. Talio usually skipped the section by habit. This time, he'd found exactly what he needed.

"This is not a hearing about the government," Talio said, addressing the audience. "The Queen's government may have brought this cause of action, but this matter turns on one individual. There." He pointed to Honell.

Cale rolled his eyes as usual. Of course, he thought Talio was trying to tug at the emotions of the audience. Such a tactic would never work on Clemente.

"I would like to read from the opening lines of Scodel's laws," Talio said. "If we might have an abridged codex brought from the Hall of Documents."

Magistrate Jilani rummaged in his robes. "You may use mine." He handed it over with a glare. "But be careful with it."

Talio started reading from the beginning, choosing the phrases he had already memorized. "'Each citizen has the right to a fair hearing. Each citizen has the right to be represented by an advocate. Each citizen is equal before the eyes of the law...'" Talio skipped ahead. "'It is better that ten guilty citizens should go free, rather than punish one citizen unfairly.'"

He closed the codex and set it down on the desk. "Note Scodel's wording. One citizen. A single citizen. Not society. Not any group within society." Talio turned and appealed to the magistrate. "By Scodel's own words, our legal system—

our Grand Experiment—is based upon the individual. These are not rights to be balanced against what something might cost the government, or the royal body. The individual, the citizen, the person who stands alone in their own life, is paramount over all else."

Talio handed the codex back to the magistrate and turned back to the official from the key division. "I have no questions at this time."

And now he had boxed Cale in completely. Typically, an advocate who reserved their statement would follow up with questioning of the witness. Talio had not done so, and therefore Cale could not now ask to redirect. Nor could he cross-examine Talio's statement. The words hung in the air.

The prosecutor's hands were twisting the vellum sheet before him, and Talio had a moment of sympathy for him. If Cale had based his entire argument on the cost to the government, his point about the primacy of the individual would serve as rebuttal each time. The prosecutor would not force Honell to submit to demeaning testimony, either. Talio knew Cale well enough on that point. What his father must have done to him, for him to refuse to allow another child to suffer.

"Then perhaps we should have Advocate Rossa take the stand," Cale burst out. "And ask him if he believes Honell is a boy or a girl." He was truly angry, color rising on his cheeks.

"Objection," Talio said. "An advocate may not be called to testify about the merits of a hearing they are arguing." The magistrate gave a curt nod in his direction.

"I request a recess," Cale said. He would not look at him, and Talio felt alarm. He and Cale had been so lighthearted in threatening to beat each other in this hearing, but the prosecutor's face was grim. Had he driven him away?

"One hour," Clemente said. Cale rose and left the hearing room.

Talio stayed at his desk and sent Honell to be with their parents. He did not look up or speak to Pazli, who sat with his arms folded, silent. The only person who approached him during the break was Emara. "Scodel would have approved of your argument," she whispered in his ear. "I approve, too."

An hour later, there was no sign of Cale. A messenger delivered an official lockbox to Clemente. "The government has requested an adjournment for the day," he announced.

Talio had avoided the Palace canteen all fall and winter, and he was tired of it. His argument in the Honell hearing applied here; it was the canteen's task to accommodate him, not the other way around. To his surprise, Pazli asked if he could join him.

Once they purchased their teas, nobody confronted them. There were no "reserved" tables. *Was it this easy?* Talio wondered.

"I owe you an apology," he said after they sat down.

Pazli nodded. "You owe me several. Which one do you bring forth now?"

"For not taking your views seriously. Your legal theories." Talio sipped his tea. "You are my mental equal, if not more. I have stolen the attention and left you in the shadows."

"Sometimes it is best to stay in the shadows," Pazli said. "I do not always want the attention of others." Talio touched the cleft in his lower lip.

A bell rang; there was a commotion at the canteen entrance. An elderly woman was swapping out the existing roster sheet much earlier than usual. Excited chatter rose from the people around the woman. Pazli rose and Talio followed him to the door, where they read the updated document.

The government had dropped the Honell hearing without prejudice. Although Talio was glad for the youth, his heart sank at the lost points. Defending a client in a matter against the government would have been worth twenty points. He might even have been able to make the ultimate argument that this was "advancing the state of the law" for forty points, enough to get his license back. No more.

"Perhaps they realized the strength of our argument," Pazli said.

"Or perhaps they looked at the cost of changing their systems and felt it was not worth pursuing." Or they knew of other Incarnites similar to Honell. Forestalling the issue was the government's best strategy.

Barring recovery of costs in the Hall of Equity, Honell was still in the same position they had been in before the hearing. Their path ahead was a narrow one. Honell could now file a claim against the government. There would be no monetary damages, but they could ask for specific performance: that the government make the changes they requested and issue a special key. The threshold for specific performance was impossibly high, but the Double Moon might be able to muster a convincing argument.

Combined with his committee work and the other minor Incarnite hearings, it could be his last chance to earn enough points to get his license back. Talio would have to check the accursed *Wayward Advocates* pamphlet to be sure.

There was one more hope for Honell, but a conversation with Gawani the following day put a stop to that at once. She asked Talio and Pazli to rejoin the committee as soon as possible. "Won't the Honell matter be referred to the committee for study?" Talio asked. "We would still be in a conflict of interest."

Gawani shook her head. "The Honell matter has not been referred to the committee." It never was.

Millions of silver coins, balanced against one child—and the other Incarnites who had so far remained silent about their own identity. Talio could stand and speak of Scodel's Grand Experiment all he wished, but nothing would change. The government would not change the identification system unless they were legally forced to. He thought of Honell and of Minka. And he thought of himself, ten years earlier, making furtive trips to the Double Moon Inn.

"Do you *believe* yet?" Pazli asked him once, without mentioning Honell.

"I am trying to," Talio said. "A little more every day." He waited for Honell or their parents to contact the Double Moon, but they kept their distance for now. It was not his place to try to persuade a client to launch a risky hearing—points or no points—and Pazli did not raise the matter after the meeting with Gawani.

In the Hall of Reference one day, as Talio was doing research on a housing matter, he ran into Cale. "Advocate Rossa," the prosecutor said.

"Are we back to a last-name basis, then?"

Cale shrugged. "You have refused me, and yet you say there is nothing between you and Pazli. Logically, I take this as a rejection."

To that, Talio could say nothing. "Will you help me with the codices, then?"

Cale gave him a lingering touch on the arm, as if he regretted having to pull away. "That is a separate matter. I will help you." He gave a faint smile. "You can be a dangerous man. Did you know that?"

Another announcement made waves: With the official end of the judicial season, the Palace of Justice would hold a gala party, and all advocates, prosecutors and magistrates were invited. Even Queen Jaconda would be in attendance. Palace staff would give tours of the building, including the Hall of Antiquities.

Talio, Pazli and Cale gathered to talk in the only space in the Palace guaranteed absolute privacy, standing in the swirling sleet and wind of the law school's square. Talio and Cale had their cloaks up around their ears, while Pazli's winter hood protected him as usual. The prosecutor had avoided Talio for a few days more after the Honell hearing, but he was a man of quick anger and equally quick forgiveness. Pazli's anger had faded to his usual supportive neutrality.

"Can we get close enough to the obelisk during the tour?" Talio asked.

Cale shook his head. "They will put it behind a rope or out of view. Or they will have some other excuse."

"The main event will be in the rotunda," Talio said. "Maybe we can slip away for a few minutes if you can get us to the Hall of Antiquities."

"There will be guards and peacekeepers and a full room. Everyone will see if we try to leave."

Pazli cleared his throat. "I believe I may have a way to leave the rotunda unnoticed. But we will still have to get past the quadruple-locked door to the Hall."

"A potential solution to those locks has occurred to me," Talio said. "I must think more on it, though." It was dangerous, but what was not dangerous about this plan? It would be the only opportunity this year to read the text on the Obelisk of Justice.

The three of them were partners now. Perhaps not in the way of a relationship, or even legally. But they were somehow bound together. And together they would solve the mystery of the codices.

Talio looked at Cale, then at Pazli. He knew there was another mystery he would have to solve eventually. But for now, the law took precedence over the human heart.

# Chapter Twenty-Three

That night, Talio thought back to the dead rat that someone had nailed to his door. At the time, he had put it out of his mind, but there was something to consider, something important. Something that could help him, Pazli and Cale with their plan.

Whoever did it had unlocked the locks on the Double Moon Inn's door without damaging them. There were two possibilities. The first was a set of duplicate keys. Vinne had always told him the Inn only had one set of keys for security. He kept them on the same ring as his identity key, and Talio had never seen Vinne without it, no matter how drunk he got.

That left the other alternative. There was some device, some mechanism for opening a lock containing false merinite without the associated key. Anyone strong enough could open most locks with physical force. But to pick a lock protected by a chip of false merinite was said to be categorically impossible. If someone had this device, they could enter anywhere, steal anything.

He considered the implications. Theft did occur, but not at the rate that would suggest widespread use of this device. If it existed, therefore, only a few people or groups had access to it. The government. Certain criminals.

Talio was not stupid enough to approach Oran Keel again. But there was another option.

The next evening, Vinne and Talio sat in chairs in front of the fireplace, wine glasses by their side. Talio explained his reasoning to the innkeeper and mentioned his need for the device but said nothing about the codices. "They are going to kill you," Vinne said. "You do realize that."

"Who?"

Vinne waved a broad hand. "They. Some anonymous 'they.' The people who have been trying to kill you so far." Of course. He had never accepted his tale about falling into the canal.

He told Vinne everything he knew about the codex mystery, but in the end, the innkeeper only shrugged. "Who cares?"

Talio raised his eyebrows. "Really. A conspiracy involving the entire Merin legal system, and you say, who cares?"

Vinne refilled his glass. "You're talking about pages in a book. They're not even the laws. They're the sentences. Who cares if someone goes to prison for one year or five years?"

"I imagine the accused cares a great deal."

Vinne's disinterest was infuriating. "Look," Talio said. "A society's culture comes from its laws. The things that tell us what we can and cannot do. What we should do." He hunted for an example. "If you want to encourage scholars, you promote mandatory education. If you want to encourage couples staying together, you outlaw divorce. Or penalize adultery."

"Like taxes," Vinne said. "Excise taxes on wine. So damn high. They do it to make people drink less. Heartless monsters."

Talio nodded. "A similar idea. Taxes and spending on the one hand, laws and sentencing on the other. You can tell what a society values by what it encourages. And what it discourages."

"What do you think the obelisk will tell you?"

"I don't know. Scodel never explained his thoughts behind the legal system. He wrote the general principles, and that was it. If he'd survived..." Talio shrugged. "I want to know *why*. Why the secrecy? Why the different codices? I have to know."

"You were like that ten years ago, too." Vinne smiled. "You had to know about that part of you, so you came here exploring." He gazed into the depths of his wine glass and continued in a quieter tone. "Me, I'd rather not know."

"Will you help me, then?"

After a while, Vinne nodded. "All right. I'll try to get something that you can use. I've heard rumors. Stories. But whatever I get, you can only have it for the night. You can't lose or damage it. I don't know what'll happen if you do." He raised his glass in a toast. "And when they kill you, I will drink an entire bottle at your funeral."

On a chilly sunny day, Talio accompanied a preoccupied Emara to the Palace of Justice for her first hearing. He had been too busy with the Honell matter to help her for a while, but the matter of Lady Safana and Physician Malmo had finally been scheduled on the roster. Emara left him for a few minutes before the hearing to visit the Hall of Registration and returned with a mysterious armful of vellum.

He thought he would be anxious for her, but Emara commanded the courtroom as if she'd been born to be an advocate. She strode right up to the magistrate—a sleepy-eyed pockmarked fellow named Denby—and made her arguments in a loud, clear voice. Her forceful, dogmatic nature that had been detrimental to her client work now turned to her advantage.

"This hearing turns on the injury of Lady Safana," Emara said. She pointed to the young noblewoman sitting at the claimant's desk, cradling her left arm. "She came to Physician Malmo for treatment of a broken arm which had not healed properly."

Emara questioned Lady Safana as to her treatment and injuries, then a reluctant Physician Malmo, and finally friends and family of Lady Safana as to the effect of the injury on her mood and lifestyle. Lady Safana claimed the physician did not tell her of any potential risks. Physician Malmo insisted he disclosed them prior to treatment, and that the lady understood and insisted on proceeding. Her arm suffered further damage as a result, which resulted in the cause of action for medical harm.

The defending advocate was an older woman who spoke dismissively of the entire matter. She brought forth evidence that Lady Safana had visited several healers in the past for complaints that could not be substantiated. The implication was that this one was spurious as well. Given Emara's raised eyebrows, Talio imagined the noblewoman had not made her privy to this information.

He was very curious as to the stack of vellum, but it did not make an appearance until Emara's closing arguments. "We have heard the evidence of both parties," Emara said. "I will not repeat it. The testimony is inconclusive and mutually exclusive." This was her way of saying that one of them was not telling the truth, without saying so directly.

Credibility, Talio thought. Who to believe? "Therefore, the hearing turns on the credibility of those giving testimony," she continued. "As stated in Verrane's pamphlet on medical hearings."

Emara had visited the Hall of Registration. They licensed physicians at the Hall. As a magistrate, Talio would not have approved of the last-minute theatrics he suspected she was about to deploy, but he was no longer sitting behind the magistrate's desk.

She waved the vellum papers bearing the Registration seal with a flourish. "The Guild of Surgeons has suspended Physician Malmo on three previous occasions." Emara turned to the magistrate. "I suggest that if you in your wisdom find Physician Malmo to be free of guilt in this matter, Lady Safana will file a civil cause of action." She gave a tight smile. "And should the lady do so, the details of the physician's previous suspensions would be admissible at that point. Even if they are outside the scope of the current hearing."

*Clever*, Talio thought. Emara must have discovered the suspensions too late to submit them as evidence for this hearing. Raising them during her closing comments served two purposes: to sway the magistrate without having to enter them as formal evidence, and to suggest that they would be determinative in a hearing for damages at the Hall of Equity. One of Scodel's fundamental principles of justice was that separate judgments for liability and damages in the same matter should have similar outcomes, to assure citizens that justice was uniformly served.

Physician Malmo conferred with his advocate for a moment. Then the woman stood and faced the magistrate.

"At this time, we move to discuss a negotiated settlement," the advocate said, defeated.

The magistrate yawned and shrugged. "Very well. I set a meeting in my rooms for the third hour after midday break."

"Excellent work," Talio said to Emara after Lady Safana thanked her profusely. "Although last-minute revelations do not give the opposing side the opportunity to give a fair reply."

Her grin was broader. "I seem to recall someone with some purple dye in a murder hearing a while back."

Talio coughed. "I have been having second thoughts about that. About tricks in general." Not to mention the question of what actually happened to Selig Ivor. It hadn't bothered him at the time, but the loose thread nagged at him now and then. Had it truly been suicide? He was sure of Dovuta and Pazli's innocence, and yet there was something he was missing.

She stuffed the vellum pages into her satchel and closed it with a snap, bringing Talio back to the present. "As long as we win," Emara said. "If we are on the side of right, isn't that all that matters?"

*But sometimes, you can't know which is the right side to be on,* Talio thought. But he said nothing.

Emara came to work the next morning all smiles, carrying a basket of flatbreads and pastries. Even with the heavy cloak over her dress, she looked like a carefree girl, swinging the basket and setting it down before them. "Am I an advocate for the Double Moon now?" she asked. "Finally?" She had hit her one hundred points. Now all she needed was a job.

He and Pazli lifted their mugs of tea to her in celebration. "Now that you're a real medical advocate," Talio said, "there's a little pamphlet you might find useful. Something by Magistrate Verrane." He smiled. "I've heard the red edition is the cheaper one."

The contingency payment for Lady Safana's hearing had been substantial, and the Double Moon Law Office now had extra operating capital. There was enough silver to hire a new scribe and their first set of legal reference materials.

Emara insisted they buy texts on medical negligence, and in the end, they bought the latest edition of *Verrane on Medical Hearings* after all—the blue one.

There was even good news from the Judicial Review Committee. Gawani made an announcement. "We have two months before the end of the judicial season. Queen Jaconda has asked us to prepare a set of formal legal recommendations for her and the legislative council."

"Will our recommendations become law?" Talio asked.

Gawani gave an ambivalent hand gesture. "Officially, the Queen and the council will review and take action on our work. Unofficially, any uncontroversial changes should pass."

Uncontroversial! The concept of intangibles was about to change the practice of law. Nothing as extensive as what Honell might have brought, but they would have to draft several new addendums. They could not touch Scodel's original laws, of course.

Emara overcame the tyranny of her points, and now Talio was about to as well. He had spoken to Gawani informally about using the "advancing the state of the law" part of the point system, and she'd conferred with the Ethics Review Committee. "They're impressed with your work," she'd told him before the meeting. "You have an excellent chance once the recommendations go through. At least something good came out of the Skyways matter." With forty points from this task alone, he would clear the one-hundred-point threshold with ease.

Talio's excitement over regaining his license was dampened by Pazli, who spent the meeting with his arms folded in silence. He caught up to him in the rotunda restroom after the session. "What is the matter?"

"I am having misgivings about my role on this committee."

They walked down the marble hallway toward the exit among the crowds leaving for the day. "You've brought the voice of the Incarnites into the legal system," Talio said in protest. "It's as if you have the ear of the Queen herself."

Pazli remained silent and spoke only once they were approaching the Double Moon Inn. "I feel they only wanted me as a member so they could say the Incarnites approve of what they are doing. I can say what I will about my people's position within the law, but I am starting to believe the problem is not with the law, but Nuciferian society as a whole."

Talio could not deny the possibility. "You sound as if you want to leave the committee."

"I do."

Rising panic swept through Talio. He could not bear any further separation. Pazli was pulling away from him, away from something he wanted but would not grant himself. This was another step that would drive them apart. He could not afford to lose the man's vote on the committee either. *Calm,* he thought. Calm.

Then he heard a child scream.

A woman stood in front of them in the blowing snow, holding a fussing toddler. The boy was three or four; he was looking directly into Talio's face and screaming. He would not stop; his face was beet red and covered with tears.

"I'm sorry," the woman said, looking everywhere but at Talio's face. "I'm sorry." At last, she turned and hurried off with the child. A crowd of people were watching him.

Pazli reached a hand toward him, but he batted it away. "It is all right," Talio said in a calm voice. "Everything is all right."

He turned and strode toward the Double Moon. All he wanted to do was get to the inn, sit down, and have some wine. Pazli was having trouble keeping up with him for some reason.

Talio flung open the door to the inn and went directly to his room. He stood in front of his bed, breathing hard, looking at the floor, hands balled into fists. He heard Pazli come in behind him and close the door.

"Talio," Pazli said. He had never called him by his first name before.

Talio spun to face him. "Don't say it. Don't even try. I do not need your pity."

The other man took a step forward, and Talio backed away until he was pressed against a wall. "Everything is all right," he repeated.

Then he burst out without thinking, "You stand there in your cloak and your hood, and you think you know what it is like to be isolated and judged." Talio shook his head. "You are an idiot, and your religion is foolish."

Pazli did not react. Talio went on. "You can walk down the street whenever you want, and nobody will pay the slightest bit of attention to you." He could not stop himself. "I have to deal with the comments. The looks. The people pretending they do not see me. I can never tell when it will happen. I can never let my guard down."

Still no response from Pazli. Talio held his trembling hands in front of him as if he could will himself to be calm. "When this happened to my face, when I was a child, I learned to put up a shield in my mind. Not to care what others think." He looked up at Pazli. "And I don't, most of the time. They look, or they comment, and I am fine. It truly does not bother me."

"And then, perhaps once every five years, it happens," he said quietly. "On a day when I am not paying attention. A day such as today." He sat down on the bed. "I was upset with you. I did not want you to leave the committee. Why did that child have to..." His voice trailed off.

"Talio," Pazli said again, gentler this time.

"Would it be so much to ask you to hold me?" Talio said in a broken voice. "To touch me as if you meant it? Not fling me onto the bed in anger. You hide behind your cloak, and..."

Then Pazli gathered him into his arms and held him. Talio buried his face in the man's cloak and closed his eyes, smelling that earthy smell he knew. No one else smelled like him. He would know the man anywhere. He relaxed into Pazli's arms, let him hold him, wrap himself around him.

Pazli pulled back and touched Talio's forehead at the point where his scar disappeared into his hairline. He drew his index finger down the scar, across Talio's nose, to where it bisected his lips. He held Talio's chin with his hand and brushed his thumb along the gap in his lower lip. There was no pity in the gesture, only acknowledgment and acceptance. For a while Talio did nothing but look at him, past the hood, past the layers of clothing into Pazli's eyes, witnessing them in his mind and the compassion he knew they held.

Then Pazli withdrew the cloth strap from his pocket. "Turn around," he whispered.

Talio felt the strap come down over his eyes, and all went dark. Then Pazli's lips were brushing the nape of his neck, kissing him.

Their previous time together had been quick and violent, with Pazli in angry command of Talio's body. Now he was still in command of him, but his touch was firm and gentle. The man's fingers carried the message: *Do you feel me? I am here with you.*

Talio heard Pazli removing his hood, his cloak, his underclothes. He turned Talio around and lowered him onto the bed, kissing him, unbuttoning his clothes. Pazli's tongue entered his mouth, insistent. And always, his hands moving, rubbing the hair on Talio's chest, pulling gently at his nipples, wrapping themselves around his back until there was no separation between them. And his hands spoke to Talio: *I have not forgotten you.*

It was like a ship coming into a harbor, being enveloped by Pazli's lean arms. Not so much a physical sensation as an emotion. The feeling of coming home at last.

When Pazli kneeled down and pulled him into his mouth, Talio felt the wiry hair on his head. His hands explored the other man's body and saw what his eyes could not. And Talio replied to the message Pazli was giving him with his own hands: *I am here, too. I am yours, if you would have me.*

It was Talio's turn to enter Pazli this time. The other man pressed the jar of grease into his hands and submitted to him. *So tight,* he thought. But Pazli knew how to move his hips, how to grip him and move against him for his own pleasure. He had learned at the hands of another man.

They ended up face to face under the sheets, lips barely touching, arms entwined, lying together as the afternoon became evening, then night. Talio had to know that Pazli was there, that he would not leave him. He could not let any part of him remain untouched. Pazli grasped his hands, kneaded them, and wrote his own secrets with his fingers on Talio's palms.

*It is a message*, Talio thought as he drifted off to sleep. Pazli was trying to tell him something. Instead of speaking the words into his ear, he was telling him with his hands and his body. As Talio lay beside him, he wondered what that message could be.

The next morning, he awoke to the faint sounds of the street. He could tell from the stillness in the room he was alone. Talio untied the strap from his eyes and sat on the edge of the bed in the silence.

Pazli had indeed sent him a message. And that message was goodbye.

# Chapter Twenty-Four

Talio pulled on his trousers and walked into the front room. Vinne was still asleep somewhere, and Emara had not yet arrived with any Incarnite clients. Pazli stood in the front room in his cloak and hood, waiting for him. He was as far away from Talio as he had ever been.

He walked over to the man and handed him the strap. Pazli folded and put it away without a word. "So this is farewell, then," Talio said.

"I cannot be with someone who is not an Incarnite. No matter how I feel about you."

Talio would not let himself contemplate that last sentence. "And if I were a woman?"

"Not even then." Pazli shook his head. "If you were a male Incarnite, I could get a dispensation from the cleric for all the work I've done here." Talio wanted to laugh. A dispensation for missing vespers, a dispensation for loving another man.

"I won't let you go," he said in a firm voice. "I will not permit you to leave my life."

Pazli's voice was suddenly cold. "No doubt you would prefer not to associate with an *idiot* who follows a *foolish religion.*"

Talio's shoulders slumped. The words broke something deep within him. He did not want to continue the conversation; he wanted to take the man back into the other room and hold him. "You know I did not mean it."

"No," Pazli said. "You *did* mean it. That is what you honestly thought. After all this time." He shook his head. "Not acceptance. Tolerance. And bare tolerance at that."

Talio could not take the words back. "You separate yourself from society," he said. "There is no need. You can be one of us."

"Us." It was a dull, angry word. "Now you are on the other side, with them. And you say my cloak and hood are the things that separate me from you."

It was going all wrong. Talio thought of Cale, of the man's openness, how he could look at him and say what was in his heart—no matter how much Talio's answers might hurt him. The shield around Pazli was so impenetrable, so difficult to pierce. It was only when the other man let him in—or was overcome by emotion himself—that Talio could reach him. What were the right words that could touch the man's heart, without immediately causing him to withdraw?

"I need you with me," he said at last. "I cannot imagine my life without you by my side." There. He did it, said the words. He could not express everything that he felt; he said what he dared. But he could see that the words had not reached Pazli. They were not enough. He did not need to remove the hood to know the man's expression.

Pazli rubbed a hand along Talio's beard for a moment: touching him one last time. "You have forced me to choose between my religion and you," Pazli said.

The moment was endless, and Talio held his breath.

"I am an Incarnite."

He could remain silent no longer. "Or there is another explanation," Talio said quietly. "You are doing this to avoid what you are feeling."

Pazli drew back. "I imagine you should be more concerned with what *Cale* is feeling."

"Cale?"

The man turned away from him. "You were at the water purification ceremony together. You often take lunches together at the Palace canteen. I imagine you have met many times."

Talio wanted to scream at him, beg Pazli to say he needed him. But instead, he forced himself to keep his voice soft and even. "But you are not jealous in the least, are you?"

"Of course not," Pazli said. "As I said, I am an Incarnite."

Talio watched him leave and closed the door to the inn behind him. He dabbed at his eyes. Vinne would be awake soon, then Emara would arrive, and the Incarnites. They had a full schedule. He would be busier than usual; Talio did not expect Pazli to return that day.

He took the small stuffed bird from his worktable and put it away under his bed, where he would not have to see it.

* * *

Pazli continued to attend the committee meetings, but his presence made the next step of their work far more difficult.

At first, the committee had five members: Gawani, Talio, Verrane, Darra, and Clemente Jilani. Any formal materials written by the committee had to be approved by a majority. When Pazli joined the committee, he made a tied vote possible.

Talio believed he could count on Gawani, Pazli, and Darra's votes, at least sometimes. Gawani was for progress, Pazli was for progress for the Incarnites, and Darra favored anything that did not cost the Royal Palace any silver. Clemente and Verrane always voted as a bloc against him.

The committee considered Kallis's recommendations on mediation for government hearings, but Darra—and presumably Queen Jaconda—felt the cost and administration involved was prohibitive. So this year would focus on intangibles. First came extensive discussions about intangibles. What were they? Was a bonnet design an intangible worth protecting? What about the text of a pamphlet? A song? A new strain of duhan plant?

*And so we went around in circles*, Gawani had once said. Talio was not about to let that happen. Who knew what would come of his hidden work with the codices, but he could force the hand of progress through the committee and help the Incarnites that way. His license also hung in the balance; he could feel the last of the judicial season slipping away. At eighty-five points, he was so close, but there was no way he could get to one hundred without success on the committee.

"Do we agree then," Talio said at one point in growing frustration, "that someone cannot make an exact copy of a document without permission? That the text of that document is an intangible?"

"What if they change one word?" Verrane asked. Talio knew he was thinking of his pamphlets. "Then they can claim it is an original work."

"Would the wording 'substantially identical' be acceptable?" Talio asked. The magistrate considered this.

"If the magistrate in the hearing can rule on what 'substantially identical' means in a particular situation," Clemente broke in.

"Substantially identical, determined at the discretion of the magistrate," Talio said, watching Gawani's scribe note his wording. "Is that all right, then?"

Verrane and Clemente exchanged glances, then nodded. That was the first new statute and it had taken them weeks. Even then, the wording would not be final until they completed the recommendations document. Talio felt the end of the judicial season approaching like the spring thaw; they were running out of time and so was he.

Sometimes Talio wanted to tell Pazli to quit the committee formally and prevent the possibility of a voting deadlock. He came close to suggesting it, but Talio could not bring himself to see even less of him. And how would Pazli react if he suggested he was no longer wanted? The man was mercurial enough to stay simply to spite him.

"The problem seems to be with the word 'idea,'" Gawani said at one point. "Is an idea protected?"

"No," Verrane said. "Not until it is written on vellum. Or expressed in some other form." Clemente nodded.

Darra finally broke in. "The Queen does not wish to protect an idea. She is concerned about spurious claims." She looked around at each of them. "Consider the Skyways matter. Imagine that two claimants file separate causes of action. Each claims the other stole their idea, and that they had the idea first."

"Then we need a way of registering ideas," Pazli said. "An organizational system."

"Too complex," Darra said. "Too expensive. And what if someone were to register a hundred ideas and never bring any of them to life? Should others be prevented from using those ideas?"

That meeting concluded with the determination that no, the law would not protect ideas. It would only protect the expression of ideas. Clemente insisted on the "substantially identical" phrasing, which Talio felt placed an undue amount of discretion in the hands of magistrates—no doubt Clemente's goal.

He stood in the hallway with his hands thrust in his pockets, frustrated. Gawani came out of the room last and dismissed her scribe. "Imagine how it was when Scodel created our legal system," she said with a weary look.

"There must be a better way," he said.

They walked down the hallway toward the rotunda. "Let me tell you a secret," Gawani said. "The work of a committee does not take place during meetings."

"You want me to go see everyone after the meetings?" As an impartial magistrate, Talio had been expected to keep his distance from advocates, prosecutors, and anyone whose presence might hint at a conflict of interest. Aside from Clemente Jilani's mentorship and Gawani's warmth, it had been a chilly time at the Palace.

"After, before, whenever," she said. "When we are all together, Clemente has his thumb on Verrane. Verrane has his mind on his pamphlets, and I do not know where Darra is." Gawani clapped him on his back. "Individually, they might be more pliable."

He did not want to visit Clemente at all. The man would strangle him...or peck him to death. Darra had the might of Queen Jaconda behind her; he felt uneasy approaching her first. That left Verrane, who had rooms by the law school wing. He taught classes every morning, so Talio caught him in his rooms the following afternoon.

"Do you regret your actions, then?" the rotund magistrate asked Talio. "In the Skyways hearing?"

"Yes, Master Verrane," Talio said. *Not at all*, he thought, *except in losing to Cale*. "But you see why I did what I did, do you not?"

The man laced his hands over his ample belly and shook his head. "To convince me to rule in your favor."

True, but honesty would not serve him here. "I wanted the same thing as you," Talio said. "To protect the intangible idea the Skyways Construction Company had for the merinite redesign. The one the government copied."

Verrane harrumphed. "Those designs were not identical, not even close." Curse Clemente and his "substantially identical" nonsense.

Talio tried another tack. "What if I read your pamphlet, then wrote a summary?" Verrane furrowed his deep brow. "I could reproduce the main points in my own words, but the text would be completely different."

"Students might prefer to purchase a summary instead of the full pamphlet," Verrane said, pondering. "We cannot have that." He frowned. "But a summary is not a copy."

"Consider it...a reproduction of the essence of the ideas in the pamphlet," Talio said. They circled around the argument for more than an hour, and in the end Verrane agreed he would think about it.

"The students have always loved your pamphlet," Talio said in closing. "It would be a pity for someone else to sell a summary of it. Especially a cheaper summary."

* * *

He sent his finest message lockbox to Darra at the Royal Palace with a request to meet on "committee business."

While he waited for her response, Talio finally got up the courage to see Clemente. It was the final examination period before the end of the judicial season. In the Hall of Education, Talio checked the lecture room by the second noticeboard, but the professor was not there. He asked a worker at the student office where Clemente was and got the answer he was dreading.

Talio had not been to the magisterial wing in eleven years. Now he dragged his feet along the marble, doing everything he could to delay the visit. A young magisterial acolyte in teal robes took a wax imprint of Talio's identity key, then ushered him down the dark hallways he remembered from his dreams.

Dark. It was always so dark in the magisterial wing. Shadows cast by the acolyte's taper flickered against the walls. The door to Clemente's rooms was open, and the acolyte left Talio there. "Come in, Rossa," the older man said from within.

Talio entered the cramped space. Clemente was eating lunch, pecking at bits of flatbread and fruit. "Master Jilani."

"You want to convince me that an idea is an intangible," Clemente said, puncturing any hope Talio had of starting with a softer introduction.

"Yes."

"No," the magistrate said. "Go away."

The frustrations of the last month of committee work boiled up in Talio's mind. "Why do you hate me so, Master Jilani?"

Clemente removed his spectacles and peered at him. "I don't like you, Rossa. But I don't hate you, either."

"Why treat me in this manner, then?"

"Because I hate what you represent." The magistrate put the spectacles back on and adjusted them until his beady eyes focused on Talio. "You are everything wrong with Merin's legal profession. Fifty years after Scodel's divine revelation, we have reached this travesty."

He advanced upon Talio, jabbing at his chest with a claw-like finger. "Tricks. Always with the tricks. No substance, no legal analysis." Clemente screwed up his face as if he'd smelled something foul. "No rigor. Anything to circumvent Scodel's laws."

Clemente took a breath and straightened his shirt. "And then you work your way onto the Judicial Review Committee, trying to change the legal system. Bringing an Incarnite with you to tip the votes in your favor."

Yes, to the magistrate, this was how it would appear. "I was asked to join the committee."

The anger in Clemente's eyes changed to disgust. "By your former wife, in exchange for defending her Incarnite student from murder. Which you did using rather shaky legal arguments, by any measure. Then she pressured the Ethics Review Committee to give you a second chance at a law license." Again, this was a valid interpretation.

"You will oppose me, then?" Talio asked. "At everything?"

Clemente nodded. "With my dying breath, Rossa. At least you are no longer pulling tricks like you did in the Mecomb and Skyways hearings. I take comfort in that one blessing. Now get out of my rooms."

* * *

Darra agreed to meet Talio in the canteen two days before the following committee meeting. She looked harried and tired. "I hope this is important. I came here especially to see you," she said. "I only come to the Palace of Justice when I need to."

He had planned his attack, but Darra had her own agenda. "I do not wish to hear of intangibles," she said once they exchanged pleasantries, handing him a set of gilded pages. "Look at what I am dealing with." It was a position paper from the Royal Palace.

The paper predicted that a new industry would arise in Nuciferia as a result of the legal changes surrounding intangibles. Within five years, they would require more advocates, more hearing rooms, more administrative staff, and more space at the Palace of Justice. The few statistics that had been gathered about hearing administration showed that the Incarnites would be more likely to bring forth hearings related to intangibles. As a result, more guards would be needed for identification purposes as well.

"We cannot afford this," Darra said. "We are already over budget for the coming year."

"I do have an idea," Talio said, thinking of the Double Moon.

"Anything. Please."

"We need more law offices. More groups of advocates working together. Pazli and I can manage more clients together than we could on our own. If we were to do something about paperwork and partnership fees..." Talio let the idea percolate.

"True. There have only been five new law offices created in the last year," she said. "The structure is in place to create more, if the incentives were there."

"Now will you listen to me about intangibles?" he asked.

She filed the pages away. "As long as it does not cost the royal body any additional silver, I will listen." And so Talio began to talk, avoiding any mention of budget or expenses. She promised that she would consider it, but he could see the Queen's scales in her mind, weighing the silver and what the net cost of adding intangibles to the Nuciferian legal system would bring.

Long after their meeting, Darra's position paper remained on his mind. The Double Moon was straining under the influx of new clients. Emara insisted on focusing on medical hearings, so he and Pazli still had to deal with the Incarnites and other Nuciferians seeking their services. With the intangibles work, the firm would grow even larger.

He would see Pazli less and less. Talio would miss working with him side-by-side, but how could he tell him he was unwilling to grow the firm because of his feelings? Because he could no longer bear to be apart from him?

The committee made it with a month to spare before the end of the judicial season. The recommendations, the research, the background material, everything was ready by the last meeting. It was the most important meeting of the year: the final one to approve all the recommendations and send them on to the Royal Palace.

Darra was not present. Gawani explained she had been called away on royal business to Rylavia. During the interim, another Queen's representative, Adan, would replace her.

The oily little man reminded Talio of Oran Keel. Adan spoke of "respect for tradition" and "responsibility," and told anecdotes of his encounters with Queen Jaconda. Talio asked if they could delay the vote until Darra's return, but there was no time.

The vote was three to three. Adan voted with Verrane and Clemente. Of course. Clemente had planned this. He must have whispered in someone's ear at the Royal Palace. Waiting until the last minute to replace Darra so Talio would have no recourse.

Gawani threw up her hands. "All that work," she said. "Very well. No recommendations for change will be put forward this judicial season."

Normally, Clemente was the first one to leave, but this time, he stayed in his seat. When Talio finally rose, their eyes met. A year's work, discarded in order to punish him and hold back legal progress. To prevent the Incarnites from reaping the fruits of their labors. To prevent him from getting his license back. Clemente accomplished so very much with one vote.

Talio's second legal career was now as dead as his first. Even if Honell brought a hearing against the government, he could not earn enough points before the end of the judicial season. He thought he should feel anger, or at least grudging admiration to his former professor, who had indeed pulled a mightier trick than Talio ever had. But all he felt was cold determination. He nodded to the man, whose face held the ghost of a smile.

*I will find that obelisk,* Talio thought. *I will discover what Scodel's true intentions were.*

*And you won't stop me.*

# Part Three: Scodel's Grand Experiment

# Chapter Twenty-Five

Two months before the end of the judicial season, Jani and Ulric brought Honell to the Double Moon offices. They were quietly defiant. "We want to file a hearing against the Nuciferian government," Jani explained.

Talio and Pazli had prepared for this. Even during the previous hearing, Pazli had researched such a hearing on the theory Honell would lose. He'd concluded at the time that a countersuit would fail and had not pursued it further.

"It is too late in the judicial season," Pazli said. He and Talio were sitting at one end of a worktable, but Talio sat back and let him handle the meeting. These were his people.

"There are still two months," Ulric protested. "The last hearing only ran a few days."

"Because the government dismissed their charges," Pazli said. "In any event, the government could simply file for summary dismissal." He sighed. "And Advocate Rossa spoke to you about remedies already. You cannot seek monetary damages from them."

"He said something about performance," Honell said. Their voice had changed, become more musical.

"Specific performance," Pazli said. "If you were to succeed in the hearing, the magistrate could compel the government to accommodate you. In theory. The bar for specific performance is extremely high. They will fight you."

"I want to be heard," Honell said.

Pazli again suggested they postpone filing until the fall. Ulric shook his head. "We are going to be moving the fair on to Damiria in early summer," he explained. "You can imagine what would happen if they held the hearing in Damiria."

"We will pay," Jani said. They were offering a great deal of silver to bring the hearing before the end of the judicial season. The Double Moon still needed the income.

Pazli conferred with Talio after the Tamms left. "Do we take the hearing?"

He turned it around on the man. "You tell me what you would like to do, Advocate Mecomb." Talio smiled. "You don't have to ask me for permission. I'm sorry if you ever thought you did."

Pazli sighed and folded his arms in the manner Talio knew so well. "An important case. A great deal of public attention. What will the magistrate think when he sees an Incarnite arguing it in the hearing room?"

Talio placed a hand on Pazli's arm. "He will see the same fine advocate I do. This time I will do the research and stay in the shadows."

Having decided, he felt better, calmer. He was no longer scrabbling in the dirt, dowsing for points. Now he was free to support Pazli and to wrap up the remaining matters for the judicial season. He would get ten points assisting Pazli in the second Honell matter, and just miss out on his license. After that? Perhaps the Double Moon Law Office would need a notary, or a scribe.

Pazli never ate dinner at the Double Moon Inn anymore, but Talio could not resist asking him to stay for a meal that night. "First vespers," Pazli said, shaking his head.

"May I accompany you as far as we go, then?" Talio asked. It was only a few minutes to where he would turn upstream to the Palace, leaving Pazli to go on to the Incarnite temple. He would take every one of those minutes. Pazli assented with a nod.

They trudged along the wintry streets in silence, Talio scuffing his boots through the piles of snow. Piles of stones marked the edge of the streets and warned of the drop-off to the canals below. "I think the cause of action will be 'unfair treatment,'" Talio said. It could fall under no other category, but he wanted to hear Pazli speak.

More than that. He wanted to touch the man, to hold him, to do anything to get a reaction. Not this passive behavior. For so long he had thought it was a fiery anger that drove Pazli to withdraw, but now Talio saw another side to it. There was pain there, a longing for connection he could not, would not allow himself to have.

"That would be sensible," Pazli said. "We cannot fulfill the requirements for requesting accommodation."

They walked on. "Are the vespers pleasant?" Talio asked in desperation. They were almost at the point where their paths would diverge.

"They are beautiful. Would you come to listen sometime?" There was no invitation in Pazli's voice, only curiosity.

"Someday," Talio said. "If you were to ask me to."

Pazli was silent. They reached the corner of the street and turned away from each other in the snowy night.

He stayed late in the library at the Hall of Reference. His carrel's taper smoked and crackled in the frigid air. He thought there might be a cause of action requiring the government to accommodate the needs of its citizens, but the statute was so narrowly drawn it was useless in this hearing. The more research he did, the more frustrated he became.

The government owed every citizen fair treatment: another one of Scodel's fundamental principles. Talio had extrapolated it into a cause of action for unfair treatment. The government had treated Honell unfairly, and they had to be compelled to treat them with fairness.

This required Pazli to prove it. Prove that Honell was neither boy nor girl, man nor woman. Beneath their cloak, they were one or the other. Honell's sincere belief meant nothing in the hearing room.

He also had to anticipate the government's defense. Would they try to impugn Honell this time? Public interest in the matter was still high. The government would not want to be seen badgering a youthful claimant in a public hearing, especially after the leaked position paper.

They would not argue policy. Cale had shown the folly of such an argument last time.

That left natural science, and the weakness of Pazli's argument. Prove that Honell was a boy or girl, and the case fell apart. As an Incarnite, Honell could not be compelled to expose themselves, even to a physician in private, but their identity key constituted circumstantial evidence.

Talio suggested the possibility of other Incarnites in the same position as Honell coming forward, but Pazli advised against it. There was an unspoken agreement among the Incarnites in general not to speak of this matter; Honell and their parents were the first to breach it. For now, it would remain the claim of one child.

The Palace of Justice did not object when they filed the preliminary notice of hearing. Talio wondered what conversations were happening at higher levels. Darra had told him Queen Jaconda was watching him. He hoped very much that the Queen was watching Pazli this time. Nobody in the legal system much cared about public opinion, but the Smiling Queen had always taken care to maintain her image in the eye of the citizens of Merin.

The Palace finally posted the roster. Cale would be lead advocate for the government on defense. To Talio's surprise, Magistrate Verrane would preside. He had expected Clemente, but Verrane's medical background suggested the nature of the government's legal argument. Yet another hearing with Cale. It would be awkward facing off against him but given the prosecutor's popularity and success at the Palace of Justice, it seemed hardly surprising he would be assigned to such a high-profile case.

Talio had never studied natural science, and he found the theories confusing compared to Scodel's laws. The aspect of natural science related to human anatomy and physiology was largely shrouded in mystery. The reference materials were laden with *ifs, possiblys, perhaps*—far different than the simple cause-and-effect describing a crime or cause of action and its outcome in a magistrate's codex. In anticipation of Cale's line of argument, he read pamphlets from the Hall of Documents late into the night at the Double Moon, summarizing them for Pazli's review.

Over the months, Talio had become accustomed to Vinne coming into his bed late at night naked and pressing himself against him, depending on his lack of sobriety. Now that he was staying up nights working on the hearing, he missed that simple contact. He could have sought out Cale, rolled around with him somewhere. But this was such a high-profile hearing that Talio did not want to risk the possible gossip. Nor did he want to give him the wrong impression.

So Talio kept to himself. Each night in bed alone he would reach for his jar of personal grease and think of Pazli or Cale, or sometimes both at the same time. It did not help. Then he started snapping at Pazli and Emara during the day. Pazli took it without complaint, folding his arms and listening silently. Emara would give him a disgusted look and walk away.

He no longer slept well. Talio was afraid someone might come in during the night and hurt him. There had been no new attacks or threats, but he still worried, still woke up from nebulous dreams of violence. He sat on his bed late into the night, watching shadows from the vigil candle dance on the wall.

He could not stop rubbing his eyes during the day. They were grainy and sore. His stomach hurt. Talio's hands trembled when he held the stylus. Sometimes, as they sat across the front room from each other at separate worktables, it seemed like Pazli was watching him. Was it concern, anger? Did he miss him?

He had to work harder. More clients, more hearings. Never enough time, never enough silver. The points were gone from his worries, but he fretted about the future. How would he earn a living? Would he have to return to scavenging merinite? One afternoon, Talio's stylus snapped, and he hurled the pieces across the room.

"Stop," Emara said, putting her hand down on the vellum before him. Her face was grim. "You can't bring in fees if you are dead."

Before Talio could protest, she picked up the vellum sheets and held them out of reach. "Tonight, you will come with me," Emara said.

"Where are we going?"

"I have been watching you for the last two weeks. You need a break, some kind of change. I've made a decision."

She pushed a scrap of vellum with an address on it at him. "There is a group of people I meet with regularly. You will take the evening off and join us."

She gave him a calculating look. "We call it a secret society."

# Chapter Twenty-Six

The address Emara gave him was in a fashionable, crowded area down by the harbor. It did not seem to him as if a secret society would make their home there. Talio had little call to visit the harbor; it was such a pity that Nuciferia had built its highest buildings in that area, blocking the view of the ocean.

"These are my rooms," Emara said, joining him on the narrow street. "We're going somewhere else." It came as a surprise to Talio that she could afford to live somewhere that expensive, but she would be the type to save her coins. She would have negotiated an excellent deal on rent, or she might have intimidated the landlord.

The second address was two streets over, still in the expensive district. She knocked at a set of double doors on the main floor, then presented her identity key and motioned for Talio to do the same. They performed the water ritual and entered the main rooms.

The inside was spacious, high-ceilinged and gilded, filled with elegant people and the splashing of fountains. The first thing Talio noticed was that everyone in the room was a woman. The second was that there were no Incarnites. Even a few months ago, he would not have noticed their absence, but he had become keenly aware of their position—and lack thereof—in Nuciferian society.

He saw Minka sitting on a couch talking to two women who were holding hands. On the other side of the cavernous room, he was surprised to see Dovuta. There was no sign of Gawani.

"Is this really a conspiracy?" Talio whispered. Minka had spoken of a group of women, and here she was. It still seemed rather prosaic to him.

"They are not plotting the downfall of Nuciferia," Emara said. "But they don't make their presence known to others." He thought of her negotiated absence from work one evening a week. She must have been coming here all this time.

A group of women clustered around someone in the far corner, and Emara led him toward them. So many secret groups in Nuciferia. These women. The network of men who preferred men. The Incarnites. The underworld of Vinne and Oran Keel. The conspirators behind the codices. These groups clearly flourished in societies where their needs were not being met.

The woman in the chair was immense, rolls of fat hanging over her sides. She had short red hair with no bonnet, spectacles and pale skin, and wore a dark shawl over her dress. Talio and Emara waited to talk to her.

Minka came over to greet Talio. "You have found us," she said to him.

"I do not know what I have found."

She laughed. "We simply want somewhere to meet and plan, once a month. Somewhere without men."

"Why?"

"I will let Avelle tell you," Minka said, pointing to the large, seated woman. "She speaks for all of us."

Dovuta was next to come talk to him. "Thank you," she said. No slaps tonight.

"For what?"

"Defending Pazli." Not Master Mecomb. "Does that surprise you?"

"He is a difficult person to warm to, even after you get past his outer shell."

Dovuta nodded. "But he is someone worth knowing. Once, he gave me advice on how to repair some crockery. And then we began talking a bit, each time he came by. A smart man. Too smart to be a junkman." She smiled. "Better to be an advocate."

This was a different Dovuta than he knew. She was friendly, composed. His former wife had spoken of the pressure her mother exerted on her. Dovuta, in a subtle rivalry with her own daughter? A pleasant woman when Gawani was not around. Much like water in the absence of fire had no reason to boil.

"I will tell him I saw you." Though he would not describe the specific circumstances.

"Let him know the new junkman is no good." A hint of the old Dovuta.

"And where is Gawani?" he asked.

Dovuta gave him a wave and walked away. "She does not believe women should be separate from men."

Talio took a moment to try to catalog the women in the room. A few of them wore the red pins of the Royal Palace. He recognized a couple of administrators from the higher levels of the Palace of Justice. There was Minka and Dovuta, and Lady Safana made an appearance as well. Lastly, he noted several noblewomen he'd had the pleasure of meeting at social events when he'd been married to Gawani. This was a powerful group. Powerful enough to influence the creation and distribution of codices.

Talio's pulse pounded in his ears. A conspiracy of women. Hadn't Minka Schell suggested as much when Talio first met her after returning to Nuciferia? *There are women in the Palace of Justice who have a vested interest in such things.* Women had only begun to assert their equality to men in the past thirty years, not counting the primacy of the queens and princesses. Perhaps Queen Jocanda was aware of this group. But what did the different sentencing guidelines in each city have to do with the rights of women? And how much danger was he in right now?

Emara finally pushed him in front of Avelle. "This is Talio Rossa," she said. "The advocate."

Avelle's chest heaved with her breaths. "I know you by reputation, of course." She added with a smile, "Welcome to our little conspiracy."

Talio would never get another chance to confront them like this. The group did not look violent, and Emara and Minka were here. He had to press his case, to find out why they were maintaining this elaborate grip on the laws of Merin. "I know what you are doing with the sentencing guidelines," he said.

She shook her head in confusion. "I'm sorry, I don't understand." Avelle waved a thick arm around. "We have advocates in our group, of course. Emara is quite keen. And sentencing is an important issue in matters of social justice."

He had to choose his words very carefully. "The different sentencing guidelines for each city."

"Scodel's laws have been both a blessing and a curse." Avelle smiled again. "No matter how different the personality of each city, the sentences the magistrates hand down are always the same across Merin. No matter how much our group presses for reform."

Then she had no idea of the secret of the codices. The women had a conspiracy of their own. *Matters of social justice*. Talio relaxed. He could not think ill of this group, not with Minka, Emara and even Dovuta among its members. This conspiracy of women was certainly intriguing, but the answers to the codex mystery lay elsewhere.

The large woman cocked her head at him. "Do you know who Amina was?" Talio shook his head. He had the faintest memory of the name from Clemente's lecture when he'd gone to see him at the law school.

"What do you know about the creation of our judicial system?" Avelle asked.

"What every advocate knows." He shrugged. "After the War of the Cities, the unified government captured the remaining merinite and subdued the rogue mages. Then it asked Scodel to bring democracy to every city."

"And the specifics?"

He gave another, slower shake of his head. There had never been much focus on this aspect. The literature treated it as a divine revelation from Felle. *Praise Scodel.* "I assume he reviewed the documents of each city's legal system, chose the best parts and combined them to form our current laws. 'Let four streams flow and may four cities bloom.'"

"Amina was an ambassador during Scodel's era," Avelle said. "She was the one who did the research. She was the one who took the historical concept of mages as arbiters and transformed the role of *mage* into *magistrate*. She was the one who presented the set of completed laws to the government. She was the one who petitioned the Sleepy Queen. And she was the one who called a constitutional convention ten years after they enacted the laws in order to ratify them permanently. She was the author of our legal system, not Scodel."

Out of the corner of his eye, Talio saw Emara frown. No, she would not believe in Avelle's story, regardless of what evidence the woman provided. If indeed she had evidence.

"Is that your conspiracy, then?" Talio asked. "Concealing the truth about how our legal system was founded?"

A group of women gathered around them. "Not at all," Avelle said. "Amina's system was brilliant, but it was created fifty years ago. Since then, Merin has become stagnant. We need legal progress, and the magistrates and law professors treat Scodel's words as untouchable." She pointed to herself modestly. "And so, we work behind the scenes, each of us, to give Merin little pushes here and there. An appointment to a Judicial Review Committee. A queen's representative with the ear of Queen Jaconda, advising against mediation for government matters. Medical hearings to remove healers preaching superstitious cures and nonsensical treatments. Even clerks who strategically lose forms."

"What do you hope to accomplish?" Talio asked. No, they were not the conspirators he sought. Much as he'd once twisted the words of Scodel as magistrate, they merely worked around the edges of the system.

"Why, what everyone who works in the legal system does," Avelle said. "To build a more perfect Merin."

His audience with her was over. The women talked of government, of politics, of the Sleepy Queen and the Smiling Queen and which one had been best for the citizens. They spoke of moral and ethical issues: poverty, medical care, the homeless, rights to waterways. The justice they discussed was the justice of doing, of obligation and charity—not merely verdicts handed down by magistrates in a marble-clad building. Once Avelle finished her talk of Scodel and

Amina, Talio's thoughts were free for the first time in months. When he got back to the inn, he fell asleep at once.

Much later that night, he bolted upright in bed with a realization. The constitutional convention had been planned for ten years after the laws went into effect. The same year that Scodel died. The only recorded skyline fatality ever, aside from Joban's test run. Nobody had ever noticed this coincidence. Merin history had Amina as a mere footnote, a long-forgotten ambassador without even a last name. And the conspiracy of women saw her as a pure and virtuous heroine.

Had someone silenced Scodel to ensure the ratification of his laws? Why would he be against his own legal system unless Amina had been the one responsible for creating it?

More than ever, Talio needed to see the words on that obelisk.

# Chapter Twenty-Seven

Pazli told Talio the Palace of Justice was going to staff the end-of-year party with Incarnites. "They approached our temple some time ago to hire us for the event," Pazli said. "I explained I had prior plans. As a guest."

He was still the only Incarnite advocate at the Palace, although they'd heard of others who were planning to apply for licenses in the fall. "The idea of a group of Incarnites serving a group of Nuciferians at a party troubles me," Talio said. "It is not a pleasant image."

The other man shrugged. "I do not imagine any of the attendees will complain. And the public is unlikely to find out."

Talio took some money from the Double Moon law firm's operating funds to buy some large-format vellum and new flints. They would need both for their plans at the end-of-season party. Cale had agreed to store the materials in his rooms at the Palace, as long as they were inconspicuous.

Vinne still had not given him any hint of his progress on the miraculous machine that could open any merinite-coded lock without a key. Every time Talio looked at him with a question in his eyes, he shook his head and said, "No." Once Talio snuck into Vinne's rooms and lifted the innkeeper's eyelid as he slept. "Still no," was the response from the immobile man.

Talio and Pazli had been discussing their plan for the party during lunches at the Double Moon. When he was sure they had a workable idea, he outlined their idea to Cale in quick whispers as the two of them stood in line for a hearing.

All Cale asked was, "Do you trust Pazli?"

"Do you trust me?"

"Very well." Now Cale looked uneasy. "I also need to discuss something else of importance with you."

"I am free tonight. But I will be busy after that until the hearing begins."

"Meet me at the hospital then," the prosecutor said. "The one by the southern exchange station. After supper. Our last meeting in my rooms landed me in trouble with the owners of the dormitory. This is all I can arrange." His expression was somber. "I apologize in advance."

* * *

The district by the exchange station was even poorer than the garment district or the area where the Incarnite temple stood. Many of the buildings were deserted; the hospital was dilapidated with a cracked front. Random broken stones lay on the street in front of it.

In a chilly room on the fourth floor, a shrunken white-haired man lay in a cot swaddled under several blankets. Cale sat before him, spooning mashed fruit into his mouth. The prosecutor looked up as Talio came in, frustration and sadness in his eyes. After rinsing his hands in the ritual basins and praying, Talio came over to the bed.

"Where is my wife?" Master Faro asked him. The man's eyes were rheumy and watery.

"She's at the exchange station," Cale said, as if reading from a summary document. "She will be back within the hour." Another spoonful of mashed fruit. "It will be a while," he whispered to Talio.

Cale's father asked him several times more where his wife was, and Cale repeated the same two sentences each time without emotion. When he finished feeding him, they found an empty room to talk. Talio couldn't help but comment. "From what you'd told me about your father, I was worried you kept him manacled. I see you are much kinder."

"Being here is bad enough for him. I used to want to get back at him for how he treated me. But I can't punish the man he once was by hurting him today."

Talio knew the hospital, run-down as it was, must be costly. "Is there nothing cheaper?"

"Of course. I have seen the facilities for the poor. They toss the patients into a large room. Strap them into beds. No gutters. No basins. Not even cups for the ritual waters, if you can believe it. They treat them like animals unless you have money." Cale's eyes were haunted.

Talio touched the man's shoulder. "Thank you for trusting me with this."

"Remember this the next time we are on opposite sides of a legal matter." Cale shook his head. "And on that note, I must talk to you about the upcoming Honell hearing. This is far enough from any prying ears at the Palace of Justice."

"It is Pazli you should be speaking with."

Cale shrugged. "He and I do not get along."

"You are hardly the only one."

"Then I should be flattered," the man said with a laugh. "He is very polite to me. Polite and proper. But it is always winter with him, and never spring."

Talio did not reply.

"You do seem different," Cale said, musing. "Has something changed?"

"He has made a decision about me."

Cale nodded. "Yes, I can see how upset you are. Behind that mask you project." He gave a sudden, beautiful smile. "Then I shall have my chance, after all."

Talio wanted to say yes, but he couldn't. Not yet. "After the party."

"Pazli has botched his chance, and I feel sorry for him. I do not like the man, but I respect him." Cale said. "That is why I want to talk to you about the Honell hearing."

"If you insist, you may speak to me instead."

"Very well. Tell Pazli the government will win this hearing," Cale said.

Talio smiled. "You always claim victory in advance."

"No, you do not understand." Cale bit his lip. "Magistrate Verrane will rule in favor of the government. They have insisted that he do so."

"That is a serious violation," Talio said. "The Ethics Review Committee..." He threw up his hands. "Of course, if the Ethics Review Committee were ever to publish a pamphlet, the cover should have a prominent drawing of my face."

"I want Pazli to know what to expect," Cale said. "When Verrane announces the dismissal, I am going to have to ask to see Honell's identity key. Right at that moment."

Talio could not understand why Cale asked to talk to him. "Then I will tell Pazli to marshal his arguments against you. And hope that he plays the game of law well."

"Is that all this is to you?" Cale burst out. "A game? Do you not care about Honell? About the parents?"

"Of course we do."

"Not Pazli. You." The man's dark eyes were intense. "What are Honell's interests? Hobbies? Hopes for the future?"

Talio could not answer. He did not know. Honell was an abstract principle, a cause of action. Clemente had been right about him, after all. *Always with the tricks.* Or the points. No sense of the people behind the case.

"It matters that much to you, then," Talio said. "What happens to that child?"

"Yes, it does." He saw the shadow of Master Faro in Cale's eyes.

"Then Pazli shall have to win an impossible hearing." Talio smiled. "If anyone can do it, I believe he can."

They sat in silence until Talio leaned forward and gave Cale a gentle kiss. "Still, I am glad you are not physically restraining your father."

Cale sighed. "If I had the opportunity to play at being a god, I would not wish this on him. He has finally taught me one thing in his old age: that I am a better person than I thought I was."

* * *

Very reluctantly, Talio told Pazli of the government's plans. Then he wished he had not said anything; he could sense the change in the man's mood at once.

Knowing that Verrane would rule against him no matter what he said or did was a damper on Pazli's spirit and creativity. He could go to the Ethics Review Committee, but given his partnership with Talio, they would slam the door in his face.

Talio asked to join Pazli on his last visit to Honell before the hearing. Cale was right; he had been treating Honell as a legal matter rather than a person. "You have to tell the Tamms," he told Pazli. "The case is hopeless."

"Is it better to allow them to dream, or to dash their hopes?" The other man shook his head. "You once told me you were fond of the truth. Very well, we will tell Honell the truth."

During the winter, Honell's family took rooms in a district near the Double Moon. They were wealthy enough that Honell had their own private space.

Pazli sat on the small bed, silent. Talio walked around it as the youth sat at a child's worktable. He looked at the paintings, the toys, the games. Then he joined the man on the bed and waited for him to speak. "We cannot win the hearing," Pazli said at last.

"Don't you think I'm right?" Honell asked.

Pazli shook his head. "It does not matter what I think. You are fighting the Nuciferian government and the Royal Palace. It is like pushing water uphill."

"I will tell my story."

"That might be even worse." Pazli pressed his palms together. "If I ask you questions, they will ask you other ones. Unpleasant questions. They will try to make you look wrong, or bad, or like a child who knows nothing." Talio held onto the belief that Cale would not pressure Honell under questioning, but if Pazli examined them, the government would force the prosecutor to cross-examine.

"What do we do?" Honell asked, sounding very young. "Do we stop the hearing? Like the government did?"

"It may be better if we lose the hearing. Do you understand?" Honell shook their head.

"It is difficult to explain," Pazli said. "Many grown-up things are. Tell me something. What would you like to do when you are an adult?"

Honell pondered the question. "Work in a building. Not the fair. Make things or tell people my ideas. Be a magistrate."

Talio smiled. "That is a respectable job, if you can get it. I was a magistrate once."

"How did you become one?" Always the same question, from Pazli, from Cale.

"I came to Nuciferia when I was a young man. A few years older than you." Talio rocked back and forth on the bed, remembering. "I had to work in construction, because I did not know how to do anything else."

Those years were so long ago, yet close enough to remember well. "I met someone who helped me," he said. "Someone who paid for my schooling. And later, I became a magistrate."

Honell didn't answer. "You would enjoy being a magistrate," Talio said. "You can tell other people your ideas all the time."

"I want to do that now," they said at last.

Pazli put a hand on Honell's shoulder. "If you lose, there may be enough of an outcry to force changes. Outside of the legal system."

Honell shook their head. "But I'd lose."

"In the short term, perhaps. But in the longer term, every Incarnite like you may win. If we approach this hearing in the right way."

Talio and Pazli walked away from the Tamms' rooms in silence. Normally Talio was the one to break the silence, but it was the other man who spoke first this time. "What are you thinking?" Pazli said at last.

"That you may be wrong in this situation," Talio said gently.

"Your usual train of thought. And, as you would say, a foolish one."

It was nearly dusk. Talio put a hand on the man's cloak. "I am glad I came today. Glad I had a chance to meet Honell and hear what they had to say."

Pazli raised his hand to Talio's, touching it for a brief moment. "You believe I should examine them in the hearing. Question them. Humanize them, no matter the cost to the youth." He shook his head. "It will not convince Magistrate Verrane. And I doubt that Advocate Faro will look kindly on this approach."

"Cale might surprise you," Talio said. "You are right about Verrane. What I am hoping is that you may end up convincing someone far more important: Queen Jaconda."

# Chapter Twenty-Eight

On the day of the hearing, there was a protracted line to get into the hearing room as other members of the Palace of Justice and the public waited for a limited set of audience seats. Talio took advantage of the delay to duck into the restroom in the rotunda and splash cold source water on his face.

Gawani entered and joined him at the basins, whispering the prayer to Felle. "I wish the Double Moon good luck today," she said, red hair neatly tucked under her bonnet as usual.

"I thought you would be on the side of the government. As a public defender."

She put a hand to his shoulder. "I am on the side of a man I was fond of, a very long time ago. And a student I remember very well." Gawani smiled. "Do you know why I asked you to defend Pazli Mecomb?"

Talio straightened his suit jacket and checked his reflection. "Because none of the other defenders would do it."

She brushed his hands away and fussed at his collar. "Nobody would take him as a client. He didn't have the silver to pay the private advocates, and the other public defenders did not want the loss on their records." She licked her thumb and wiped at a spot on his cheek. "But later I realized that was not the real reason."

"You wanted to see me again?"

She shook her head. "Only you would make sure things came out right, no matter what. No matter how you had to twist everything around. I knew you would exonerate Pazli no matter what."

He stepped away from Gawani. "I did not do the right thing ten years ago."

Her face held the wistful smile he'd known so well. "With the benefit of hindsight, I believe you did. But that is something for us to discuss once this hearing is over."

There were so many spectators the guards finally left the doors to the hearing room open and placed additional chairs outside. Honell and their parents sat at the plaintiff's desk while Talio, Pazli and Emara removed their papers from their satchels. Pazli had the idea to bring Emara onboard, in case Cale or Verrane directed the hearing into medical territory. "Are you ready?" Pazli asked Honell. The youth nodded.

Attendants roped off a small part of the audience area. Talio was curious about who reserved it until he heard a commotion outside the hearing room. A guard appeared, lifting her upturned hands twice to indicate that everyone should stand.

It was Queen Jaconda. Paintings of the queen hung in every hall and public place, and Talio had last glimpsed her during the ceremony to proclaim him magistrate thirteen years earlier. She looked now as she had then: small, fine, with delicate porcelain features and braided black hair. The right side of her mouth twisted in a permanent wry smile, or a smirk. She led her group to the roped-off area, and they sat, followed by the rest of the audience. *No pressure*, he thought.

Talio thought of all the Incarnites who could not or would not be there today. All those who believed as Honell did. The ones who were waiting for one person to step forward, to succeed on their behalf. No pressure, indeed.

Magistrate Verrane shambled to his desk, settling his bulk in the chair and pushing up his spectacles. Talio had come to realize Verrane was not a terrible magistrate. On the Judicial Review Committee, he tried to be judicious and impartial—as far as Clemente allowed. At the hearings they'd worked on since Skyways, Verrane had given him ample time to develop and present his arguments. If it were not for his cursed pamphlets, Talio might even like him.

"We pray for guidance," Verrane intoned. "And wisdom. May your knowledge flow through us and grant us the ability to make the correct decision in this legal matter." After he called the hearing to order, Pazli rose.

"Magistrate, I wish to make a request at this time. I ask the Crown's mercy in not requesting identification from the plaintiff during the hearing." He had explained to Talio that if the government forced Honell to produce their identity key before the hearing started, Cale would argue the issue was moot, since Honell suffered no obvious harm.

"If the advocate for the defense has no objections." Cale shook his head.

The scribe read out the summary document. There were no surprises. The cause of action was straightforward; Honell claimed that the Nuciferian government had failed to accommodate their sincere belief that they were neither male nor female, had not provided them with a way to record this in official documents or their identity key, and had threatened them with arrest. Honell sought specific performance as a remedy.

Talio was unused to being a spectator at a hearing. He was nervous for Pazli. But the man stood before the crowded room with confidence; when he addressed the magistrate, his voice was clear and firm. He never had anything to worry about. This was exactly where Pazli belonged. Just as Talio and Emara belonged by his side. She sat alert and watchful beside him. He felt a swell of pride then, for all three partners in the Double Moon law firm.

Pazli reserved his opening statement, as did Cale. They were both treading gingerly at this point. Talio imagined Cale was still smarting from the outcome of the previous Honell hearing and did not want to repeat that catastrophe.

"I call my client, Honell Tamm, as a witness," Pazli said.

Whispers stirred in the hearing room. Pazli had no other choice. Fighting on the grounds of policy or natural science was like trying to swim upstream.

Cale was leaning forward, waiting for his moment.

Pazli stood before the desk and addressed Honell. "How old are you?"

"Eleven."

Honell answered his questions about where they lived and what their parents did. Talio wondered how far Cale would let him go in his questioning. Pazli's goal was to humanize the youth, to make the audience aware of what was at stake for a single, unique citizen. Verrane would rule against Honell regardless, but Pazli had the weapon of public opinion.

"Are you a boy or a girl?" Pazli asked.

"Objection," Cale said, rising. "That is a matter for an expert witness to decide."

Pazli spoke to him in a grave voice. "Is it, Advocate Faro? If I were to ask you if you were a man or a woman, would we require an expert witness to examine your trousers? Or would you be able to tell us yourself?" Talio winced. Pazli was letting his feelings about Cale rise to the surface.

Titters in the audience. "Magistrate," Cale said to Verrane, "the defense's argument rests upon proving that a person must be either male or female. This is an attempt to prejudice your opinion through the testimony of a vulnerable minor."

"I shall endeavor not to be prejudiced," Verrane said. "Overruled."

Pazli repeated the question. "Neither," Honell said. "Not a boy, not a girl. Something else."

"How do you feel when someone asks you for your identity key?"

"Objection," Cale repeated. "This is an attempt to play on our sympathies. Specific performance will not be awarded based on how Honell *feels*."

Pazli shrugged. "In the last related hearing, Advocate Rossa used a defense based upon our fundamental legal principles of individual sovereignty. As a result"—here he pointed at Cale with a finger—"the government dismissed the hearing against Honell. This advocate was quite happy to waste everyone's time preparing for a hearing that ended immediately. I can only assume that Advocate Faro and the government both agreed with my colleague's reasoning. Today, I will show how failure to act upon Scodel's general principles has harmed this citizen emotionally and deprived them of their rights physically. This follows directly from the previous argument. My question about feelings goes to the matter of emotional harm. If the government—and the tireless Advocate Faro—agreed with the reasoning in the first hearing, I should hope they would agree with us now. Or perhaps I need to rephrase this in simpler terms." When Cale shot him a look, Pazli added, "I believe the scribe is having trouble keeping up with me."

Pazli had no other options. Verrane would still rule against him, but this was a goad for Cale to act. Did the government want the testimony of a helpless child read into the record? Pazli would question Honell for days if necessary to make his point. His voice was even and calm, but certainly Talio was not the only one to see his anger roiling below the surface.

One of the royal peacekeepers stood and approached Cale with a note. Cale read it and looked at Pazli in frustration. Then he said to the magistrate, "At this point, we request summary dismissal." Talio closed his eyes. He had made the right decision after all. Even if he'd taken on the hearing, he would never have gotten his license back.

The voices in the audience were loud enough to drown out Verrane rapping on his desk with his fingers. "Order. There will be order. In the name of the queen, we will have order!"

The hearing room quieted down again. "The matter before us is simple," Verrane said. "Honell has been asked to surrender his or her identity key for identification and has refused to do so. I have seen the preliminary documentary evidence, and I remain unconvinced that there is some third alternative between male and female." He shook his head. "A belief must be reasonable. In this matter, I find that Honell's belief is unreasonable. The hearing is summarily dismissed, costs to be determined in the Hall of Equity at a later date."

Talio placed a hand on Honell's shoulder, and the youth shrugged it off. What could he say to them? There could be no success in a hearing room. This was the only lever Pazli could pull to sway public opinion.

"As representative for the Nuciferian government," Cale said, "I request that Honell present their identity key at this time." Talio had been expecting this. The government had to make this public, to drive home that nobody was above the law.

"No! I won't!" Honell was on their feet in an instant. The youth raced down the aisle and out of the hearing room. Their parents ran after them in front of the bewildered audience.

A few minutes later, a peacekeeper dragged Honell back into the room and stood them in front of the defense desk, an angry Jani and Ulric trailing behind. "Please give me your identity key," Cale said in a gentle voice.

Honell gave him the key. Cale examined it, nodded very slightly at Pazli, then turned to Verrane. "The child has provided satisfactory identification."

"Then we are done here," Verrane said. "Unless the advocate for the plaintiff wishes to use his deferred statement at this time."

Pazli turned to face the audience. "I am aware that appeals are rare in our justice system," he said. "I would hope that in the government's infinite wisdom, such an appeal will be heard, no matter how high it must go." He said this last while looking toward Queen Jaconda, who gazed back with her penetrating green eyes and smirk. Magistrate Verrane rapped his fingers to draw the hearing to a close.

Jani and Ulric pushed past the peacekeeper and held Honell in their arms. "You're all monsters," Ulric said. "Monsters." Nobody else spoke as they walked out of the hearing room.

The queen and her retinue were next to leave; the audience rose and waited until she was gone before they filed out. There was a dismal feeling in the air.

Talio, Pazli and Emara went to the restroom by the rotunda. Inside they found a youth in an Incarnite cloak and hood sitting in one stall, the door to it ajar. "What happened when my friend gave up her key?" Honell asked.

"Your friend was very brave," Emara said. "The defense advocate didn't question the key."

It had been a trick, but a trick in the service of one citizen's dignity. When Honell ran out of the hearing room, their Incarnite friend was waiting in the restroom to change places with them. It was that girl who surrendered her key. Talio had suggested the idea to Pazli; he'd gambled on Cale's ethics and his compassion for a helpless child, like the one the prosecutor had once been.

"Maybe he didn't see her name on it," Honell said.

"No. Advocate Faro saw the girl's name on the key," Pazli said. His voice no longer had the undercurrent of anger; he merely sounded sad. He placed a hand on Honell's shoulder. "I believe he simply did not want to punish you any further."

* * *

The next day, Talio returned to the Palace in search of Gawani. He wanted to put their past behind them, to see if they could tear down the wall that still separated them. He would never stop feeling guilty for what he had done, but perhaps they could still be friends.

At the service desk, the stooped elderly man behind the counter nodded and smiled at him. "I'm looking for Gawani Balsamo," Talio explained. The man opened a large register to the last page and reviewed the entries.

"She's reserved a gathering room for herself," the man said in a quavering voice. "Through those doors. She should still be there—it's booked for the next hour."

He had little else to do, so Talio followed the man's directions. The door to the gathering room was ajar, and the room was dark. He pushed the door open. It was empty.

*But she signed in*, Talio thought. He had always signed in and out of the register as a student, as a magistrate, and now as an advocate. As with the message keys and lockboxes, these were rickety social systems that depended on everyone participating voluntarily. Of course, there was nothing to prevent Gawani from signing in retrospectively, or signing in and leaving the Palace for a while without recording her absence...

An awful, terrible idea was forming in his mind. He remembered Gawani's words before the Honell hearing: *I knew you would exonerate Pazli no matter what.*

He raced through the administration building to the Hall of Commerce, hoping Emara would be there. She was leaning against the wall behind the scribe's booth, doing combat exercises with a baton. When he approached, she gave him a wave and stuck the baton under her arm. "Give Pazli my congratulations," she said.

"Are you willing to do something unsavory?" Talio asked her.

"If the money's right."

He explained what he needed, then hung back as she marched up to the administration service desk. Emara complained in a loud voice that she had lost her identity key in a hearing room, that the old man must let her into that hearing room, and that she would not leave him alone until he helped her.

While the man was occupied, Talio stepped up to the service desk and pulled the register toward him. He flipped the pages back to the date of the murder of Selig Ivor.

Gawani's name was also on the register for that day. She had signed in that morning with the note "Judicial Review Committee meeting—morning," and had signed out at day-end. A perfect alibi. Except that Talio knew from experience Judicial Review Committee meetings only took place in the afternoon. Enough time for her to leave the Palace, return to the Balsamo manse, and be back before anyone noticed. There was no risk of her running into the other members of the committee: Darra only came to the Palace of Justice for the afternoon committee meetings, and Verrane taught morning classes. Talio, Pazli and Clemente had not yet joined the committee when Ivor was killed.

He left the service desk and gave Emara a nod. She disengaged from the old man at once. As he walked toward Gawani's cozy rooms, Talio felt the tumblers of his mind slide into place. It was like opening a door with many locks; all you needed was the right set of keys.

Gawani looked up from her worktable. "I was sorry to hear about the Honell matter. Just as I am sorry to hear that you have been unable to earn enough points toward your license."

"Thank you." He sat down across from her. "But I would like to tell you a story now."

Gawani smiled in anticipation. After making love—in the early months, while they still made love—one of them would tell the other a story. Some tall tale from the history of Merin.

This would be a story of a different kind.

Part of him could not bear to speak of it. The words almost died on his lips. It would be easier for him to walk away, to ignore what he suspected. But Talio had to know for sure.

"This is a story about Selig Ivor." No response from Gawani.

"The Ivor family was wealthy, once," Talio said. "Selig and Dovuta knew each other long ago. Perhaps very well. Perhaps well enough for an affair of some kind." The smile was now frozen upon her face. "And then your mother became pregnant with his child."

The shame. The scandal if it were to be revealed. "Your mother could not have a baby out of wedlock. Perhaps Selig even refused to acknowledge that it was his."

"Your mother's family sent her to Rylavia on the pretext of doing charity work," Talio said. "While there, she gave birth to you and brought you back as a foundling."

"Some months ago, Selig had no money and no hope. But he remembered your mother. He decided to ask her for money, threatening to expose her secret." Talio had to continue. "The records of the Rylavian orphanage might confirm his claim. She could not take the chance."

Each word was torture. He had said such things many times to an accused. But this time, it was to someone he'd once loved more than anything else. Each word was a step away from her, forever. "She agreed to see him at the manse. You found out somehow. And you would not let Selig Ivor tell the Balsamo family secret."

"No," Gawani said at last in a horrible rasp. "None of that is true."

He remained silent. It did not matter either way. Gawani always wore gloves. Nobody would have checked her hands after the murder. All these months later there would be no evidence of any staining on her fingers. Would the Rylavian orphanage even release thirty-five-year-old records based on one man's hunch?

Gawani came around the worktable and sat next to him. Up close, he could see dark rings of fatigue under her eyes. "Listen to me. I am not Dovuta Balsamo's daughter by blood," she said with emphasis. "I was born in a Rylavian orphanage. The birth records are at the manse."

That was not the entire truth. Talio could always tell when she was withholding something.

"Do you remember Father?" Gawani asked. What a strange question. He remembered him quite well. Though they'd only known each other for a brief time, he'd made quite an impression on him.

"Lord Balsamo? He was already sick by the time you and I started courting each other."

"Sick. He was always sick. A sick man with a sick mind." Her face was suddenly animated with loathing. "I hated him. Mother detested him. He had a reputation for doing perverse things with perverse people. She only found out once it was too late."

"And Selig Ivor?"

"He had information. Proof of what my father had done all those years ago. With all sorts of people, all sorts of terrible things. Simple infidelity would not have been a problem. My father's...adventures...went far further. Nothing illegal, but enough to bring down my family. Ivor wanted more money than mother and I could afford."

"Gawani," Talio protested. "That was more than ten years ago. Who would care now?"

She tilted her head and gave him that affectionate, frustrated look he remembered quite well: the one she'd given him when he'd used the wrong fork at a dinner party or had greeted a commoner before a noble. "The Balsamo family has been holding onto our reputation for a very long time. You believe being a noble is such a simple thing." Gawani sighed. "Did you never wonder why I work as a public defender? The daughter of a noble family?"

She had once told him it was because she wanted to stay busy. "We have barely enough money to get by," she went on. "I need to work to supplement what little we do have. Any breath of scandal, any hint of impropriety and we could end up like the Ivors, or worse."

*And so, you killed him.* She'd had the idea herself, or Dovuta had asked her to. It did not matter. A thought struck him, "Pazli could have gone to the gallows."

Gawani shook her head with a sad smile. "As I said, I knew you would exonerate him. If anyone could do it, it was you. I made sure neither he nor my mother had dye on their hands."

"Your mother could have fallen under suspicion."

"Would they have accused a noblewoman without clear evidence?" Gawani asked. "And would they have found her guilty if they had? Her hands were clean—literally and figuratively."

Talio had no answer to that. As a public defender, Gawani had taken the same course in logic as he had. Her reasoning was sound with respect to her mother—but she had gambled Pazli's life on Talio's defense skills. He was not sure whether to be flattered or horrified.

"Did you kill Selig Ivor?" he asked at last. "Or did your mother?"

"Mother wanted to get rid of him. She told me she was going to do it. Of course, I begged her not to. I am an officer of the court, after all." He could see her thinking back to that conversation now. "I even threatened to go to the peacekeepers, but it was no use."

"She poisoned Selig Ivor?"

Gawani shook her head. "I could not persuade her not to do it. She would have made a mess of it. It would have been so obvious that a magistrate would have had to find her guilty. She would have been hanged and our family name destroyed. Ivor was going to die, one way or another. I could at least prevent suspicion from falling upon us. So, I told her I would do it instead. Bonnet dye is quite easy to obtain."

Talio had no response. It had been the utterly logical thing for her to do, after all.

Gawani gave a heavy sigh. "Now that you know, what will you do?"

He got to his feet. "I do not think there are any steps I can take. Or want to." He had lost her ten years ago, and now he had lost her all over again.

"Tell me then," she said with a wan expression. "If it had been you in my place, what would you have done? Would you have saved your mother? Your family's reputation?"

He shook his head. "It would be easy for me to answer a hypothetical question. Far more difficult if I was faced with the actual situation." Scodel's laws did not take family obligation into account. Or love, for that matter.

Talio had come to her to renew their friendship, their affection, everything they'd meant to each other short of love. But there was no way he could ever trust her again, now. Some part of him wanted to laugh. He was claiming the moral high ground. She'd had other options open to her than murder. Unpalatable options, perhaps, but she'd rationalized killing Ivor in a way that he never could have.

He pressed his hand to hers, one last time.

"Goodbye, Talio."

"Goodbye, Gawani."

# Chapter Twenty-Nine

The night before the Palace party, the innkeeper finally drew him aside. "I've got something for you."

Talio expected some device or contraption, with wheels and dials. Instead, Vinne gave him a velvet bag that held two simple silver cylinders. "Is this it?" he asked.

"It's taken me weeks to get these," Vinne said. "You could go to prison for looking at them. Yes, this is 'it.' There's one spare, though Felle help you if you need it. Let me show you how they work."

Vinne gave a demonstration on one of his message lockboxes. He pressed a button on the end of one of the cylinders and a thin wire tipped in milky-blue merinite slid out. "This merinite is the real thing," he said. "Someone could buy and sell you with one of these." He inserted the end of the wire into the keyhole. He pushed it in further so that the cylinder was flush with the keyhole. After a few seconds, the lock popped open with a click.

Talio still could not believe it, that such a simple thing could so easily defeat something every Nuciferian relied upon. "Show me."

It took a few minutes for Vinne to instruct him. The first lock was easy to open. The next one refused to budge until Vinne showed him again.

"You're pressing down too hard," the man cautioned him at one point. "You'll crack the merinite, and then our heads will be on the block. Gently. You won't get anywhere being rough."

Talio raised his eyebrows at him with a sly smile. "It's a lock, not a lover," Vinne said. "Didn't know you liked it hard. Learn something every day."

Talio turned back to the lock. "Me neither, until recently." The innkeeper snorted.

When he unlocked all of his message lockboxes, Talio beamed. "We are ready for tomorrow night."

The burly innkeeper shook his head. "I also borrowed some stronger locks." He drew five heavy locks out of the velvet bag and spread them across the bed. "The ones on the Hall of Antiquities are probably going to be more heavy-duty. Better try these, too."

Talio had no problem opening four of them, but neither he nor Vinne could open the final one. "Luck of the draw," Vinne said. "Here's hoping."

The remaining things they needed were already in Cale's rooms at the Palace. Now they were ready.

* * *

The Palace of Justice had provided vouchers for all guests to arrive by canal. Candlelit boats floated upstream starting at dusk. The Palace staff had cordoned off the administration rotunda and decorated it with vellum flowers, garlands and vines. They had diverted and filtered one of the streams from the return gutters to the rotunda to form a multi-level waterfall. Musicians played formal Damirian marches as advocates, magistrates, and other high-level staff circulated around the large room.

And everywhere, there were Incarnite servants in saffron robes, serving food, pouring drinks, and clearing tables of used plates. After Talio and Pazli accepted glasses of soft wine from a passing Incarnite with a tray, a drunken advocate who Talio did not know accosted Pazli, "Where is that rabbit you were going to get me? The rabbit skewers? They were all out."

Pazli pointed to the silver advocate's pin on the front of his cloak and did not reply. Talio gave the drunken man a not-so-gentle shove away from them.

Gawani was speaking to a group of fellow public defenders. Verrane had a group of law students around him, no doubt regaling them with tales of his pamphlets. Emara was holding an animated discussion with Clemente Jilani, of all people. He hadn't even been aware they knew each other. She had studied under him, of course, but Clemente was notorious for keeping his distance from the students. Odd. The Queen's representative, Adan, flitted from one group to the next, but Queen Jaconda was elsewhere.

Cale approached them, resplendent in a dark green cloak. He was anxious, coiled with tension. "Are you ready?"

Talio nodded. "Where's your cousin?" he asked Pazli.

"He is awaiting our signal." Then Pazli asked Cale stiffly, "When will you go?"

"I saw the guards on their rounds a moment ago. We can leave now."

Pazli went over to another Incarnite and touched hoods. They walked toward the restroom and disappeared inside.

Talio grasped Cale's shoulders and turned him around, so they were both facing away from the restroom. "Aren't you the slightest bit curious?" the man asked.

"We promised them we would not look."

"I imagine he has a big nose," Cale said.

They stood facing the wall until Talio felt two taps on his back. He waited another minute, then nodded at Cale. Trying to be casual, the two of them walked to the restroom.

It was empty. Talio bent down and drew out the cloaks and hoods Pazli and his cousin stowed under a cabinet. Cale was retrieving the bag he had hidden earlier that day.

Pazli and his cousin had entered the restroom and removed their hoods and cloaks. Now, Talio and Cale were struggling into the unfamiliar Incarnite clothing. There were two of everything, but Talio knew Pazli's clothing; it smelled of him.

Initially, Talio had suggested simply hiding a pair of Incarnite outfits ahead of time, as they'd done with the vellum and styli. "Each cloak and hood is custom-sewn for the wearer and blessed by a cleric," Pazli had reminded him. "They may not seem holy to you, but they are to us." And so, this roundabout method had been the best solution they'd been able to devise instead.

The Incarnite outfits were constricting. He could barely see in front of him through the slit in the cloth that hung down over his face. The only parts of him showing were his hands. They had agonized that someone would notice they had no hand tattoos, but if someone saw two men in saffron hoods and cloaks, would they think they were anything other than Incarnites? They took the contents of the bag Cale had secreted and put them in their suit pockets under the cloaks: tapers, the large-format vellum, and several styli. Talio also had the lock tools and flints.

"Are you ready?" Cale asked. Talio nodded, and they rejoined the party.

The crowd parted before them. Nobody was looking at him. It was an unusual feeling, not being noticed or judged because of his face. No, he was being watched, but in a way he'd never felt before. Ignored, but scrutinized at the same time. So, this was what it felt like to be an Incarnite.

A part of him was also excited. Pazli was here in the room with his cousin. At this moment, neither of them wore a cloak or a hood; they had come to the party dressed in formal cloaks under their Incarnite outfits. Now they looked like any other partygoers.

"Nobody may look upon me and know that I am Pazli Mecomb," Pazli had told him and Cale. "This is from our catechism. But if I remove my hood and cloak, nobody will know who I am. For an hour, I will dress as a 'regular Nuciferian.' For once." There was amusement in his voice. "Yet another costly dispensation from the cleric. He is allowing me to reveal myself once in this lifetime. In the name of justice."

Talio wanted to look around, to find Pazli, to see him at last. But he and Cale had promised they would not try to figure out who the two Incarnites were without their garb. "We have a little less than an hour," Cale whispered. "We must go."

They each picked up a tray of food and walked toward the far rotunda exit. As Pazli had recommended, Talio kept his hood angled downward in deference.

Once they were outside the rotunda, they abandoned the trays and followed the winding path Cale had plotted through the administration building. Even if someone stopped them, they could claim they were servants who had gotten lost.

Talio saw a peacekeeper approaching. *Be calm*, he thought.

"Your chest!" Cale said.

"What is it?"

"You are still wearing Pazli's advocate's pin. Take it off!"

As the peacekeeper came closer, Talio tugged at the pin. It would not come loose; the clasp was stuck. Pazli must have been unable to remove it. He yanked at it in panic, but the woman was upon them. Talio ended up placing his right palm flat over the pin.

"What are you doing?" the peacekeeper asked, looking at his hand. She was short and tough, like Emara, with a stiff expression. He prayed she did not notice the absence of a tattoo.

Cale pointed to Talio's hand. "He is giving you our traditional blessing. Praise be unto you...from the Incarnites."

The peacekeeper nodded at Talio. "Very well. Thank you for the blessing." She strolled onward.

"Have you ever known a single Incarnite?" Talio asked Cale, shaking his head in disbelief, as they continued forward.

"Only the jealous one you work with."

Talio managed to pry open the clasp of the advocate pin at last and stowed it in Pazli's cloak pocket.

He had not seen the Hall of Antiquities since he returned to Nuciferia, but the entrance was much as he remembered it: dusty, dark and imposing. They removed their hoods, and he used the flint to light a taper, giving it to Cale to light the way.

As expected, the massive door had four heavy locks. Talio retrieved the tools Vinne gave him. "Will those actually work?" Cale asked. Talio shrugged his shoulders and started on the first lock.

The first three went smoothly. Cale stared in amazement as Talio pressed the cylinder with the metal wire to the keyholes and each lock popped open. The last one would not budge.

"Push harder," Cale urged. Vinne had told him not to, but here they were. Talio bore down, and the wire broke with a snap, falling out of the lock.

"Find it!" he said to Cale. "No, keep the light focused on me." He was under strict orders not to break or lose any of these devices. Each of them was probably worth more than the entire Double Moon Inn, land and all. What would the people who owned these tools do to him? Probably try to kill him, like everyone else. They would have to find it on the way out.

Using another cylinder, Talio was able to open the final lock. The Hall of Antiquities was a vast space, cool and dark. After they shut the door behind them, Talio felt comfortable using the flint to light a taper for each of them. They examined the contents of the hall through flickering candlelight. There were coffins, goblets, swords and old documents. The entire history of Merin was laid out before them in artifacts. Scrolls and potions from the time before the War of the Cities, when a mage could determine innocence or guilt simply by touching an accused's forehead. Gowns of royal succession, designed for kings and princes before the queens had assumed their rightful place on the throne. Talio could see himself spending half a lifetime in here.

But there was no obelisk.

"Do you think they moved it?" Cale asked.

"I don't know. Keep looking." Time was slipping away from them.

Cale found a second door. He called Talio over and they stood in front of it. There was no lock. It would not move even the slightest amount when they pushed on it. There was a blue disk of merinite on its front at waist height, covered with symbols.

"Ancient Merin," Talio said. "Did you take the elective?"

Cale shook his head. Neither had Talio; he'd taken a course on ethics instead, of all things. If only he'd brought

Emara. She'd told him she knew Ancient Merin the first time they'd met.

He contemplated the disk. He knew the four ancient symbols around its edge; they represented the Four Cities. Other symbols he did not know appeared at random across the disk. He tried pressing on one symbol and discovered that it slid to one side. The symbols were on a series of concentric rings.

"I suggest we line up the symbols for each city," he said. Aurania was the City of Compassion. He found symbols for a heart, clasping hands, love, a lotus and a feather, then slid the rings so the symbols lined up with the correct cities. The door would not move.

"We do not have time for this," Cale said. "And why would sun and wind be symbols of compassion?" Talio shushed him and tried to think.

It had to be something else. Something easy enough for one who knew the secret, but impossible for a stranger like himself to discover. He thought of Queen Jaconda's smile. The Smiling Queen. Less a smile than a cruel smirk. Tricks. Always tricks.

He slid the rings around again. Aurania was called the City of Compassion; in truth they were the weakest of the four. He lined up the symbols for a broken bone under Aurania. Then, the other cities. Damiria, City of Honor, was cruel: a plate of food below a mouth, but far enough below that the person could not reach it. He knew little of Rylavia, City of Equality, but he assumed the answer would be that it was unequal: a triangle and square, the representational symbols for false and true merinite. And finally, Nuciferia, City of Strength, would be weak. But Aurania was already the weak one. No, the trick of a strongman like Nuciferia was to be a bully. The symbol for an upraised closed hand could also be the symbol of a fist.

The door still did not open. Talio swapped the symbols for the broken bone and the distant plate; cruelty and weakness were very similar. That was enough; the door swung open with a hiss of air. There was no time to explain his reasoning to Cale.

The small chamber was silent and pitch black. Talio held up his taper and took three steps forward. Then he saw it. The Obelisk of Justice.

It was a little taller than he was. At the top, starting with Rylavia, the name of each city appeared. Then came an illustration of Scodel against the stylized rays of the sun. The principles and statutes began below it.

Talio sank to his knees before the obelisk, holding the taper before him. After all this time, he was in awe of the monument before him. An entire legal system, etched on a single structure. Scodel had chiseled these words, the laws which had dictated the course of all of Merin. *Let four streams flow and may four cities bloom.*

"Start reading the sentencing guidelines," Cale urged him. "They should be at the bottom."

They had decided with great reluctance not to bring Cale's codex or the ruined pages with them. If someone caught them, things would already be bad, but being caught with codices on them would mean imprisonment and perhaps a charge of treason. Talio had done his best to memorize a few sentencing rules from each document. He ran his index finger down the engraved text on the obelisk.

Cale moved away from him further into the chamber. None of the sentences Talio read matched what he remembered from the codex or the pages. How could this be?

After a long moment, Cale called to him in a strange voice that held a mixture of awe and dread. "Come here. You must see this."

Talio got to his feet and walked around the obelisk. When he saw what Cale found, he dropped the taper in shock. It rolled away and guttered into darkness, but Cale's taper was still enough to illuminate the scene before them.

There were three other identical Obelisks of Justice in the chamber. Scodel's laws were inscribed on all of them.

# Chapter Thirty

Talio retrieved his dropped taper, relit it and examined the obelisks. "Maybe they are all the same. Each city could have their own copy."

Cale shook his head, examining one more closely. "Then why are they here in Nuciferia?"

"Continue examining them. I have other things to do." Talio started digging through his satchel. For the next part, he would need a sheet of large-format vellum and stylus.

After a moment, Cale jabbed a finger at the obelisk. "I have it." He pointed to the top. "This one has Aurania at the top of the list of cities." He walked over to the first one. "And this one has Rylavia at the top. You are right. Each obelisk belongs to one city."

A suspicion was dawning on Talio. He put down the satchel. "Read the sentencing portion for the Rylavian one," he said. "I will look at the Auranian one. Tell me if you see anything unusual."

A brief time later, Cale looked up. "These are unusual sentences. Community service. Working for the victim of a crime, even. I can't imagine a magistrate in Nuciferia imposing these regularly."

Talio glanced over from his obelisk. "And these are rather gentle."

"Auranians are compassionate people," Cale said. "Compassionate sentencing for a compassionate city?"

"No." Talio felt a growing excitement. "I understand now. It's the reverse."

He pointed to the obelisk with his taper. "This was Scodel's Grand Experiment. Four obelisks. Four separate sentencing systems. The Cities were no longer at war. Scodel gave each city a different obelisk and waited to see what would happen. Which one of these approaches would be the best for all of Merin? Each city's society developed based on their unique sentencing guidelines: restoration, kindness, cruelty, perhaps forgiveness." Had it truly been so, though?

Was fifty years long enough to change entire societies through sentencing guidelines alone? Talio thought back to the historic folk art and encouraging banners of his childhood in Aurania. Perhaps the four cities had always had these inclinations, and Scodel had merely used the different codices to nudge their tendencies along.

There was no time to theorize further. Talio retrieved the vellum sheets and styli. He positioned the vellum over the sentencing guidelines on the Nuciferian obelisk. Then he began rubbing the side of the stylus against it to make a copy. "It's not working," he said after a time.

"Let me try." Cale added his effort, but to no avail. The vellum was too rough and thick, and the engraving too fine to make a clear impression. Their plan hinged on them finding proof of their theory, and now that proof would have to wait.

They could not stay. "We have done what we could. Now we must get back to the party."

They bundled the supplies into their satchels and closed the door to the obelisk chamber behind them. Talio had a moment of panic when he realized he did not remember the original position of the merinite rings. He hoped nobody would notice.

He and Cale spent a frantic few minutes outside the door to the Hall of Antiquities searching for the wire from the cylinder device. At last, they heard a guard approaching, and had to abandon their hunt. It had to have rolled away under a display case. Talio could not even imagine what he was going to say to Vinne.

Nobody disturbed them on the way back. Cale and Talio stood in front of the rotunda's restroom in their Incarnite wear for a full minute to signal Pazli and his cousin that they had returned. Then they entered the restroom and removed their cloaks and hoods, hiding them and the satchels where they found them.

Once Pazli and his cousin assumed their Incarnite clothing once again, he rejoined Talio and Cale. "I will leave you to discuss the finer points of jurisprudence," Cale said, tipping his glass at Talio and ignoring Pazli. He went off to join a group of prosecutors, each bearing the violet pin of their profession.

Talio quickly described their discoveries to Pazli. "Have we succeeded, then?" the man asked.

"Somewhat," Talio said. "We know there is a separate set of sentencing provisions for each city. We think we know why. But there remains the question: why keep up this pretense after fifty years? What benefit is there to continuing to have four separate sentencing systems? Would Scodel have not meant for his Grand Experiment to conclude at some point?"

"It must have felt remarkable to make such a momentous discovery," Pazli said.

"Everything is momentous in the Hall of Antiquities. I wish you could have been there." Talio gave him a smile. "It has been a long evening."

Three royal peacekeepers appeared before them, accompanied by the Queen's representative, Adan. "Good evening," he said to Talio with a grave expression.

"Good evening."

The man gave a little bow. "Advocate Rossa, the queen has requested your presence for an audience. Will you please accompany me? Alone."

* * *

The queen and her retinue commandeered one of the larger gathering rooms. Banners of royal red hung to her left and right in the frigid air. Queen Jaconda sat on a stuffed, ornate chair. She watched Talio as he entered. Clemente Jilani stood to her left, arms behind his back. None of this could be good.

Talio bowed, then took a knee. "You may rise and approach," the queen said.

Up close, he saw something he had never noticed in the drawings of the queen. Each of her eyes looked in a different direction. The flaw was slight, but once Talio noticed it, he could not stop glancing from one eye to the other. How she must hate her subjects' darting eyes; did she even realize the reason? "Your Majesty," Talio said.

"Your law office has put me in an uncomfortable position," the queen said.

"I apologize, your Majesty."

The queen leaned forward. "No, I do not believe you are sincere." Talio stole a look to his right at Clemente. The man was expressionless. His presence worried him a great deal.

"I understand you are one who likes tricks," the queen said. "And so let us talk of tricks tonight. We disapprove of the Incarnite's handling of the second Honell hearing."

"There were no tricks in that hearing." Talio hoped dearly that Cale had told no one of the true nature of that identity key.

"Your law office insisted on bringing an unwinnable cause of action. You wanted us to dismiss the hearing to garner sympathy for the child," the queen said. "The boy. The girl. Whichever."

"As you say," Talio commented. "A cause of action that Advocate Mecomb could not win. A predetermined outcome and a predetermined verdict." It had been Pazli's case. Why had the queen not requested his presence? He knew the answer all too well.

Clemente came forward. "It was necessary," he said. "Strictly from a financial perspective."

Talio looked at him, the birdlike man in his ill-fitting magistrate's robes. "Then why allow a hearing to proceed at all? You wanted to drag Honell through the sewers. Tarnish the credibility of a child."

"Silence," the queen said without raising her voice. "This is not a hearing room, and you are not making a closing argument." She frowned. "By filing this claim, you and the Incarnite ensured that the court of public opinion would weigh in on the matter. And this we do not like."

"The Incarnite has been infected by Advocate Rossa's excessive enthusiasm," Clemente said.

"Enthusiasm and zeal are very close to each other," the queen said. Then to Talio, she added, "I need some way of making this matter go away. Of making this Honell disappear. Something that will not cost us millions in silver."

Talio was about to speak, but the queen waved a hand at him. "Do not interrupt. There is a solution that will do several useful things. As the commoners say, it will 'kill two fish with one spear.'"

The gathering room seemed very warm. Talio wanted to tug at his collar, but he stood stock-still. The queen stood and approached him. She was as tall as he was, but her regal air gave her the appearance of added height. "Talio, we would promote you to the Royal Palace as a legal advisor." She paused. "The unofficial title would be Legal Advisor for the Incarnite Question. They are growing in number, and we must deal with them. Welcome them into the royal body. It will provide a useful distraction from the Honell matter. For a while."

The chance to influence policy at the Royal Palace. A way to change the circumstances of the Incarnites directly. But Talio had an acute awareness of Pazli and all of the other Incarnites who had not been consulted. "Might there be a place for an Incarnite as well?" he asked. "To bring their unique perspective to these matters?"

Queen Jaconda shook her head. "Incarnites do not belong in the Royal Palace. We need the perspective of a worshipper of Felle."

"Involving an Incarnite would do a great deal to deflect their concerns," Talio said. He recalled Vedan's mission. "Now that they are planning on building temples in other cities, it would make sense to have them on your side and avoid any...unrest. Your Majesty."

Her eyes were the cold green of deep water. "Very well. I assume you are referring to Pazli Mecomb."

"I am."

A curt nod. "He shall be your assistant, with no named title. He may only work with you outside the Royal Palace. We will listen to his suggestions." Listen, but not implement.

"Yes, your Majesty." The queen had said nothing about the Hall of Antiquities or the obelisks. Had he and Cale managed to escape unnoticed?

"I am sending you away from Nuciferia," the queen said. "You and the Incarnite. Clemente feels that Kallis's ideas regarding mediation might be better used to administer Incarnite justice, instead of hearings against the government."

Clemente nodded and stepped forward. "Kallis is another legal mind with excessive zeal. The Incarnites would be best served with a more compassionate approach, however." He gave a little smile. "I have been at the Palace of Justice long enough to know just how compassionate Auranians can be."

It was all too much to take in, but he had to try to focus, think about this new opportunity. "Thank you, your Majesty," Talio said.

She gave the slightest incline of her head, then turned away and walked back to her chair. He had been dismissed.

Clemente did not meet his eyes. Talio bowed in the direction of the queen's back, then an idea struck him. "Your Majesty. About Honell. I have a suggestion."

The queen turned back, face impassive. He went on, "Choose one small area of government affected by the issue. Start with a minor change. There could be an additional mark on identity keys—nothing that needs recording in the organizational system. Similar to the one for intersex individuals. See how disruptive the change is." He smiled. "It may relieve some pressure from public opinion. And we may find that accommodation is not as expensive as the royal body might think." Or that the expense could be amortized over all of the Incarnites in the same category as Honell. If they came forward at last.

"As you say, Talio, we will consider it. You will leave for Aurania two days hence."

The royal peacekeepers accompanied him back to the rotunda, where the party was still in progress. Pazli rejoined him. "What did the queen want?"

Talio relayed the conversation as faithfully as he could, cringing when he got to the part where the queen had offered him the position at the Royal Palace, with Pazli as his untitled assistant. Then he waited.

"Your assistant," Pazli said, contempt evident in his voice.

"It sounds terrible, but I could work on the Incarnites' behalf more effectively at the Royal Palace. And I would consult you regularly. There might even be room for you there at some point."

"The Incarnites are not a question." Pazli stood with his arms behind his back, a still form among the party guests. "And we do not need your help."

"But you do," Talio said in surprise. "I have been doing nothing but help, for months now. You asked me to. The Incarnites lined up outside of the Double Moon to seek my services."

"We are not children. We do not need you to take care of us."

The wine was going to Talio's head. "No. You have misinterpreted everything. I have done what I could to assist you. Not to patronize or control you."

"You had another goal." The bitterness was unmistakable; Talio had not heard it for so long.

"What goal is that?"

"Winning," Pazli said. "Power. You defended me in order to erase the blot on your legal career. You took advantage of the Skyways hearing to strike a blow at Master Verrane and his pamphlets. You used Honell as a springboard to raise your profile, and now the queen has taken notice of you."

"That is an unfair interpretation." Talio sensed another feeling underlying Pazli's anger, something that drove the man onward. He was poking at the story of the last several months, trying to find a string that he could pull so that it would all unravel. How much easier for Pazli to attribute Talio's actions to ambition, to push him away, than to admit the feelings they shared.

Pazli broke into his river of thought. "Would you have ever taken up the Incarnite cause if it had not ensnared you by circumstance?"

He could lie to him, but Pazli was right. Talio would have continued to live a comfortable life far from the Incarnites, thinking of them as nothing more than a blight on the city. He bit his lip and remained silent.

Pazli folded his arms. "Don't do that," Talio said softly. He wanted to reach over and spread the man's arms apart, but they were only a symptom of what was going on behind his hood and cloak. "Please don't run away."

"Would you ever have pursued me?" Pazli asked in a quieter tone. "Or perhaps you prefer someone with no troublesome religious beliefs." He could not deny his physical attraction to Cale. He would not deny it if Pazli asked him. The man was tormenting himself because he would not accept what he felt for Talio. It was so obvious, yet Pazli was blind to it.

"Please do not do this," Talio said. This was neither the time nor the place for this discussion, but it was agony knowing Pazli believed this. "You are letting your feelings cloud your judgment."

"My feelings?" Anger was now rising in Pazli's voice. "You are the one who cannot bring yourself to choose between me and Cale. Incarnite or Nuciferian. Sif or Felle. You have always wanted more than your share."

All he had to do was say he felt nothing for Cale. That he cared for Pazli. But with a sudden pang, Talio realized what that would mean. Pazli would be forced to choose between him and his religion.

He hesitated, unsure of how to phrase his reply. It was a hesitation he would remember for the rest of his life. Into the silence came an elderly woman who tapped Pazli on the shoulder. "Would you get me another one of these fish cakes?" she asked. Talio glanced at the bare front of the Incarnite's cloak; Pazli had been unable to repair his silver advocate's pin.

He ignored her and spoke to Talio instead. "I will see you at the skyline station in two days." Then he was gone.

# Chapter Thirty-One

"Are they going to kill us?" Talio asked Vinne much later that night.

The innkeeper pawed through the lock tools and clucked. "They will cut your head off. Your pretty little head." He gathered them in his hand and rolled them up in the black velvet. "Me, they're probably going to throw into a canal along with a giant stuffed wyvern."

Talio had gotten home late from the party, but Vinne had insisted on retrieving the tools at once. "How much silver is the missing cylinder going to cost?" Talio asked. Could he approach Gawani somehow? Get a loan? Ask the Incarnite cleric for a dispensation?

Vinne mulled it over. "About ten silver, give or take. I'll have Emara get it from petty cash next week."

"I don't understand." Talio sat down on the bed. "Aren't the devices powered by merinite?"

"False merinite," Vinne said.

"You told me it was true merinite."

Vinne winked. "You're always losing things. Forks, knives, glasses, men—everything goes missing around here. Figured I'd keep you on your toes."

"They might have found us while I was busy scrounging for that broken piece."

"No chance," Vinne said. "You're the impatient type. How you spent ten years digging for merinite, I'll never understand." He was not about to press the innkeeper on what had been, after all, a clever trick of his own.

Now that the excitement was over, Talio was exhausted. "I'll leave a morning meal outside your door," Vinne said. "But there is something else we have to talk about at some point."

"What is it? Don't tell me. *You* are the secret head of the conspiracy."

Vinne shook his head. "Your neck is safe, for once. But it's time for you to leave the Double Moon."

He sat down next to Talio on the bed and put a paw around his shoulders. "No," Talio said. "Please."

Vinne gave his shoulder a squeeze. "You're running out of space here. Emara keeps asking for more rooms, more chairs. The two scribes can't keep up."

He couldn't bear the thought. "Why didn't she tell me?" Talio asked in a small voice.

"The season's over. She knew you had things on your mind. So, she talked to the guy who sweeps up when everyone's gone."

Talio put his free hand on Vinne's. "I'll think about it during the summer."

The other man gave a rolling shrug. "There is nothing to think about. I'll kick you out if I have to." He struggled to his feet. "People have started asking me for rooms. Men. Women. Even some of our hooded friends. Can you believe it? What the Incarnites painted on the wall outside came true: we're somewhere safe for people. A refuge."

When Talio said nothing, Vinne shook his head. "It's time for you to grow up. You can't stay here forever."

As Talio expected, Pazli did not come to the Double Moon the next day or send any message lockboxes. Emara was busy at the hospital with clients. The only visitor they had was a messenger that evening with a gift bottle of wine for Vinne. "One of my admirers," he said shrugging. "Better sample it to make sure it's not poisoned." Off he went.

A bit later, there was an unexpected knock at the inn door. Talio opened the door to find Cale, locs covered in snow. "May I come in?" the man asked.

Talio was dressed in his shabbiest clothes, but it was Cale, after all. He'd seen him clothed, naked, in Incarnite garb, in prosecutorial robes. Talio stood back and waved him in; the prosecutor had his hands behind his back.

"I'll get you a cloth for your hair," Talio said, and brought one out for him.

Cale brought his hands forward and gave Talio a small package. It was wrapped carefully in cloth, tied with string and damp from the falling snow. Talio pulled the package gently apart.

A single perfect flower. Red, with heart-shaped waxy petals and a yellow center. "Where did you get this?" Talio said, marveling at it. "No. Don't spoil it."

He hadn't seen any flowers in months, or any greenery for that matter. It smelled of spring, of summer, of walks in the Palace law school square and the Incarnite harvest festival. He looked up from this marvel into Cale's face and smiled. "Thank you. This is wonderful."

Cale used the cloth to briskly rub the snow and damp from his hair. Talio suspected the man did not want him to see his face at that moment; much as Talio concealed his true feelings most of the time, Cale bore them for all to see.

Talio stood the precious gift in an empty wine bottle filled with source water. Placing it on the table between them, he and Cale sat across from each other in the flickering candlelight.

Talio explained what happened at the meeting with the queen and Clemente. "Will Pazli even go with you to Aurania?" Cale asked.

"I imagine the queen's request carries some weight. Even with a worshipper of Sif."

Cale nodded, then grinned back at him. "You did it, you know."

"We did it. The three of us."

The man shook his head. So handsome, always so handsome. "No, this was your adventure and your scheme. You managed to solve a mystery spanning half a century that nobody even knew existed. A bet Scodel made on the laws of Merin."

Talio shook his head. "Not quite. We know the four cities share the same legal system. The bet was about sentencing. Punishment, you might say. Cruelty for Damiria—or retribution, to use a more objective term. Compassion for Aurania." He thought of Emara's parents. "Perhaps fairness for Rylavia. And for Nuciferia? I'm not sure."

"Nuciferia has been blessed, regardless of our sentencing," Cale said. "We are the effective capital of Merin now. It wasn't always so."

Blessed. Divine intervention. As always: *Praise Scodel.* Talio recalled the eerie feeling he'd felt standing in front of the first obelisk, the compulsion to fall to his knees. "We thought Scodel had the answers. But he was stumbling in the dark, just as we are. It's comforting to know he was only human. It is all right to question the writings of a human, somehow." They sat for a while in the shadows of history.

"That is not why I came here tonight," Cale said at last with a shy smile.

The flower. This private meeting. It was the prosecutor's story to tell, now. He could sense the man gathering up his nerve, and at last Cale grasped Talio's hands with his own. "I can finally argue on my own behalf. I do not want to let go of you, ever again. After all this time, you have managed to capture my heart."

He had thought it might be this, had hoped it wasn't. But the prosecutor would never hide his feelings. "Cale," Talio said, stricken.

"I had hoped for a different reception." The man's damp locs sat around his face in disarray. "Would it have been better said in the Hall of Antiquities?"

Talio shook his head but did not trust himself to speak. Of course he cared for him. He admired Cale's ability to speak his mind and heart, and his dedication to the truth as he saw it. The drive he had—to do what he needed to in order to attend law school, argue a hearing, fulfill his family obligations or pursue someone he wanted. How could he not feel affection for him? But in this moment, when he had lost Pazli forever—that was when Talio knew where his heart lay.

"I love you as a brother, and always will," Talio said at last. "But Pazli is the man I cannot live without." *Even if he never speaks to me again.*

"Why?" Cale asked, and Talio could hear the man's heart break in that word. "Why him? Why not me? What does Pazli Mecomb have that I do not?"

The realization came to Talio at that moment. "He is an Incarnite."

"You don't believe in their religion."

He shook his head. "No, I do not. But he does. He believes. No matter what, he believes. Most people in Nuciferia hate the Incarnites, but he still believes. He worships, he prays. He uses his religion as the measuring stick of his morality, and he lets people come to his church on their own terms. Through all that, he continues to believe." How could he explain this to Cale? "I will discard whatever belief I must in order to win a hearing. Pazli will never lose his principles. He gives me a goal to aspire to, someday. The one belief I cling to is that I love him. No matter how he feels about me."

"But I'm—" Cale protested, bringing a hand up to his face. He fell silent. Yes, Talio thought, you are certainly the most beautiful person I have ever known. For all the times a good-looking man had turned his head, he had somehow managed to fall in love with someone whose face he would never see, except in his dreams. It mattered so little, in the end.

Cale had always been attracted to him, despite the scar. Pazli had seen something in Talio as well. He was more than his scar, just as Pazli was more than his cloak and hood, and Cale was so much more than his good looks. Talio felt his heart start to heal, the part deep inside that had been injured along with his face thirty years ago. It was like hearing a long echo fade away at last.

"Have you seen him?" Cale asked. "Do you know what he really looks like?"

Talio squeezed the man's hands. "I suppose you could say that." He glanced down at the flower, a spark of beauty in the somber inn. "Would you like your gift back?"

Cale shook his head ruefully. "Do you know what I had to do to get it?" He laughed at Talio's expression. "No, not *that*. I had to trade some favors. Pour honey into the ears of the right people." He let go of Talio's hands. "I'll leave it with you. So you will remember that beautiful things also have their place in this world."

As Cale was about to leave, Talio placed a hand on his shoulder. "If anything should happen to me and Pazli..."

Cale's face was grave. "Then I will see that justice is done. I will break down the door to the obelisk room with an axe, if I must." The smile that followed was like sun on a summer day. "But nothing will happen to you. I will be there the day they dedicate a statue to you in the Palace of Justice."

Talio laughed. "I hope not. I'm only human, after all."

The man hugged him tight. "Just like Scodel was."

He could not sleep that night. Thinking of Pazli, Talio shook his head. How had he concluded all Talio cared about was power? Winning? Like the other Incarnites, the man had withdrawn himself, pursuing a river of thought until he'd convinced himself Talio was a monster. If he had learned anything, it was to surround himself with friends: Cale, Emara, Minka, even Gawani until recently. Pazli might remain his partner in law, but Talio worried he might never again be his friend. Or anything more.

And his anger about the legal advisor position at the Royal Palace? It was not his fault that the queen offered Talio the position. He was better placed to help the Incarnites. Progress was a slow, agonizing process, as the committee had shown. Pazli wanted to cross a wide stream in one leap, rather than hop from stone to stone.

Talio thought back to his meeting with the queen and Clemente, how they'd discussed the fate of the Incarnites. Making decisions that would affect thousands of lives without consulting them, without giving them the simple dignity of being seen or heard. The queen would not listen to a single Incarnite. He would have to stand in their place instead.

Pazli's words echoed in his mind: *We are not children. We do not need you to take care of us.* Now he felt uneasy; no matter how much he might consult the Incarnites, it would still be his voice in the Royal Palace, his opinions and his guidance. Was it his place to speak for them?

But it was obvious what the Incarnites needed, certainly. He did not need Pazli or anyone else to tell him. Talio turned this last thought over and over in his mind, and it came to him at last what an ugly thought it was. So many things to apologize for, so much forgiveness to ask. How could Pazli ever absolve him?

He had one more thing he needed to do before the trip to Aurania. From the inn's stationery cupboard, Talio took out a sheet of formal vellum, a high-quality stylus, and a jar of quick-sealing wax. He sat at his worktable and thought about the message he wanted to send.

*Gawani*, he wrote in careful handwriting:

> *Thank you for trusting me with the Pazli Mecomb case. I am pleased that I could guide the legal system to the appropriate conclusion.*
>
> *I have enjoyed my time here in Nuciferia. As you once said, I belong in the practice of law. I have done my best to fight on behalf of the Incarnites— within the bounds of Scodel's laws, as always—to bring them some measure of justice.*
>
> *I have also enjoyed working with you on the Judicial Review Committee. Nuciferia is changing, and the laws must change with it. Scodel created the Obelisks of Justice as the source of our laws, but they were not meant to be hidden away in the Hall of Antiquities, never to be seen, never to be updated. You are someone who can bring their true nature into the light.*
>
> *Lastly, thank you for the time we spent together all those years ago; I did not deserve it, but I look back on it with fondness even now. Maybe we found a way to forgive each other somehow.*

He paused at the end of the message. He would normally sign the letter with *Yours faithfully*, but given their history, it seemed in poor taste. *Talio* seemed too flippant. He compromised by concluding with *Advocate Talio Rossa* and his signature.

Talio folded the vellum and poured out the quick-sealing wax from the jar onto it. He pressed his identity key into the wax and a moment later, the seal hardened.

Referring to "obelisks" was as far as he dared go. If anything were to happen to him, he hoped she would divine the message beneath his words. He could leave no other clues. He slipped it under Vinne's door. The innkeeper would make sure it was delivered without opening it. Between her and Cale, justice would be served. They were both dedicated to rooting out the truth, regardless of their own occasional moral lapses.

Later that night, Talio bolted upright in bed from the middle of a deep sleep. He heard a soft scuffling in the front room. It was not mice or rats; the cats in the alley behind the Double Moon took care of them quite efficiently.

He extinguished the vigil candle with two fingers and opened the door to the rest of the inn. Darkness, illuminated only by a wedge of starlight coming from outside. Someone was slowly opening the outside door.

Talio looked around for a weapon. The big stick Vinne kept by the front door was out of his reach. And now he was too late. The figure entered the Double Moon Inn, shuffling a bit. They were stooped over, as if they were very tired.

Their eyes met across the main room. "Hello, Rossa," the figure said.

"Hello, Master Jilani."

# Chapter Thirty-Two

Clemente eased himself into a chair. "You are fortunate you did not encounter Vinne first," Talio said, seating himself across from him.

"The bottle of wine I sent earlier had an extra ingredient," Clemente said with a little smile. "I doubt he will wake before midday."

He dropped a small, heavy cylindrical object onto the table. A lock-picking device, similar to the ones Talio used at the Palace. Clemente knew, then. There was no more need for pretense. "I know there are four Obelisks of Justice," Talio said.

"My people found the broken wire in the Hall of Antiquities yesterday evening." He fixed him with a pointed gaze. "Was the Incarnite with you?"

"No," Talio said. "Not him."

"You've discovered Scodel's experiment, then," Clemente said, stating it rather than asking.

Talio nodded. "Fifty years ago, when the royal body asked him to design Merin's legal system, he and Amina created four separate sentencing systems, one for each city. To see which system was the best."

"Do you know why it continues to this day?" Clemente's eyes were hawk-like and piercing.

*Because forty years ago, someone sabotaged Scodel's skyship?* "I have no idea."

Clemente sighed. "I was not at the Palace of Justice back then. Despite what you may think, I am not that old. But I heard the stories from some of the professors that had stayed on. The ones who were able to make the change from instructing mages to teaching magistrates."

He went on. "Scodel had no problems designing the skyships and skylines. All that merinite. It must have been quite inspiring. A legal system, on the other hand..." He tented his fingers. "The rumor was that Amina suggested the four sets of sentencing guidelines. You might say it was a bet."

Talio was not sure he heard the man correctly. The Merin legal system had been founded on a bet? Clemente saw his expression and shook his head. "Not a simple wager. She and Scodel each had in mind a sentencing system they thought would be best. But they could not be sure without trying all of them out."

"'Let four streams flow and may four cities bloom,'" Talio said.

"Yes. This was intended to operate for a limited time. They had planned for a constitutional convention to take place ten years after the system was first put into place." Clemente shook his head. "Ten years passed, and by then I was working at the Palace. You cannot imagine the commotion when Scodel died."

"Was it Amina?" Talio asked quietly.

"Her people." Clemente waved a hand. "I was part of that group by then, but I did not pull the lever, as it were. My work lay in instructing the young legal minds of Nuciferia."

"Why kill him?"

"Well, you see, after ten years of their scheme Amina realized something very interesting."

"Nuciferia was winning," Talio said.

"Indeed," Clemente said with a small smile. "Economically. Politically. Even socially. It was the best of the four legal systems. Here we had our proof. No doubt we were divinely blessed. Amina was a Nuciferian to the core."

*Praise Scodel.* "What happened to her?"

Clemente waved a gnarled hand. "Disappeared. Probably went to Rylavia. Nothing good ever comes out of Rylavia." Or Clemente's people had tied up a loose end.

"What would you have me do?" Talio asked, quietly. The darkness of the Double Moon inn pressed down on him.

Clemente gave him a serious look. "You will help us, of course. To maintain the system. Conceal the secrets. You will have a brilliant second career as an advocate. There is no alternative situation where everyone you care about remains alive. The Smiling Queen will remain blissfully unaware." He gazed skyward. "And one day, when you and I are long gone, I imagine someone will come along and truly reform the system. Our little Judicial Review Committee has been a wonderful distraction."

"I have a skyship to catch to Aurania," Talio said unsteadily. "With Pazli."

"The Incarnites." Clemente sighed. "We won't allow them to keep prospering. Not for much longer. Ours is a system based on identity. Anyone who won't show their face in civil society cannot be a part of it." He got to his feet and gathered up the cylindrical device. It seemed as if Clemente were almost regretful. "Mediation. Such a brilliant way to handle the firebugs. No need to follow Scodel's laws. Properly done, the Incarnites won't even see the system turning against them. They have always had a persecution complex."

He got to his feet slowly and moved to the door. Talio could not see his face in the dark, but he heard the smile in Clemente's voice. "Do say hello to Magistrate Kallis. He is not one of ours, yet. But he will be."

After the man left, Talio checked to make sure Vinne was all right, then sat in front of the main room's fireplace the rest of the night. He and Pazli had to make it safely to Aurania; there was no other option. Clemente Jilani's influence could not extend everywhere. He had to gamble that they could alert authorities who were not yet compromised...if he could figure out who they were.

On his walk to the skyship station, Talio debated what he would say to Pazli. It would have to be his greatest argument ever: to persuade a man that he loved him, and that he was worth loving in return.

There could be no tricks this time, no appeals to policy, no legal principles. If he were like Cale, he could say the words simply, with sincerity, as they came to him. Dear Cale. But he was not like the prosecutor; he had to consider his words first.

He could not ask Pazli to forsake his religion. Just as law lay at the center of Talio's heart, being an Incarnite lay at the center of Pazli's soul. That said, if Scodel's laws had taught him anything, it was that every reasonable system of beliefs must make allowance for mercy. For compassion. And even for love.

There had been a break in the snow the previous day, and now it was a bitter, wintry morning with a deep blue sky above the streets and frozen canals of Nuciferia. Pazli stood in the skyline station in front of the inspection area. His cloak and hood were the same as always; his arms were folded in front of him. But there was a coldness to him, a palpable message of separation. He was a different man.

"Good morning," Talio said. Pazli nodded. It would be like that, then. He nodded back.

Talio waited while the attendants checked Pazli's hand tattoo and key. "He is not usually so morose," Talio whispered to an attendant. "Often, he is worse."

Once the attendants identified, recorded, and weighed them, he and Pazli were on their own. Now it would be a silent trip. Unless his words could somehow unlock the other man's heart.

The climb to the platform was grueling, but it was worse with Pazli climbing ahead of him. Talio had hoped he would walk behind him, speak words of support, or even touch his shoulder, but there was no communicating with the man. He had to convince him, somehow.

The platform was even colder, but the air was still. An attendant priest sat each of them on opposite sides of the aisle. "It will be some time yet," she explained. "They are clearing ice from the end of the launch platform."

He heard the priests speak the prayers to Felle behind the skyship. Then it was the two of them, alone, the waters of the skyline restive around them. Talio had gripped the far handrail as soon as he boarded, but now he unbuckled his safety belt and slid along the bench toward Pazli. *I can convince anyone of anything,* he thought. *Why should I fear speaking now?* He knew the answer. He could not let this man leave his life.

"Pazli." The other man turned to him, impenetrable behind his hood.

He wanted to tell him he loved him. He wanted to tell him how it hurt to see him so far away, yet only across the aisle. He wanted to tell him so many things.

Instead, Talio thought of a time long ago, before the scandal, before he'd met Gawani, before he'd become a magistrate. Events that had set his career in motion. It was time to speak of them at last.

"You asked me once how I could afford law school when my parents were scavengers," Talio said. No response. "I was not able to afford it."

All the details came back to him. "When I arrived in Nuciferia for the first time, all I could do was work in construction." Talio heard the saws and hammers in his mind. "There were always jobs for manual laborers. Especially healthy young adult males.

"A group of us went to work on a building project outside of Nuciferia. One day, the owner came to visit. I caught his eye. He found ways to speak to me alone. To ask questions— about work, about me."

Talio buckled the safety belt around him. "I was not naïve. He wanted me. I had worked hard that summer and had a fine body. He cared little about my face." He shrugged. "And so, we found places to go when I took breaks for meals. At first, he treated me like a living statue. A thing made of muscles. And then, after the first few times, we began to talk.

"He was lonely," Talio said, as if this excused anything. "He was ill. His wife would not touch him. His daughter despised him. He hated his work. But he liked me, and I gave him the chance to get away, a little bit at a time. So, he gave me things in return. Money, gifts. When he learned I wanted to go to law school, he offered to pay the fees. On the condition that I tell no one." An easy promise to keep, until now. "He loved me, or what I represented. An escape. A path not taken."

Talio wished that they could be airborne before he spoke of the next part. "That man was Lord Balsamo. Gawani's father. I did not know her then. When I met her in law school, I did not realize the connection at first. I had already fallen in love with her before she brought me to the manse for the first time. And there he sat in the gathering room."

The only thing that Pazli had done was clasp his hands; Talio could see his tattoo in the faint morning light. "I did not know what to do. I loved Gawani, so I pretended it had never happened. I took the coward's way out and said nothing. After that, he and I never touched each other again." Not that either of them had ever wanted to, after that shock. "Lord Balsamo died while I was finishing the magisterial track."

Talio wanted to put his hand on Pazli's, but the aisle was in the way. "I never told anyone that story before." Would Pazli not speak now? Would he not say anything, ever again?

"That is not the worst thing I have done," Talio went on. "While I was married to Gawani, I let Cale Faro seduce me. I slept with other men besides him during my marriage. I have bent and broken the truth so many times, in and out of the hearing rooms."

There—was Pazli's hand moving? Was he reaching toward him across the aisle at last? "We are all guilty of these things. Cale slept with me when I was a magistrate so he could get into law school. Vinne has his own secret, one I do not believe he knows himself. Gawani...well, Gawani is the one who killed Selig Ivor. I know it to be true. And I know who is behind the conspiracy of codices. Finally, after all this time." Silence from the other man. How could he remain mute in the face of these revelations?

Now came his summation. "None of us are perfect. Even Scodel had his dark secrets. We are each sailing a ship through the dark, blindly." Talio started to reach for Pazli's hand. "I need your help to find my way. I will not make it without you."

Their hands were still so far away from each other. "You have a fine legal mind," he said. "I will step aside so that you may come out of the shadows. Others will see you the way I do. As an advocate and an Incarnite."

The icy wind came up at that moment; it blew across the skyship and tousled the hairs of Talio's beard. He drew in a deep breath of the clear winter air and waited for Pazli's response.

There was no scent. No scent at all.

Talio sat very still. Whoever sat beside him, whoever was beneath that cloak and hood, it was not Pazli Mecomb.

With a sudden jerk, the skyship glided away from the platform and launched itself along the waters of the skyline. They were alone.

# Chapter Thirty-Three

The frozen canals and snow-covered buildings of Nuciferia flashed by below. He had to think. Who was sitting beside him?

Whoever it was had managed to bypass the security at the skyline station, using a false hand tattoo and identity key. It was someone who had seen Pazli's sullen moods, the way he would fold his arms and grow silent. Someone observant enough to impersonate Pazli's movements and posture. Someone with a keen, watchful eye. Someone living in rooms far too expensive for their income. Someone roughly the size of Pazli's body. Someone who knew Ancient Merin. Someone who would do anything for the right price. Someone he had trusted until this very moment.

He could not postpone the confrontation any longer. "Take off the hood, Emara," he said quietly.

Talio felt her stiffen beside him. Then she pulled the hood from her head. Emara had tied her long blond hair back in a bun, which gave her a severe look. She took a sharp, ugly knife out of her cloak pocket. Talio did not know how she'd gotten it past the guards, but it mattered little.

He had told her everything. Everything! "Where is he?" Talio asked. "Where is Pazli?"

Emara gave him a stricken glance. "I'm sorry." For a moment he saw the young woman, the girl she had once been, before her own shield had closed around her. "They had to get me aboard the skyship. He had to be eliminated."

"No," Talio said, confidently. "He is not gone." If Pazli had died, would he have not felt it? Would his world not have come loose from its moorings at that very moment?

"I saw his body." Her voice was unusually quiet. "They copied his tattoo onto my hand. I took his identity key." Again she said, "I'm sorry." But a chill was creeping into her tone. She was pulling away from the realization of what she had been a party to.

He could not contemplate it. He would not allow himself to think of it. But when Talio spoke again, his voice was weak. "Why? Why would you help maintain this horrible system?"

"Fifty years ago, Nuciferia was the smallest, poorest of all the Four Cities. Now we are the greatest, because of the advantage Scodel gave us. Divine intervention. We will not give that up. Ever."

Her eyes were shining. This was the true face of religious zealotry, then. Not Pazli's quiet devotion, but the sick fervor of perceived superiority. "*We?*" he asked.

"Others. Master Jilani. Powerful people in the Palace of Justice. Not the conspiracy of women. Not a conspiracy at all." She gave a terrible smile. "We are working to preserve the world that Scodel built. We start early. Approach certain students in the law school. Ones we think are sympathetic." They had tried to tempt Cale down the same path. What had he said all those months ago? *The price had become too high.*

For once in his life, he could think of nothing to say. There was no way to persuade her, to convince her she was wrong. Emara's face was a locked door. Her expression held no opportunity, no hope. Only a halt to progress, forever. There would be no changes to the law, no help for the Incarnites. No support for Honell or those like them. Scodel's Grand Experiment would continue to strangle Merin.

"Eleven years ago," Talio said dully. "The scandal and my codex. Was Jilani responsible?"

"He and the others who came before me. They were watching." She pursed her lips. "You were trying to get around Scodel's words. Handing out your own justice. But you are not Scodel. You are not divinely inspired." The statue. Worshipping a flawed man for fifty years. Turning him into a folk hero. A god. *Praise Scodel.*

Emara shook her head. "He created the perfect legal system." Was there a plea for understanding in her eyes? "The people of Merin are the ones who are flawed. Criminals. Outcasts. Religious cults. Deviants. Our group is the only one that can prevent chaos." He could understand her perspective. He had done everything but pray to the altar of

Scodel himself while he had been at law school. But hadn't Talio's career been one of chipping away at an imperfect system? As he had said to Cale long ago: *My task is tearing down what he spent years building up.* Scodel's laws were far from perfect. And those who resisted progress would always have excuses. As long as the doors to Merin were closed to the Incarnites, Scodel's system could never deliver true justice.

"Now what?" Talio asked. "You planned all of this to get me alone aboard this skyship. What happens when we reach Aurania?"

Her hazel eyes now held nothing but determination. "Now you jump."

"What will they say when you arrive in Aurania alone?"

She smiled, but it was a grimace. "You're not the only one with tricks. I will pretend to be Pazli, and I will confess to killing you out of religious madness. Then I'll present his key and show the tattoo. They will arrest 'Pazli' for murder. They wouldn't dare unmask an Incarnite. One of our loyalists in Aurania will release me at some point. Some forged documents and I will be on the next skyship back to Nuciferia." Emara lifted the knife. "Get up."

Clemente had never planned to let him escape alive. Why risk Talio unburdening himself to the wrong people? Better to send a vivid message to anyone who might oppose him— like the "conspiracy" of women. Pazli would take the blame for such a high-profile crime, further turning public opinion against the Incarnites.

Talio was shaking. There was nothing he could do. He would not jump. He could try to fight her off, but she was far stronger. Logic led him to an inexorable conclusion: for any chance of survival, he must attack her first. He unbuckled his safety belt and rose to his feet. The skyship gave a slight lurch. "Step back to the edge of the ship," Emara ordered.

He backed away from her toward the left side of the skyship until his calves were pressed against the edge of the copper hull. They faced each other across the seats and aisle that separated them. The white of the Impassable Forest below them was blinding. Shadows of horrible creatures moved in the fog. "Jump," she said.

Talio crouched down and sprinted forward. As he leaped across the aisle, Emara leaned nimbly aside and he crashed onto the floor of the skyship in front of her, shards of pain ripping through his shoulder. She unbuckled her own safety belt and stood over him with the knife, looking down with disgust. "As you wish, then."

He was dizzy. He could not continue. The skyship seemed to tilt around him. Then Talio saw the skyship was actually tilting. With both of them on the right side of the aisle, the skyship was leaning toward them, the left side tipping upward as it became unbalanced in the waters of the skyline.

Emara looked around in panic. Then she scrambled across the aisle onto the left side. The skyship stopped tilting toward the right, but it remained at an alarming angle.

Talio kept his eyes on Emara and that knife. Was this what had happened to Scodel forty years ago? Would the skyship slide off the river of the skyline and plummet to the ground of the Impassable Forest, repeating history?

Emara backed away to the left edge of the skyship hull, trying to balance it. He had to do something. Talio looked to his right. There was the last seat, then the canted edge of the skyship hull, and then nothing. Beyond that lay empty air. Tens of spans to the monsters and the forest floor below.

He had to stop Emara. She had a knife. Talio could not overpower her. But he could throw her off balance. Tip the skyship further to the right so she would drop the knife. Or fall. Or—

He could not do it. It was impossible. Unthinkable. But once again, the logic was inexorable. He had come to the end of his available options.

He grasped the rough frost-covered edge of the hull to his right with as firm a grip as he could manage. He said a prayer to Felle, to Sif and any others who might be listening. Then he leaned to the right, letting himself fall onto the very edge of the skyship. Talio's weight came down heavily on the edge of the hull and he closed his eyes in terror.

The skyship gave another sickening lurch to the right, and he thought he must surely tumble over the side. Talio gripped the frozen edge of the hull as hard as he could. He wrapped his legs around the edge, felt the skyship tilt and tip toward him. It would fall out of the sky.

Then water rushed into the right side of the skyship and soaked him as the edge of the hull dipped below the skyline's surface. Talio was covered in torrents of rushing icy water, and he did his best to hang on.

Emara screamed and tumbled past him, grabbing at his clothes, trying to hold on. Then he could no longer hear her voice against the wind. Talio dared to look up. The skyship lay perched on its side, flying through the sky. He climbed up the three vertical seats on the right side of the skyship, but could not surmount the aisle itself. Below him, the right side of the hull skimmed through the torrents of the skyline, throwing up water at him. Talio clung desperately to the legs of the seat by the aisle with all his might. Far below, the white forest and its shadowy monsters sped by. Emara was gone.

He moved his body back and forth as much as his grip would allow, hoping he could swing the skyship back into a horizontal position. It would tilt no more in either direction. The skyship was now stuck in a new equilibrium; Talio could not right it.

He could not see Aurania, even on the horizon. Talio did not know how far he was from it. The entire trip took three hours. Was he an hour away? Two? Less? He had focused on saving himself. And now he was going to die. He would fall from the skyship, or die of exposure from the water that was soaking him.

The skyship flew on. At first his hands cramped from the chill, then agonizing pains shot through them. Every time he moved the smallest amount to tighten his grip, Talio could feel the splinters and rough wood of the seat legs dig into his palms. He thought that sweat was slicking his hands, but when he looked down at them, they were covered in blood. No matter. He would hold on as long as he could. To the very end. He could not stop shivering.

An empty skyship would arrive in Aurania, but the mystery of the codices would not die with him. Talio had seen to that. Cale would carry on their fight. And even if they got to Cale somehow, there was always the message for Gawani. The truth would be heard somehow. The disappearance of every Double Moon advocate would not go unnoticed. They had been notorious enough that the outcry would be deafening.

What he would have given to speak with Pazli one last time. The man he'd fought with, had stood beside, had come to love. A man swept away by the tide of history, all in the name of words carved into four obelisks fifty years ago. Everything came down to words, in the end. There were so many words Talio had never managed to say to him. Pazli could not have known the depth of his feelings.

No, that was not true. The man had heard every one of his unspoken words, just as he'd known the silent message within Pazli's heart.

As to Cale, he and the prosecutor had had their conversation on the matters of the heart. There was nothing more to say to him. He could have loved him, had he not met Pazli. And yet, they would not have shared what he had with the other man. Pazli had changed him. That was the true nature of love; to be so altered by it that he could never go back to the man he had been.

Just as Emara had been forever changed by her love of principles. She had told him what mattered to her, so many times, and he had never listened.

He had never suspected her, because he had never understood the meaning of her words or the beliefs that lay beneath them. Why had she joined the conspirators? Talio could ask himself the reason a thousand times, but he knew the answer. Nuciferia had been winning, and the other three cities losing. Such was the fundamental flaw of an adversarial legal system: one party had to win, and the other had to lose. Her group had decided that in order to preserve Nuciferia's supremacy, they had to win at all costs. Just as he had decided that in order for him to survive, Emara had to die. He had killed her, with deliberation. A capital crime.

The frigid wind and watery spray from the skyline battered his face, forcing tears from his eyes that spread along the sides of his face as he gripped the seat legs. Was it indeed murder? Self-defense was an acceptable defense at a murder hearing if the accused had a sufficient expectation of impending death.

He imagined himself arguing his defense. He would suggest that the magistrate consider prior hearings. Situations where the fact patterns were similar, the classic approach to circumventing Scodel's prohibition on legal precedent. He had reasonably expected Emara would kill him. She had told him to jump. She had brandished a knife.

The skyship tore through the sky, scooping water from the skyline and casting high curving walls of water behind it.

He was losing his grip. His hands were in agony, and the seat legs were slippery with blood. Talio opened his eyes and gave one last look past the skyship. The snowy forest surrounded him, filled with the fog and beasts that separated the Four Cities. There was nothing but desolation. He closed his eyes once more. He did not want to see the moment when he lost his grip and fell. He would concentrate on the hearing instead.

If he were the prosecutor, what arguments would he use? One could argue Talio should have waited until the moment when Emara attacked. By attacking her first, he had assumed there was no alternative. He had subverted the doctrine of self-defense.

And so, his arguments continued—for and against. Anything to distract himself from the reality of the situation and the peril he faced. He concluded he was guilty of a lesser charge of manslaughter. He would argue for a commuted sentence, given his service to the Nuciferian legal community.

He could no longer feel his hands, or the seat legs. The only way Talio knew he was still gripping them was that he had yet to fall.

Then he heard voices. Shouts.

He opened his eyes. The outskirts of Aurania lay beneath him, streets and buildings and chimneys and parapets. He could see people below him pointing, waving, shouting. "Hold on!" he heard faintly from several of them. *That is an excellent suggestion,* he thought.

His arms were being wrenched from their sockets. Talio could no longer hold on. "Source of all things," he murmured. "Quencher of fire. Cleanse my soul and purify me." Then he lost his grip entirely.

The skyship glided to a stop at the Auranian skyline station in a rainbow spray of water, still tilted on its right side. Shaking from the cold, hands bloody, Talio tumbled down the side of the skyship, past the seats, over the edge of the hull until he landed on the station platform and everything went black.

# Chapter Thirty-Four

He awoke in the middle of the night in an unfamiliar bed, shivering, not knowing where he was. The decorations on the wall were Auranian; after a moment, Talio recognized the place. It was the inn they'd stayed at when the committee had sent the delegation to visit Magistrate Kallis. Where he and Pazli had shared a bottle of soft wine.

A taper in a bowl of water illuminated the face of a very young, very blonde woman. For a hopeful moment Talio thought it was Emara, but then he remembered. This woman wore a peacekeeper's uniform and was dabbing his forehead with a damp cloth.

"Minka Schell sent me," the woman whispered.

"Already?" Talio croaked. "How long—"

She patted his bandaged hand. "Two days."

He just looked at her. "She said to tell you that Neri says hello, and to avoid your mother-in-law's tea." Talio smiled weakly. That was Minka, all right.

"It's a lot to ask you to put your trust in me," the unnamed woman said. "But we need to know everything."

Talio did not know what was happening. He did not know if he could truly trust this strange woman. He had trusted Emara and Gawani to his detriment. But he had also trusted Cale, and Pazli and Vinne. He had thought himself such a tremendous judge of character. Now Talio realized that what he had seen in Emara and Gawani had not been goodness...but their potential for goodness.

Scodel had turned Nuciferia into a city of fearful, mistrustful people. That had to end.

Shivering still, Talio began to speak. At some point, much later, he fell asleep. When he awoke it was day. Late-morning sunlight streamed in through a window, and faint sounds of foot traffic and horses came from outside. He sat up, groggy. He was no longer shivering.

Talio pulled himself to the edge of the bed. Strips of white cloth swaddled his aching hands. He did not want to look under the bandages. He did not want to do anything.

Pazli was dead. Emara was dead. The Double Moon Law Office was gone—at least the two advocates who had been its living, beating heart. Even Vinne wanted him to leave.

Talio did not want to start over a second time. He could not bear the thought of walking into an unfamiliar building without Pazli to make a sardonic remark or Emara to list her concerns with brisk efficiency. Or Vinne to commiserate with him about love and the price of wine.

Emara had been his friend, once. Talio could not believe that she had simply gotten close to him in order to monitor him, to plot and scheme. He had watched her work, heard her laugh, seen how she had helped him and the Incarnites. Even her victory in the Lady Safana hearing. That was the woman she had once been, the person she'd had the chance to show him. The Emara from the skyship, with her anger and certainty—that was the inevitable result of her belief in Scodel's infallibility. In principles and laws instead of the people behind them.

A knock at the door. "Come in," Talio said in a dull voice.

An Incarnite servant entered carrying a tray of food. The midday meal. Talio waved a bandaged hand. "Thank you. Leave it on the table."

He stopped and looked. Then he looked again.

Then he leaped from the bed, throwing the sheets aside. Talio ran across the room and flung his arms around the Incarnite, burying his face in the man's cloak, in his scent. The tray clattered to the floor. He ignored the pain in his hands and pulled the man tighter to him.

"It is good to see you again, too," Pazli said.

Talio shook his head. "She said...she said you were..." The last word was so horrible he could not say it.

Pazli set aside the remains of the meal tray. Then he took Talio by the arms and led him back to the bed. One of his bandages had come loose; his swollen right hand was a mass of red-purple bruises and shreds of torn skin. The man re-wrapped the bandage as he spoke.

"The night before our trip, they sent one of your message lockboxes summoning me to the Palace of Justice," Pazli said. "It was not written in your usual illegible scrawl, so I did not fall for their first trap. Then I heard from an unexpected source."

"Cale?"

Pazli shook his head. "Chief Physician Minka Schell. She has friends, women in the Palace who continue to feed her information while she is on leave. They heard of plans to poison me that night in the temple cloister. And so, I devised a trick."

Talio managed a faint smile. "You have learned well."

"Nobody knows what I look like. At my suggestion, one of Minka's spies obtained a dead body from the Palace morgue. They dressed the unfortunate man in my cloak and hood and copied my tattoo onto his hand in ink. All that remained was to put my identity key in his pocket and make sure the conspirators found him in my rooms at the cloister."

A false tattoo. The same trick Emara had used. Pazli went on. "Nobody thought they would try to kill you aboard the skyship itself. I was still in hiding, but Minka's people were waiting for your arrival in Aurania."

"The peacekeeper you spoke to last night arrived in Nuciferia this morning," Pazli said. "She informed Queen Jaconda of the events of your skyship journey. Jilani and most of the conspirators were quickly apprehended. The Palace of Justice is in an uproar, as you might imagine."

He could hear the smile in Pazli's voice. "I believe the Queen would like a quick hearing when the new judicial season starts. Perhaps you would defend him?"

"Let him hang." Talio was surprised by his own vehemence. "I will pull the lever myself, given the opportunity."

"I believe Prosecutor Faro has also been assisting, in his own way," Pazli said grudgingly.

"Oh?"

"Someone broke down the door to the Hall of Antiquities. Nobody has taken responsibility, but Cale was summoned to the Royal Palace for questioning. No doubt he is headstrong enough to do such a thing."

Talio smiled. Headstrong, indeed. Cale would have beaten his own forehead against the merinite lock if that was what it had taken to break through the inner door. Or perhaps his own letter to Gawani had alerted her to the secrets within the Hall. She might not have acted so quickly, but if Dovuta had found out, he could well imagine her mother taking an axe to the obelisk chamber's door.

Pazli released Talio's hand and dug into his cloak pocket. "Here. I have something for you."

It was a folded, sealed sheet of vellum. The paper's quality far surpassed the formal vellum Talio used on special occasions. He broke the seal and unfolded it, then stared at it for some time without speaking.

His law license. Not provisional, not probationary. Bearing the text: *In Recognition of Advocate Talio Rossa's Service to the Queen.* And below, in swirls of red ink, the signature of Queen Jaconda. "Is it real?" Talio whispered.

"Darra gave it to me herself. It is quite real. You are finally an official advocate."

They sat in silence. "And now we come to a more difficult subject," Pazli said.

"The night of the party, the queen offered you the position at the Royal Palace. Legal Advisor for the Incarnite Question." Pazli shook his head. "We are not your problem to solve. We are not your story to tell, or your question to answer."

"I realize that now. I was so eager to help the Incarnites, but I never thought to ask you the best way to do so. Or if you wanted my help at all. You need only ever ask for my assistance. As a legal advisor, or as a friend." *I am yours. If you would have me.*

Pazli stroked the back of Talio's hand. "I was so angry. Furious. But later that night, I remembered the day I saw you for the first time. We had worked together for months, but I had not truly *seen* you until that moment."

"It was the day when the child screamed at you in the street. When you ran back to the Double Moon. And you said those things to me."

"I will keep saying I am sorry for that. Forever, if I must."

Pazli shook his head. His voice was soft. "That was when I realized I had been pushing you away all this time because I was afraid. Afraid of my feelings. Afraid of letting you into my heart. Afraid of desiring someone who was not an Incarnite. And most of all, afraid of confronting my religion."

"I am sorry I forced you to make that decision," Talio said.

Now Pazli's grip on his hand was firm, though still mindful of his injuries. "For the first time in my life, it occurred to me that the Incarnite catechism might not be perfect and accurate after all. Like a document written by another famous man, fifty years ago."

Talio smiled. "I had to learn that lesson myself."

"I *saw* you that day on the street. All of you. How you strive for perfection, imperfectly. How you care for the Incarnites. You take risks and say things I wish I had the courage to say."

Pazli traced the circle of his tattoo with his fingers. "I do not believe any god—Sif or Felle—would want me to suffer. There had to be an answer. I spent the next two days studying the Incarnite tenets. Unlike Scodel, Peyor understood the perils of complexity. Our catechism is watertight."

"I will always support your beliefs," Talio said. "I do not want you to give up your religion."

"Good. Because I will not."

Pazli sighed. "The choice was between my religion and you. I thought I could not have both. And then I remembered your question about Peyor's hands." He held up his own. "He was willing to expose a small portion of his body when the alternative was death. For him, it was better to remain alive and continue practicing his beliefs."

His hands gently turned Talio's face to him. Pazli cradled him, stroked his beard. "I faced the same choice. The alternative here was death. The death of my spirit if I chose to live without you. And so, I accept this minor infringement upon my religion, so that I may continue to survive."

His deep voice took on the storytelling tone that Talio knew so well by now. "Scodel did not know everything. Peyor did not either, or Lady Zielle. They were only human." Pazli lifted Talio's hand gently to his hood, brushed his beard against it. "*I am like Sif, I am like fire*. But I am also a human."

"*Cleanse my soul and purify me*," Talio murmured.

Pazli's voice grew intense. "When I met you, I was an angry, bitter man. Every closed face I saw in the street was a rejection. I was a victim, and I thought the Incarnites were victims. Working with you helped me realize we were not victims at all. It made sense for us to fight for our rights, to challenge the very system that stood against us. We did not have to accept how society saw us. At the fair, you asked, 'Why not work to change the circumstances of the Incarnites?'" He shook his head. "You did not believe in our religion, but you still cared. About my people, about me. It was at that moment I knew I loved you. I could not say the words then, because of my beliefs. Because of the wall around me. I say them now. At last."

His hands were so gentle. Talio had never expected to feel their touch again. "Is there anything I should tell you about Cale?" he asked.

"Should I have any reason to be jealous of him?"

Talio shook his head. "None whatsoever." He smiled. "I care for him. I really do. But you are the man I love. The one I have been searching for all these years, even if I never knew it. You have given me something to believe in, after all this time."

"I would very much like to kiss you now."

Talio got to his feet, bandaged hands at his side. "Bind my eyes with the strap."

Pazli stood in front of him and shook his head. "I trust you. Close your eyes. I know you will not open them." Talio shut his eyes and heard Pazli remove his hood.

And why would he open them? He had already seen every part of Pazli, every aspect, every hidden corner of his fiery soul. As the man lowered his lips to his, Talio received the final message Pazli had to give him.

Where they came together, where their hearts met, there was no need for words, for statutes or catechisms. No need for religion or law, belief or logic.

They were fire, and they were water.

ACKNOWLEDGEMENTS

Thank you so much to my wonderful beta readers, who pointed out errors, omissions and other problems with the story, as well as providing suggestions and appreciating the good parts: Allison C., Brittany M., Hannah P., Josef C., McKenna L. C. Greene, and Rob M.

Thank you also to the sensitivity readers who reviewed the story and provided invaluable feedback on gender matters, Talio's facial scarring and the Incarnites and their religion: Lwazi V., Mikaela M. and Syeda A.

I could not have done it without you all. Any errors or inaccurate depictions that remain are my own responsibility.

Thanks must also go to my publisher, Space Wizard Science Fantasy, and William C. Tracy who did a fine, supportive developmental edit on the manuscript.

# ABOUT THE AUTHOR

J. Alexander Cohen graduated from law school in the early 1990s and worked in legal publishing for several years. He still looks upon his legal education somewhat fondly, even though he never practiced law. He's also surprised as to how much he actually remembers of what he learned. His first novel, *Bear Like Me*, was published in 2003 and reprinted in 2011. After 16 years as a caregiver for his elderly parents, he returned to fiction writing with the Lavender Tavern podcast telling gay fairytales. He lives in Toronto, Canada and works as a technical and marketing writer. To read more of his works, visit www.jalexandercohen.com

Please take a moment to review this book at your favorite retailer's website, Goodreads, or simply tell your friends!